ROBBY RUN

★ ★ ★ ★ ★

A NOVEL OF BLOOD AND AMBITION IN THE ANTEBELLUM NAVY

SUTTON STERN

South Town

www.southtownpress.com

ISBN: 979-8-9853893-2-6

PART ONE

CHAPTER 1

The engine cut and the *Union* hushed. Smoke from her stack died away as she drifted into a channel. Her wheel stopped rotating but the slosh from inside the drum persisted as a phantom in Roebuck's ear. Low islands dotted the coast, cypress trees overhanging their banks and coastal birds shoveling through mud for a meal.

The crew relaxed, riding the current and then dropping anchor at the harbor known as Port Leon. On a map you could barely find it, but here it was at the bend in Florida's elbow. Roebuck scratched at mosquito bumps and waited for the launch crew to row him ashore. Waiting didn't bother him because he was here where he wanted to be.

After some time a midshipman arrived and said, "The gig is ready, Lieutenant Roebuck. Commander Hurley asks that you climb aboard with no delay." This was the sort of fare-thee-well Roebuck as an officer in the Revenue Marine, not the Navy, expected. He nodded a serene goodbye and climbed down into the launch.

On shore he sought for information, a cloth duffel over his shoulder and a banjo case in hand. The instrument reminded him of his freebooting days on the Chesapeake. He and his pals always trying to turn a dime into a dollar, raiding crab pots and emptying tobacco barns. Those days had taught him how men who use waterway can evade the law. He knew the minds of such men, knew the instincts of smugglers. When he realized two years ago that this was an advantage, he had secured an extended leave from the Navy, where his progress up the promotional ladder had stalled. Or rather where he had made no progress at all. This leave had been easier to obtain than he had ever imagined, for the Navy it seemed was as happy to be free of him as he of it. The transfer was effected and he restarted what had been a failing career as an officer, in command of the revenue cutter *Louisiana*. That day was as clear in his memory as yesterday, for it had come on his twenty-first birthday—May 5, 1843—and started a two-year run of success.

Sweat streamed down his face as he walked, beading on the tip of his nose and dropping away. When a fat one formed, he shook his head like a wet dog and laughed. It was very hot, yes, but he was here with a new command. Why not laugh?

Roebuck stopped to watch a pair of mules pulling three cars down a rail track and wondered what came down the rail that these people couldn't get from ships? Maybe the cars were empty, on their way to be filled with the world's bounty.

The town was called St. Marks and the harbor Port Leon, rather grand names for settlements such as these, but Roebuck could appreciate the ambition they represented. He found a merchant in the harbor village who agreed to hold the bag and banjo and who penciled a map to Roebuck's next stop: the St. Marks Customs House. Like the Revenue Marine, customs houses were part of the U.S. Treasury. The orders from Washington that he carried in his pocket told him that the customs agent here was called Abel Van Diemen and that Abel Van Diemen would have information about Roebuck's new station and, most importantly, when and where he would find his crew and cutter.

Twenty sweaty minutes later, Roebuck found the customs house. It wasn't much. In fact, it was meager, especially compared to the one he was used to in New Orleans. He never tired of walking through the massive oak doors of that big columned beauty nor of walking over the cool marble of its floors. Now there was a building that should be printed as a picture in a book. It probably was, many times over.

This one here rested on pilings and wouldn't be more than a few rooms arranged off a dog trot, the porch bigger possibly than the rest. There was a palmetto in front shorter by a foot than Roebuck was.

He cut across a weedy patch, climbed four wooden steps to the porch, and opened the door without knocking. Two men sat on either side of an end table topped by half a bottle of amber liquid and two nearly empty glasses.

The one man looked at Roebuck's jacket and said, "Revenue Service," not making it a question and not getting up.

Roebuck felt like this required a response. "That's right," he said. "Are you Abel Van Diemen?"

"That's right," the man said.

The other man smiled.

Van Diemen manipulated a gold watch chain and looked at Roebuck with big pupils, a man who didn't like surprises. He said, "Has something happened?"

"I'm Lieutenant Robert Chase Roebuck. I have been assigned to this station and am reporting." Why did he sound like such a moron?

"Well, Robert Chase Roebuck," Van Diemen said. "I am in possession of bad news."

The second man began to worry the brim of a felt tarpot hat.

Roebuck noticed a cushioned chair across from them. It looked very comfortable.

Van Diemen continued, "There's not a ship in St. Marks for you to report to and no command."

Roebuck fished his pocket for the crinkled paper of his orders. "Here sir," he said, "Dated June seventeenth, 1845."

Van Diemen didn't take it.

Roebuck wanted to be certain the man understood, saying, "The cutter *Massachusetts* is mine and I am to command a new Revenue Marine station here." Sounding repetitive now in addition to moronic.

"You are expecting a complement to be filled and waiting for you," Van Diemen said. "Their heads bowed in deference to our Revenue Marine hero, Bobby Chase." Van Diemen, not wasting any time, was using Roebuck's nickname and reputation to have some fun with him. "And your ship bursting with provisions?"

This customs agent was turning out to be a very uncordial man, but it came as no surprise. If Van Diemen did not want the Revenue Marine nearby, he would not be the first or last man in his position to feel that way. Most of these agents wanted to be left to their own devices.

Roebuck said, "Sir, I was told…"

"You have already explained what you were told," Van Diemen said. "But I say that I myself watched as the *Massachusetts* was broken up for timber two weeks ago. I am surprised you didn't know."

Had the information passed him as he shipped here on the *Union*? "Broken up?" Roebuck said, not sure why he needed everything repeated all of a sudden.

Van Diemen turned to his friend with the tarpot hat. "The Mandarins in our Treasury Department are zealots, Captain Roux. The idea," he said with a mournful shake of his head, "that we need a revenue cutter in this village."

Captain Roux said, "I am told how smugglers overrun Mobile Bay."

"Indeed they do, sir," Van Diemen said. "A fact which does not seem to move the Revenue Marine."

These two were laying it on thick. Roebuck sensed that Van Diemen was more than a mere bystander in the events he was now reporting. He said, "Why was my cutter broken apart?"

"She arrived taking on water uncontrollably," Van Dieman said. "The lieutenant in charge, Mr. Gosling, deemed her unfit for service. And I have word that there will be no Revenue Marine station here until there is a ship. And that the Treasury Department in its frugal wisdom has no plans to acquire or construct any ship besides those already in commission."

Roebuck was stunned. He wanted to ask if the Treasury Department knew how much he had been counting on this. And as for Gosling, Roebuck knew him. A Revenue Marine officer who had been put to court martial twice in connection with the black markets of Charleston and twice acquitted—dubiously, as the story went.

"Where is Gosling, now?" Roebuck said.

"The port of Wilmington in North Carolina. His new station." Van Diemen motioned to his companion, who rose to his feet. "Captain Roux, as you have heard, this is Lieutenant Roebuck."

Roux's smile was impressive.

Roebuck tried to match it tooth for tooth. "Captain," he said, nodding slowly.

Roux said, "It is a pleasure, Lieutenant." His speech was smooth and accented in French.

Van Diemen said, "Roux captains the *Hilaire.*"

Roebuck said, "Her cargo?"

"Sugar," Roux said.

"Captain Roux is now loading his ship with cotton."

Roebuck said, "Come down by that rail?"

Roux and Van Dieman both smiled and nodded.

Cotton, of course, was the explanation Roebuck had earlier sought in his mind about the rail cars. He turned again to Roux. "You're headed north?"

"You have surmised it, Lieutenant," Roux said. "My destination is Newport."

The Frenchman sat down again and the two of them stared up at Roebuck. No one spoke.

"If you need a bunk," Van Diemen finally said, "Madame Galdos has a boarding house half a mile toward town. It is one of the few respectable lodgings we have."

Roebuck was being dismissed. He left them and stood stunned in the middle of the road, if you could call the red clay dirt-way a road. Gone was the command in New Orleans that had brought him fame, not to mention the lightning-fast cutter *Louisiana.* These were lost to him because he had believed he would master a new cutter here in St. Marks to go along with a brand-new command. Now all he mastered was a pile of broken timber somewhere here on this remote edge of the Union.

***

The Galdos place was marked by a shingle hanging in front:

GOOD BEDS

This House is strictly First Class

For single men only, by permission of Mrs. J.S. Galdos, Proprietress

Next to it hung another that said the same thing in Spanish.

It was the first house Roebuck had seen in St. Marks with a fence that separated yard from road. A path lined by flowers led to the door. He knocked. A woman in a pressed black dress—buttoned up high, no hoops in her skirt—answered. Her shoes were flat. A widow.

"Señora Galdos?" he said.

"Who else?" she said, squinting.

He introduced himself in Spanish and she replied in Spanish, "I have rules, Lieutenant. They are good and fair."

Good and fair for whom, he wondered.

She said, "You are Catholic?"

This question normally put him on his guard, but not this time. "Yes, ma'am."

She sort of nodded, not looking convinced, and said, "Supper is served at four. Breakfast at six. You must make your own bed, because I am His servant, not yours. The front door is bolted at eight each night. If you arrive at 8:01 you will be obliged to find another bed."

Roebuck said, "There are other beds?"

"There is a rum palace in the harbor village, but it is no place for a man with a good name. I cannot recommend it."

"Perhaps you could just name it, then," he said.

"Posey's Inn," she said, "The province of two-bit harlots."

Roebuck had an idea of what two bits bought in New Orleans along the waterfront, where the famine girls set up shop, but who knows what it would buy here. A breeze stirred at his back. He said goodbye to Doña Galdos and returned to the merchant to gather his luggage.

Although small, Port Leon was busy. There were four ships at anchor and the village was active. Van Diemen had done well to land himself here amidst so much commerce and wealth to be captured in duties.

The largest of the four ships was Roux's *Hilaire*. She had the remnant of a mizzenmast stepped immediately behind her main mast, a configuration he didn't often see at anchor. She was wider than most brigs although the same length, cargo the reason for the extra girth. Most shipwrights Roebuck knew and many seafaring men would call her a snow, a version of the brigantine he knew to be admired by slavers.

The *Hilaire*'s crew was looking at him, his uniform attracting their attention. That was something. He took her measure slowly and then turned back toward the village, a picture forming in his mind. The *Hilaire* making the middle passage with a belly full of contraband.

***

At Posey's Inn, the place Señora Galdos had named but not recommended, Roebuck took an upstairs room with a window, which he hoped might disperse some of the July heat gathered there. He changed into a civilian blouse, britches, and straw hat before descending to the tavern. The kitchen was serving shrimp stew with a half-loaf of bread. He added an ale and looked around.

While it appeared to be true that Roebuck's ship had been broken up, he was still an officer in the Revenue Marine until he heard otherwise. The tavern would be a place to swap stories as drinking men do and gather information that might be useful on the water.

The bar had a shine that comes from years of men leaning the elbows of their shirts or the backs of their waistcoats against it. Roebuck added a little of his own polish, picking out an open space to lean on.

Sunlight filled the room. A long mirror opposite him offered a view of the straw hat on his head. He'd acquired it on a whim at Cisette's Emporium, captivated by the New Orleans splendor of its red grosgrain trim. Certainly not the sort of hat a revenue officer would wear. He felt disguised.

In an hour, fishermen arrived in search of refreshment. They stayed for no more than a drink or two, doubtless limited by their early mornings. A tide of sailors came and went without interruption—guided to the place by celestial hands it seemed, probably in search of something more than refreshment—on shore to blow off steam after a long voyage or maybe to gird themselves before one. Roebuck drank and talked, learning plenty and hoping what he was bound to forget wasn't the important part.

As he chatted with a man who'd shipped out of Norfolk, a group of whores entered the room in a tidy line, reminding Roebuck of the infantry. The last of them was a round, very round, red-faced woman. She stomped one foot and the others stopped cold for a second before squaring up to the bar, a maneuver intended to fetch cheers from the onlookers, which it did.

A very small dark-haired sailor rose from a table and began walking the line. It wasn't long before he stopped and smiled up at the round woman. She twirled impressively, Roebuck noting a thin spot in the back of her golden wig where a patch of brownish hair peaked through. Job-related wear, he supposed. She grabbed the sailor by the hand and pulled him out the door toward someplace where they could consummate whatever it was that had united them.

Another girl came in and limped her way along the bar. She wasn't a foot-dragger like he'd seen among palsied beggars in New Orleans; more like she had broken a bone or maybe twisted up a joint. He turned to the barkeep and ordered a rum. Then he felt a tap on his shoulder. The girl with the limp was looking straight at him. She was lovely.

"*Buenas noches, marinero,*" she said.

Roebuck was getting used to how conversations here started in Spanish as often as they did in English. He said, "*Hola, guapa.*"

She shifted most of her weight against him, telling him in Spanish to buy her whatever he was drinking.

He ordered a rum in English and she said, "You are American."

He said, "Aren't you?"

"Yes, of course." She delivered the words in a way that suggested otherwise, yet she was game to keep the English going. Before long, Roebuck and Rose, as she called herself, were in the street walking toward what he knew would be a bed. They passed a porch lit by a sputtering lantern where a negro in a narrow frock coat stood, a shiny beaver top hat upon his head.

"Marse!" he said, "lookee here." He pulled a young negro woman or possibly a girl out onto the porch. "I have something fresh for you. That one," he said, pointing at Rose, "she humps like she walks—ooof." He said it as if shaking off a bad memory.

Rose said, "Angel, I know what make you happy."

Her grip strengthened and they continued on until reaching a long rough building assembled from mud and log. It was dark inside but he could see that it was full of canvas bunks tethered to posts that reached up to nothing. No roof. By the sound of it half the bunks were *ocupado*.

"Let's see the harbor instead," he said, interested in another look at the *Hilaire*.

"On my back or my feet, Angel, it's the same," she said, rubbing two fingers against her thumb.

He paid her a half dollar.

"More," she said.

"My pockets are empty."

She stuck out her hand and smiled so he fished around and found a penny.

"Next time," she said, "bring more."

At the harbor, the *Hilaire* rested at close anchor. The land breeze had petered out, replaced by one that built from the sea.

Rose looped her arm in his and they walked, a limping lady and her gentleman. Sniffing the air she said, "What a funny smell."

"Vinegar," he said.

"Why I smell this, Angel?"

Roebuck shrugged. There were captains of stinking ships who scoured their decks with vinegar. He wasn't sure whether that was to clean the planks or mask the smell soaked into them, but something about how Rose put the question suggested she was ahead of the answer. Their promenade continued until they reached the water-front, where another smell met them.

Rose backed up and said, "*Que bestial.*"

Bobbing gently in the moonlight, the *Hilaire* set an attractive profile at odds with the powerful stink of urine coming from her decks.

Rose pulled at Roebuck's arm and said, "Let's go back, Angel."

"Wait," he said, nose upturned. Urine could be a very stubborn smell. Planks of softwood, like larch or pine, absorbed it. Vinegar might help but only time did the job of ridding those planks of that odor.

On patrol, Roebuck had learned the difference between a prudent slaver and a careless one. Prudent slavers deployed necessary tubs throughout their cargo. It made a difference when it came to the solid waste but not the liquid kind. They couldn't keep the cargo from pissing on the deck. The cargo's way to demonstrate against the hell of it.

Had the *Hilaire* picked up Angolas or Loangos along the Guinea coast? Perhaps Roux had sold them in Recife, or maybe he'd hauled them as far as Havana, the price per head increasing in proportion to the distance travelled. Roux had said the *Hilaire* hauled sugar and there's no separating sugar from slaves.

Had Roux found a way to smuggle them all the way to the United States and into this new state of Florida, admitted to the Union just three months earlier? Naval ships and revenue cutters on patrol would make the attempt risky. But Roux flew a French jack, and the Navy Department preferred that its officers avoid offending the pride of France and inviting the intimidations of her navy. Why wouldn't Roux take advantage?

Rose tugged his shirt sleeve, pulling him off balance. She had a carpenter's wrist. "Come on, Angel," she said, "I no like it here."

Roebuck sniffed the breeze once more. Urine, sure enough, and not a sea of vinegar could hide it.

***

When Roebuck awoke reluctantly, the morning was half gone. A wiser path would have been to desist last night from the last several of those rums. Snake-bit, with the basin water too warm to help, he left his uniform coat draped over the chair back as he dressed, wanting to avoid the sort of attention it had attracted from the *Hilaire*'s crew the day before. Today he would be in shirt sleeves and Cisette's straw hat.

Downstairs, he finished a slow breakfast and was tempted to return to bed for a nap. Against this was a niggling feeling about making his confession. It was overdue. Last night he had noticed a little stone church on the way to the waterfront, so off he went to find it.

His mother, Josephina, was a Spaniard by birth and raised Catholic. She would be very pleased to see him making this journey. His father, Martin, was also Catholic but only in name, baptized as a condition of his marriage. Martin attended mass once a year, skipping Christmas in favor of Easter, manifesting a preference for the redemption in the risen Christ over the miracle of the born one.

Roebuck's own Catholicism was something he did not talk about in the Revenue Marine. There were men in that service who complained about the influence of what they called a Popery. These were men lacking the imagination to consider that one of their comrades might be among those so dangerously influenced. Roebuck said nothing when the subject came up but wanted to tell them how little there was to fear, given the Episcopalian readiness to build steeples higher than anything else in town, which matched a preference common to the American parishioner for objective measures when choosing a faith. Moreover, he knew it was just a matter of time before Florida got on the Methodist circuit and that there wasn't a pope known to history could resist such a force as that.

He turned a corner and when he turned another he found a line of penitents wrapped around the little stone church's ground and into the street, as if the place had grown a tail. The breeze was too hot to give relief and it raised swirls of red dust into the air. The idea of breathing in particles of clay until it was his turn to confess sins most men would pay to hear about was a nonsense. So he returned to Posey's, a tavern being the second most likely place to find a priest if you truly needed one.

CHAPTER 2

St. Marks was alive with news of a naval ship's arrival. The U.S.S. *Macedonian* had dropped anchor in Port Leon that morning. Roebuck knew the ship, a frigate that patrolled the islands from the tip of Florida all the way to Brazil. He knew her by sight because he happened to be there once when she took shelter from a gale off of Fort Jefferson way down in Florida's islands.

Two days later, the *Macedonian*'s illustrious captain, Matthew Calbraith Perry, sent an invitation to Roebuck, but the thought of how a conversation with Perry might go knotted his stomach. *So, Lieutenant Roebuck, tell me about your command,* or maybe *What does one do with oneself in St. Marks?* But Perry was a prodigious figure in the U.S. Navy, by no means a man to ignore. The next morning, Roebuck brushed his jacket, shined his boots, and was welcomed aboard the *Macedonian* at four bells in the forenoon watch. At 10:20 he was still waiting outside Perry's cabin, and after another ten minutes he told the steward he would not wait a minute more for a man who had invited him on a schedule but lacked the manners to see him at the appointed time. The steward looked thunderstruck before managing to explain that this was a time of day the captain read the Book of Books and would finish soon enough. Roebuck said he'd be at Posey's Inn when the captain finished with whatever thing of things he was up to.

Just then Perry opened his cabin door and said, "You are an impertinent young man."

Book or no Book, the captain had been listening. Roebuck said, "Yessir." Perry had a prodigious head and jowls to match. He was impressive looking, if not handsome, and with an impressive wave he motioned Roebuck in, leaving the door for his steward to close. There they stood in the narrow room looking at each other. Roebuck hoped this particular phase would end soon.

Perry said, "I have invited you into my cabin as a courtesy. I thought it proper to recognize the service you have rendered to our country," building to a climax Roebuck anticipated would be along the lines of *and you repay me with starchy, conceited behavior.* But Perry surprised him, muttering, "Well, never mind," looking dissatisfied but making an effort not to. He nodded toward a black lacquered chair, and Roebuck sat down. Perry sat on a sea chest.

They had started like alley cats, but Roebuck sensed a sympathy in Perry. Then suddenly and mysteriously Roebuck surprised himself by blurting, "You have heard of my father?"

Perry held Roebuck's eyes and nodded.

"Then you know we Roebucks are in the business of disappointing the Navy."

Perry's face registered nothing. "You put yourself in the same category as your father?"

"I am in that category, no matter where I put myself."

"Yes." Perry joined his hands and rubbed.

His was a famous naval tribe. Perry's father had reached the exalted rank of captain. His elder brother, Oliver Hazard Perry, had whipped the British on Lake Erie some thirty years ago, throwing the nation into a swoon. The U.S. Congress had gone so far as to mint a coin in commemoration.

Perry said, "You see our lives and relations as different?"

"Night and day, sir."

Perry said, "Darkness and light," sort of grinning. While not exactly snaggletoothed, his mouth was pretty crowded.

Roebuck said, "Yes, sir."

Perry said, "You believe our family connections have had one effect on you and another on me." He stood up. "But I have been called Oliver a thousand times, my own mother included."

Roebuck wanted to nod but he wasn't sure what Perry was saying.

Perry said, "You have a brother?"

"Yes, sir. Three years my senior."

"Has your mother called you by his name?"

Roebuck thought about it for a second. She never had but he remembered how she'd called his brother, Peter, by Robert. He'd never thought about that until now. Perry was making some kind of point. "No," Roebuck said, wondering when the captain was going to say something about his taking leave from the Navy in favor of the Revenue Marine.

All Perry said was, "Yet we both live in shadow."

How strange, shocking even, to hear of Oliver Hazard Perry and Martin Roebuck referenced even obliquely in the same breath, one a national hero and the other a disgrace.

Back on shore, Roebuck watched several fishermen standing in the shallows cleaning the day's catch. Mackerel, the striped backs and fanned tails said so, a very good fish to eat when salted. The fishermen knifed through the bellies, scooping offal and tossing it to hogs gathered in expectation on the sand. The men took care to keep the spines in the meat, mackerel having a very neat and useful spine. Roebuck smiled. Such an abundance here in St. Marks.

CHAPTER 3

The sheets were down around Rose's waist, and the sound she let out rhythmically was not a snore exactly but would be, he predicted, in about ten years. He tried to get out of bed without disturbing her, but she grabbed his wrist without opening an eye. *Jesus, that carpenter's grip.*

He said, "Rose, I have to go."

"Where you go, Angel?"

He stood up and pulled on his drawers.

"Come to your Rose," she said.

He dressed in his civies again and leaned over to kiss her lips. The night before, Roebuck had asked in Spanish what Rose's real name was. She had answered in English, "My name is Rose. I'm your flower." Roebuck thinking of thorns. She was from Tampico and limped because of a drunken captain from the Tuxpan *batallón* who had shot her in the hip one night after she had resisted his violent advances one in the family parlor. Rose's mother had hit him in the head with a large and heavy tortilla skillet and in return he killed her. Rose explained that her father was too liquored up most days to be much use, so she had left home. Six years had passed since then, two of them here in St. Marks.

When he was dressed he said, "I'm going to see Mr. Garrison in the boatyard. Tomorrow when the tide is low I'll look at the bay south of the harbor." He was hoping Garrison could map him some of the hazards, or at least show him where to look.

"Me too," she said. "I show you the way."

Now she was on her feet. Her smooth skin, biscuit-colored breasts, round belly, and black patch beneath it. She came on with that hitched step and wrapped her arms around him, adding pleasantly to the morning's heat.

He said, "You aren't exactly light on your feet and I don't want to carry you."

"I need to make sure you no get lost, Angel. You get so confused when you have to use your feet instead of a boat. I come in the morning," she said. "We go together."

"You'll be asleep."

"I'll make you breakfast."

"I don't want breakfast."

"No? Oh yes I know, Bobby Chase, you no eat, *El Fantome*, how you say in English?"

Where had she heard about his nicknames? Even the Spanish one. This town was smaller than he thought, much smaller. He said "Rose, you tell me something."

"Why should I when I can't see the bay with you."

"Tell me something and we'll go together."

She smiled a little.

He said, "What was the *Hilaire*'s cargo?"

She said, "We no talk about that."

"You know what it was."

"Nobody talk about it with you, Angel," she said. "You think you put on a straw hat and walk around, the people no see you? *El Fantome*, Ghost."

Roebuck reddened. He must have looked ridiculous skulking around the village thinking himself disguised.

She said, "They look at you and they look at him."

She meant Van Diemen. He wasn't sure how but he knew.

She said, "They ask who will be here next month and the month after and the next year? *Este hombre*," she smiled. "He no going nowhere. Too much money here in St. Marks. But you? Maybe you leave tomorrow."

Roebuck said, "People know what he's doing?"

She laughed again, shaking her head. "Angel, that man, he pay everyone. *La negra* we saw on that porch in the harbor?"

"The young one?" he said.

"Yes, that one. That house full of *negras*, little ones, big ones, half of them just arrive."

"From the *Hilaire*?"

"I no need to tell you because you a clever boy." She shrugged. "Who you think makes the money?" She was telling him that Van Diemen prostituted negroes and traded in slaves. Roebuck had more or less believed the importation of black Africans into this country was over. But Rose was saying no. It continued in remote places like St. Marks. He wondered how many black markets thrived on the edges of the Union.

***

At dawn the next morning, Rose surprised Roebuck just as he was leaving Posey's. She had packed some tortillas filled with a mixture that smelled good enough to start his stomach turning.

"We'll eat them by the water," he said.

They drifted down the St. Marks River in a skiff borrowed from the boatyard. The water was low but fast on a retreating tide, banks of oysters jutting up along either side. More abundance. When they reached the bay, he beached the skiff and hid it in the brush.

Rose said, "Why you want to walk along the bay? Only a crazy man walks here in the summer."

"I'm crazy then."

"*Sí*, you my *demente*," she said ahead of him, picking out a path he had not seen. "You walk far enough, you think the water changes? It's blue here, but there," she pointed to the east, "it's green? Water is water, Angel."

"Thanks for telling me."

"I tell you because someone has to. You crazy."

"No, sugar," he said, "I'm in love."

"Same thing,"

He said, "Maybe you forgot how you said to me: 'Take your Rose so I can walk in the sun with my crazy *teniente*.'"

She laughed. "It's true, I say it. I crazy but here I am with my Angel, so maybe not so crazy."

Rose was not crazy. She had talked him into paying her to join him. Her time was like a lawyer's—valuable.

Roebuck had already walked the Apalachee Bay's western shore at low tide. That side had a sandy bottom and, save for a few grass flats peeking through, wasn't much to worry about, even for a pilot that didn't know it well. He had seen a chart of the east side, where they were now. Something about the markings caused him to doubt the chart's accuracy. He preferred his own eyes to judge and expected the low morning tide to reveal plenty.

The path took them away from the coast up to a piney rise and then turned southward. When they had a good view they stopped. The sand and mud of the bay's bottom was exposed. Birds hopped from one mouthful to another. Jagged limestone rose from the bay's floor. A high tide would conceal those jags. Roebuck imagined sailing into the top of one and tearing a hole in his boat. But he could also imagine how snapper fish would shelter at their base. Good fishing, he thought, if you could navigate through. It was tempting. Why not fish here and send the bounty up-rail to the inns of Tallahassee? The living could be good.

Rose scrambled over the trail's occasional shelves of limestone with a goat's equilibrium. The path became narrower as they headed east. Eventually they were thicketed in and followed a stream out, finding a cool shady spot where the water was deep. Roebuck stripped off his clothes and waded in.

"Join me, sugar," he said.

"I no like it," she said.

The pool was deep enough for him to swim upstream. He rolled over on his back and drifted down again.

"Stand up and take off your frock," he said.

"Angel, I no like the water."

"It's cool, feels good. I'll show you."

So she stripped too.

"Those two," he pointed at her breasts, "could float you back to Tampico."

"I know you like them, Angel," she said, climbing onto his back.

He waded her in. She wasn't heavy and he swam her around the pool until she was laughing.

"It's so good on my skin," she said.

When his limbs tired, they splashed in the shallow.

"It's nice to feel something new," she said. "The water is cool."

"You're my Rose," he said.

"I'm everybody's Rose."

"My Sugar, then."

"I can do it too." She waded out onto the narrow beach and twisted water out of her hair, leaving a trail in the sand. Then she sat down and opened her sack, pulling out a Mexican pepper. "Give me your knife," she said, and cut the pepper open, taking out some seeds and setting them on a smooth rock. She offered three to him saying, "Chew."

He did and in moments he felt a searing in his mouth. His eyes watered and he dipped his hands into the stream to drink, then splashed water on his face. "You just made me your fool," he said thinking she had probably done that a while ago.

She laughed and then crushed a seed between her teeth, moving its essence around her mouth and did the same with two more, untroubled by their heat. "Lie back," she said and began to stroke his prick, which quickly stood up. "My *Teniente* is ready for battle."

Then she put it in her mouth and he felt the heat, her tongue a wet flame. He inhaled and said, "That gets your attention."

She took it out and said, "Stop talking."

Afterward they ate lunch and shared two bowls of the tobacco he kept in his pouch. She liked smoking from his clay pipe. Then they napped before returning to town.

CHAPTER 4

D on Justo ignored Doña Belén in favor of his own face, which was reflected very handsomely in the mirror. This vanity, although repellent, was the least of his problems.

"My dear," she continued, despite this lack of interest, "it is your brother, after all, who has asked us to take her in."

"This is something you have told me before, darling," he said. "More than once and more than twice."

"She is your blood, Justo."

He shifted attention from the mirror to an open bottle of brandy, lifting a glass and saying, "If you would be so kind."

How well he staged his indifference.

"You know her by sight," she said. "I do not. You must be the one to greet her when she arrives tomorrow. And recall, my dear, she has agreed to come here because she is fascinated by her roguish uncle Justo. If you are not there to welcome her we will have a bad start to something very important to us both."

"I am occupied," he said, shifting his eyes to the window. "As for my niece Anita, she is a pig with stringy black hair. When you see a girl who fits that description, you have found her."

Belén said, "Your elder brother has forced this journey upon her because of the decline in our fortune. Yet you feel no obligation?"

Justo fiddled with a stack of papers.

Their business, one of Montevideo's oldest trading houses, had a problem. Its receipts could no longer keep pace with Justo's gambling, whoring, and acquiring every beautiful object that caught his eye.

"My Justo," she said, softening her voice. "Just this once."

He said, "I wish to be left alone, my sweet. What more do you want?"

"What I want," she said, "is for you to stop giving in to the disorder of your mind and act like a man."

***

The next day, Belén watched as passengers disembarked from Anita's ship. They moved with surprising ease down a flexing plankway. *Sea legs*, she thought, smiling. Most were met with hugs, others with tears of joy. A few wandered off alone into Montevideo's old city. Not one of these passengers answered to Justo's unkind description of his niece.

Belén was not normally a woman given to worry but today, watching for Anita, her nerves jumped each time a girl stepped from the ship. She wanted her niece to like her because she was lonely, and, to her surprise, grateful for the small affection that had grown with each letter she and Anita had exchanged. At the age of twenty-nine, she knew many men but had no close friends who were women.

After nearly an hour, the flow of passengers stopped. Belén looked down the length of the wharf. At its end, near the ship's stern, she saw a girl brushing dust from the folds of her skirt. This same girl had debarked thirty minutes ago, looking too much like a woman to be her niece. Now Belén hurried over and said, a little anxiously, "Anita?"

"*Sí*, I am called Anita. Tía Belén?"

"*Sí*, Anita, how beautiful you have become!" It was true, she was a beauty. Even so, Belén half expected her niece to color at the extremity of the compliment.

Anita showed nothing. Instead, she put a hand on her hip, pointed to the old city of Montevideo, and said, "It is as I told Papa it would be, a cow pen."

"Come, child," Belén said, kissing her once on each cheek. "I cannot tell you what a pleasure it is to see you."

"And I am glad to see you, Tía." Anita said, "Where is Tío Justo?"

"I'm sorry, my dear, Don Justo wished to welcome you in person, but urgent business has taken him away."

Anita pursed her lips and said, "Business? I have come all the way from Cádiz on a ship full of paupers smelling of lard and beans and he is not here?"

Anita was more interested in Justo, of course. Every person of her sex was. It made Belén sad. This niece had become a woman. Her brown eyes had a fetching shine. Two mother-of-pearl combs held rich mounds of black hair in place. Belén was suddenly conscious that she presented an unfavorable contrast, with her long black hair pulled in a tight bun and without time to change out of her riding clothes. What should Anita think of her?

Belén said, "You are grown up, niece."

"Grown up?" Anita said. "Why, yes, I am so grown up that I can be traded away as if I were a barn animal at a meet."

"You are tired, my dear," Belén said. "Things will seem different once you rest." But she understood how Anita felt.

Several months ago, Don Justo had learned that a Creole who operated the largest wheat and barley exchange in Rio de la Plata was looking to marry his unwed son. Justo put this news into a letter and sent it to his elder brother Cornelio who had three unmarried daughters. Most South American Creoles cherished a desire to improve their line with noble blood from Spain. The kind that ran through Justo, Cornelio, and Anita. This trading family especially so, and they were counting on their son to do it. As Belén had borne no daughters, indeed no children, Justo resorted to a most unsentimental trade, coming to an agreement with the Creole merchant to swap Anita for a lucrative position in the wheat and barley exchange. Don Cornelio had wasted no time in delivering his daughter.

Walking arm in arm with Belén toward the coach, Anita abruptly stopped to say, "Tell me about Mr. Wheat and Barley. Is he handsome? How does he dance?"

"I have heard nothing but good words about his character," Belén said, and that was true.

"God save me," Anita said. "It is tragic." The coachman helped her up and when they were on their way she said, "How far is Nahomi?"

"You know the name of our estancia?"

"We all know it, Tía. We know that it holds 200,000 head of cattle and sheep and a stable of the pinto horses you favor. We know this because it pays for the life we enjoy in Cádiz."

Belén said, "Estancia Nahomi is some way east of the old city, but the road is smooth, so you can sleep."

"Tell me about Tío Justo," Anita said.

"He is fine, my dear."

Anita said, "I have a clear memory of his last visit to Cádiz. Yvette—do you remember her?"

"Your elder sister."

"By four years," Anita said. "Her friends were visiting for dinner and when Tío Justo walked into the room, they all fell silent. He was so perfect it took the words right out of their pretty mouths. Is he still that way?"

Belén said, "He still likes to walk into a room full of girls."

CHAPTER 5

Another message had arrived from Captain Perry inviting Roebuck to tour his frigate. Roebuck knew the *Macedonian*'s anchorage was next to the *Hilaire* and wondered what he might see looking down into Roux's ship from the vantage of Perry's portside deck.

A lieutenant met him as he came aboard and guided Roebuck down to the orlop, the lowest of the ship's three decks. The lieutenant pointed and mumbled his way through the tour, looking interested only at the ship's stern knees and breast hook, bleating about how the planks were fastened with a very hard iron and very neatly plugged with wood.

Roebuck yawned and asked to be taken above, where he stopped amidships and peered over the rail down to the *Hilaire*, observing her goings-on. There wasn't much to see. A few cotton bales loaded, not yet stowed below, no one paying attention to them, purposely left there, he decided, to announce themselves as the ship's cargo.

Down in the captain's cabin, Perry waited with a pot of tea. He and Roebuck spoke aimlessly for a while before Roebuck said, "Sir, if you will forgive the question, what is it about St. Marks has you leisuring here?"

Perry sipped from a cup, which looked overwhelmed in his racoon-trap hand. "During the six months of our patrol," he said, "there were outbreaks of fever among the residents of several islands in the Caribbean."

Not a promising beginning.

"I do not like shore leave in the first place, too many temptations, but with the fever at hand I could not allow a man ashore, not one. We were ship-bound without exception for close to half a year, and the men felt it to an extreme."

"Have you lost any to the fever?"

"Fortunately, no."

Roebuck, impressed, said, "And they give you no thanks?"

"Men are no more capable of taking note of their good health than they are of noting the hair on their head."

"Until they begin to lose it," Roebuck said.

Perry smiled—an unusual sight, Roebuck guessed.

Perry said, "I am giving my sailors two weeks here before we finish our voyage."

Roebuck said, "Why St. Marks?"

"There is no fever here," Perry said. "And diversions enough without being too many. And something else that should not be under calculated. Here, the men are far enough from the naval station in Pensacola to be sensible of real liberty. I believe they can be themselves in St. Marks in a way they could not have been in Pensacola."

Roebuck had the feeling there was more to it. He suspected that Perry, like most captains, had to fight to keep his seamen from leaving the service. The Navy had been out of favor with the public for at least two decades and starved by Congress. "Are you concerned," Roebuck said, "about re-enlistments?"

Perry said, "A captain is concerned with little else. Seamen have many advantages these days in the midst of such abundant merchant opportunities. Re-enlistments suffer. And yes, you are correct, my friend, St. Marks is a concession."

Roebuck had been paid a small bonus when he transferred to the Revenue Marine. He said, "Why not pay enlistment bonuses?"

"The Navy depends on the U.S. Treasury. We might as well ask a cat to share a sardine. Our men have not been paid half of what they are owed and they are unhappy. One day, months ago, on a calm sea and a sunny day just out of the harbor at Nevis, every seaman on the *Macedonian* stopped working for an hour. They just sat or lay down wherever they were."

Roebuck said, "Goddamned mutiny."

"I didn't see it that way, Lieutenant. The leader of this demonstration had communicated the plan to me through the sergeant-at-arms. So I knew when and for how long it would last. To prevent it would invite trouble, so I didn't."

"They wanted you to know they expected to be paid."

"It cleared the air," Perry said.

A thought excited Roebuck. He rose and said, "May I show you something, sir, up above?"

Up on the main deck, Perry with Roebuck at his side moved in a way that was stately and calm while Roebuck wanted to bound forward.

At the right place, Roebuck said, "Here, sir."

Perry stopped and the two of them looked down onto the *Hilaire*. Roebuck pointed and said, "See that chain there, along the portside bulwark."

Perry lifted his chin a little and said, "I'm not blind, Mr. Roebuck."

"Can you guess its purpose, sir?"

Perry's face assumed a granite quality. All naval captains could do this. Roebuck thought it might be part of their examination.

Perry said, "Just tell me."

"That chain," Roebuck said, "is used to restrain male slaves by their leg irons."

Perry looked at the ship from end to end and said, "She smells like a slaver."

"Piss and vinegar," Roebuck said.

Perry said, "We do not profane the main deck on this ship, Mr. Roebuck."

"No sir," Roebuck said, then said nothing and just waited, putting his blank subordinate's face on.

Perry said, "Go on, Lieutenant."

"Her captain's name is Roux and he is a friend of Abel Van Diemen's."

"The customs man?"

Roebuck nodded.

Perry surveyed the *Hilaire*. He wouldn't like how Roebuck, a Revenue Marine officer, was educating him and yet he would want to know the truth.

After some time, Perry said, "You think Captain Roux sold contraband here?"

"I do."

"And you do not trust Van Diemen."

"He is a criminal and St. Marks is his enterprise," Roebuck said.

Perry said, "The United States made the importation of slaves illegal forty years ago. And we in the Navy endeavor at sea day in and day out to end that trade. Yet you, Mr. Roebuck, presume the Navy has failed?"

Roebuck appreciated the question if not exactly the words. Why should Perry believe him? If their roles were reversed, Roebuck would be skeptical until the case couldn't be denied. The prestige of the Navy, while not exactly at stake, was part of the story. He said, "The navy has ended the slave trade among ships flagged with our jack and many others also, but Captain Roux flies a French jack."

"How could they sell fresh negroes here?" Perry said. "Ones who are so obviously contraband with no English or civilization."

"Captain," Roebuck said, wanting to return to the point. The *Hilaire* has engaged in illegal trade on our shores, and you will find between 10,000 and 30,000 dollars in gold aboard her."

"You suggest I impound the *Hilaire*."

"It is your duty, sir," Roebuck said. "But you'll not find the loot unless you open her up timber by timber. Yes, threaten to impound her. Give the captain a choice: show me the gold or lose your ship and the gold."

Perry looked doubtful, but it wasn't long before Roebuck was watching a detail from the *Macedonian* board the *Hilaire*. He knew what would happen next. An obsequious mate holding them off until the captain arrived with honeyed words and a cooperative demeanor. But when he realized there was no talking his way out of it, this captain would become offended and belligerent. It enraged such men to realize how nothing would come of all the risks they had made to get to this point. Risks, Roebuck believed, which included the ruination of their soul.

If he was right about the *Hilaire*, the Navy now understood what was happening here. In the future it would be harder for types like Roux and Van Diemen to hide from view in St. Marks. It gave Roebuck pleasure to know that a Revenue Marine officer like himself could subvert the enrichment of a son of a bitch like Van Diemen.

Roebuck recalled one slaver in particular he'd boarded as commander of the *Louisiana*. An American Guineaman out of Newport in which the contraband, shackled two by two, right wrist and ankle of one to the left wrist and ankle of another, were forced to live in hog-pen feculence. The ship's officers had gratified themselves with the females, who were obviously mortified by the arrival of Roebuck and his fellows—more white men, thus more violation. This fear considerably dampened Roebuck's exhilaration at capturing this slaver, especially how that fear might outlast everything else in their lives. Another slaver also came to mind. This one from Boston, the captain saying how he needed the proceeds to pay the dowries of his three daughters. His contraband had slept without cover, their skin rubbed away to bare bone at the elbow and knee, a consequence of under-planed timber on the deck planks. Sights and smells of these boardings remained vivid to Roebuck and showed no signs of fading from his mind.

He and Perry watched Roux, tarpot hat on his handsome head, emerge from below. After some back-and-forth with the *Macedonian*'s boarding officer, Roux began to grimace, the bitterness setting in.

Roebuck said to Perry, "What will you use the coin for?"

"I will count it," Perry said, "record the amount in the ship's log, and pay my men what they are owed."

CHAPTER 6

Justo and a circle of associates—they could hardly be called friends—gathered in his study during some evenings. They were there tonight. Doña Belén knew he would entertain them with cigars and French brandy. They used Justo's study because they had started to draw unwanted attention in town. Meeting here, at Estancia Nahomi, kept them away from prying eyes.

Although she thought of Justo as weak and trifling, lately she wondered if he might be more than the harmless garden snake she had supposed. One of the men who joined these evenings was the French Admiral LeBlanc, a man who owed her over 1,500 reales. Or rather owed those reales to La Compañía de Comercio de Overo, the trading business she ran, ostensibly with Justo, although he was worthless. The admiral had not paid for any of the provisions, from mutton and beef to grain and rum, delivered over the last three months to the ships in his squadron. There was something strange about LeBlanc. He could have stepped right out of a portrait hanging in France's halls of glory, a handsome picture of the gallant French naval officer. Yet his dealings in Uruguay were muddy, and she wondered what it was exactly that had tempted him down here. Of course, Justo, prancing fool, had not lifted a finger to collect the money LeBlanc owed them. At least he had given her this chance to claim what was rightfully the company's, for she was resolved tonight to ask the admiral about the money he owed her.

She and Justo maintained a small office in town peopled by two clerks, but Belén much preferred to spend her working hours in the larger main office her father had installed years ago in an outbuilding on the estancia, across the courtyard from the main house, where Justo hosted his cronies this evening. She left her office and slowly crossed the courtyard, warming to the prospect of surprising them. Besides LeBlanc, she knew she would find the Sardinian officer Lechi, a narrow faced beady-eyed cutthroat, a man who had made a series of blunt and repulsive passes at her.

The night was still and humid, kept from total darkness by woolly shafts of moonlight penetrating the moisture in the air. The quiet caused her to wonder if Justo's gathering had broken up early. Hopefully not. She walked slowly, savoring an image of consternation on her husband's face that she knew her visit would produce. And she enjoyed the anticipation of admiring looks she could expect from the other men. Justo had noted these looks too. She could see that in the way his eyes narrowed and his posture hardened whenever she met them. He didn't like it. But he never said or did a thing to discourage it. It was as if these men owned him.

A horse whinnied. She looked toward the hitching post by the entrance. Nothing there. So she walked to the east side of the house, shaded from the moonlight. The horse snorted. Once her eyes adjusted to the darkness she realized two horses were hitched to the lowest branch of a tala tree. Justo and the others were using extra caution.

She walked through the entryway and down the hall. The study door was ajar. A column of lantern light showed through the crack and set aglow tobacco smoke drifting through the opening. Justo had broken out his Cuban cigars.

She heard Justo say, "Garibaldi is worthless!" That was him putting on his bullying voice.

She recognized the voice that answered as Lechi's. "Garibaldi has moved men to revolution, led them in battle. But he fails to impress you?" Expressing the word *you* as an insult. Lechi's Spanish was accented, and not in an attractive way. Justo sometimes imitated him to her for a laugh, adopting the accent of an Italian rustic. *El Cafone*, or the boor, is what Justo called him, only never to his face.

"He is naïve," replied Justo, "and leads brutes to political suicide. The hallucination of Republicanism."

"You judge Garibaldi?" Lechi said. "You, a creature who came into this world as a measure of pus drained from a boil on your mother's hairy ass."

Belén stopped and slid into a dark nook where a portrait of her father hung. She smiled at it, knowing how much he would have enjoyed hearing what she had just heard. She would listen a little longer.

"You compare a man of such refinements as the don to drainage from a boil?" That was LeBlanc, his Spanish accented but graceful.

"Is that unjust?" said Lechi. "Perhaps he was just farted into the world."

Belén wondered what Justo would say. He was probably waiting for LeBlanc to save him from the humiliation, but LeBlanc might have been waiting too, because the room remained quiet.

LeBlanc finally spoke. "The don is right that Garibaldi leaves a wake of chaos wherever he goes." The words might have soothed Justo had LeBlanc not waited so long to utter them, the pause announcing that while Justo may not be a boil on his mother's ass, neither was he man enough to defend himself from the insults of this *cafone*.

When Belén thought about LeBlanc, it wasn't just about the mystery of his presence in Uruguay. She wondered about his life in France. Was he still married? She had heard rumors about difficulties and debt but wasn't sure if those could be credited. And Justo said very little about the admiral, reserving his scorn for Lechi.

LeBlanc was a gentleman with an easy authority, and he was attractive. She wondered how he managed to keep such a strange collection of men together. Justo the Spaniard, a royalist fantasizing about returning Uruguay and the Argentine Confederation to Spain. Lechi, a comrade of Garibaldi's, a so-called fighter for freedom. But those who knew Lechi called him Garibaldi's sword, a killer who helped Garibaldi first in Italy and now here to advance his cause on waves of blood. And then there was a man they called the American. That one had not been to Nahomi yet, but she could guess at which American he was.

These were dangerous times in Uruguay, indeed throughout the region, all the way down to the southern tip of Argentina. Civil war surrounded them, but in LeBlanc she saw a man who might have the nerve and guile to navigate through and emerge the better for it.

She sensed that somehow Nahomi, their estancia, was at stake with these men. Her father had entrusted it to her and Justo. Despite Justo's incompetence and weakness, it was still a place of wealth and enormous potential. There were twice as many cows in Uruguay as people and three times as many sheep, and Estancia Nahomi was pasture to a great many of them. She could see no other reason for LeBlanc's interest in Justo save Nahomi. And she knew she should fear him for this, but she didn't. She was attracted to something in him.

She heard LeBlanc say, "Mr. Lechi, can you explain to me why we are disappointed yet again by the yield in silver from La Gaucin? These disappointments come too often, my friend, and I would be a fool to tolerate them any further."

Lechi said, "The captain of the *Eliza Davidson*, he doesn't cooperate. He makes trouble, slows his men from working. They fill the wagons with rock, not silver."

She knew the *Eliza Davidson* was one of two American trading ships LeBlanc had captured on the pretext that it had violated a blockade, which the French had imposed against the Argentines. Practically everyone she knew in Montevideo was made uncomfortable by what seemed to be LeBlanc's indifference to keeping personal ambition separate from military policy. What good could come to them by antagonizing the Americans?

LeBlanc said, "Beat him."

She could not see him but could imagine the admiral leaning back as he said this. Maybe even crossing his legs.

"We did. He's little but he doesn't give in like you expect from an American."

LeBlanc said "You are an expert on Americans?

"Money-grubbers, merchants, not men."

LeBlanc said, "Beat him harder."

Lechi said, "We broke his teeth, but it does not move him."

"Break his arm." LeBlanc said this as an uncle would chide a wayward nephew.

"No, I don't think so. We need every pair of hands for the mine."

"Cut out his tongue. If he tells them to do things which slow us down, then we will make it impossible for him to speak."

They were silent for a while. What could Justo be thinking? How could he believe that he was anything but LeBlanc's toy?

LeBlanc broke the silence. "I recall there were two boys captured."

Lechi said, "Yes, that's true. Two boys, little ones, can't work so much."

"Kill one," Leblanc said.

"Kill a boy?"

"That's what I said."

Justo still quiet as a mouse.

"Which one?"

"There is usually one asking for it more than the other. Tell the captain if he refuses to cooperate, we shall kill the one who isn't asking for it."

Lechi said, "So I tell him, help us or we kill the boy?"

LeBlanc paused, maybe thinking about it, and said, "You form his crew in a line, call the boy out. Say that you are tired of the captain's games and say, it's your fault that this boy must die. Then slit his throat."

"His throat?"

"Do you understand me, Lechi?"

"Yes, sir, I do. Kill a boy."

"Yes, but just one. Keep the other in case we have any more trouble."

Belén decided that collecting the debt from LeBlanc might not be as urgent as she had thought. Her footfalls away were as quiet as she could make them.

***

Belén and Justo left their office and headed into the evening. The black cobbled streets were still warm with the day's sun. They walked toward the Londres, a club she loved not only because it served lamb from her pastures but because the chef knew how to prepare it so that the meat retained its juices. And there was no better place to be seen among Montevideo's foremost citizens, not to mention catch up on the week's gossip. Tonight they would dine with Admiral LeBlanc. At the club's entry, she and Justo nodded their way through an excess of friendly greetings from the doorman and the commissionaire before turning toward the back room where LeBlanc held court.

"Doña Belén, how fabulous to see you." This greeting was offered by Senator Montcalvo, who smiled at her in a way she trusted instinctively. Turning his back to Justo, he took Belén's hand and raised it to his delicately mustachioed lips. Montcalvo was powerful in the Senate and a man who openly expressed doubts about the presence of so many Europeans in their capital during Uruguay's civil war.

Belén said, "How lovely to see you again, Senator. How is Doña Teresa?"

"She is very well indeed, madame, but would be better yet with a visit from you,"

"I have not seen her in so long," Belén said.

"A terrible shame," he said, and they grinned together.

What a beguiling man and not just in the usual way of those with power. "Yes," she said, "it has been too long."

Montcalvo said, "Will you dine with the admiral tonight?"

"You know I will," she said.

This seemed to cut the man's good cheer in half. He said, "The American consul general Houghton is dining with him this evening. Why don't you ask them about the Americans."

She smiled, about to take a step toward LeBlanc's table, but hesitated, a question forming in her mind. *What about them?*

Justo grabbed her arm and yanked her forward, not giving her a chance to ask. "That man," he said, "is a cretin."

Montcalvo had mentioned Houghton. She had first met Hilary Houghton two years ago at an assembly of suppliers to American ships. Houghton and the consulate had hosted the affair, serving a dinner that was unappetizing in a way one of the merchants, who was French by birth, characterized as uniquely American. He had said that Americans could mix any ingredient no matter how fresh or how fine into something that would appall any palate but an Englishman's.

A waiter led them to the back table. Justo was about to sit at the open seat next to LeBlanc, but the admiral who had risen, waved him off and said, "Doña Belén, come sit beside me, my dear."

The French naval captain Dufour, an enormous man, had also risen and bowed a greeting. Pure formality she realized because his expression was pure indifference. When he sat down again and grasped his glass of wine, the size of his hands made it seem like a thimble.

She didn't have to ask about the Americans because the subject came up quickly, introduced by Houghton, who said, "Our

Commodore Nicolson has called for at least 50 guns from the U.S. Navy to sail down here to confront the French."

"They are going to fight the French?" LeBlanc said. "I doubt it."

"They will confront you, sir," Houghton said, "for taking their merchantmen, *America* and *Eliza Davidson*. While it is true the Americans do not realize you no longer represent France, it is a mistake to doubt they will confront you for so openly disregarding their maritime rights."

"You have made an insult to their flag, Admiral," said the Sardinian, Lechi. "May I salute you." He raised his glass.

Houghton hesitated, carving patterns with a knife into the gravy on his plate before saying, "They might send a ship of the line with seventy-five or maybe a hundred guns."

LeBlanc shook his head slowly in dismissal rather than disagreement, "No time for a ship of the line, Mr. Houghton. They will send something fast with as many guns as they can fit on it. And should they send fifty guns, we will greet them with one hundred."

"Greet them?" Houghton said. He stopped playing with the gravy.

"More like sink them, I suppose," LeBlanc said.

Houghton swallowed some wine, not looking very happy. Belén had not discovered the reason why, but Houghton always had a seat at LeBlanc's table.

Lechi said, "Dead men tell no tales, Mr. Houghton."

Belén said, "What you mean when you say sink them is kill them, no?"

"When I say dead men, is the meaning not clear madame?" Lechi answered for LeBlanc, superimposing his own enthusiasm onto the admiral.

"What if it is two ships they send?" asked Houghton.

LeBlanc answered, denying Lechi the chance. "It won't be two ships, Mr. Houghton, so you may sleep soundly tonight."

"It's not tonight I'm worried about." Houghton resumed carving the gravy.

This time it was Captain Dufour who spoke. "The Americans will not fight," he said. "They only confront those weaker than themselves."

There was something about how nakedly they discussed their crime that Belén knew should affront her, but instead she felt a thrill to hear them.

Dufour said, "Even in the event they challenge us, we control the sea here. They are no match and their Commodore Nicolson knows this. Why else have they done nothing so far? This is where the American heart is. They do nothing because they are afraid."

Houghton, who seemed to be feeling better about the conversation, stabbed a piece of mutton and gulped it down before saying, "It would be better if we gave them a good reason."

"Reason for what?" Dufour said.

"For doing nothing," Houghton said. "Your Gallic magnificence and the nature of your invincibility may not be as well known to them as it is to you, Captain. And in their ignorance they might very well fight you."

LeBlanc said, "What do you propose, Houghton?"

"They must believe that their merchant ships have sunk and their crews are lost. If they are given reason to believe that the *America* and *Eliza Davidson* are gone, there will be less pressure for their government to do the thing you say they don't want to do, which is fight the French."

"You mean fight us," Dufour said, clearly making a distinction.

Houghton nodded, his mouth full of gravy-soaked bread. He said, "Not even France knows yet of your rupture with her," projecting bits of bread from his mouth as he did.

"Rupture," LeBlanc said as if smelling burnt coffee.

"Liberation," Houghton said, balancing a smile with the act of chewing. "The Americans still believe that to fight Admiral LeBlanc is to fight France."

"They will not believe the ships and crews are gone. Why should they?" said Dufour.

Houghton said, "They will be glad for the excuse and accept it."

LeBlanc said, "Dufour, you will command three ships to intercept any American naval vessels headed to Rio de la Plata."

Dufour grinned. "With pleasure, my Admiral," he said.

"Insurance, Mr. Houghton," LeBlanc said, "nothing more. We shall follow your advice and expect your countrymen to do exactly as you predict." He turned to Belén and grinned. "Now, my dear, tell me about your herds."

CHAPTER 7

On Roebuck's next visit to the *Macedonian,* he caught a lighter carrying barrels of salted fish and pork to her. Perry shouted a greeting as Roebuck climbed the Jacob's ladder to board. This was the first time Perry had come out to welcome him. He looked almost genial. Together they backed down the main hatch ladder to the gun deck, where they met two of the *Macedonian's* lieutenants and a gunner named Jaffe. Perry and Roebuck walked the deck side by side while the others hovered, looking more like attendants than officers.

Perry pulled out a white glove and tugged it onto his right hand. Stopping at each gun, he dragged the tip of his pointing finger along the barrel. Then, without looking, he showed the finger to his officers. The number eight and number twenty-one guns must have shown too much grime because the lieutenants went off to find their gun crews.

In the captain's cabin, Perry filled Roebuck's cup from a teapot, saying that it was his finest blend. "Lieutenant Roebuck," he said, "we pulled twenty-two thousand dollars in gold out of the *Hilaire.* I reported to Abel Van Diemen what we discovered."

"And also what you did with that discovery?" By that, Roebuck meant using the gold to pay the *Macedonian's* seamen and officers.

Perry leaned back in his chair and said, "So I did, so I did." Showing those teeth again, grinning.

"I wish I had been there to see his face."

"Mr. Van Diemen does not meet with your approval."

"No, sir. Neither does syphilis."

"I wanted to ask him why he had come to such a small port," Perry said. "He seems a man with larger ambitions."

Roebuck said, "Have you seen his gold watch chain?"

"I have."

"Or sat on those cushioned chairs?"

Perry nodded.

Roebuck said, "Customs agents like money. They like to collect it, handle it, count it. And I've met some who like to keep it for themselves."

"Mr. Van Diemen seems . . . more enterprising than that."

"He takes the biscuit," Roebuck said. "With a name like that I'd say he's a Dutchman, the moneymaking kind who eats tin to shit gold."

Perry frowned before saying, "I believe your presence here concerns him," opening the real purpose of their conversation. "And I must admit, I am puzzled by it. Secreting yourself in this village when a man of your gifts should be serving his country."

Just what did Perry think finding $22,000 in gold was if not serving his country?

"Men with a record of success are in short supply, in your service or mine," Perry said. He exhaled. "Outcomes are what we need. The bigger the better. You have a sort of legend and you know as well as I that our people love a legend. They will pay for ships sailed by legends. The Navy is where you belong. You know it as well as I do."

Roebuck shrugged.

"Listen carefully to what I am about to tell you, Robert."

Perry had never used his Christian name and it set the hair on Roebuck's neck to standing.

Perry said, "I believe there's going to be a fight very soon. I have just received word that two American merchant brigs have been captured off the coast of Argentina and the Navy has asked me to send fifty guns to join the Brazil Squadron and assist in freeing them."

"Who captured the brigs?"

"The French."

Such a provocation. Roebuck said, "Why, in God's name?"

Perry's thick gold epaulettes glittered as he rose from his chair. "A peculiar alliance with the British against President Rosas in Buenos Aires has emboldened the French into conduct even more arbitrary than usual. For so long we have taken British sea power for granted. And in our weakness we have counted on it to restrain Gallic high-handedness. Now in the South Atlantic that restraint is gone and American trading ships suffer the consequences."

Roebuck did not want to encourage any lectures. "What are the two brigs?"

"The *America* and the *Eliza Davidson*. Both were boarded and their cargo seized."

Calculating the distance between here and Rio de la Plata, Roebuck said, "It will take a month and a half for your fifty guns to reach Rio de la Plata. By that time there will be nothing to do."

Perry said, "A ship in Pensacola will soon be available to set sail. The *Savannah* is the Navy's fastest frigate. With the right captain she'll make up the time required and join her guns to the squadron."

"What of her current captain?"

"The *Savannah's* commanding officer, Captain Fitzhugh, lost a brother to yellow fever several weeks ago who left behind a wife and three children. She is quite frantic, I am told. Fitzhugh must go and tend to their affairs. We have no other captain close by to be activated."

Roebuck said, "But, sir, that's a command for a senior captain."

"Yes, I know it. I wish there were one at hand, but there is not. It's you I've got and you I intend to send."

Roebuck shook his head and said, "The *Savannah* must have a first lieutenant. The command should fall to him."

"But the Navy needs men like you. That is why you are here in my cabin."

"You have officers, plenty of them."

"I will remind you, Lieutenant, that you are still an officer in the Navy despite your present position."

Roebuck nodded. He couldn't deny this.

"Besides, you are fast and you like to fight."

"And the others don't?" Roebuck knew any senior officers presently serving on the *Savannah* would not accept an interloper like him. "To be kicked down the Navy's captain's list by a Revenue Marine lieutenant would be something hard to swallow."

"I'm not making you a captain," Perry said.

"You take my meaning."

"Captain's list, pshaw." Perry said, working the tip of his nose. "You speak of the administrative navy." He sat down again. "The one that says organize your ship, parade your men, and we will be obliged to you."

"White glove over a gun barrel," Roebuck said, connecting with this man.

Perry barked a laugh. "But you know the sea does not care about parade-ground efficiency or dirt on a gun barrel. Neither do the French once the fighting starts. We are in an illusory calm, my friend, and not prepared for heavy weather. It will come and when it does we will face it with a corps of bewildered men consumed by administrative trivia."

He rose again to pace the narrow canyon of his cabin. "We send ships around the world to extract agreements, stop slavers, or bombard weak states. That is far, far from combat."

Could Roebuck take this conversation at face value? The idea of returning to Perry's navy was impossible. He said, "And what do you suppose I know about combat?"

"How many times have you exchanged fire with pirates?"

"Three times."

"And how many times have you captured them?"

"The same."

"Casualties?"

"Yes."

"How many?"

It was obvious and irritating that the captain already knew the answers to these questions.

Perry said, "Death is instructive, Lieutenant. I suspect you know what a combat-ready ship is."

"I know what it isn't." Roebuck said and looked around for effect.

"Remind me," Perry said, "what that ship from the Mexican navy was called, the one harassing trade through the Gulf. I read about it in the *Army Navy Chronicle*.

"The *Cuauhtémoc*."

"Did she not turn her broadside on you as you chased her into Corozal Bay?"

"She fired two rounds and it was over. Four of her shot bounced off our side. I believe the Mexicans are in the habit of undercharging their guns."

"Not enough powder?"

"Their army gets the powder," Roebuck said, "and their navy makes do with leftovers."

"She had three times as many guns as you. But you prevailed, based on a calculation of risk."

Roebuck poured his own tea this time.

"It was a fight, Mr. Roebuck, initiated by an aggressive officer pursuing his martial duties according to their original meaning."

"If you had been there you wouldn't describe it as a glory."

"But it is whether you admit it or not. The reason your reputation has grown is the same reason naval officers resent you."

And because of his father's infamy, but he and Perry had already covered that ground. Roebuck said, "You want a lieutenant in the Revenue Marine to command one of the Navy's treasures?"

"I want someone to sail down to Rio de la Plata and free those Americans. I don't care if he does it in a dingy with a slingshot."

"But you are not recommending a dingy with a slingshot. Rather, you propose I take command of the U.S.S. *Savannah* without consideration of her officers or the morale of her seamen."

"Are we back to that? Your advocacy of the administrative navy surprises me."

"I advocate nothing."

"You are an officer in the fighting navy, Roebuck, why in heaven deny it? It is the only navy that matters. Congress, the president, even our own Cabinet secretary and the officers who serve at his discretion forget how close the fight is. How it's always close. Our survival as a service depends on victory. It is what inspires Congress and the people to buy more ships. We cannot survive without men who don't just fight but win."

CHAPTER 8

A little past four was when the thunderstorm broke the afternoon heat. This was a favorable sign in Roebuck's book so he decided to try the tavern at Posey's Inn to see what he might find. One thing he knew he wouldn't find was an invitation from Captain Perry. Those had stopped coming after Roebuck's last visit, which had ended with Perry berating him for his indifference to the plight of the Navy. Men like Perry had trouble with the notion that not all seafarers wanted the same thing. What Roebuck wanted was to be left alone, maybe more than that the thing he didn't want was to have anything to do with the U.S. Navy.

At the tavern, he took his place against the bar thinking about not much. He liked St. Marks. Liked Rose even more. The longer he stayed the more he liked the idea of staying and believed it would be no challenge at all to make a living here, filling barrels of fish and bushels of oysters. He ordered an ale then another then switched to rum, asking the man tending bar, "Is there a game in the back?"

The man nodded. "Full of uniforms tonight."

Naval uniforms. Euchre was the game officers in the U.S. Navy played and Roebuck had been relieving them of coin ever since the *Macedonian* had anchored. He walked to the back.

When a seat at one of the tables opened he nosed in. Roebuck recognized the *Macedonian*'s purser among his opponents. And he saw the purser was partnered with one of the ship's mates. His own partner across the table was a Spanish merchant from Port Leon called Fernandez. Roebuck knew from past experience that he played tolerably well. The purser smoked a thick cigar and both he and the mate handled tall glasses. A Marine lieutenant, also from the *Macedonian,* stood and watched.

After three hands, Roebuck had won nearly seventy dollars. He was playing with the kind of freedom he knew resulted from the drinks that had gotten him started at the bar. The purser and mate won ten dollars back before Roebuck went in alone and took the hand by three tricks, each of those worth ten dollars plus two more in ante.

The *Macedonian*'s men grasped their glasses. The purser's cigar cooled in a shallow clay bowl. Roebuck looked on as they began rubbing their necks or noses, a poorly disguised form of cheating. Roebuck didn't know which bothered him more, the fact that they were doing it in the first place or that they assumed he'd be too stupid to know. If the purser rubbed his nose it meant he had the cards to play the first trump turned over from the deck. If he rubbed his neck it meant he didn't and the mate should consider naming a different trump instead.

After watching this charade for three consecutive hands, Roebuck said, "Rub your snot noses after we know the trump, or I walk from this table and say good night."

The mate said, "He's not man enough, too afraid to give us a chance to win back what we've lost."

The purser pointed to the merchant playing as Roebuck's partner and said, "Your little greaser plays a strong hand. It's like watching a monkey count."

Although tempted, Roebuck did not respond in kind. This was a sign of progress in the development of his character and was praiseworthy, so he congratulated himself, pocketed his winnings, said, "Good night," as he rose to his feet.

The Marine lieutenant, who had slipped behind Roebuck, put two hands on his shoulders and shoved him back down. This made an already unfriendly feeling in Roebuck's heart toward these men even less friendly. When the Marine took his hands away, Roebuck leapt at him, swinging his fists and toppling him backwards. Then he turned back toward the others just in time to duck a chair hurled by the mate, who now scrambled over the table toward Roebuck, shouting bloody murder. Roebuck drew his knife from the sheath on his belt and knocked a handful of teeth from the mate's mouth with the brass knuckles of its handle.

The Marine tackled Roebuck from behind. The purser started kicking at his face, so Roebuck covered up and rolled to his right, elbowing at the Marine until he let go. He jumped to his feet and ducked a fist from the purser, punching the brass knuckles into the man's side. Out of the corner of his eye, he saw the Marine swinging a thick-glass bottle like a club, then he felt a bright flash of pain, then nothing.

***

Roebuck awoke on the dirt floor of a hasty-looking arrangement of log and mud walls. He leaned his back against a post and pulled his knees to his chest. It was hot, with no window to let in the air. Iron shackles chafed his ankles. It seemed he was out of favor with the local constabulary.

After what Roebuck guessed was an hour of consciousness, Van Diemen arrived resembling a cat recently fed. Skipping any sort of greeting, he opened with, "This is not a happy day for you." Roebuck could almost see him licking his paws.

"It hasn't started well," Roebuck said. He wanted to stand, but that was complicated, so he took it slowly. The pain was sharp when he bent to his left, as if someone were jabbing him with an ice pick. His temple throbbed.

Van Diemen said, "You were in a brawl over a card game."

"If that's what they told you." Roebuck tried to remember the details of the fight. The rum bottle was one thing he had no trouble recalling. He touched a raw and stinging knot just above the eye socket. It would be some time before he forgot it.

"Do you have another story?"

Roebuck didn't answer.

Van Diemen said, "Do you know where you are?"

"Captain's quarters?"

"You are in jail." Van Diemen was standing close now, crowding Roebuck letting him know who was boss. "You didn't know that I perform the role of county sheriff, did you?"

Another one not to answer.

Van Diemen said, "Tell me what that makes you?"

Roebuck rattled his shackles, "Probably not your deputy."

Van Diemen smiled. "My prisoner."

"What about the others? The *Macedonian*'s purser and the Marine lieutenant?" Roebuck vaguely remembered a third man but wasn't sure about it.

"You mean the victims of your assault?"

"They told you that?"

"They didn't have to. Your card partner, a Mr. Fernandez, has provided a written statement."

"He's lying," Roebuck said. He was beginning to get a sense of his disadvantage, which was categorical.

"He is a disinterested and therefore impartial witness."

"And now on your payroll, probably twenty dollars richer."

"Well, to be frank—and what reason is there to be otherwise?" Van Diemen said. "The inducement was closer to fifty dollars. And of course the threat of violence is also persuasive."

***

Two days later, Van Diemen let Perry into Roebuck's cell. When Van Diemen left, Perry said, "He doesn't like you."

Roebuck looked at the door, still open, and said, "I am an acquired taste."

"You are the canker in his orchard, Lieutenant Roebuck. Because of you, some of Mr. Van Diemen's felonies are known to the Navy. It is his intention to hold you here until you become sick and die."

"I'm tougher than I look."

"I hope so."

"No one has told me what I am charged with."

"Public drunkenness, assault, attempted murder."

"Attempted murder?" Roebuck laughed.

"You drew a knife. Which is now on the *Macedonian* in my cabin."

Roebuck said, "I'd like it back."

"I have told Van Diemen that your crimes were against the United States Navy and that you will answer to me. Your attack on the *Macedonian*'s officers demonstrates clearly the threat you pose."

"I'm a threat?" Roebuck said, "Me? The one who helped you to pay your crew in gold?"

"You who have knocked the teeth from my purser's mouth and broken the ribs of my sailmaker's mate."

"Ah, yes, the mate. I was trying to remember who the third cheating son of a bitch was," Roebuck said, looking at the dirt as though he might see a picture in it.

Perry said, "Do you know why I am here?"

Roebuck shrugged.

Perry said, "Do you know why I am here?" He would get his answer.

Roebuck didn't and said so, but he was glad the captain had come.

Perry said, "I have asked something of you."

"To return to the Navy. That what you mean?"

"It is."

Roebuck could hardly believe his ears. "You want me to join the Navy, yet?"

"And command the *Savannah*."

"I have nothing new to tell you, Captain Perry. I do not wish to join the Navy. And apart from yourself, I'm sure the Navy has the same wish."

"You would refuse command of one of the world's finest sailing ships, one rated for forty-four guns, in favor of this." Perry kicked up dust.

Roebuck said, "I'll get out," although he hadn't figured out how, hadn't even come close.

"I don't think you will, at least not without my help. Even if you were able to perform that particular miracle, what would you do without a career in the Revenue Marine?"

The idea that his career now hung in the balance had occurred to Roebuck, more than a few times. Perry had come to the same conclusion, probably. News of Roebuck's St. Marks comportment—fighting was just one of his questionable choices—would likely ruin his standing in that service.

Roebuck thought of Rose and said, "Maybe I'll fish for my keep. Maybe raise a patch of tobacco. Sell it to men like your purser. He seems to enjoy a cigar and he'll need something to do with his mouth now that his teeth are gone."

Perry squinted at Roebuck as though trying to make out something very small and said, "You are a young man in serious trouble."

"I know it."

Perry's face was a jowly slab of granite and he shook his head. "You have a duty, Lieutenant Roebuck. There are wrongs, tyrannies of all kinds. Your Abel Van Diemen is right in the center of one. You and I cannot yield to rascality such as his, nor can we yield to our own weakness."

Perry was no fool. Roebuck wondered why he seemed so determined to sound like one. He said, "You and I and the Navy?"

"You in command of the *Savannah*."

"You have my answer, Captain Perry."

Perry said, "It is no longer a request."

Roebuck stood up. "This isn't Shanghai. I'm as free a man as you." He said this without conviction. Thick-headed and baboonish though he may be, it was clear even to him that there was no path now but the Navy.

CHAPTER 9

Rain sheeted out of the mist as Roebuck waited on the *Savannah's* quarterdeck. Waiting was an aggravation and naval commanders did a lot of it.

A half-inch of water already stood on the *ship's* deck, and with the help of the wind, rain was finding its way under his tarpaulin and soaking his uniform. He could imagine the scene on shore where the gale would sweep back the fronds of palm trees like a nasty boy jerking his sister's hair. That wasn't so bad; out here in the open water, ships would founder under an accumulation of swells, sailors cartwheel from decks, and lungs fill with water.

Second Lieutenant Aaberg approached the quarterdeck and began his report, but Roebuck was distracted by the cascade spilling over the brim of the lieutenant's hat. Roebuck missed what Aaberg had told him, so he leaned in with a cupped hand over his right ear. Aaberg stopped, filled his lungs and said it again, almost shouting how the carpenter had tightened the mast wedges but wasn't done with the hatches because he was short seven battens.

Good God, thought Roebuck, *what an unready ship*. He wondered how they would reach Rio de la Plata if they could barely cross the Caribbean. He said, "He's cutting them now?"

"His mates are, yes sir, in the workshop."

On a frigate a carpenter had mates. In the Revenue Marine ships had no carpenter. He had done all the woodwork himself aboard the *Louisiana*.

"Have them cut twenty," Roebuck said. "What about the jib?"

"The boom is in, sir, and we've rigged lifelines on deck."

"Very good, Mr. Aaberg." Roebuck nodded his dismissal, but Aaberg did not move. A question hung around his eyes. "You have something you'd like to ask me, Lieutenant," Roebuck said.

"Well, sir." Aaberg sounded stiff and careful. "The lieutenants wonder when you intend to bare poles and put the yards a-weather." He puckered a little, like the words had soured his mouth. "Or maybe scud the ship?"

Roebuck said, "Bare poles or scud?" as a way to stop himself saying to hell with any lieutenants who didn't trust him to manage the ship in this storm. The *Savannah* rolled over a big swell, both men instinctively widening their stance. "Mr. Aaberg, you know how far it is to Rio de la Plata."

"More or less I do, yes, sir."

"And that to make our rendezvous, we must maximize our speed through each minute of every day?"

Before Aaberg could reply, they shot up another swell, steeper than the last. Roebuck readied himself for the crest, for that feeling of the bottom falling out. He called, "Hold fast!" to the four new hands who had not yet gained their sea legs and had passed the last four hours shitting through their teeth over the port rail.

He knew the feeling. On the rise your feet were set on solid oak, but the first floating second of the fall ballooned your stomach up through your chest and into your throat before it dropped back down, a churning bag of *I'm gonna puke*. Then that taste, like sucking iron nails.

Those four wouldn't be able to think of anything but their stomachs until the storm had passed, at least this would be a distraction from the more unnerving thoughts of drowning or having flesh torn from your bones by toothy sea creatures. The *Savannah* crested and hung there for a moment as one of the four men dry heaved, stomach empty of everything but the sickness. Then she plunged and another heaved, not dry and not over the rail.

"On the deck again, will you?" said Edwards, the boatswain, eyes a blue wrath. "You slobbering bastard, do you want Captain Roebuck to wade through your mess?"

Roebuck turned toward an urgent call of "Belay! Belay!" It was the *Savannah's* sailing master. The ill-temper in the man's voice gave as much away. Roebuck turned, squinted through the spray, and saw the man shouting at a group of seamen at the ship's waist.

"First you must tie them down, you nackle-assed sons-of-the-dirt." The sailing master's name was Cherry but not because he was sweet.

The topmen had triced a pulley of blocks and halyards to lower yards being stripped from the top. There was too much power in this storm to keep sails set. Cherry was watching as several seamen received these yards in a way that must not have pleased him. Like the four puking over the rail, these were fresh recruits, about as ready for the sea as ten cows in a pasture. Many of the new hands had been rounded up from Pensacola gin mills. Perry had even blessed enlisting the least promising kind of men: noontime drinkers. Others were supernumeraries from Fort Pickens. These last were generally a better sort of man, but all of them were now too frightened to do anything but fumble what came to them.

"Hurry now!" shouted Cherry, a worthless command if there ever was one. Roebuck went toward them to sort things out, but a shearing wind jerked the ship and the men tumbled over like a rack of ninepins. Blue-black water broke over the rail, staggered Roebuck, and washed the fallen men into the starboard bulwark.

Gravity lost its center and Roebuck's feet seemed to bear no weight. He repressed a shout of fear and then the familiar pull of ballast righted them between two waves that looked like a pair of snow-capped mountains.

"God damn," Roebuck said. Was Aaberg right? Should they lay up and try to outlast the storm or even run with the wind, even though that would take them back in the direction they had come? Roebuck called to the boatswain. "Mr. Edwards!"

"Sir?"

Roebuck nodded toward Cherry's detail. He and Edwards watched them scramble to their feet and chase the spilled yards from one side of the deck to the other, about as sure-footed as deer on ice. Edwards took the cue, calling his mates to leave topping up the davits to take over for the new men, but even they struggled as swells continued to climb over the rails.

Roebuck thought of his orders, thirty-five days to sail the *Savannah*'s fifty-two guns down to Montevideo. Thirty-five. Did Perry know what that took? The risks? He slowly rubbed the ridges of his right ear with three fingertips, feeling them but not hearing. That had changed in the last fifteen minutes, the wind so loud now and the sea like a thousand tons of sliding snow.

As if to answer his question, the main mast produced an eerie groan loud enough to hear through the storm. He listened, but the sound did not repeat. Perry had said the *Savannah* was fit and ready to sail, but she wasn't. The running rigging in particular. Roebuck had asked to replace it in Pensacola but Perry said there was no time. The *Savannah* was relying, in this gale, on lines spliced and sealed with black pitch so often they looked crusted by morbid growths. A storm like this could part the soundest cord and the *Savannah*'s was far from sound.

Roebuck said, "Lieutenant Aaberg."

"Sir?"

"Double any stays in danger of parting and ask the sailing master for punch mats. Mat any chafing. Tend the bunts of the furls in particular. They give a nasty rub." Roebuck glanced over to see if the lieutenant had heard.

Aaberg shouted, "Aye aye, sir," and moved off, the wind forcing his white trousers against the outline of his thighs and calves.

Minutes later, the mast produced a shriek, higher than Roebuck recognized, like cork twisting against glass.

"Mr. Aaberg!" Time to learn what kind of lieutenants Roebuck had.

"Here, Captain."

"Rig the storms'ls."

"Aye aye, sir."

When Aaberg returned to the quarterdeck a gust tore the glazed hat from his head, bouncing it into the starboard rail. In seconds, the curls of his blond hair were soaked flat.

Roebuck said, "Mr. Aaberg, we'll press on under the fore tops'l. Haul in all sails from the main and mizzen."

Doubt hung from Aaberg's brow. He would be thinking the foretopsail shouldn't remain set, thinking of the danger.

"Headway, sir," Aaberg said. "In this?"

Roebuck was making a decision against the wishes of his lieutenants. They wanted to lay ahull or run before the wind. Any hesitation in their progress, Roebuck knew, would make it impossible to reach the destination of Montevideo Uruguay in time to reinforce Nicolson. Perry had chosen Roebuck because he sailed faster than his naval counterparts and because he wouldn't stop in a storm.

"No time for anything else," Roebuck said. "We need to make way. The foretops'l's how we'll do it. The storms'ls will keep us upright and ease nerves among the new men." He was about to say more, but he was the commander and did not need to explain himself.

Aaberg offered a half nod, conveying no confidence, but that was his problem, not Roebuck's.

They rolled up another big swell and the sea stormed over the port rail, driving Roebuck back to the helm and overwhelming the officers on the quarterdeck. Frothy water blanketed the deck, bright flecks tearing off into nothing. A broad sheet of white flowed into the starboard bulwark, piling up and folding back on itself. It drained through scuppers, and so did Aaberg's hat.

"Lost your top, Lieutenant," shouted Roebuck, returning to his place, pretending calm.

"Aye, sir." Aaberg flattened the sound of his voice and forced the corners of his mouth to match.

"The sea claims another victim." Now Roebuck was twisting his lips into a smile.

"Never cared for that hat, sir."

The wind shifted. Rain stung Roebuck's right cheek. He imagined Aaberg's toes curling down, trying to grip deck planks through boot soles. The chaos of a storm frightened most men, but Roebuck had other fears, like the prodigal twins of this command: doubt and expectation.

He watched a clutch of seamen pull on the halyards, crowding in for leverage. Aloft the hands worked to set the long, triangular storm sails fore and aft. He felt unexpected relief at passing from uncertainty to action, risky or not. Behind him, a third helmsman had been added to the wheel to keep it steady. Roebuck turned to the three of them and said, "We're going to steer through this weather, boys. There'll be plenty to see very soon but no matter what your eyes want to do, keep them on that tops'l and keep it full."

Out of the corner of his eye Roebuck saw a dark figure pull himself up through the main hatch. Bernard Malvey, the ship's first lieutenant, an Englishman by birth, formerly a petty officer in her majesty's service. Experience, not to mention rank, had made him a logical next in line to command the *Savannah* during Captain Fitzhugh's leave. But Perry had installed Roebuck as the ship's commander instead and Malvey thundered around the *Savannah*'s main deck like a bipedal advertisement proclaiming the unjustness and stupidity of this decision.

Malvey strode onto the quarterdeck, took his position next to Roebuck, and said, "Feels like we're breathing water up here, sir." He had a confidence that about sliced the gale into bite-sized wafers.

Roebuck said, "Mr. Malvey, have you confirmed that the gun lashings are secure?"

A simple question, but Malvey held himself back, letting it molder a moment before his yes sir. Then came another groan from the mainmast, this one louder and longer than before. Roebuck looked up. Malvey didn't.

Roebuck said, "If you please, Lieutenant, collect the cable required to twin the mainmast's standing rigging."

Instead of moving off to fulfill the order, Malvey nodded gently and twisted his whiskers in his fingers, a philosopher in repose. "Captain, soon your lone square sail will be on the foremast. Why stay the mainmast when your sail is set on the fore? I know that creak may put a little scare in you, but a stout heart and a little sailing sense will get us through."

Roebuck had entertained the same thought earlier. There was not enough cable to double the stays on both masts, so he had to choose one. The mainmast was groaning, not the foremast, so that is the mast he wanted to secure whether there was a sail set on it or not. He felt a sudden surge of fear. Malvey was speaking with the voice of experience and proposing something sensible even if it was against Roebuck's judgment.

Roebuck repeated the order. "Lieutenant Malvey, double the stays on the main, if you please."

Malvey responded as if Roebuck had asked his opinion. "Pressure's piling up on the fore, sir. If your aim is to make headway in this storm, you'll want proper support where your sail is set."

Roebuck looked to the foremast and then back to Malvey. The brim of the lieutenant's hat was pulled down against the weather and covered his eyes. Headway is what Roebuck needed, Malvey was right about that, and he seemed to be endorsing Roebuck's decision to move forward in the storm. Roebuck had gathered from Aaberg that all the lieutenants, including Malvey, did not see wisdom in that decision.

But maybe Malvey was an exception.

Roebuck said, "We must keep that mainmast upright, Mr. Malvey, no matter what." Roebuck's tone had lost a fraction of certainty.

"The storm's leaning on the fore, sir," Malvey said, backed by twenty years of service in the Royal Navy, the world's greatest navy, none other even close.

Roebuck said, "Well then, double stays on the fore but do it now, with no more talk, if you please."

"Very good, sir," Malvey said, moving off and shouting orders loud enough to be heard through the storm. He quickly formed a detail of the ship's best topmen and set them to work.

A swell hit the *Savannah* dead on as another crashed into her port bow. In a high pitch of fear, the foremast captain yelled, "Watch out for war, boys! The bow chaser shed her ties." He waved and jumped as he said it. "Tend ye now! TEND YE NOW!"

One of the guns from the bow was loose and swiveled violently through the crew. The ship tilted and the gun jerked around, smashing into a broad-shouldered seaman, knocking him down. The front carriage wheels jumped as they rolled over his right leg and jumped again over his left. The man screamed and writhed in pain.

Another swell pushed up the *Savannah's* bow, and the gun rolled toward the quarterdeck. Three gunnery mates chased it with handspikes, but it crashed into the fife rail before they could reach it, splintering a stanchion. The mates took advantage of the gun's pause to wedge their spikes under three of the wheels, holding the carriage in place as two others lashed it down.

"Take him below!" yelled Malvey about the stricken man. "Let's see if he comes back up with either of those legs. Lash a gun like you lace a moccasin and we'll be using legs as gun stops all the way to Argentina and back."

The men stood gaping.

"I said below with him, you little flowers, get on with you!"

Several men hurried off for a stretcher.

Malvey had said the guns were secure, but they weren't, at least not that one. Roebuck wondered about the other fifty-one. "Mr. Aaberg, have the gunner recheck all the gun lashings immediately."

"Aye, aye sir."

He called for Malvey, reconsidering the order to lash the fore-mast, thinking he was right about the mainmast and suddenly confused by the thought that Malvey might be more than just a son of bitch. He might be a lying one.

Malvey did not answer.

Roebuck called again, and again nothing. He looked up at the *Savannah's* telltale banners. Each was swept stiff as copper by the wind.

"Mr. Edwards," he called. Roebuck would have the boatswain find Malvey and help stay the mainmast. The ship's best topmen moved up and down the rigging like demons, doubling threadbare cables and matting stays. The wind would catch on everything with an edge or pocket, so several topmen, pressing their soles into the footrope and leaning into mainsail's two long yards, tucked in dog-eared furls and loose rope-ends.

There was a loud snap and Roebuck jumped. His ears knew immediately what his brain wanted to deny. The mainstay had parted. All he could do was stare as the 150-foot mast wrenched backwards. The topmen hung on, yelling for help as the mast bowed and bowed before whipping back, flicking them off all at once—the *Savannah*'s best men—like beads of water from a flexed line.

There was a cleaving in Roebuck's mind. One part thinking *stop, stop and search*. The other knowing that they were gone, that to launch a boat in this storm would be madness. Those men were gone. He made an effort to hear them, their calls or their thrashing in the water, but there was nothing outside the whistle of wind through rigging. Then a noise, even louder, wood under stress, a great crack chilling him to his heart, a 44-rate naval frigate losing a mast—not the son of a bitch Malvey's foremast but the mainmast. a sound as the fracture and fall of a great tree.

CHAPTER 10

It was now three weeks to the day since Anita's arrival. She had done little but offer one excuse after another to avoid meeting Señor Wheat and Barley, as she called him. His family was starting to have their doubts.

Doña Belén raised the subject with her niece once more at breakfast. "My dear, you are at an age to marry. You have a man of means in hand. It is time for you to meet him."

"Tía Belén, I scarcely know a thing about Montevideo or your people. I need more time."

"It is what you always say, child, and yet you do nothing about it."

"Tell me, Tía, my mother often said it is you, not Tío Justo who runs Nahomi. Is that true? She says I am to become a woman of the New World like you."

"You change the subject as usual, Anita."

"Tell me, please."

"And what does your mother think is so wrong with the Old World?"

"She says it is dry, nearly dead, and will soon be as a fallen leaf, rotting into the earth."

"You do not need to concern yourself," Belén said, "with this world or that. You are here to marry. There is no better place for you to do so well and comfortably than Montevideo."

"This is what my father wants," Anita said. "I know."

"As mine did for me."

Anita became agitated. "I hate it. That my life and my marriage do not belong to me."

"Whether your life is yours has nothing to do with your marriage. It is a choice, darling. If you cannot have the life that you want, you must make whatever life you have your own. Something that cannot be taken from you." Belén paused for a moment. Her words would be wasted on Anita, but why not try? "For any woman not content to live according to the wishes of men, this is the only way."

Belén thought of Justo. She did not remember him as someone other than what he was, a man indifferent to anything but his own pleasure. She had been sixteen and he twenty-seven on the day of their wedding. Her father had pursued the match because although they had over 150,000 head of cattle and sheep, and their tenants produced bushels of grain by the tens of thousands, Don Justo's family was one of the oldest in Cádiz. Not only that, they were also connected by another marriage to its largest trading house, one that happened to be in need of a reliable supplier of cowhide, tallow, and grain. Belén and Justo's union was intended to secure the future of all three families in one connubial stroke. It was a hard lesson for Belén that for so many men, marriage was but a means to power and wealth.

She thought about her father, a good man. She loved him. He never once complained, as some do, about not having a son; he told her he had exactly what he wanted, a friend. It was true—besides blood, friendship was what they shared. To his great sadness, her father had seen clearly that the marriage he had arranged for her had become a trial of humiliation for Belén. His face came to be deformed by regret. And while Belén felt desolation on the day he passed, she was relieved for his sake.

When she first saw Justo, she felt the sort of infatuation Anita seemed to feel now. His manners were exquisite and he combined head-to-toe beauty with a casual intelligence and charm that made him desirable even to her young eyes. He was gentle on the night of their wedding in a practiced sort of way, her virginity something he understood better than she. He had administered pleasure with a vague distance, like a physician during an examination.

Throughout the first year of their marriage, Justo seemed more interested in Belén's reaction to their lovemaking than in the lovemaking itself, another reflection for him to enjoy. At the passing of that year, almost to the day, their bed turned cold. Soon after, she learned that he was sleeping with their youngest servant while at the same time keeping a woman in the old city.

***

After breakfast, Belén waited in the stables for Justo. When he did not come, she sent her servant Rocío to find him. He finally joined her but had not bothered to pull on riding boots. Instead, he had selected a single pink rose for the top buttonhole on the lapel of his coat. This was his theater. She was his audience, his way to say he was not going to ride with her after all.

They were supposed to look in on a tenant who had failed to harvest his wheat in time. Belén said, "Justo, you are dressed for town."

"What powers of observation, my little bird," he said. "Tell me, what do you think of this?" Opening his arms and puffing his chest. "A new cravat."

"We were to visit the tenant Gómez this morning. Do you remember? He has lost the harvest again."

"He is a fool."

"I think we are the fools. It is the second year in a row and the third time in five years. Have you forgotten your promise to tell him we are terminating his tenancy?"

"That is rather harsh, Belén. You are too young to become a shrew."

They had already gone through this. And Justo had agreed many times. She said, "It is our accommodation that keeps the man in drink. Can you not see that we must give him a reason to look at his life and amend?"

"I am kind to the peasants," Justo said.

"You are indulgent. There is a difference," she said. "And again I must ask you, my dear, to refer to our tenants as something other than peasants. They are not bonded to the land. They resent the word and it is not accurate."

Justo said, "Let us give the fool Gómez another chance and not waste this lovely day."

Belén's father had once told her that the excess of Justo's leniency for men like Gómez was based on a consciousness of his own weakness. "Gómez must no longer till our land," she said, "because we can no longer afford his failures. How can we keep you in velvet cravats if we allow men like Gómez to continue?"

"Silk, my darling, the cravat is silk. And what of La Gordita?" It is what he called Anita: "the little fat one," a gratuitous unkindness which did not describe her in the least.

"In her room. She complains again of her stomach," Belén said.

"Wake her up, put her on a horse, and let her help you kick Gómez into indigence. Is she not supposed to learn under your Spartan tutelage?"

She said, "You will meet with your fellow schemers at the club?"

He said, "I am going there now."

"People are talking about your meetings, Justo. Senator Montcalvo mentioned to me that some of his colleagues describe them as suspicious. They think you are in league with Madrid."

"We play cards and commiserate on our lot among the barbarians down here, not a thing else."

"Cards." Belén laughed at that. His game was girls, and if none were available, women.

Justo said, "Tell Gómez, next time I see him I'll stand him a drink," and exited stage left through the stable door.

***

Belén rode to see Gómez with the estancia's overseer, an Englishman named Guillory. After awhile, her pinto pulled up lame and she returned on Guillory's mount for a replacement.

Coming up to the main house, she noticed Justo's horse tied to the post in front. That was strange—he always stabled his horse, never tied it. She went inside to see what was wrong. Before she reached the front door a vague suspicion that had been with her for weeks became clear. Until lately, Justo never bothered to hide anything, his fornicating with their servants, his indifference to the fate of their business, but now he skulked around looking guilty. She walked inside. Her head rang with the sensation that her husband had crossed into hell itself.

"Don Justo?" she said, entering his study. There was a half carafe of Mendoza on his desk. Letters, mostly unopened, were strewn about. She went into the kitchen to ask the cook what was happening. The cook shrugged. When Belén pushed open the door to Anita's room, Don Justo had his trousers down and was mounting his niece, skirts bunched up around her waist, from behind.

***

There was blight in the apple orchard. Guillory had topped about one quarter of the trees in the fall to stimulate fruiting and she supposed this may have stressed some, making them vulnerable to disease. She was on a ladder examining the branches of one that might be stricken and sure enough there were cankers. Now she would have to see how many of the trees could be saved.

"Madame, be careful."

"Admiral LeBlanc," she said. She knew his voice without turning to see him, his easy French-accented Spanish. She didn't feel surprised or even afraid, which seemed strange given what she knew about him. She backed down the ladder and extended her hand for support, which he quickly took.

"I have never seen a woman wear breeches before," he said, peeking at her legs and raising an eyebrow.

"Don't look so surprised," she said with a laugh. "My dress-maker makes two pairs for me each year. They get torn and soiled out in places like this so quickly, I must have new ones every January." How had he known where to find her?

He smiled. "I'm sorry to surprise you this way, but I thought it would be useful for us to talk."

"You know that my husband has gone to Buenos Aires?" As she said this her face became hot, the image of Justo and Anita still a grease fire in her heart. Was this humiliation, anger, or both? She had sent Anita back to Cadiz without delay, refusing to inhabit the same continent.

"Of course," LeBlanc said. "It is I who sent him."

She wondered if he had heard about Justo and Anita and, if so, was he inviting her thanks? The servants could not keep their mouths shut and the admiral seemed like the kind that would know.

"He would not tell me what his business there was," she said.

"You are his wife and what is more you run the trading house, so you should know."

"Justo has secrets and you know many of them, Admiral."

"You are a woman with extraordinary powers of perception."

"Do not flatter me, sir." She turned back to the apple tree. "It gives me no pleasure."

"This is not flattery, madame. It is understatement," he said, pushing his smile toward her. The smile was not warm but she thought he was hoping it might be. "Your husband is a fool," LeBlanc said. "This observation will not surprise you."

Here was something that required no response. She turned toward him again and waited.

LeBlanc said, "He believes he can restore Spain to its original position of power here." LeBlanc shook his head as if to say *poor little fool.* "He has begun this quest in Argentina, believing he will have the support of my ships and Lechi's soldiers when he needs them. But, madame, he will have neither. And he will fail."

"That is his gift," she said.

"He will be arrested, I am sorry to tell you." LeBlanc offered this news without any sign of sorrow. "Then Don Justo will be shot for insurrection, which brings me to the reason for this visit. I am here to say that together you and I could rise to a position of power and wealth the likes of which the people of Uruguay have never seen."

She was not quite ready to move on from the pleasing subject of her husband's demise, but the admiral did know how to get a woman's attention. She said, "What makes you so certain that Don Justo will be arrested?"

"Because I have arranged for it. You and I can now be as one and when we are, there will be no limit for us."

This was a man who would stop at nothing. She knew she should be repelled, that for her own good she should stay away. Yet there was something about him. He was pure temptation.

CHAPTER 11

For the past five days Roebuck had been trying to write a report, which the Navy required after the death of a crewman—or, in his case, six crewmen. He was daunted in his writing of this report by the knowledge that his first challenge as a naval commander had resulted in the death of the *Savannah*'s best topmen, the ruin of its 150-foot main mast, not to mention twelve days lost to refitting at the Jamaica Dockyard in Port Royal.

The *Savannah*'s officers had been guests of the yard's British commandant—the most smug man Roebuck had ever met, which was saying something given his three years in the U.S. Navy. But the man and his dockyard could not be avoided. There was no other reasonable place to raise a replacement for the *Savannah*'s mainmast. All of this taken together made the report difficult, even painful, to contemplate much less write. Over the seventy years since the Continental Navy had been born during the war for independence, Roebuck could not think of an American commander who could claim so thorough a disaster outside of battle. And here he had managed it in his first week. Roebuck was unsurpassed.

With his right hand, he twisted a screw into the corked top of a port bottle. With his left he covered the cork in a thick canvas rag. When the screw was deep enough to take hold, he pulled hard, easing as the cork came free from the mouth of the bottle. The canvas muffled its pop. He poured and sipped with one hand, while dipping the nib of his pen into India ink with the other, a drop of which bled off and splashed onto the sheet of paper, the first mark on it.

After staring at the wall for a while, he decided to address it, saying, "Commander Robert Chase Roebuck, known by the title of Captain aboard the *Savannah*." He took a generous sip of port before completing the thought, "Captain Roebuck," reminding himself that despite what had happened, he was due—for now, at least— every courtesy and every ceremony by which captains were elevated above all others on a ship. *Cheers*, he thought, and took another sip. This elevation by virtue of his rank was no doubt a hard pill for the *Savannah*'s officers to swallow. But swallow they must for their navy needed what it needed, sympathies of its officers aside. And what it needed was the *Savannah*'s fifty-two guns in Rio de la Plata as soon as it could have them. And he was the one to get them there, not Malvey, not Aaberg. If that meant a journey of nearly six thousand nautical miles through contrary conditions on a ship with threadbare rigging, officers that did not believe in him, and an inexperienced crew, so be it. He missed Rose.

He wanted to take another sip yet knew that what was needed was concentration on the problem of his crew. During the week that had passed since the gale, the *Savannah* seemed to have lost the discipline needed on a military vessel. The new men in particular were full of muttering and complaints about the food, the heat, the stale taste of barreled water. This called for a firm hand. He was certain of that, yet lately what he wanted more than anything else was to be left alone in his cabin.

Roebuck rose, crossed his cabin in four steps, and then turned to face his desk. He tried to focus. To call the state of mind among the crew a problem might be an understatement. It was more properly described as a threat. He took four steps back and sensed that his glass needed freshening. He swallowed what was in it and poured another. Soon, fine warm fingers of port spread themselves out inside him, fortifying a feeling that this cabin was a splendid place. No doubting eyes or resentful mouths here. Roebuck drained the glass and was leaning toward the bottle for another when there was a knock.

He called the name of his steward. "Lilywhite?"

"Aye sir," said the steward. "I have Captain Pemberton with me, and he says that he must see you."

Pemberton was the senior Marine officer and in charge of the ship's security. He was not likely to be bearing glad tidings. Roebuck called, "Mr. Pemberton?"

"Here, Captain," Pemberton said, projecting his low voice through the closed door.

Rather than open it, Roebuck said, "Off with you then, Lilywhite," and waited a moment before saying, "Mr. Pemberton, I'm sorry to disappoint you, but I am deep in review of our charts."

Pemberton said, "The charts are in the greater cabin, Sir."

This made Roebuck angry. "How did you know that?" he said. "I alone have the key to that cabin."

Pemberton said nothing, somehow making it obvious that he hadn't known it before but did now.

"I would ask you in, Pemberton, but there's no chair for you and I am engaged in something that keeps me here."

"I brought a stool."

"Ah, very well." Roebuck corked the bottle, pushed it into his sea chest and rinsed the goblet at his basin. He said, "Damned if you can take a hint," unlatching the door.

"Thank you, Captain." Pemberton nudged the door open and ran his eyes over every object in the room, his face neutral as a Dutch merchant's.

Neutral was good because Pemberton usually looked mean enough to cause a Comanche to pluck the feathers from his war bonnet and turn to beekeeping. Roebuck liked Pemberton and knew he needed someone onboard he could trust, someone who understood the ship and its crew.

Pemberton's mother was Chickahominy, a tribe from the Virginia tidewater, his father from Edinburgh. He had just two facial expressions, one angry the other not. These replaced each other about as often as England changed her sovereign.

"The stool?" Roebuck said, looking at Pemberton's empty hands.

"Thought I'd stand instead."

Pemberton was known as a man to avoid if you felt like making trouble, and his presence robbed most of the ship's seamen of whatever troublemaking courage they might develop. This suited Roebuck's antipathy toward traditional methods of discipline, flogging in particular. But he also knew that the *Savannah* was no revenue cutter. Her complement numbered over four hundred, almost ten times what Roebuck had commanded on the revenue cutter *Louisiana*. It wasn't just the number of men here, it was the type. So many of them freshly weaned from the nipple of a gin bottle. Pemberton had been reminding Roebuck of this each day for nearly a week.

"Well?" Roebuck said, irritation in his voice.

"Sir, yesterday there were four thefts reported."

"Captain Cook used to shoot islanders for theft," Roebuck said.

"Then I might need a pistol that can shoot straight."

"Your job is to prevent them from stealing, not shoot them when they do."

"It isn't just stealing, sir. There's disobedience. The crew is losing respect for the ship's authority."

Roebuck nodded.

"And neglect of duty. Yesterday three men, mizzen topmen, each one an experienced sailor, failed to sheet the to'gan's'l, and it tore. They were sleeping in the top."

Roebuck's mind wandered back to his report.

"Neglect of duty, sir, can sink a ship," Pemberton said.

"What do you intend to do about it?"

"Have I mentioned intoxication?" Pemberton said.

Roebuck shrugged and sat back.

"There is more whiskey aboard than what was provisioned. Men have smuggled it on. They drink more than their ration." Pemberton reached over to touch Roebuck's sea chest. "Drink ruins men and ships alike."

Roebuck said, "You're being obvious." The hint at his own drinking was awkward but probably unavoidable.

"Would you prefer a subtle Captain of the Marines, sir?"

"The ladies in our Temperance Society would applaud your scruples, Captain." Roebuck stood up, antsy all of a sudden. He knew he must establish control of his ship. Here he was, installed as a naval commander whether he liked it or not, so why not set the record straight that the Roebucks, his father included, knew their business and that their business was to command sailing ships. But how? All these men with no faith in him—against him, even.

Pemberton said, "One more thing, Captain, if I may?"

"Go on."

"Lieutenant Aaberg sends his compliments and says conditions will need your attention. We are five degrees north of the equator. The wind is growing milder with each hour, and—"

"—the glass has fallen below 30.20," Roebuck interrupted. "Lieutenant Aaberg fears we will lose what remains of the breeze."

Pemberton looked around—looking for a barometer, that was obvious.

Roebuck said, "Tell the lieutenant there will be no breeze in a matter of hours. Those five degrees he quotes leave us fat in the doldrums, where we will drift until the wind returns, and there is nothing he or any other of those pretenders on the quarterdeck can do to change it."

***

As Roebuck had predicted, the *Savannah* soon lost her breeze just north of the equator in the seaman's netherworld known as the doldrums, a loss that left them without anything to do but whistle for wind and broil under a sun that seemed to take up half the sky. If this did not portend the end of the mission, he didn't know what could.

The atmosphere of Roebuck's cabin was hot and moist and he wore it like a freshly boiled suit of clothes. With some effort he focused his mind away from the heat and toward the words written on the sheet of paper topping the stack on his desk. It read:

Here the gods becalmed me twenty days without so much as a breath of fair wind to help me forward.

This was the opening line of a short dramatic performance proposed by the *Savannah*'s midshipmen. They had shown the wisdom to adapt it from Homer's *Odyssey*.

Roebuck had developed the idea of a theatrical contest shortly after Pemberton's warning about the ship's eroding discipline. A lot of work went into such a contest. Stage and scenery had to be constructed, music selected and practiced, and of course there were the acts themselves. Roebuck hoped the activity would divert the collective attention of his crew away from what he thought of as the underlying causes of their unrest: boredom, frustration, misery.

Pemberton had in his way let Roebuck know that he believed this plan was a trifle, something to be done at anchor in a harbor, not out in the open ocean. Roebuck himself knew that it wasn't exactly a hardheaded plan, the kind a commander might need, yet he preferred to see the *Savannah*'s indiscipline remedied through the soul rather than through blood and body.

It was late and Roebuck had spent the last three hours reviewing proposals for performances, his men hoping to persuade their commander to give them some time on stage. Two proposals remained, although he hardly had the energy to read them. The *Odyssey* from the midshipmen and another from the gunroom's mates, a group led by Lieutenant Malvey. After Roebuck finished the first, he began the second. Malvey's choice for the subject seemed benign enough, a comedy based on Washington Irving's *Rip Van Winkle*. As he read, the heat continued its rise and it soon pressed him out of the cabin and up the hatchway ladder where an updraft of musty air caught him. Afternoon heat was drying out the sodden world below, raising hot vapors that irritated a red heat rash starting to form across his back and the insides of his elbows and knees. He scratched this rash with the pommel nut of the knuckled knife Perry had returned to him the day the Savannah weighed anchor in Pensacola harbor. This made the rash worse.

Itching like he'd been given a hundred lashes with the stinging tendrils of a nettle, Roebuck took his place on the quarterdeck with the officers on watch. They saluted. It still surprised him, the situation of his being just twenty-three years old and master of one of the U.S. Navy's finest ships, disrepair notwithstanding. He knew it surprised his lieutenants too, and not in a good way.

The ship's fourth lieutenant, a man named Brimblecorn, mumbled, "Afternoon, Captain Roebuck." For someone so elaborately named, Brimblecorn had a simple face that you didn't expect. Regrettably, his mind was even more simple than his face.

Roebuck nodded to the Lieutenant and surveyed the deck. Malvey was absent, although it was his turn to preside. "Where is the First Lieutenant?"

"Readying the launches, sir."

Roebuck was about to respond by saying that he had given no orders related to the launches but didn't.

Brimblecorn seemed uncomfortable in the silence that followed because he soon said, "The doldrums is what the Navy has steam ships for, isn't that so, sir?" apparently unaware of his commander's distaste for steam-powered ships.

When Roebuck received his commission in Pensacola, Captain Perry had mentioned that the *Mississippi*, a new steam frigate, had been considered for this mission. But the fiery demise of her sister *Missouri* two years back had caused Perry to choose the *Savannah* as a more certain option. To Roebuck steamship captains were kin to greasy teamsters, commanding two shitting steers with a goad. However, now motionless here in the doldrums, he wished that this was the *Mississippi* and not the *Savannah*. If it were he'd steam out of here, wind or not.

Brimblecorn was content to carry the subject forward, saying, "I once spent eight days in the doldrums without a breeze, eight god-forsaken days. Have you had that misfortune, sir?"

Roebuck said, "I have." He hated the idea that the *Savannah* was abandoned by the Atlantic's breeze. Without wind, they had no motive force and without that, this mission had no chance. The thought of this failure attaching to the Roebuck name, another indelible mark, made him miserable.

He watched the sails hanging on their yards like drying laundry, heavy and barely moving with each shallow roll. A whiff of burnt sweetness in the air caught his attention and he looked around to see a tar kettle bubbling over a makeshift brick fireplace on deck. A seaman carried a bucket full of water toward the fire. Four buckets just like it sat there already—a measure of caution on a wooden ship filled with explosive powder. Water spilled and began to steam up from the deck planks as the man set the bucket down.

Other hands pulled long strands of yarn through the tar kettle and hung them from brackets over the ship's rails until the tar pitch hardened. The strands looked to Roebuck like bunting with the banners burnt away. When the yarn was nice and stiff, crewmen would twist the strands into cables and replace whatever of the ship's standing rigging had parted or was close to it.

The boatswain oversaw this work. Roebuck called to him, "Remember, Mr. Edwards, fire not so hot it burns any yarn touching the bottom of that kettle."

"Aye sir, and not so cool the tar clumps and clogs," Edwards said. "I remember."

The current had been against them since leaving Pensacola and would be until they crossed the latitude where Brazil stuck its fat rump into the Atlantic. The odds against making the rendezvous with Nicolson's Brazil Squadron had always been high. Each passing hour at rest here was ruining them once and for all.

Roebuck looked up to see Malvey coming toward the quarterdeck like a rooster walking his yard. Roebuck half expected the Englishman to cock-a-doodle-do.

"Sir," Malvey said. "Shall we hoist the launches, then?"

Roebuck recalled his own weak-mindedness the last time Malvey made a suggestion of this importance. The price had been very high. He was not quick to answer.

Malvey used his hands to pantomime the question in a gesture of impatience.

"Hoist," said Roebuck, sounding puzzled.

"Aye sir, we've raised the boats and the men are waiting to go," Malvey said. His confidence was suffocating.

"Hawsers and kedges?"

"Stowed an hour ago, sir." Malvey's singsong delivery suggested he might be addressing a child.

Maybe he was because Roebuck wasn't sure what to do about it.

Malvey said, "I'll pull us out of this, sir," referring to the kedging operation he'd advocated since daybreak. "I've seen it done on the H.M.S. *Medina,* under Captain Wiggin—Lord Wiggin now, a man with the heart of any ten commanders. I'm not afraid to try it, sir, no fear troubling Bernard Malvey. Give us a fairer chance than leisuring here."

Roebuck said, "If you were on an oar, you'd be troubled enough, Mr. Malvey." Any decision Roebuck took now would be blind. Yet he knew, as everyone knew, that it was a commander's job to make blind decisions. It was also true that nothing could unmake a commander quicker than such a decision gone wrong. Malvey he realized would be counting on that.

Kedging was brutal work, requiring one boat to row an anchor out ahead and drop it at the limit of its cable while sailors at the capstan wound the ship to it, a second boat doing the same farther ahead, both repeating, on and on.

"I've pulled oars-a-plenty in my time, Captain."

"Maybe you'll see fit, Lieutenant, to share with me where you think 'out of this' is?"

"Out of the doldrums, sir, of course."

"Which is where exactly?"

"Not more than a few leagues, sir." That delivery again, talking to a little boy. "Call it a seaman's hunch." Malvey's eyes were fixed somewhere beyond Roebuck's right shoulder.

"And the heading?"

"You wouldn't have me do a sailing master's work, now, would you, sir?"

It was true, setting their course was sailing master's job and Roebuck's responsibility, not Malvey's. And if kedging failed to raise a breeze, it would be Roebuck's fault. He looked over the rail. The ocean was still calm enough to have been painted with a brush of perfect sable bristles. No horizon in sight, just unbroken blue sky blending into the sea. "Lower the launches, Lieutenant," he said, without knowing what to do other than not doing whatever Malvey said.

"Do nothing then, sir?" It was more announcement than question, delivered with enough volume to be heard up and down the deck.

"Not nothing, Mr. Malvey. Lower the boats."

Malvey didn't move. "Try the kedge," he said.

Roebuck balled his fists. "You will address me as Captain or sir."

"Aye aye."

"Say it."

Malvey said something that might have been sir, or maybe something vulgar.

"We are becalmed, Mr. Malvey, but that is no reason to turn the *Savannah* into a galley of slaves at the oars for what could be days."

As Roebuck said this he noticed for the first time that the crew had stopped their work to listen. Malvey had sucked him in and made him look like a ditherer without the sand to try freeing them from this dead-still misery.

"Lieutenant," Roebuck said, "You were the *Savannah*'s first lieutenant before my command, were you not?"

Malvey hesitated, knowing Roebuck already had the answer.

Roebuck continued, "An officer of your considerable experience and ability right here on the *Savannah*."

This time Malvey was quick to say, "Aye sir. I was here and my ability is considerable."

Some of the crew laughed at the impertinence.

Roebuck said, "Yet they passed you over."

"Well, sir—"

"Found someone else, not even a captain and not even from the Navy."

"I have had occasion to wonder what possessed them." Malvey paused a moment before saying, "sir."

Roebuck said, "They must have found someone better."

***

Holman was the last of eight midshipmen to arrive, walking self-consciously through the open glass-paned doors of the ship's greater cabin. The *Savannah*'s four senior lieutenants were waiting in a line looking grave.

The third lieutenant, who was named Cockrell, said, "Mr. Holman, you must be an eminence spun way past your rank to keep Captain Roebuck and his four lieutenants waiting." They all glared at Holman.

"I beg your pardon, sir," the young man said. He turned to Roebuck and bowed a little, looking like he had no idea what he was supposed to do. Then he somehow got a clue and turned to the lieutenants. "I'm most sorry," he said, "you've had to wait on my account, Mr. Malvey, Mr. Aaberg, Mr. Cockrell, and Mr. Brimblecorn," nodding to each as he said their names.

Roebuck said to the room, "Be seated." As they sat, he said to Holman, "Not you." And the midshipman jumped back up, coming to attention.

Roebuck nodded to Aaberg, who stood with a lacquered pointer in his right hand that reminded Roebuck of one a teacher of his had used. Roebuck had briefed Aaberg beforehand, believing that this information would be better received coming from the second lieutenant than it would from either himself or Malvey. Roebuck felt somehow compromised by the hostility he and Malvey so obviously had for one other and thought these officers might feel the same way.

Aaberg said, "As you know, our destination is the River Plate estuary. The Dagos call it Río de la Plata." He indicated a location on the chart resting atop the table. "Here at the harbor of Montevideo in Uruguay. We have a range of seven days, during which Commodore Nicolson and the Brazil Squadron will be waiting for us. The last day in this range is ten days from today. If we do not arrive by that day, the squadron will move off and resume its normal operations." He spoke in a low voice with a Norwegian accent and he never lifted his eyes from the chart. The Commodore will be forced to abandon the mission." Aaberg paused to let that part sink in before saying, "Added to this is the requirement that we avoid any encounters with the French navy along the way."

"What is the consequence of abandoning the mission, sir?" Brimblecorn said.

Roebuck said, "You mean if we fail, Lieutenant."

"Aye, sir."

Roebuck kept his eyes on Brimblecorn's vaguely mindless expression. "We cannot allow that to happen, Lieutenant."

"No, sir."

Malvey yawned, his mouth wide open and his eyes closed.

Midshipman Rowan asked the obvious question. "Why are we at odds with the French, sir?" Roebuck not having shared that information yet.

"Because they are garlic-eating reptiles," Malvey said, "who would sell their mums for a glass of the emperor's port."

"Mr. Aaberg." said Roebuck, feeling uncomfortable in that moment with his own appreciation of port Aaberg said, "The French have captured two American traders, the *Eliza Davidson* and the *America*. They are holding crews, cargo, and ships. The French falsely claim that the vessels violated their blockade of Argentina. Our government cannot accept this. So we are to assist in the liberation of the ships and their crews."

"Unless we never get there," Malvey said.

Roebuck wondered how Malvey would look in the ocean with a 42-pound shot chained to his leg.

Cockrell said, "Sir, once we clear these doldrums, I suggest we take the trade route. The currents are favorable and the breeze constant."

Roebuck shook his head. "I am instructed that patrols have grown over the past year along those routes. We must avoid them at all costs."

When Roebuck dismissed his officers, he expected that their minds would be full of thoughts about the rare chance to fight and the prospect of glory, the clods.

***

Alone in his cabin, port bottle open, Roebuck resumed his efforts to write the Navy's report. He was hoping for inspiration, filling and emptying his glass five times. Unfortunately none came. A loud voice suddenly interrupted, shaking Roebuck free from this uselessness. "Captain!" Then three startling knocks.

"Who is it?"

"Midshipman Watt, sir. Major Pemberton sends his compliments and word of a scrap on the orlop deck."

"A scrap? Be clearer, man."

"Can you open the door, sir? Please."

"I can hear you fine with it closed."

"Major Pemberton insisted I ask you to open it. He says you would be very glad if I did."

"And you believed him?"

"Well, sir." Roebuck knew Watt, a passed midshipman waiting for an open lieutenancy, was a calm presence among the younger officers. "He seems honest, for a Marine anyway."

"Not all he is," said Roebuck under his breath.

"Sir?"

"I'm coming." Roebuck was up now if a little unsteady.

"Captain." Watt sounded a little impatient.

Roebuck let him in and said, "What about it?"

"It's a big one, sir. And it could spin up into a riot." Watt's voice was cool, no panic.

"What is the cause?"

"The chaw bucket, sir."

The last fight to break out was between some Marines who were well corned and several of the fore royal topmen. Each side claimed exclusive use of a big oak bucket as a receptacle for their tobacco juice.

Roebuck said, "Why can they not empty their buckets when full and use them in common?" He was the commander, not a constable. Commanders had important things to do. "Next, someone will come knocking to demand I make porridge when the cook decides he can't manage on his own."

"Probably be an improvement, sir," Watt said.

Roebuck looked at him. Watt was just nineteen but had a world-weariness about him. "A witticism, Mr. Watt?"

"If it pleases you, sir."

"It does not."

Roebuck's cabin was at the stern of the *Savannah*, below the main deck. The fight was another deck below. Roebuck followed Watt to the main hatch, where they lowered themselves. The port made this dizzying work. As his feet touched the orlop deck, he heard what sounded like animal snarls. Pemberton, his sergeant named Mace and several other Marines were trying to keep two groups of men from punching and gouging each other.

As Roebuck began to say "Stop as you are," he tripped on something heavy, knocking it over. He fell and hitting the deck, slid in a cloying warm liquid. Tobacco juice. What he'd knocked over, the big chaw bucket, had spilled all around him, soaking the left leg of his white trousers to a shade somewhere between red and brown, and the same with his white blouse. Spit dripped from his face. It matted his hair.

The two groups of fighting men stopped cold at the sight of their commander sprawling between them in a slick of the day's expectorations. Roebuck sat up, feeling disjointed and ponderous. The port was having a surprising effect on his limbs. Best remain seated and deliver his command quickly. His bottom was in a puddle. That was too bad but not the main thing. He shouted, "Stop as you are!" And tried to follow the words with something commanding but nothing came, his mind as empty of words as that goddamned bucket.

CHAPTER 12

Why military bands couldn't resist "Hail Columbia" was a mystery to Roebuck. The *Savannah*'s band was playing it now as an opening to the evening's theatrical contest. The polished brass of their instruments reflected lantern light. Flynn the carpenter and his mates had finished building the stage and the performers were ready. The crew body and mind had been diverted for a week preparing for this moment.

"Hail Columbia" sawed on. Roebuck imagined the composer as a man who tells the same joke over and over. Aaberg sat to Roebuck's left. To Aaberg's left sat the ship's clerk. Next to him was the ship's surgeon, Benoit. Perry had described Benoit as the Navy's best bone-sawer, saying the *Savannah* was lucky to have him. The sort of luck Roebuck hoped never to try.

The four of them were judges, seated together in order to convene at the evening's end and choose the contest's winners. A double ration of grog for the next week would be the prize.

The band played the last note, lanterns dimmed, and the crew whooped and clapped in anticipation. Roebuck hoped the evening's performances would help the crew put bad memories behind them, particularly the one concerning his recent chaw bucket bath. He wanted to forget it too, the feeling of that muck on his skin, the smell. The whole affair still stuck to him like a greasy film. He saw it in the eyes of the crew and officers every day.

The curtain rose to reveal a simple elevated platform framed by posts painted to resemble white columns. Midshipman Watt had a reputation as an artist and Roebuck had seen the young man mixing paint and taking a brush to those very posts two days ago.

After a song by Glad Thistle, a ship's boy with a strong contra-tenor singing voice, two old-timers took the stage. One was a wrinkled, bronze-faced sheet-anchor man called Murdoch. He had salt-and-pepper side-whiskers below his ears thick as wood blocks and carried a fiddle. The other was a hand named Kerr, slack as a loose cable and gripping a banjo.

Thistle yelled out, "Don't just stand there, youngsters, do something!"

They started a version of "New York Girls." The evening was proceeding well enough although the heat was still extreme and the men, packed so close together, had begun to shift uncomfortably.

The last of the evening's performances was Malvey's *Rip Van Winkle*. The humor in the vignette had seemed harmless to Roebuck when he had reviewed it. But now, as the curtain rose, nerves seemed to be swimming a relay race in his stomach and he wondered why he had given Malvey what would in effect be the last word. The stage was dark except for light shining on a boy holding a kite and facing a man with the string in his hand.

"Rip, she just can't seem to catch any wind," said the boy.

"Ach, how 'bout now," said the man. He wore loose white clothes and his long black wig was tied back.

The boy shook his head as if to say "old fool," and dropped the kite. "Lookee!" he said, pointing to a leather pouch resting on stage.

Rip said, "Coins! I'll stand you a dram!"

"Mother says I ain't to drink with ye."

When Rip dropped to his hands and knees and crawled toward the pouch, the light shifted to several boys pulling a string and keeping the pouch just out of Rip's reach. This continued back and forth with the first boy following Rip and mocking him. Then the entire stage lit up. Two men sat at a table to the right. Each had a shiny copper buckle above the brim of his rounded hat.

One said, "Derrick, yonder crawls Rip Van Winkle in the dirt. I've seen children play one thousand tricks on him with impunity."

"Ya, Nick, he's inherited little of the martial spirit of his ancestors."

The pouch finally came to a resting place. Rip lunged and grabbed it, splashing down into what was meant to look like a thick pool of brown mud.

"I got yer," Rip said. "Well den, less see what we haf here." He sat up, turning the pouch upside down. With a dull clink, a few scraps of iron fell out. "Ach, well I guess dey'll be treating me for a dram, heh, heh," he said pointing toward the men at the table.

There was a collective gasp from the deck as Rip stood up straight. Roebuck was mortified.

The left side of Rip's white clothes were stained a reddish brown, knee to shoulder. Mud dripped from his cheek. The black hair of the actor's wig was loose now and fell to his shoulders. He pushed it back behind his ears in a gesture that mimicked one Roebuck often made with own black hair. There was nothing in the text of Malvey's theatrical that said *look yonder, Rip Van Winkle stands covered in mud just like Captain Roebuck soaked in tobacco juice.* But that was the message, plain as the soil on Rip's white clothing.

Roebuck watched as Rip Van Winkle drank his way through the rest of the performance. *As Rip, so our captain* was its theme. Each new piece of satire stuck to Roebuck like the mud had done to Rip. The crew devoured it. When Rip drank too much and fell asleep for twenty years, it brought the house down. Roebuck had never imagined how far Malvey was willing to go.

It finally ended. Malvey and his players took their bows amid applause twice as loud as the thing deserved. The crew didn't bother to restrain themselves, as though what they'd just seen gave them license to shed whatever discipline remained on board.

A group of drum and fife players marched onto the stage to wrap up the evening, forming a line and playing "Sailor Boy." It was a bad choice. Fife and drum was fine music on shore, but it put the crew in mind of calls to duty on a ship. They whistled and jeered. A group of Marines stood and shouted for the players to get offstage.

Malvey stood up to speak over the crowd. He was riding on the wing of his triumphant Rip. "See here, lads," he shouted to calm them, asserting authority, "here now!" His Northumberland burr seemed to hide its R's down some hollow in his throat. "Lads," Malvey said, like the ship was his, "we can liven this up. Can anyone dance a hornpipe?"

Three volunteered to dance the jig English sailors held so close to their hearts. One was a Briton, one an American who'd served on a British merchant vessel, and one was a needle-thin negro from St. Kitts. The fifers and drummers resumed but this time playing the English jig, and the three men stamped away. Malvey clapped the rhythm, trying to get the crew to do the same. But they didn't. What they did was abuse the dancers.

The hornpipe was a slow, disjointed affair. The oaths and whistles from the deck grew. Malvey tried to soothe the men. But he didn't know them, not really. He hadn't grown up rubbing elbows and skipping stones with their like. He was English and an officer. And the hornpipe carried a strong whiff of the British navy. While U.S. seamen might have a warm regard for their British counterparts, not so for British officers, who, as most on board knew, manned their ships with men pressed into service against their will, including, at one time anyway, American sailors.

Roebuck, sensing an opportunity, stood and shouted, "Murdoch! Kerr!"

Surprise robbed the crew of their voice for a moment, or maybe they were still embarrassed by the memory of their commander soaked in tobacco juice. Roebuck said the names again, louder, calling the fiddle and banjo up.

Murdoch stood first and began a slow walk to the stage.

Roebuck hopped up onstage himself and said, "Let's show them a dance." That got a little sound from the deck, as if the men might even have liked the idea if it had come from anyone but him. "Any buckaroos onboard?"

Silence. Roebuck's flesh grew hot, his rash feeling like he supposed an old dog might feel mange. Murdoch climbed up. Kerr was on his way.

"I say again, can't someone dance the buck here? There's an extra ration of grog for any flat-footer that tries to win over this sorry lot!" Roebuck pinned a smile to his face. The mention of grog got their attention. It never failed.

Midshipman Watt stood up and shouted, "Captain Roebuck, Ten'til dances the buck."

Ten'til was a fore-topman, nicknamed for the way he smoked a little corn cob bowl. He always held it in his teeth at an angle to his nose like ten minutes 'till the hour.

Ten'til was known for the way he bounced up the *Savannah*'s ratlines as though each crosstie was hinged with a spring. He went aloft in any kind of weather, taking the place of less steady men when it blew hard. And the crew loved him for it. Roebuck asked the two musicians, "You boys know 'Groundhog'"?

"I know I like to eat it for supper," Murdoch said.

The crew laughed. Kerr just nodded. Ten'til reached the lip of the stage and stepped up.

Roebuck said, "Well then."

One of the crew shouted to Murdoch, "C'mon, Granny, wake 'em up."

Roebuck nodded and they started to play. After four stately bars, Ten'til was shuffling toe to heel and then the reverse, mixing in easy combinations. But Roebuck could see he was holding back, waiting for a little more of something or other. This was going nowhere and the crew could see it. Before Roebuck realized what he was doing he half-sang, half-shouted the next verse of the song:

Whet up your axe, whistle up your dog
We're off to the wood to hunt groundhog

His ear was good enough to stay in pitch and the song was a favorite of the boys he used to pick with on the Eastern Shore.

Some of the crew from the deck shouted the refrain, "O' Groundhog."

That was good, how simple it was to sing. Others could join in to sing the refrain. Roebuck sped up to the next verse and Ten'til responded easily, nodding with a slight grin to his commander. The men cheered him. Man could dance, no doubt about it.

Yonder comes Sam with a ten-foot pole
Roust that hog right outta his hole

Twice as many of the crew sang the refrain now. But most of them were still holding back. Then Watt grabbed a handful of sand from a fire bucket and spread it under Ten'til's feet. It added a scuff and a music to the rhythm of Ten'til's taps. Energy built in Ten'til, waiting to get out. The crew seemed to feel it. But Kerr was a slouch, too damn slow. Roebuck needed to make this work, conscious of its strange importance.

"Come on now, that ain't nothing," a Marine called.

Roebuck sang a verse that always made people laugh.

Up stepped Sally with a snigger and a grin
Groundhog juice running down her chin

Murdoch had no problem with whatever pace Roebuck set, but not Kerr.

"Kerr," Roebuck said, "faster."

Kerr's expression hardly changed, saying in a low drawl, "Sorry, sir."

The song ended to more whistles than cheers.

Roebuck reached across and grabbed the banjo fret above the drum. Yanking it out of Kerr's hands, he said, "I'll pick a chord or two."

Kerr slunk off. Murdoch had stuck the whole night to the key of G. That suited Roebuck and he pulled a few chords from the banjo. Sounded good so he took off on his own with "Cripple Creek," playing fast, releasing Ten'til. Murdoch followed, throwing in neat turns on the fiddle, lifting them up. Murdoch leaned toward Roebuck, head bobbing, shoulders dipping and rising. He looked twenty years younger. That was all Roebuck needed. He let go in a moment of musical fury, playing as fast as he ever had but not losing time. Ten'til's head went back a little, eyes looking up. Between the speed and the sand, it was like he floated, the sound of his toes and heels tapping out the rhythm. He kicked his feet high forward, then to the side and back again, put one in front of the other, and then reversed.

The crew went silent, maybe sensing they might see something good now. Murdoch took another break on fiddle, hitting every note, fingers pressing and releasing strings onto the fret with the precision of a machine and the heart of a man who'd spent his last twenty years at sea. He leaned forward still, but sometimes sprang back on a chord change that touched him. When he did, some of the crew raised their voices to push him on, and he slowly leaned forward again, loading the spring before breaking out once more. When he finished his break there was a whoop all around. Then the crew turned back to Ten'til. The young man seemed to feel it, kicking out an impossible spiral and moving in a way that lit a fire on board.

When Roebuck's break came, he kept his back straighter than the new main mast, his eyes locked on the fingers of his left hand and their work on the fret, flicking down and back, pressing strings to lacquered wood and releasing faster and faster, again and again bringing it back to those chords, combining in that way every crewman who'd ever heard a banjo knew, a musical totem that they cheered for its feeling of home. Roebuck took off, changes boiling up, never far from those home chords, feeling that old feeling, all the while holding himself stock-still.

His eyes wanted to close to shut out everything except the music but he refused them. A part of him wanted to move like Murdoch, but he'd long ago conquered the urge of his body to sway and jerk when he played and instead he concentrated on pushing Ten'til. The crew could see it and seemed to feel something coursing through them altogether.

In his memory Roebuck saw the stains of iron nails bleeding into porch planks where he used to play this same song with his free-booting pals. He could almost smell the sweet vines of honeysuckle climbing porch ends and see green shutters against whitewashed boards. He felt the humiliation and failure lifting like a poison fog. He hoped the crew did too.

Yells came from the deck, different than before, deeper, reflexive. Roebuck lifted his eyes to Ten'til, who kept everything from the hips up as steady and cool as the deepest part of a wide stream. The crew was with them, the rhythm and feeling of this wild tuneful music in their movements, surrendering their bodies to it.

When they finished, full-throated cheers washed over them. Roebuck felt like he'd just fed a starving man. Cockrell came out, yelling, "Do we have a winner?" The men shouted. And Cockrell said, "*The Odyssey*?"

Crew shouting, "No!"

"*Rip Van Winkle?*"

"No!"

"Tell me boys, how about the captain, Mr. Murdoch, and this man?" raising Ten'til's right hand as if he was announcing the winner of a boxing match and John Paul Jones's victory over the *Serapis* at the same time. The deck roared.

Something had been restored. Not order, far from that, but a balance, and Roebuck knew that there was a chance for him now, that respect for command and discipline might be teased back onto the *Savannah*. First, however, he had to let these men feel what they were feeling tonight for as long as they felt it and he shouted, just before the cheers began to die down, "Roll out the barrels! Fill their cups, by God."

CHAPTER 13

Roebuck watched the white heart of a flame snap in the lantern. He removed the glass shade. The flame shuddered and then settled. He hoped it would shudder again, a sign of some breeze through the open porthole. It didn't. He drew very close, but the flame did not care.

Then came the unmistakable and irritating knock of his steward. Roebuck said, "Come in."

Lilywhite entered, his shoulders in the permanent hunch of a tall man in a low-ceilinged world. "I have your supper, sir."

"Put it on the side table."

Roebuck was famished but needed to review the ship's logs and to fully consider all that had happened on this strange night. The contest had ended in excitement, which the extra grog elevated. The crew might be on his side for the moment, but they would soon recall his chaw-bucket bath. And the full force of the heat would be back in the morning. Indiscipline still threatened his command.

He pulled off his blouse to eye his itching rash in the mirror. It had spread, brilliant red against his pale skin.

Lilywhite came with a cup of tea, put it gently on the table and stared at Roebuck's red and swollen flesh.

"Sir," he said, "maybe a glass of sherry to take the edge off."

"Not tonight," Roebuck said as he cleared his desk and grabbed the tray of food. A plate of putrid cheese greeted him with a smell that used to turn his stomach before his years at sea had inured him. Lilywhite called the thin strings floating in the bowl of warm water beef, but they could have been anything. Roebuck leaned over to grab some hardtack and tapped it for weevils. None. That was promising. Must not have hatched yet. Once they did, seamen would break up the biscuits, drop them into their morning coffee to float the larvae to the top, skim them off, and slurp the mixture down.

Another knock came, loud and quick this time.

Lilywhite snarled, "Captain's at his supper, come back in thirty minutes."

"I have to see the captain." The door swung open, revealing Midshipmen Rowan, his chest heaving and face flushed. "Captain the Marines are fighting, sir, thrashing some of the crew."

"Let's go then."

"The sergeant-at-arms has broken them up and put them in irons. Major Pemberton instructed me to tell you when he finishes with them, he will come here to report."

"What was it about?"

"The Marines were inebriated, sir, and they assaulted two mates on patrol below." Rowan filled in the scene with a few more details before leaving.

Soon after, Lilywhite announced that Pemberton was waiting on the afterdeck. Roebuck knew the Marine captain would be here to discuss punishment for his six violent and drunk Marines; in particular their leader, a big talker called Vermont, nicknamed for his home state.

Pemberton entered and said, "Captain Roebuck."

Roebuck said, "They still drunk?"

"Yes. Some of them will stay that way for hours. They can barely hold themselves upright."

The steward arrived with two cups of coffee. Roebuck sipped. It was weak and didn't smell like anything in particular, probably brewed from used grounds. The ship's provisioning had been woeful.

"Mr. Watt has been detailed to locate and confiscate any contraband whiskey. With luck, sir, he'll have it all by dawn," Pemberton said.

"Very good. Have the Marines told you anything yet?"

"Not directly."

Pemberton had something on his mind and was laboring to remain composed.

Roebuck said, "I don't think they realize how close they've come to swinging."

"The bastards might yet, sir."

Pemberton was not a man capable of selective enforcement. It was one reason he commanded respect. Another was the way he could drop an unruly seaman as fast as most men cracked a walnut.

"They're about as seditious as four monkeys in a tree," Roebuck said. "And it would be hard for a man to hang for too much whisky."

"What the bastards did was threaten the ship's order. The patrol was acting under your command, your authority."

"They may have talked themselves into something foolish."

Pemberton held Roebuck's eyes. "Or they may have been talked into it. They're still corned with liquor and loudmouthed, and they've mentioned Lieutenant Malvey several times. He may be the source of whisky."

"Lieutenant Malvey?" Roebuck said.

"You aren't surprised, Captain?"

"Let me free you, Mr. Pemberton, of any notion that Lieutenant Malvey be subject to discipline for this."

"And if that arrogant son of a bitch arranged for the whisky?"

"Malvey handles the guns better than any officer in this navy. He has no equivalent on board—no one is even close."

"The United States Navy has a code, Captain, and there is no question of my Marines' guilt," Pemberton said. "They need to be punished publicly."

"What do you have in mind?"

"One hundred lashes each."

"No flogging," Roebuck said. "It changes nothing in the guilty man, except to leave scars on his back. I don't know why officers are so quick with the lash."

"Order, sir," Pemberton said.

"Not on the *Savannah*."

"Yours is the first ship I have served with neither lash nor rod," Pemberton said. "Discipline on a ship is simple. There is the offense, the offender, and the law. And in this case, we have all three."

Roebuck said, "There is not a man in our navy that does not admit, at least to himself, that the harshness of our discipline keeps free Americans of all kinds from enlisting. You above anyone must know that men from the tribes would never submit to the lash. So they do not serve on our ships and we go without the advantage of their fighting quality."

"Start with problems here, Mr. Roebuck. You can save the Navy later." That rolled around between them for a few seconds before Pemberton added, "Why would you suppress punishment?"

"I wouldn't. Crewmen who violate the code are punished on this ship."

"The penalty must address itself to the body—if not, it fastens to nothing. Doubling a seaman's duty or docking his pay is not enough. Worse, it hides both crime and penalty. The crew hears about it, but it is not real to them. What they see is real, what is done to the offender, to his body. Those scars portend something to them."

"Torture."

"If you like, yes. On a ship, the scales of justice matter less than her blindfold. When we apply a single standard for everyone, we are just, sir, and we have discipline."

"Flogging, the gauntlet—these are carnivals of pain, Major Pemberton. Discipline should not be public spectacle."

"Maybe not, but punishment should."

"What if a man steals because he is hungry, or he spits on the deck because he is sick?"

"Maybe it's difficult for you to accept the chance that those who serve under you associate this kind of spectacle with your reputation as an officer, or even as a man. But those shitty drunken Marines were threatening the authority of the ship, threatening the Navy itself. They are as much a danger to the crew as any enemy could be."

"I don't see the good in it."

"It clears any doubt from his mind about what is permitted and what is not. The appearance of law must be sustained most of all while it's being broken."

Given the pleasure Pemberton took in swearing, it was surprising how easily he found words that seemed true as soon as Roebuck heard them. He was eloquent.

"One of the costs a commander must bear is the occasional commission of injustice," Pemberton said. "It is a weak officer that consoles himself with a perfectly clear conscience."

Pemberton was staring into Roebuck's eyes and it was all Roebuck could do not to look away.

"How can I resist such an onslaught of reason, Major Pemberton?" Roebuck said, suddenly wanting this Marine out of his cabin. "We'll have it your way." He rose from the table. "But I decide what those men will suffer."

***

Four Marines stood on the spar deck, shackles around their ankles. Malvey directed a group of crewmen to pump bilge water into buckets and hoist them up to the hands ready on the ratlines. Most of the crew had turned out, and the deck was full of their unsmiling faces. Next to Roebuck stood Captain Pemberton who surveyed the crew and said, "What do you suppose is on their minds, Captain?"

"Some of them will enjoy it, I suppose, and see the punishment as entertainment. But most will be troubled." Roebuck had assigned Malvey to supervise. If the lieutenant had instigated this little revolt, as Pemberton suggested, Roebuck wanted him to demonstrate which side he was really on, the side he would always be on.

Malvey addressed the assembled crew, saying, "These men were caught drunk and fighting," his voice as full of bravado as ever. "Every one of you will empty two buckets, one after the other, on these miscreants. You will do this forcefully. Those of you up in the shrouds," he looked up at the men perched in the rigging like big birds on a line, "will empty your buckets upon their heads." Malvey glared at the four bound Marines.

Malice was in Vermont's eyes as he returned Malvey's glare. There was something between them and Vermont was making sure everyone knew it.

Malvey resumed, "You will do this one bucket after the other until I tell you otherwise. Anyone who makes his part of the punishment easy will be inviting discipline himself. Understood?"

"Aye aye, sir!" said the crew in a single muddled voice.

Pemberton called out, "Fall in!" to his Marines, who quickly formed six lines, one facing each of the shackled men. The major had insisted that the Marines be first on the buckets, his way of endorsing the need for discipline. Roebuck heard Pemberton instruct his men to do their best to drown the rascals bucket by bucket by aiming for their noses.

"Carry on," Malvey said. The crew used all the spare buckets on board, filled in advance, dumping them on the offenders, a bucket detail refilling them as soon as they were emptied. Roebuck required that each of the six would suffer one hundred violent douses.

At first the men jerked their faces left and right in an effort to avoid the worst of each bucketful. Salty fetid water would penetrate their noses, eyes, and ears again and again. When one of them opened his mouth for air, it would immediately be half filled with water and he would gag and spit, desperate for a clean breath.

Soon the offenders gave up moving their faces. There was no use in it, nothing to do but stand and wait for the end. At sixty buckets, some were delirious, confused about whether they were above the sea's surface or below it. Trimble, a Marine with thick blond hair, began to scream, "Here, mates, here, toss a line" in a state of panic, believing he might be drowning. Two others followed him, his shouts a confirmation of their own fears. So the buckets shifted to other targets until the two regained their senses. When they did, the punishment resumed. By eighty douses the four hung limp, held up by fellow Marines, yet the buckets continued.

Eventually Malvey yelled, "Avast! Avast!" It stopped; the men were taken below. Malvey took a position beside Roebuck on the quarterdeck, saying, "Well, sir, it's done. I doubt there have ever been seven cleaner Marinesin the history of the sail."

CHAPTER 14

No wind, no rain, no ships, nothing disturbed the *Savannah* as she dozed in the dead calm. Equatorial heat had transformed her into a fifty-two-gun oven. In the late afternoons, some of the crew used belaying pins to flick heat-addled rats on deck over the rails. Each time a rat plopped into the glassy ocean surface, they cheered. What else was there to do? The cheers were weak, the men somewhat heat-addled themselves. Roebuck began to envy the rats. Maybe he'd go over the rail himself and swim for Brazil.

A detail of hands was making a racket aloft, driving nails into the mizzen top. Roebuck had ordered the carpenter to widen all three of the mast tops. More men in the tops firing carbines and tossing grenades was, he believed, an advantage in a fight.

Others of the crew were strengthening stays, front and back, blacking them in a fresh coat of pitch, to bear the extra weight of the widened mast tops. The ship was starting to feel the way he wanted, not that this did anyone much good at the moment.

A few Marines were already crowded up there practicing their throws from both main and foretop, using one-pound balls left over from days when the *Savannah* had pivot guns mounted on her rails. They were trying to hit empty barrels strung together and bobbing in the sea. Vermont, dried and recovered from his water-bucket punishment, was hitting the farthest ones. Man had an arm to go with that mouth.

Malvey leaned against the fife rail, shifting his weight and crossing his arms like he was watching himself do it, a little self-conscious now, less of the strutting rooster.

Roebuck was learning to read Malvey and guessed that the man was waiting for the right moment to deliver a quip. Why let him? Roebuck said, "Mr. Malvey."

"Sir?"

"You want to say something?"

"Aye sir, it's just that I never knew a captain who preferred throwing shot to firing it out of cannon."

The crewmen working nearby stopped their work and chuckled.

Roebuck said, "They don't throw grenades in the Royal Navy, Mr. Malvey?"

Malvey snorted.

Roebuck said, "You know we are short on powder, Lieutenant." Half the gunpowder loaded in Pensacola had turned out to be spoiled. There had been no time to check the seals on the kegs before weighing anchor. Roebuck did not want to waste a single gun charge. Malvey damn well knew it.

Malvey said, "No amount of powder can make up for unpracticed gunners." And looked around to see who was listening.

Roebuck said, "Our gunners are far from that."

"Not far enough for me, sir. Practice and more practice are what make a good fighting ship. And not the kind of practice we've done here with no live rounds."

The sun was behind Malvey and Roebuck squinted to see his expression. Roebuck said, "We run out of powder against the French and we'll end up fighting with knives and forks while they send us 32-pound balls and exploding shells."

"Knives, forks, and your grenades, sir," said Malvey, nodding toward the Marines throwing shot into the sea. A couple crewmen laughed out loud.

"Lieutenant Malvey, sometimes the choice a commander has to make is between something he dislikes and something he dislikes intensely. I do not like the fact that you cannot work the men on the guns as much as you wish. But I like the prospect of fighting without enough powder even less."

"Hallo there, deck!" came a call from the maintop watch. "Cloud off the starboard quarter."

"Distance?" shouted Roebuck.

"Two leagues, sir," the watchman hesitated, "or a little beyond that."

The telltales hung limp. Roebuck looked through the telescope, adjusting the focus until the white smudge on the horizon grew into beautiful hard clarity. He recognized what he'd imagined each of the last five nights as he closed his eyes to sleep. Tall clouds, downy and white like enormous balls of stacked cotton. His heart rose so fast he closed his mouth to keep it from jumping out.

Aaberg jogged toward them, holding himself back from an all-out sprint. "Captain Roebuck! Do you see the cloud, sir?"

"I hardly see anything else, Mr. Aaberg!" Roebuck said. "Lieutenant Malvey, call the launch crews to the deck, prepare the towlines. Four boats." And turning again to Aaberg, "We reach one of the clouds, Mr. Aaberg, and we'll find our breeze."

Roebuck lifted the glass again and saw the cloud light and high. Here was their chance; if they were fast, they might catch some luck. "Bo'sun," he called.

"Here, sir."

"All hands."

Edwards piped the men up and soon they filled the deck and scrambled up the rigging.

"Take in all but stays'ls, jibs, and spankers," said Roebuck.

The crew was quick, animated by the gravest desire to get this dead stretch of the Atlantic behind them.

The boats were soon up on their davits. Roebuck said, "Launch them, Mr. Malvey, and see that the men pull those oars as if their lives depend on it."

CHAPTER 15

The clouds had yielded a breeze and the *Savannah* was underway at last. Spirits on board had gained in proportion to their headway and the ship was a gladder, much gladder universe.

Charts covered a table separating Roebuck from Cherry. Aaberg stood beside Cherry, his eyes pearled over and his head, Roebuck knew, full of thoughts he would keep to himself.

"The clipper route will save us four days, sir, maybe more." Cherry's face puckered as he pleaded, nostrils wide as his eyes. "How else can we gain on lost time?"

The current in Cherry's clipper route was fast but it was also full of merchant ships, and Roebuck's orders were to reach Rio de la Plata undetected. A speedy clipper or packet ship could overtake them and carry word of the *Savannah*'s impending arrival to officials in Montevideo who would certainly tell their allies, the French. Roebuck didn't know how hostile the French were, but if they were hostile at all, they'd do whatever it took to keep the *Savannah* from adding her fifty-two guns to Commodore Nicolson's squadron.

"No, Mr. Cherry, you must chart another course," Roebuck said, looking at the fleshy creases and wiry black brows crowding the man's rheumatic eyes.

Cherry resisted. The clipper route was one he knew well and the prospect of traveling a course out of his routine unnerved him, but after considerable encouragement, if that was the word, he came up with an alternative and they began to chart it.

Lilywhite entered with a knock and said, "Sir, the officers are gathered in the greater cabin."

"Supper?"

"Aye sir, as you asked. Boiled peas, and the cook managed a version of black pudding from dried apples, salt pork, cheese, and the last of the onions."

"Thank you, Lilywhite." Roebuck turned back to the charts.

Lilywhite said, "The officers have been waiting for close to an hour, sir. They're beginning to complain."

The ship was moving, the crew happy. Roebuck did not want to spoil any of the good feeling the breeze had brought with it. He said, "Mr. Aaberg, let us join the others."

Walking toward the greater cabin, the two of them passed the boatswain and Roebuck recalled something. "Ah," he said, "Mr. Edwards, kindly remind Mr. Cherry that he must be careful to account for any deviation in the binnacle compass when he sets course."

"Aye aye, sir."

The windows of the greater cabin doors afforded Roebuck a view of his officers seated around a long table, a thick bank of pipe smoke floating above them, Virginia leaf by the smell of it. Roebuck swallowed and entered.

The officers rose to attention.

Roebuck said, "Sit down, gentlemen, please," taking his own seat at the head of the table.

The four midshipmen puffed away on clay pipes. Cockrell hung a lacquered corncob bowl off his eyetooth. Aaberg smoked from briarwood. Pemberton was too busy talking to smoke.

Roebuck had his own leaf—no shag, thank you—that his mother sent him from the family patch, and he'd rolled a few cheroots for the evening. Malvey smoked from white Meerschaum. His face was neither scowling nor ironic, anticipation of drink perhaps mellowing the son of a bitch in him.

Roebuck said, "Quite a bowl on that pipe, Lieutenant Malvey."

"Aye, sir, it's carved in the likeness of Admiral Nelson himself."

Cockrell laughed.

"Someone say something funny, Mr. Cockrell?" Malvey said.

Cockrell said, "What's that on his head?" pointing to the bowl.

Malvey said, "It's an admiral's hat. See the peak? It's how admirals prefer them."

"Ain't like any admiral's hat I know," said Cockrell.

Malvey turned to the midshipmen and said, "Mr. Cockrell wouldn't know an admiral's hat from a handbag."

"I see what you mean, Mr. Malvey," Cockrell said, "It does resemble what Mama used to keep her comb and her tithing coins in."

"A saintly woman," Roebuck said.

Cockrell said, "Yes, sir, she was that, certainly."

"It's a turban, not a hat," a rare sentence from Pemberton that didn't feature swearing.

"With a Turk's pointy beard," Brimblecorn ventured.

Malvey said, "No, Brimblecorn, it's no beard. Nelson was endowed with a prominent chin," and pulled deeply on the pipe.

"Where did you acquire the pipe, Mr. Malvey?" asked Roebuck, Meerschaum having the quality of being found among the Ottomans and nowhere else.

Malvey mumbled something that sounded like it might have been Istanbul and nodded at Cockrell, saying, "My friends, here we have a man smoking a cob of corn with all the seeds eaten off and yet you think my pipe is strange."

"Kernels," Aaberg surprised the table with this act of speech.

"What colonels?" Malvey said.

"I do not mean, however, to correct you, Mr. Malvey," Aaberg said, not quite getting it right. "They are referred to as kernels, not seeds."

Malvey stared.

Cockrell said, "This is no common cob of corn. It is our first president, General Washington." Pulling the pipe from his mouth, Cockrell with a sense of gravity pointed to its front. "A great general, but a little beady in the eye."

Rowan snorted, and the other midshipman laughed, which caused Roebuck to frown. They straightened up. Time had come to open the evening, so Roebuck stood and said, "Let us raise a glass together. Lilywhite, if you please."

The steward uncorked three bottles and emptied them into the most capacious decanter Roebuck in his short life had seen. After that Lilywhite opened a fourth bottle and, plucking each man's glass from the table, splashed in just enough of the wine to top it off without ever spilling a drop. The skinny little rake was showing off. Roebuck raised his glass and said, "To the *Savannah* under sail again, may the wind fly her all the way to Argentina."

"To the *Savannah*."

Roebuck said, "Lilywhite, the punch?"

"Here, sir," Lilywhite said, emptying two bottles of Madeira into a large glass bowl. The cook had already half filled it with lemon juice, sugared water, ginger, and cinnamon. It had a tempting fragrance.

The officers smoked their bowls and tipped their glasses. A boy entered to hand a red-hot poker to Lilywhite. He stirred it into the punch, which hissed and steamed, its vapors adding a whiff of burnt sugar and lemon to the smell of tobacco in the cabin.

"It's better hot," Lilywhite said.

Roebuck was delighted to see how Lilywhite made such an occasion of it. Eight boys entered, two large white china serving dishes in hand, each dish heaped with peas and black pudding. Not appetizing, exactly, but it would do.

Before they were too deep into the evening, Roebuck had intended to confirm Cherry's heading at the binnacle, but now realized that his own compass was buried under a pile of blue coats shed by his guests. How would it look, him already into his third cup, digging through the clothing of his juniors? Not inspiring, he was sure of that. The responsibility was Cherry's in the first place and a good officer must not overbear his inferiors. So Roebuck didn't.

Midshipman Holman spoke, handsome face smiling. "How did you know the wind was there in the cloud, Captain Roebuck?"

Roebuck had never tried to explain this to anyone before. It was just there inside him.

"Rivers," Roebuck said, and looked quickly around the table. Detecting nothing to inhibit him, he went on. "The rivers do it, I think. I learned to look for clouds like that after a cool rain up rivers."

"Which rivers, sir?" Midshipman Watt interrupted.

"Susquehanna most often, then the Choptank or the Potomac."

They were nodding.

Roebuck said, "The mouth of the Amazon is to our west."

Watt said, "You believed she would send some weather?"

"I wish she had sent it sooner," he said. "But she keeps her own time."

CHAPTER 16

The *Savannah* continued its progress, carrying seven knots on the strength of a southerly breeze. Brazil was nowhere to be seen on the Western horizon and Roebuck congratulated himself for crossing one of the world's most traveled sailing lanes undetected. If the wind and their luck held, the rendezvous might yet be within the universe of possibility.

"Boy," called Roebuck, starting from a daze the sprout on watch whose nose was sprayed with freckles.

"Yessir?"

"My compliments to Lieutenant Aaberg," he said. "Ask him to join me here."

"Aye aye, sir."

Roebuck knew it was Aaberg's supper hour but had also learned how the man was never bothered by impositions of the kind Roebuck intended.

Malvey stood a few paces away. He and Roebuck had not exchanged ten words over the duration of Malvey's turn as officer of the watch, an improvement, Roebuck believed, to Malvey's conversation.

"Mr. Lieutenant Malvey," Roebuck said, scratching an ironic itch, "Mr. Flynn is yet to fill in these screw holes." He nodded toward eight large holes in the deck's planks, all that was left of the theatrical stage. "Would you be so kind as to go and ask him what ails?"

Malvey clenched his teeth. A natural reaction, for this was no task for the officer of the watch. Malvey's teeth unclenched. An indication perhaps that he was about to start chewing on somebody. Roebuck for instance. But Malvey surprised Roebuck, a calm somehow welling up from his snotty depths, saying with matter-of-factness, "My watch is not over, sir."

"And," Roebuck said, "I would not end it early if there were the least chance of anything to disturb this run of headway." Was he being peevish or was he asserting himself and how does an officer tell the difference?

Malvey nodded and walked away after a marble-mouthed "Aye aye, sir."

In minutes, Aaberg appeared on the quarterdeck and said, "I beg your pardon, Captain." Aaberg still sounded Norwegian but carried himself like a Tidewater planter. It never mattered how arbitrarily Roebuck imposed himself on the man, Aaberg never failed to greet him in a way that sounded like an apology. Roebuck could be three sheets to the wind speaking Latin backwards in just stockings and a feathered cap and Aaberg would make like he was talking to the Archbishop of Baltimore.

"Mr. Aaberg, good day to you," Roebuck said.

Aaberg nodded and smiled, creases kinking a face that had seen more years at sea than on land.

"Gather the watch for drills, if you please."

Aaberg nodded and said, "Aye aye, sir."

"Pardon me." It was Cherry. "I beg your pardon, Captain sir." He'd snuck up on them.

"What is it, Mr. Cherry?"

"We just shot the noon sun, sir, and well, Captain, what the chart says, and this will no doubt be a surprise and not a pleasing one to you, we've gone a terrible way off course."

The hair on Roebuck's neck stood up. "Continue," he said.

"Well, sir. We mistook our heading when starting the new course last night. And we've come to be long six degrees north and short three to the east."

"Wrong direction?"

"Aye sir," Cherry gulped, and said, "The binnacle compass was off, sir."

Roebuck's face was hot and he felt pressure building at the top of his skull. He said a quivering, "Well?"

Cherry explained but the explanation did nothing to change the fact that they were off course in a way that played havoc with their schedule. Roebuck had trusted a man nearly everyone onboard knew could not be trusted and had done it for the least of reasons. Now he would pay. He said to Cherry, "I will join you in the chart room in five minutes to decide the heading back to the clipper route. For now we shall add three points south-southwest." They had no choice but to use the swiftest route possible. The risk of detection was secondary to speed. Everything was.

Cherry's "Aye aye, sir," was enthusiastic.

Cherry waddled off and Roebuck turned to the binnacle, putting his hands on its big brass head, squeezing hard as if to collapse the metal, his way to exorcize the black anger from inside him. Still shaking with the effort, he wiped the binnacle glass with a sleeve and wrote down the reading. His compass was no longer buried beneath a pile of blue officers' jackets, so that excuse was no longer available to him. He went to retrieve it and check the reading against the binnacle.

When he'd done this, he sat at his desk wondering if a man like Cherry or anyone else on the *Savannah* could for a second realize how humiliating it had been to grow up a Roebuck on the Chesapeake Bay? With no possibility of respect from a single soul on either shore. Not from his neighbors, not from the parents of his friends. Growing up with a dishonor that hung off each member of his household like something scarlet and ulcerating.

***

It took eight hours on the new heading to join the fast flow of the clipper route. And in no time the *Savannah* encountered a merchantman headed north. And soon after that another heading, Roebuck guessed, to Bahia. It troubled him to think how many more there would be to come. A packet ship heading in the same direction as the *Savannah* might expose the facts of their presence and heading to those hostile toward his mission.

On the forecastle, the crew gathered to watch an initiation of first-timers into the league of sailors who had crossed the line of the equator. Murdoch, the old fiddle player, took on the role of Neptune, making his entrance seated on a gun carriage, a group of powerful Tritons pushing him along. He directed the proceedings with godlike solemnity, using a makeshift trident to point here and there.

In keeping with an apparent naval tradition, the first-timers, polliwogs as they were called, offered up their rears to the great Neptune for a whipping. Each had shaved his beard under a generous emollient of fish fat. The great Neptune forbade washing it off so the stink of it would stay with them for days.

When the solemnities ended, Murdoch deemed those whose rears had been whipped true seamen in the U.S. Navy, thereafter to be called shellbacks. It surprised Roebuck to see pride on the smelly faces of these men as they thanked Neptune for his divine ministrations.

When the diversion ended, Roebuck's mind went involuntarily to what he sensed was going to be an encounter with the French. He didn't know exactly where the *Savannah* stood in relation to the navy of that nation, but something told him there would be hostility of the kind that led to violence. Perry had spent an afternoon and two pots of tea telling Roebuck how a rare alliance with the British against President Rosas in Buenos Aires had emboldened the French to bullying conduct at sea. British sea power had been the lone restraint on French high-handedness for decades. But no longer, at least in the South Atlantic. The *Eliza Davidson* and the *America,* boarded, their cargo seized, were among the first to suffer the consequences.

The Savannah was a fast ship but she was powerful too, originally rated for 44 guns, the Navy had found a way to add eight more, including two long 24-pound chasers. The broadside batteries consisted of twenty-eight 32-pounders and twenty-two 42-pound carronades, an ugly snub-nosed gun that carried a powerful punch at short range.

Roebuck joined the watch. "Hello, Mr. Aaberg."

"Good afternoon, sir."

"How does she sail?"

"Never better, sir, oil on ice. We have put more sea behind us in the last two hours than in the previous three days."

They had finally caught a favorable current. Roebuck was silent, trying to empty his mind of unhappy thoughts.

"You've seen the long swells, sir, starting to show, coming north-northeast?" Aaberg said.

Roebuck had and he nodded. The swells were a curiosity under such a cloudless sky. He hoped they wouldn't last and said, "Soon we'll have the southerlies at our shoulder and we'll make better time still."

"Aye, sir."

A voice rang out from the foremast top.

"Deck, sir! Sail-ho! Three points off the port quarter!"

Roebuck snapped the telescope out and raised it. A ship heading north, square sails, low mizzenmast, longish yards. He couldn't make out her colors. Aaberg took a long look through his own glass, Roebuck waiting to hear what the man thought.

Aaberg stopped looking and resumed his previous attitude.

Roebuck said, "Lieutenant Aaberg."

"Sir?"

"Do you have an opinion?"

"Aye, sir."

Roebuck waited some more, Aaberg seeming in this moment more like a sideshow mute than a ship's lieutenant. He said, "Do you mind sharing that opinion?"

"No sir, I do not." Aaberg paused as if something just occurred to him. He stepped in the direction of the watch log, hesitated, and asked, "Shall I tell you my opinion, sir, or log it for your review?"

"Now, please, Lieutenant. I am trying to make up my mind whether or not to sail over and blow that ship into kindling and ribbons."

"Well, sir, you won't catch her. She's a tea clipper, Aberdeen built, I think. Do you see her bow taper?"

Roebuck looked again and saw what Aaberg meant. She was cut with a little more shape than a Yankee clipper.

Aaberg said, "Yes, sir. Long and with some rake to her masts. Built for speed."

Roebuck said, "Hard to find any margin running opium into Canton on a slow ship." The clipper was lovely and they watched her make way. "She'll be full of tea for the ladies in Boston." Deliver opium, take home tea; Roebuck was familiar with the formula.

"Or London," Aaberg said.

American shipbuilders had designed speedy clippers to outrun blockades from the British and French during unfriendly times. The Scots took the pattern and built their own for trade in the British Isles and these had been improved upon to elude Chinese war junks and Malay pirates. They were very fast and maneuverable but couldn't handle much cannon weight. As a consequence, they weren't normally built under naval commission. So Roebuck did not worry about this one.

"We'll see others along this route, sir," Aaberg said.

"And naval traffic, too. Patrols," Roebuck said. A trickle of sweat ran down his back and he realized with relief that for the first time in five days he felt no urge to dig fingernails into his skin. The heat rash was down. "Lieutenant Aaberg, do you like a French or a British frigate?"

"Like?"

"If you were a captain, which would you prefer to command?"

"For what purpose, sir?"

Roebuck said, "What sort of purposes can you imagine?"

"Imagine?"

"Lieutenant Aaberg, why do I feel like I'm talking to a bag of rocks?"

"Are you referring to me, sir?"

"Let's try these purposes," Roebuck said. "Battle with another frigate, battle with a lower-rated ship, battle with a higher rate, patrol, chase and capture, rough seas, low wind, escape."

"Well, sir, for speed, it's hard to beat the French. When the British capture French frigates they examine the hulls to copy their shape. The French are clever, sir, none cleverer; and they've discovered ways to prove their designs in water before splitting wood for a single plank. But the British have better masts and hulls. It's the timber there, sir. Their own woodlots have been exhausted, but they have found other sources, such as Canada or India. The French cannot avail themselves of such timber." Aaberg looked like a new man, talking about ships. "The British ships are sturdier, 'cause where can the French find good timber? And the British understand how to rig a ship," he said, peeking at Roebuck, looking for something in his commander's expression to suggest that he was talking too much. Whatever he saw there he interpreted as no. "So I guess as far as a rough sea, British; low wind, French; easy seas in a chase, French. Any kind of fight, British. The French make smart guns, very smart, probably the best, but their ships can't support enough of them. They don't like the weight, most already hog and sag."

"Inferior timber," Roebuck said dry as popped corn.

"Right you are, sir. Old as well."

Roebuck smiled, watched the tea clipper sail out of sight. Their course might bring them into contact with the French and when it did, he would have to test Aaberg's notions.

Aaberg said, "How about you, sir?"

"British, I suppose. You can always get more speed from a ship, good hull or bad. And it's true that the British rig a ship as well as anyone."

"Except the Americans," Aaberg said.

Roebuck nodded, thinking, *We'll find out soon enough.*

CHAPTER 17

The *Savannah* passed another swift hour on the current, which had carried them to the edge of Brazil's coastal shelf. Sea captains heading south loved the shelf for both breeze and current, the very reason Roebuck had wanted to avoid it. His orders were to keep out of sight until he reached Montevideo. But now he believed he must risk exposure and discovery in order to make up for lost time. At the same time he knew if they were sighted from shore a warning might travel by Brazil's coastal signal towers all the way to the French in Rio de la Plata. If those towers were good, the message would be there in hours. A packet ship overtaking them could have the same result. But what else was there to do?

Roebuck sat in the chartroom, looking through an open porthole. A light rain had begun to fall. Pressure was for the moment holding just past twenty-nine. That was down a notch, a storm ahead but not close, maybe even spent. The chart room was cool. God knew Roebuck needed cooling to help him concentrate. So he thanked God. His rash was almost gone

. Was that ever a welcome change.

The swells ticking up from the southwest had grown taller. Roebuck had been certain that the opposite would happen, that they would diminish and eventually stop. But no, each of them was large enough now to lift the *Savannah* up and pitch her over, slowing their progress by half at least.

His blue sack coat hung from a hook. Six-buttoned and half-lapelled, the kind lieutenants wore. Only this one had the straps of a commander attached to the shoulders. The sewing had been done in haste and these the straps were a little cockeyed. He wondered if that made the overall effect as shabby to others as it was to him. At least Roebuck liked the embroidered eagles on those straps, how their wings were spread as if feeling the wind. An infantry colonel he met at Fort Pickens also had shoulder straps decorated with an eagle, although his was a more stern-looking bird. Roebuck imagined it looked that way because infantry colonels had no idea on earth about the feeling of wind against a wing. A bull or maybe an ox would have been his choice to represent that branch of the U.S. Army.

His hat followed the same story. While Roebuck was pleased to find a spare officer's hat after he had been breveted at Pensacola—blue wool, decked with a trim black visor—it was too big by a size and a half. He had to push it up sometimes so it didn't cover his eyes. His trousers were his own white ducks rather than the blues of a commander. He wore them because of the fit. Perry had given him a pair of blues, but they turned out to be loose at the waist and sagged around his rear. It wasn't just the uniform. He could tell that there were men onboard with doubts about his experience, and more than just a few. Nothing in a commander's coat or a hat would change that.

Lilywhite's voice interrupted. "Captain, sir," he said.

Man never rested. Roebuck said, "What is it?"

"Lieutenant Cockrell sends his compliments and requests your presence on the quarterdeck."

"Did that cotton-picker tell you why?" Roebuck wasn't finished with the chart and was annoyed with himself for becoming distracted.

"Ships, sir."

"On my way." Roebuck pushed the door open and was past Lilywhite almost before the steward had finished the words.

Through the main hatch and up on the spar deck he saw Malvey jawing at Cockrell while Cockrell kept his eyes fixed eastward.

"Lieutenant Cockrell," Roebuck said.

"Sir, there are two of them, square rigged, three masts, long yards. Seems like they're together, with near two or so leagues between them. One broad to our port quarter about five leagues and the other a point forward of that."

"Colors?"

"French."

"Thank you." Roebuck had to push southward, French or no French Malvey said, "Let us go straight at them, sir." Roebuck was *sir* all of a sudden. "Like crossing lots."

Roebuck said to Cockrell, "Bearing?"

"South of our heading, sir."

Malvey said, "We do them away, Captain, and it's smooth sailing after that."

Roebuck looked again through his glass, bringing one then the other of the ships into focus. He said, "How long are we from sunset?"

Cockrell wasn't sure and Malvey didn't bother answering. The French ships were closing on the *Savannah*, both of them a-port. Would they try to box him in? They might keep to the wind and put him at a disadvantage. How easily would they turn together? And the main question hovering over everything: Was he out of his depth?

The *Savannah* was so big compared to any of his previous commands. And these ships were smaller, but oh brother they would be bigger by far than anything he had tangled with.

He turned to Malvey. "What do you see, Mr. First Lieutenant?"

Malvey took Roebuck's glass. "They're French rigged, sir, as Mr. Cockrell had it. Corvettes, same trim with speed to make it a tough race."

Roebuck said, "Who said anything about a race?"

"We'll fight them then?" Malvey said.

Roebuck said, "How many guns?"

"Corvettes have at least twenty-four, sir," Malvey said, and sounded pretty certain about it. "The Frogs haven't made a corvette rated lower than that in decades."

Roebuck said, "Save your history lessons for the midshipmen and tell me how many guns you see."

At that Malvey began to slow down, taking a second leisurely look at the closer of the two ships. A drizzle of rain pebbled on the cylinder of his spyglass. Malvey's eye stayed on that closer ship. He obviously enjoyed the other officers' attention and was performing for them. When he finally spoke he said, "Twenty-two guns, sir, ten there on the starboard battery, and chasers, probably nine pounders. Two of them on the bow and I'd wager another two on the stern."

Roebuck nodded, if the other corvette had the same number of guns, the two combined would match the *Savannah*'s battery.

"What position gives them an advantage?" Roebuck hated asking Malvey in front of everyone, but God he wanted to know.

Malvey said, "They'll hold their position to the weather if you let them," making it sound like Roebuck would have a choice.

A French corvette was a famously maneuverable ship, and in this case could take whatever position a French captain wanted. Malvey's giving voice to the idea that the *Savannah*'s commander could do anything but make the best of the position he was handed was pure fiction.

Roebuck turned to Cockrell and said, "What is our speed?"

"About eight knots, sir. We'd be faster if not for these big white horses."

Cockrell meant the swells continuing up from the south. They had grown and were now topped with angry white crests. Remnants, Roebuck now believed, of a distant and massive storm.

He watched the corvettes for a while and saw the loose angle they took across the wind. They did not appear to be trying to intercept the *Savannah* as quickly as they could. Rather they were aiming to converge with her at a spot over the southern horizon. The curve of the earth almost certainly hid something good for them down there.

"What do you think, sir?" asked Cockrell.

An obnoxious question is what he thought and didn't answer. Instead, he watched the two sister ships, each of them quick. The one nearer sailed close to the wind. Was she well captained, her crew smart? At this distance Roebuck couldn't tell. Her consort was farther away but coming on. No changes visible to her direction or trim, her captain probably thinking they had plenty of time.

"Simple," Roebuck said to himself, except out loud. Then before Cockrell could respond, he said, "Signal flags?"

Cockrell said, "No, sir, the topmen have been watching for any signals between them but ain't seen a thing."

Cockrell was thinking of the important things. That was good, if a little surprising. Roebuck said, "Don't need them."

Cockrell said, "They don't, sir?"

Malvey said, "Because each already knows what the other is going to do."

"And," Roebuck said, "might be there's a third ship or, who knows, a squadron waiting past the horizon."

Neither lieutenant spoke. Was fear causing their commander to imagine ships that weren't there, as a child imagines monsters in the closet?

CHAPTER 18

Roebuck and the *Savannah*'s two ranking lieutenants, Malvey and Aaberg, were leaning over the charts below. Earlier he had checked the almanac to see what the moon had in store for them that night and learned there was to be no moonrise before midnight. There was already a dense covering of cloud overhead so it would be a very dark night before the moon was up. Roebuck hoped to use the darkness.

Aaberg looked dubious.

Roebuck said, "To encourage them to doubt our speed and question our competence, we will change course with plenty of looseness and hesitation. Naturally they will close the distance between us. But when the sun sets and we are hidden in the dark we'll change our heading."

Malvey said, "What would that heading be Captain Roebuck?"

This of course was the question and the only thing that mattered. The *Savannah* had made a swift move to the clipper route in order to accelerate her way to the rendezvous. Now it seemed the only choice was to abandon it and it's advantage in speed. "If they do," Roebuck said, "We cannot allow them to slow our progress, they will have succeeded in keeping the *Savannah* and her guns from helping to secure the release of the *American* and the *Eliza Davidson* and their sailors."

Malvey waited. Roebuck felt ridiculous for exposing his logic rather than answering the question. It must be obvious to his lieutenants that he didn't have an answer, that he was dithering. He found himself wondering if there were sailors aboard the French ships who knew the *Savannah*, had seen her before and could tell their captain of her speed and if so how that might render the notion of a feint and swift escape unlikely. He checked the charts to learn just how far the clipper route was from the Brazilian shore. The route moved toward and away from the shelf off of Brazil's coast for many leagues. He said, "East'-sou'-east, Mr. Malvey. We will make our feint into the open ocean."

Back on the quarterdeck, it wasn't long before the foretopman called out, "Hallo deck, sir, three masts a point off the starboard fore!"

Roebuck had feared there were more hostile ships on the far side of the horizon. Here was a case when he'd rather that his instincts had been wrong. Through the glass, he followed a dab of white against the southern edge of his view. "She's hull down," he said. "Can't make out her size," and waited for another ten minutes before looking again. He said, "A goddamn razee," nerves talking before he could quiet them. The first razee he'd ever seen was British and anchored in a small Tobago bay, that jewel of an island. What he now saw through the glass was similar, the ship's lines telling a story of their own, how she once had three gun decks but was cut down to two, navies of Europe following the American preference for ships quick and maneuverable yet with enough firepower to defend the convoys.

Malvey took the glass. "So it is. That'll mean at least fifty-four guns. And she's to the wind of us. That's trouble to you, sir, no arguing that."

With the addition of the razee, the three French ships roughly doubled the *Savannah*'s guns. Roebuck looked at one of the corvettes zipping along then the other. They were fast, agile, and gaining. He had only four days remaining to make his rendezvous with Nicolson's Brazil squadron. It was time to change their direction.

"Haul to the wind, Mr. Malvey," he said. "Ten points a-weather."

Malvey turned to the quartermaster and helmsman, saying, "On my command, east-sou'east."

"Ready for stays!" Malvey called.

The mast captains took the cue, calling, "On the main!" "On the fore!" and "On the mizzen!" The crew scrambled into position.

"Mr. Malvey, we'll brace about and finish right next to the wind," Roebuck said. And remember, loose and slow."

"Aye, aye, we've prepared the men to make us look as hopeless as you'd like."

Roebuck nodded.

Malvey said, "How will you slip her back alee in the dark, sir?" He pointed the eyecup of the spyglass, "That corvette, when she draws close, the sound of us wearing around will reach her."

"Did you have a suggestion Mr. Malvey?"

"Just can't catch sight of it, sir. You might just as well raise a white flag, sir, and walk us over to them here and now."

***

The *Savannah* had sailed east-southeast for hours. The corvettes were close now, very close, and Roebuck had been trying to choose the time to reverse their heading again and leave his pursuers behind. The hourglass told him that the last of the day's sunlight had been gone for just over an hour. The darkness had become as close to complete as it could be. And while he knew the French were near, it was impossible to tell how near. *Now or never*, he thought. Roebuck gave the order to extinguish all lanterns.

"Humph." Roebuck felt a sharp pain in his side. "Who is that?"

"It's me, sir, Holman, midshipman of the watch."

It was too dark for Roebuck to see the young man's handsome face. Hopefully there was a trace of fear in it for having jostled his ship's commander. "Keep your elbow out of my ribs, if you please, and spare Lieutenant Aaberg the greeting you've just given me."

"Aye aye, sir. Sorry, sir."

"I'm over here, Mr. Holman," said Aaberg. "You may take your position beside me."

Hoffman's boot soles shuffled forward then stopped. It was quiet again. Roebuck allowed the midshipman's eyes to adjust to the darkness before saying, "Mr. Holman, gather the mast captains to the quarterdeck. And look alive this time. Mr. Aaberg, let us prepare to haul a reverse."

Aaberg waited for some time before saying, "Captain, sir, might it not be to our advantage rather to put her stern through the wind and jibe, given this darkness and our proximity to the French?"

Roebuck could almost see the pins knitting Aaberg's brows. "Backing the ship will give us our best chance to avoid those people," He said, pointing in the direction of the corvettes. He stopped. Was there a more useless gesture in darkness? He was about to explain another advantage of backing but stopped. *Just say it*, he thought, *and let them do it.*

Aaberg said, "Sir, it might be—"

Roebuck said, "Enough."

Holman arrived with the mast captains.

"Gentlemen," Roebuck said, "We'll soon bring the ship around on her heel."

"Sternway, sir?" said Murchison, the ship's eternally impatient foremast captain.

"That is correct, Murchison, so your men will have the lion's share of the duty."

Murchison said, "We've backed her plenty of times before, Captain."

His peers each grunted their agreement, probably wondering why they were on the quarterdeck in the first place discussing something so routine.

"Yes, but now you must do it with no lamplight and in silence. I want us to come around with the mid and after yards nice and easy."

"And quiet," Murchison said.

"That's the idea," Roebuck said.

"Aye, sir, we'll just need a care on the helm. Another helmsman maybe to keep her smooth."

Roebuck nodded, liking Murchison. No questions about what, just how.

"We've practiced it in the dark sir, but in silence?" It was Bayless this time, the mainmast captain.

"You and Lieutenant Aaberg can work that out in the wardroom," Roebuck said, recognizing Bayless's doubt as a cultured seaman's response.

It wasn't very long before Aaberg reported that the mast captains and crew were ready. But Aaberg again expressed his concern, calling attention to the fact that the *Savannah* was closer to the French than ever. French voices now clearly within hearing.

Roebuck was concerned also, but saw no choice. They were doing what they could to avoid detection, the crew shoeless now and padding around the deck in bare feet and whispering when they had to.

"Captain, sir?" whispered a voice Roebuck didn't recognize.

"Who is there?"

"Marine Corporal Vermont, sir. Major Pemberton sent me to you." Vermont, the drunken troublemaker.

"If there is more trouble, Vermont, it can wait."

"Yes, sir. Only there's no trouble. It's that I hear the French."

"We all do."

"But I speak the lingo, sir."

"You speak French?"

"I'm Acadian, sir."

"You don't exactly follow a pattern do you, Vermont?"

"Try not to," Vermont whispered.

Roebuck hearing for the first time a vague French twang in his voice. "Go on," he said.

"I heard the French gunner telling his crews that they must be ready to fire the moment they see us. And the other two ships have the same orders, but this man wanted his guns to be the first.

"With our timbers they're unlikely to sink us," Roebuck said.

"They'll try, sir. I can promise you that. And the gunner said that when the *Perle* joins them soon, they'll send us to the bottom."

"*Perle*," Roebuck said, "must be the name of the razee," thinking if it wasn't already, the balance would soon be against them. "You can leave us, Mr. Vermont," and then said to Aaberg, "Square the head yards."

Aaberg gave the order and the words quietly traveled all the way up the mast tops. Aaberg and the mast captains had worked out a way to pass commands by a nearly silent relay.

Roebuck said, "Has Mr. Edwards raised all hands?"

"He has, sir."

"Let us run up into the wind then."

Darkness hid the sails, the sea, everything. The only way to bring the *Savannah* around would be by feel. Roebuck fixed his mind and body on her shuck and flow, sensing the breeze against her canvas and the press of her rudder. "Bring us up," he said to the two men on the helm, "and to take us into the wind."

Aaberg said, "Now the after yards," his words once again relayed quietly over the deck as the ship swung to the wind's eye.

They reversed the *Savannah*'s sails to back her and she began to groan, too loud. Too goddamn loud. "Ease those braces," he said, attempting to growl and whisper at the same time.

Gradually, the nimble frigate made sternway, her bow falling off quickly and the rest soon following.

"Good girl," Roebuck whispered, hearing nothing apart from a vague creak in the planks. She was where he wanted her, retracing the narrow arc she had followed into the wind, backwards.

"So far so good, sir," Aaberg whispered.

These were the words Roebuck had not permitted himself to think, much less say, wanting to avoid invoking the hostile spirits of foul luck. "Not another word, Aaberg," he said.

They backed the ship close enough to rub snot from any French seaman with his nose over the rail sniffing the breeze. It was a memory Roebuck would keep, how they came around and made way in pure darkness and utter quiet.

CHAPTER 19

Darkness is never perfect at sea, but tonight it was pretty close. The sky was a Roman concrete of cloud. That was good, because without it the constellation Virgo would bounce its light off the undulating sea and silhouette the *Savannah* for French eyes.

Lantern light on the closest French ship became dim over the water as the distance grew. Roebuck's heart was still in a sprint, and he said, "Pray she keeps moving sou'ward, Mr. Aaberg," his voice cramped and nervous.

Aaberg said, "I have been doing just that, sir."

Roebuck had demanded silence, no pumping in the bilge, no extra line and cable harping in the wind. Had the French figured them out anyway?

His eyes and ears were useless in the silence and darkness, but not his nose. And he had never been more aware of the harsh charred smell emanating the ship's galley stovepipe. Would the French sniff them out? Would the stink of their bilge water betray them? The odor that reminded him now as never before of so many rotting corn stalks in a flooded field,

***

Morning light revealed that the *Savannah* was alone and free, at least for now, to make way southward.

"Pardon me, Captain," Aaberg said.

"Lieutenant?"

"I'd like to remain on deck through the next watch, sir."

Aaberg's watch duty was ending but he was too much of a sailor to miss this cat and mouse game. "Gladly," Roebuck said.

A loud scuff of boot heels sounded as Malvey, who's style of walking put Roebuck in mind of the hop of a crow, took his turn on watch. "Top o' the morning to ya', Captain," he said, touching the visor of his cap.

"Tip-top, lieutenant," said Roebuck.

"No frogs in sight, sir, I just asked the watches," said Malvey, causing Roebuck and Aaberg to lift their spyglasses at the same time to confirm this piece of news.

"I guess you managed to get yourself away, sir. Not something we did much of in Her Majesty's service."

Malvey would sound smug reciting the Lord's Prayer. Roebuck managed to swallow an unfriendly reply.

Minutes passed before Malvey spoke again. "Sir, may I ask you something?"

"What is it?"

"Why do the frogs want to stop us from having an agreeable holiday in Argentina?" Malvey sounded amused.

"A holiday, Mr. Malvey?" Roebuck said, trying his own version of that sound. But it was like forcing custard up a tight sphincter. "I reckon they know we are here to take back the *America* and the *Eliza Davidson.*"

Malvey leaned over and caught Aaberg's eye. He said, "So we really will be fighting for America then, Mr. Aaberg," laughing at his own pun.

Aaberg said, "I may not sound like it, Mr. Malvey, but I am an American citizen. It has been so for almost half my life."

"There are worse things I suppose," Malvey said.

Although the rain was irregular and light, the swells had continued their curious rise and slowed the *Savannah's* progress. Roebuck knew that without a favorable current they would not reach Rio de la Plata on time. "Gentleman," he addressed the quarterdeck. "We will resume our course on the clipper route."

"But those three ships, sir," said Aaberg. "Will they not expect this?"

"The French can't threaten us now," Roebuck said, doubting his own words. Yet the risk of another encounter was secondary to the ticking clock.

Malvey said, "As soon as the French realize we have gone, they will spread like wolves. and they know where we are headed."

"The Atlantic is a big ocean, Mr. Malvey, with plenty of room for them and for us. Our time is nearly up and I'd hate for us to come all this way to miss out on the fun we'll have when we take back those two brigs."

Aaberg and Malvey met the feeble remark with silence.

Chapter 20

A day passed since they resumed their course on the clipper route. The barometer was down, but not the swells. They had grown to a size Roebuck could hardly believe. Added to this was the rain, which now engulfed them, falling in sheets. Roebuck had joined Lieutenant Cockrell on watch and Cockrell turned to Roebuck, hollering through the weather, "Swells are bouncing us around like beans on the boil, eh sir?"

"How do you like her in a storm, Mr. Cockrell?" Roebuck said, returning the shout.

"Much more than I do in a calm."

"Ha! True!"

"She'll cut through any comers, sir. She balances on her keel like an acrobat." Cockrell drew closer. "But the extra weight of her guns can make it hard to stay that way. Poor girl's rated for forty-four guns but carrying fifty-two."

The men loved the *Savannah*. Roebuck heard it in the way they described her. Even the old tars liked to scoot out onto the bowsprit when the *Savannah* sailed free, turning to watch her in mute admiration.

That was well and good, but Roebuck saw it another way. To him there was something infernal in a ship the *Savannah*'s size with all her demands, the hundreds of her crew crammed together, the ceaseless activity. And then there was the thought of the *Savannah's* guns trading broadsides at close quarters, decks washed in blood and caked in flesh. Malvey liked to describe his experience in big-ship combat, descriptions that revolted Roebuck. Or was it fear? Fighting had never scared him. The chaos of it didn't interfere with his thoughts and reactions the way he had seen it do to others. But on a fifty-two-gun ship and against opponents likewise armed? That sounded like butchery, not a fight.

He thought backwards to his days at sail on the Chesapeake, one hand on his skiff's tiller and the other pulling a sheet, that sensation of flying and dodging. He liked to consider that he might soon feel it again, once he had fulfilled whatever duty, or maybe it was a debt, Captain Perry seemed to believe he owed.

A topman called from the mainmast, "Hallo deck, sir. Masts dead off the port beam!"

Roebuck was startled. It had to be a different ship, a merchant-man, not one of the corvettes. He looked through the glass. At first he could just make out the shape of the sails but kept looking until he saw the entire ship. The ship's top-hamper showed. She had the bit in her mouth, one of the corvettes, there could be no doubt, and not more than a couple of leagues away.

Malvey walked over, stumbling a little as the ship topped a swell, his hat brim down against the wind and rain. "Well, sir, they're back," he said. "Can't say as I'm surprised."

"We haven't seen but this one," Roebuck said.

"They hunt in packs, sir. The others will be in view soon enough."

Thirty minutes later Roebuck cringed at the foretopman's second call. He looked through the glass, not wanting to but trying to raise a ship. When he couldn't he called, "I see nothing but gray clouds." The lookout peered out again, all the officers on the quarterdeck waiting, standing still enough to have been painted there.

"Aye, sir," the topman shouted, "I believe you are correct. It must have been the wind whipping up the shape of sails out of the clouds. Sorry, sir."

Roebuck exhaled. Cockrell did the same.

Malvey's face maintained its pale color and go-to-hell expression. Then his lips parted. "We ought to turn on that corvette and give her the devil. We double her guns."

A suggestion that Malvey himself knew was ridiculous, but it forced Roebuck to respond.

"Mr. Malvey, you yourself said we would soon see her consorts."

"Aye, sir, but if we take this one out first, we'll have a fighting chance once the others arrive."

"Our chance is to keep moving south."

Malvey said, "Any officer in command of one of Her Majesty's ships who'd run from a fight as easy as this might be hanged for cowardice." He paused before adding, "sir."

There it was, now Roebuck wasn't just too green to command but a coward as well. Count on Malvey to seize the moment and give the ship's wags something big to gossip about. Roebuck ignored this blatant insubordination but only because he didn't know what else to do. As for the other French ships, Malvey was probably right. They wouldn't be long. The question for Roebuck was what he might do to escape them once they appeared.

"Mr. Cockrell, call the sailmaster Mr. Cherry and let us review the charts once more."

Before Cockrell could answer, another shout came down from above. "Two sets of sails sir. Port quarter." This call came down from the mizzen top. Roebuck again raised his glass. The storm was thick, but after a couple of heartbeats, he saw the second corvette heading their way. And the razee was now visible in between them.

"Lieutenant Malvey." Roebuck hated to ask the son of a bitch, but no one knew better. "What will be the effective range of their long guns this morning?"

"Not far, sir, in this sea. If they have stern chasers they'll be long nines and won't throw shot accurately over a limit of two cables. I can't pick out what the razee has on her broadsides. Could be carronades, maybe some longer guns like ours. With these swells, those will have to be closer, less than a cable. I never like to be farther than five hundred feet sir, even on a gunner's sea."

Roebuck said, "Lieutenant Cockrell, how long before we are at five hundred feet?"

"The closer of the two corvettes runs near two knots faster than we do, I'd guess," Cockrell said. "Four hours, sir, a few minutes past that maybe."

Roebuck believed it would be sooner than that. He said, "Call all hands. Let us make our way to the shelf," hoping that the French commanders would not risk a move to the shallows in this ugly sea. Hadn't Aaberg said that French timber was old and inferior? They might not risk the extra violence a shallow seabed caused.

This would be a risk to the *Savannah* as well. Over the shelf in shallower water, Roebuck would need to be careful. A gust coupled with a move landward might see the *Savannah* stuck on a sandbar or mud bottom. Worse she might catch on a crop of rock and open up her hull.

For the fourth time in the last three days they would change course, a fact which did not exactly flatter a commander's firmness. He listened to Edwards calling the crew to their stations. The mainsail snapped out loosely, and the sight of it, the waste of speed that it implied, incensed him. He wheeled on the helmsman. "Keep her full, goddamn your eyes."

The man nodded, glancing up at the sail.

Roebuck turned to Malvey. "I'll manage this, Lieutenant," he said, taking control of the quarterdeck, not entirely sure about his first lieutenant.

"Go ahead, sir," Malvey said. "Was you, after all, that got us into it."

Roebuck said, "The men may be in a fight for the first time, Lieutenant Malvey. Here's your chance to show us how well you handle the guns rather than just telling us about it."

"Fight?" Malvey said, his eyes dark and unreadable. "Only thing we'll be fighting, sir, is these swells. I'll give odds to any man who'll take them. We'll be running all the way to Argentina and back."

Roebuck leaned into Cockrell and said, "Let go the sheets and braces."

Cockrell yelled the same to the sheet-anchor men.

Roebuck watched as they freed the yards of the *Savannah*'s big square sails.

Cockrell said, "Brace up at the cro'jack." And then turning to the helmsman, "As she comes to, meet her." When the *Savannah* was loaded for her turn, Cockrell called, "Ready about!" The crew cleared the way for the big yards to swing. Next came, "Mains'l haul!" But the breeze was stiff and swept the yards around on their own, no hauling needed. The hands had only to draw in the slack and keep everything clear, a bit of luck. They'd need more of it.

Roebuck glanced at the streamers to check the wind's direction in relation to their new heading. He called out, "Haul aft the jib-sheet, brace up at the fore, and haul forward the port fore tack." Waiting until he felt her loaded again before calling, "Down helm," all the *Savannah*'s sails over now and collecting the breeze on a starboard tack. He noted the pout on Cockrell's lips and understood why, having just superseded him.

"That first corvette will do nothing but trail us," Malvey said.

"But not close enough for us to bring our battery to bear," Roebuck said with the undertone of a question.

"Aye, she'll wait until the other joins her for that."

"The razee isn't gaining," Cockrell said.

The corvettes kept themselves to windward, a position that allowed them to choose when and in what position to fight. Roebuck wanted to see them break off, would do anything to see them give up the chase, praying to himself that they wouldn't follow the *Savannah* over the shelf. The others on the quarterdeck watched him nervously.

"I think the worst case, sir," Cockrell said, breaking into Roebuck's silence, "is the second corvette catches up and turns us."

Malvey was having none of that. "Hardly needs to turn us," he said. "If they keep to the wind and match us gun for gun, we're just toeing their line. Or worse, if one cuts underneath, she'll have us to rake."

Raked from behind, one of the corvettes firing down the *Savannah*'s length. Roebuck had been picturing this, knowing that it was the best way to use the two-ships-to-one advantage the French had, maneuvering one set of guns into a position the *Savannah* couldn't answer. It fit a well-known French preference for targeting an enemy's rigging, taking down masts and cutting up canvas rather than punching it out with broadsides. If the French pressed that advantage effectively the *Savannah* would be in a situation Roebuck had no idea how to manage.

CHAPTER 21

"Halloo deck!" the foretopman began his call but Roebuck didn't need another word. He moved quickly to the foremast, climbing its ratlines. Looking west he saw something lovely: a sharp rise of the waves. It was the shelf and he hoped it meant safety. The *Savannah* would certainly reach it before the French could catch and turn her. He clung to the notion that French ships were not sturdy enough to sail into the chop over the shelf. If that were true it wouldn't matter that they had come so close, the *Savannah* would escape.

Ten minutes passed before the *Savannah* climbed and plunged ferociously over the shallower bed's first steep swell. The mast top whipped back and forth and Roebuck was thrown down, taking a painful bounce off of his ribs. It was a pain he welcomed and he said, "We're over the shelf!"

"Easy enough to feel it, ain't it, Cap'n, sir?" said the topman, maybe not sure what else to say in the face of his commander's tumble.

God, please turn them back. Roebuck was occupied by that thought alone. It felt like he would never have any other thought again. "Turn them back," he said aloud. "Turn them back." His reputation, the rendezvous, hanging on those words.

"I think they're getting ready to do just that, sir, judging by the bustle on their decks."

Roebuck looked through his glass. It was true. French seamen were at the halyards, but he saw immediately they weren't readying to change their heading. "They're taking in tops'ls. They don't want to carry too much breeze up high on this sea."

The topman said, "Chasing us still."

Roebuck nodded.

The corvettes did not hesitate over the shelf and Roebuck's heart sank. Their timbers were apparently not as lousy as Aaberg had imagined or he had hoped. It was foolish wishful thinking, that much was obvious now. He watched the two quick French ships for five minutes before focusing on the razee in the distance as it bore down.

All those days as a youth chasing and being chased under sail had given him a feel for pursuing vessels, their movements, the angles they took. And these feelings had their own feelings, having taken root so early in his life. He needed them now. Boy did he need them.

The big swells made the ride a rough one, but the squall hadn't backed up north, thank God. It was playing havoc, cascading the rain down on them and blowing in unpredictable shifts, but as long as it filled his sails he knew they had a chance.

Another hour passed and Aaberg replaced Cockrell on the quarterdeck. Malvey said, "In range, Captain," his eyes on the nearest of the two corvettes, which had closed to a position off their port bow. The far corvette was also portside, but farther back. She too would soon be within gun range. The wind shifted into Roebuck's back, forcing rain over his collar, down the space between his shoulder blades. Good, at least it was out of his eyes and in theirs. For the first time, he made out the name on the near corvette's stern as she pulled ahead, *Badine*, carved and painted white on the blue band of its escutcheon.

"They're slowing, sir," Aaberg said, looking at the second corvette.

Roebuck said, "Take us broad on the starboard bow, helmsman," hoping to keep the *Badine* from cutting across their bow. "Mr. Aaberg, get us a little more trim, if you please."

Aaberg's mouth was set so tight, his upper lip flattened into the plane of his face.

Roebuck said, "Mr. Aaberg? You have some doubts?"

"Aye, Captain. May I ask how you see the risk?"

Roebuck said, "Of what, sir?"

Aaberg said, "Of a starboard tack, landward."

"As you see it, I'm sure, although there is probably a difference in degree."

"The risk, sir—"

"—Is leaving our keel behind on a crop of rock," Roebuck said, "or sucked into five feet of mud," a weak don't-worry smile on his lips.

"Well, sir, we know we're giving away fathoms on this tack. And there'll be no sounding on this sea."

"You believe we'll run aground."

"The thought has made itself known to my mind, sir," Aaberg said.

"Insistently."

Aaberg nodded.

"The charts for this coast, as we both know, allow a number of leagues for us to play with."

"I wouldn't put it past three, sir, if that. The chart has the bed high over a great deal of sea here."

"Charts printed from plate shrink, Mr. Aaberg. The date on our chart has it printed over five years ago, allowing ample time for a half-inch of reduction in any direction. That is enough to cause your estimation of the distance between here and when we start scraping bottom to be short."

"If the paper shrinks, then the scale also shrinks. So I cannot see the error."

Roebuck said, "No error if the chart is used in a direction parallel to itself. But otherwise there will be an error. Paper shrinks differently in two directions."

Aaberg said, "How can you be sure that the error is in our favor?"

"The lines and the numerals printed are thinner and smaller where we now are on the chart than in any other section. The difference may appear marginal, but it is not."

Aaberg didn't look impressed. "The corvettes have a shallower draught, sir."

"Your tongue's gotten loose, Lieutenant," said Roebuck, who was irritated by Aaberg's switch to this new line of reasoning. "The swells will climb as we move closer to the bottom. If they get higher all of a sudden, we'll take her back out."

"Yes, sir." Aaberg's doubts must be extreme, given that he made no attempt to hide them.

"What do you think they are angling for?" said Roebuck, nodding toward the *Badine* just ahead of them now and running fast.

"I wish I knew, sir." Aaberg raised his spyglass toward the ship. "My God, they're readying to fire one of the bow chasers."

"Impossible," Roebuck said.

It was true. A French gun crew was loading a cannon—how ridiculous, this smaller ship, not even in a position to take a clean shot across the *Savannah*'s bow. But then there it was, a gun's unmistakable discharge, smoke and fire out of the muzzle. The corvette had not even bothered to gain a decent position before sending this universal signal for a ship to heave to, to give up. It was less a message than an insult. The round shot skipped weakly away. Yet Roebuck sensed a change on his deck, something in the crew. Nerves maybe, or fear. The *Savannah*'s honor had been challenged.

"Second corvette's upon us, sir," said Aaberg.

Roebuck pivoted astern to see it, both French ships now well within range. His stomach was churning. Why now? As if the storm in the Caribbean and the doldrums hadn't been enough. Why on his first major command, the Navy's eyes upon him, possibly even the president's. It was infuriating to think of it all happening now. He'd been consumed with the rendezvous, getting there in time. Now he might not get there at all.

"Steady, man," Roebuck said, not completely sure whether he'd said it out loud or just thought it. Turning to the helmsman, he said very loudly, "Steady." Damned if he'd heave to. He turned to Watt, the midshipman of the watch and said, "The sailmaker has a *tricolore* in storage. Go and fetch it."

Watt hustled away.

Malvey said, "Sir? We can hardly expect to fool them now. They know us. Our ensign's been flying since we weighed anchor," assuming his commander's idea was to deceive the French by flying their colors.

"I won't ship under no French flag." It was Murdoch by a mainsail brace, eyes like slivers of ice, perpetual half-smile upside down for once.

Roebuck ignored them and waited for Watt and waited some more. Had the sailmaker used the flag for something else? He suddenly remembered the man asking him about using its silk in the midshipman's play. How had Roebuck answered? He looked over the *Badine's* deck, her crew pawing the lashings of its twenty-four-pound guns.

"Here it is, Captain, sir." It was Watt, *tricolore* in hand. Roebuck shook it out. Its dingy white band was stained on one end and half its red faded to orange, but it was still the pride of France.

"Hoist it by the red, not the blue, and at half mast, you understand?"

Watt smiled and hurried aft.

In a few moments the French flag was up over their stern, flying upside down, red, white, and blue instead of the French blue, white, and red, and it was stopped halfway up the line, far below the Stars and Stripes. The crew was quiet, needing some time to decipher.

Then Murdoch shouted, "The *tricolore's* flipped, boys, and she's under us where she belongs!" The crew cheered.

"They have their answer!" yelled Roebuck.

The men cheered again, and then jeered the French.

Roebuck said, "Beat to quarters, Mr. Malvey."

The Englishman called the drummer boy, and the runt came rapping out the call for the crew to take their fighting stations. A stream of men came through the hatches, many carrying their folded hammocks to slot into the nets above the gunwales, meager protection against musket fire and the deadly spray of splinters likely to fan out over the deck once French shot began to split the *Savannah's* timber.

Roebuck sent an extra watchman up to each of the three mast tops with instructions to keep an eye out for big swells.

Aaberg called, "The second corvette is close, sir, off our port quarter."

That was dangerous, the corvette nearly in a position to wear underneath and rake them. Another shift of the wind and she'd have the means to do it.

"Mr. Aaberg, if she prepares a change of course, tell me immediately," Roebuck said, thinking about what he'd do if he were in command of the corvettes. It was one thing to have an advantage, something else to make it good. Their captains would be asking themselves how long could they manage the wild sea, asking should they try to cross the *Savannah* or stay to the weather? Intuiting their uncertainty gave Roebuck heart. The shot across the bow had been weak, desperation maybe.

He looked at Watt. The proceedings appeared to have no effect on his self-possession. "Mr. Watt, keep your eyes on the *Badine*. If she starts to back sail, pipe up."

"Aye aye, sir."

He called to the main topman, "Any big swells?"

"Well, sir, about eight hundred yards, there's one a-coming."

"How big?"

The man shouted with effort to be heard over the squall. "Big, but we'll get another one, sir, bigger, I'm sure of it."

"You damn well better be."

A look at the streamers told him the wind was off their port quarter now. If it veered anywhere starboard, they'd go with whatever wave they got. He would use these high seas. Today they might be his friend.

The *Savannah* began an abrupt climb on the swell the topman had seen. Roebuck counted to eight before her bow cleared the crest. She slid forward then down. That was plenty damn big. He turned to the wall of water they'd just topped, not seeing much of the *Badine* behind it in the trough behind, just the bare tops of her masts.

"Mr. Aaberg," Roebuck said.

"Sir."

Roebuck grinned. "On my command, we'll jibe as far as the ship will allow on the downside of a swell." They'd take the *Badine* by surprise, and use a wall of water to conceal their change of course.

"In this wind, sir?" said Aaberg.

"Unless you can find us another."

Roebuck was conscious of Malvey listening.

The Norwegian spoke. "Sir, on these swells, we catch a gust and we'll be over and foundering. I've seen a ship tip on the far side of a big swell without even trying to come about."

"Noted, Mr. Aaberg," said Roebuck, "We'll do it on the biggest swell we can."

Malvey turned to Aaberg, looking directly at him, cutting Roebuck out, a couple of old hands trading … what exactly? A memory of the Caribbean and those six drowned topmen? But Aaberg turned away, putting an end to it.

Roebuck felt good. Chased by three ships, mission in doubt, outgunned, and no real idea about what came next had put him on a swing between anger and exhaustion for the past thirty hours. But now he knew what was going to happen and he knew the French did not. All he needed was a shift of wind and a very big wave.

"Mr. Malvey," he said.

"Sir?"

"We are going to cross their bow soon, and when we do you will put twenty shots into their rigging."

"These are no conditions for the guns. How do you expect to hit anything on swells like these?"

"By sailing between the swells as long as we can."

"We'll spray well over half the rounds into the ocean," said Malvey.

Roebuck stared into the lieutenant's gray eyes.

The Englishman closed his lids and then opened them, saying, "How far away, sir?"

"How close do you need to be?"

"How many chances will we have?" Then realizing the obvious, Malvey said, "Just one?"

"One's all."

"Can you get me a start at thirty yards, sir?"

"A gust at her back and the *Badine* will plant her bow in our side at that distance. We'll say eighty, Mr. Malvey. But you will have to fire on your aim, not the distance. Those eighty yards will narrow quickly."

In minutes, Malvey had the gunners working at the ship's mix of carronades, deadly from close range, and longer-ranging thirty-pounders. They moved as quickly as the towering sea would allow. Malvey would use bar and chain-shot to shred the *Badine*'s rigging.

Roebuck waited for the wind to shift. It didn't. He guessed that they only had a few more minutes before both corvettes were in an ideal position to press their advantage. Was his plan ludicrous? With so little time and so much beyond his control he had to be crazy to try it.

"Captain Roebuck, here comes your big one!" It was the watch on the mizzen-top this time. "Maybe seven hundred yards." It didn't matter that the wind was still against them, they had to take the wave.

"Guns, Mr. Malvey?" he called to the lieutenant.

"Half are loaded and plugged sir. Half not."

"You have three minutes, do not disappoint us."

"Need at least one more than that."

"Time to back up that mouth of yours, Mr. Malvey, or I will make you suffer."

Malvey swung violently around to face Roebuck, saying, "It's not in you, laddie."

Before Roebuck could reply, Malvey was gone back to the gun crews, shouting at them, telling them to finish up or face a beating. Roebuck was depending on Malvey and the thought made him sick.

Roebuck said, "Ready about," to Aaberg.

Then it happened, the wind veered once more, not perfect, but good enough, giving them a starboard tack if they were quick enough.

"Lee-oh!" shouted Aaberg. Looking uncertain but sounding as unperturbed as ever. Aware that jibing in this weather would seem to experienced seamen like an example of their commander's insanity.

"Bring the wind to our quarter," said Roebuck to the man at the wheel, "and then steer three points forward on the port beam."

The man looked at Aaberg, frightened at the danger.

"Now, goddamn your eyes," Roebuck said, "or I will let the sea have you," then back to Aaberg, "We won't heave to, do you understand?" Roebuck wanted to fully harness that wind, its speed. They were already without the royals and topgallants, so he would need the full spread of mainsail and topsail. And that is what the helmsman and Aaberg feared would have them tumbling over as they cut across the face of the swell.

Edwards gave the command and the men threw themselves into it, releasing a wave of energy pent up through the last thirty tense hours.

In an instant, the *Savannah* was falling away too quickly as she dove down the far side of the wave.

Roebuck said, "Ease off two points."

The helmsman turned the wheel back a few spokes, blunting the angle of their descent.

"Wait now," Roebuck said. "The big one's coming."

They would surprise the *Badine*, shock her with this maneuver, but only if they could make the turn. His control of the ship had to be down to the inch.

The quarterdeck was silent, the attention of its officers alternating between the great swell rolling toward them and their commander. When it took them, the ship gave a violent lurch. Roebuck said. "The headsails are nosing us over, Aaberg. We'll be sideways, goddamn you." He called to Murchison on the foremast, "Ease the sheets fore and jib." Aaberg looked relieved to let Roebuck give the commands. "Spanker windward."

The *Savannah*, recovering, shivered as the swelling wave took hold. She carved a diagonal across its massive face. Nothing to see over the starboard bow but sky as they crested, the ship slackening, her bow hanging in the air for a time that seemed endless. All at once she was over and plunging down the other side.

"Sheet all! Hard alee!" Roebuck's own voice seemed to come from the sky, sounding over the entire ship at once.

The *Savannah* swung across the wind, sails now pushing her toward the *Badine*, helmsman yelling saying he could wheel her no further, calling for the boatswain's mates to help him. The *Savannah* slid, tipping on her starboard beam, falling now, too fast, going over, men shouting, shouts bleeding into screams.

"Hold fast, you Nancys, hold fast and you won't be taking no salty baths," yelled Edwards the boatswain, but not soon enough for one seaman working a tipping line. The sudden drop loosened his grip and he fell, bouncing off the deck. Someone yelled, "You've kilt him!" Roebuck gripped the taffrail hard.

The ship was almost sideways. A sprawling mate slid past Roebuck, who tried to grab him, but the man was moving too fast and slammed into the gunwale. It saved him from going overboard.

"We're going over!" Each word trembled out of a young seaman's mouth.

"Shut your trap," yelled Edwards, but his own eyes were two orphaned children so full of fear.

The breeze stiffened, tilting them further, combining with gravity in a deadly push. Two sharp bangs sounded from below followed by a third, the inert weight of cabin doors turning unstable and slamming shut one by one. Then a louder sound but deadlier, the screams of three seamen aloft, panic slashing its way to Roebuck's ears as they dangled on a line, kicking free over the ocean. Aaberg asking, "Can we heave to sir? Isn't she's over well enough, sir?" A cask bounced by and hit the rail, splintering off a stave, spilling its liquid.

Roebuck looked over the starboard rail. Sea had replaced sky. It seemed close enough for him to reach out and scoop up. He caught a glimpse of Aaberg holding the mizzenmast ratlines tightly. The Norwegian wore an unsettled look. He didn't realize what Roebuck knew. They would not pass that murdering threshold. They would not go over.

The *Savannah* slid off the swell, leaning heavily under the wind but not tipping. She righted herself, leveling on her keel. It staggered everyone on the quarterdeck. And just like that she sailed free.

His officers gasped, the sound of it perceptible through the squall.

"Square away and let's run," said Roebuck to the quartermaster.

After nearly tossing them over, the massive swell now kindly hid them behind its enormous dark wall of water.

Roebuck again instructed the quartermaster, "As soon as the *Badine* tops that swell, fetch us athwart," wanting the *Savannah* perpendicular to the *Badine*'s bow, in position to fire down her full length.

"Aye aye, sir."

"Mr. Aaberg?"

"*Badine*'s holding her tack," said Aaberg.

"She won't do it," said Roebuck, meaning change her heading over the big swell. Her sails were already too fat and straining.

"No, sir, not unless her captain has lost his mind," Aaberg said.

By *lost his mind*, Aaberg implied that Roebuck had lost his. He laughed at Aaberg's boldness for saying it.

The *Badine*'s crew would be desperate to keep the *Savannah* in their sights through the wall of rain and spray. But the *Savannah*'s highest sails were in and the canvas of her topsails wouldn't present more than thin white shadows.

The two ships drew together, one expecting it, the other not.

Mr. Malvey?" called Roebuck.

"Almost ready, sir!"

"You have thirty seconds."

Roebuck turned away from Malvey just in time to see the *Badine* showing her bow as she sliced through the huge swell's top. Right there.

"At my command." It was Malvey, standing motionless. His feet seemed to be glued to the deck, the emphasis of his Northumberland vowels loud with their own particular authority. His presence sucked the fear off the deck. The gunnery captain, a lieutenant named Horsley, was watching him through the main hatch from below, his battery ready to follow Malvey's command.

The *Badine* was gaining her own speed on the downside of the huge wave and nearly level with the *Savannah*. She fired a chaser from the starboard bow. The shot ploughed nothing but the sea.

"Nerves have them firing early, lads," Malvey said. "Not us. We'll be wasting no shot. Hold fire 'til we're close enough to bang a penny off her captain's forehead. Hold fire, lads."

He strode forward to the aftmost gun, saying, "On my command!" to its crew, setting himself behind them, sighting down the barrel, waiting as the *Savannah* glided slowly in the trough between swells toward the *Badine*'s path. "Ready!" Malvey said. "*Fire!*"

The intensity of Malvey's voice caused Roebuck to start. The first gun sent a column of flame and smoke toward the *Badine*, chain-shot clawing through her rigging. The second gun immediately followed.

Malvey was at the third gun, calling, "Fire!" and then again at the fourth. Smoke began to darken their view. Roebuck's ears were ringing. And so it went as the gun crews fired nine more times down the line.

The *Savannah* rose on another swell and her firing battery tilted downward.

"Fire!" Malvey said with that unusual volume of his voice. Two guns discharged, but the decline was too much, shot and chain burrowing into the sea.

The *Badine* responded with another chaser, a well-aimed shot to the *Savannah*'s stern, snapping off her spanker gaff. The sail and the ship's ensigns flapped worthlessly. Yet this was small revenge.

They were near the swell's crest and again Malvey gave the command to fire, and again shot, chain-shot and bar-shot mauled the *Badine*'s rigging. He had worked in all three types of ordnance.

The *Savannah*'s stern cleared the *Badine*'s bow. They were past her.

"Hold your fire!" called Malvey, Horsley at the main battery below echoing the command.

"Re-rig those colors, if you please, Mr. Edwards. And send one of the boys to tell the carpenter we've lost the gaff."

"Aye aye, sir."

The smoke thinned and Roebuck surveyed their work. Half the *Badine*'s foremast yards were shot away, a quarter of the same were broken off from the main and mizzen masts. Her top-hamper was ripped and torn. Braces hung loose. Every tar on the *Savannah* had found the top of his voice and was cheering.

Malvey came bounding back to the quarterdeck, saying, "One more corvette to go, eh, sir? The lads are reloading."

"Quartermaster, steady on course, south-southeast," Roebuck said, avoiding the Englishman's eyes. "Mr. Malvey, we're going to Rio de la Plata."

"But she's ours for the taking, sir. We let her off, what's to say she won't chase us again with the razee?"

"I say," said Roebuck, aware that the last time he sounded so sure of himself was his flimsy prediction that they'd lost the three French ships in the night. Malvey would be remembering the same.

"You cannot say that with any certainty," Malvey said.

"She follows us, she'll lose sight of her fifty-gun partner. We're too fast for that razee. That means your corvette is chasing a ship that doubles her guns."

"We run, sir, and the boys will be disappointed," said Malvey.

"They'll recover."

"Where's the glory?" Malvey drew closer. "These boys have the heart to fight on, not run from a ship with half our guns."

"My duty is not to glory, Lieutenant. It's to the squadron in Rio de la Plata."

"But we've missed them, you know it as well as I do."

Inches separated their faces.

"Mr. Malvey, you will assess and report the damage to our ship." Roebuck was fighting the urge to draw his knife and cut open this shit-sack lieutenant. They stared at each other. And then Malvey saluted, turned with exaggerated sharpness, and walked away.

No other ship's captain would have imagined much less tried what Roebuck had just done. But thanks to Malvey, the talk on board would be about how their commander didn't have the sand to fight.

Aaberg approached. "My compliments, sir. It was a surprising piece of sailing."

"Surprising to you or them?" Roebuck nodded back toward the *Badine.*

Aaberg smiled but skipped past the question. "We're headed downstream to Montevideo?"

"That's right."

Once the second corvette realized the *Savannah* did not intend to fight, she hove-to and gave up the chase.

Roebuck wouldn't give another thought to French patrols. There was nothing to do but sail as straight and as fast as they could to Rio de la Plata and hope that Commodore Nicolson might still have use for them.

CHAPTER 22

The squall was dying, the swells down. The crew had secured the guns and the ship was making good time southward. Roebuck watched a mate patch the jib. So far, Mr. Flynn, the carpenter, had failed to emerge from his workshop with a replacement for the spanker gaff. This irritated Roebuck. The sailor who'd fallen from the rigging had broken his leg and Benoit the surgeon had set it. If Benoit had enough time to set a broken leg, what excuse was there for Flynn? Roebuck walked down ship to the poop and stared at the broken gaff. *Goddamn.*

The *Savannah* would miss the rendezvous, the chase having cost them too much time. They'd be late by two days easily. This thought somehow made the missing spanker sail all the more irritating. Without it, the ship tended away from the wind, forcing the quartermaster to use the rudder to stay close to it. It was a small subtraction in speed, but enough to have Roebuck pacing the deck and greeting passersby with a snarl.

He went below to see Flynn. The carpenter's shop was open and lamplight shined through the doorway. Inside, one mate fed wood into the scroll saw, the other pumped with his foot.

"Where is Mr. Flynn?" Roebuck said.

"In the storeroom, sir. Forward."

He walked on, past the closed door of the boatswain's store-room, then to the gunnery storage. It was open and several of the gunner's mates were there re-crating unused rounds of shot, their backs turned to Roebuck. He paused and listened to their chatter.

"Me'be next time we'll stay past the first round of the fight," one of them said.

The other said, "My bait crawlers have more spine."

"He got no stomach for fighting," the first one said. "I heard all 'bout what they call him, 'Bobby Chase,' how he chased down smug-glers and sech like near Domingo. But I cain't see that Bobby Chase business for how he goes a-runnin'."

"He needs a name what suits him," said the other. "You heard them stories about his Pappy, ain't you?"

The others nodded.

"If he ain't Bobby Chase, what is he?"

"I know what."

"What then?"

"Robby Run"

PART TWO

CHAPTER 23

Nothing slowed the *Savannah* over the final stretch of their journey as she made way on a chilly but enduring wind out of the northwest. Roebuck wondered how things might be different down here in the South Atlantic, so close to the world's edge. The French were here, that much was the same, and apparently had strength enough to effect a blockade, or at least try. And yes, the British were hovering, but this was not Europe. Montevideo was no Gibraltar and Buenos Aires was no Marseille. The cold granite waters of Rio de la Plata were far from the sapphire blue Mediterranean, that fountain of what the Old World liked to call civilization.

Robert Chase Roebuck was tired of the Old World, tired of sailing the oceans by permission of the Old World, tired of deferring to great ships of great powers as they carried the breeze right past him out of one anchorage after another. Rio de la Plata's recently established states of Uruguay and the Argentine Confederation were part of the New World, his world, and he wondered if anyone down here would feel as he did.

He looked to the west, where coastal bluffs formed a thick, dark line. Seamen floated across the *Savannah*'s decks in giddy anticipation of landfall. Not Roebuck, he dreaded meeting Admiral Nicolson and explaining why his arrival was two full two days past the hour of the rendezvous. He carried this dread inside him like a lead weight.

The Atlantic was a cool gray. Uruguay's headlands came together in a point like a craggy finger pointing east toward Africa. Grass-robed hills glowed in morning light. This was Punta Este, according to the charts, just north of the capital city of Montevideo, their destination.

"Take us a-starboard," Roebuck called to the wheel. He nodded to Aaberg who called sail-trimmers to the braces.

The rudder bit and the *Savannah* rounded the point, where he expected to be greeted by a vision of relief, a place to gather fresh water and food, a port where his men would be delivered from the abjectness of this badly provisioned ship. But oh, was he disappointed. The reality did not match this hope. He adjusted the focus of his glass to be sure. It brought a wasteland into view, the aftermath of a terrible storm. The same one he knew immediately that had endlessly pushed those enormous swells northward.

Piles of debris were scattered along the shore as if the sea had heaped them together for removal. He watched several men climbing over a jagged mass of uprooted trees. Skiffs and jacks were piled up further in, bound by remnants of fishing net and cord, Most were shorn of their planks, with keels and beams exposed like skeletons. The coast was dotted with the wreckage of ships.

As they drew near the harbor of Montevideo, Roebuck saw clay-built houses with their fronts missing and their insides scoured clean.

"A terrible storm," Aaberg said.

Roebuck said, "A hundred-year storm."

"That must be why there are no ships."

Except for two ships at anchor, one a brig of war flying the *tri-colore*, the harbor was empty. Nothing of the blockade and none of Nicolson's Brazil Squadron that the *Savannah* was here to join.

"Gone to escape the storm," Roebuck said.

"I pray they succeeded."

The scene was utterly different than the one he had prepared for. His orders had been specific and clear but had no relation to what he now saw.

Roebuck said, "the estuary bed will be changed now with storm shoals and banks. And the cross current," Roebuck paused as if to give Aaberg a chance to feel it, "will be hard at our beam as we come around toward an anchorage."

"If there are channels, sir, we'll find them," said Aaberg. "We can sound as we stand into the harbor."

The thought of inching in, dropping a lead line every yard of the way in search of the bottom was not what Roebuck wanted. He was worried about being blocked in by unfriendly ships that might be lurking over the horizon. And who knew what the situation of the shore battery was.

Roebuck said, "Let's not get too close yet."

Aaberg saluted and turned toward the mates. "Grab the lead and leather boys," he said. "We'll be sounding out the harbor," and then he turned back to Roebuck, "This must change things, sir."

Roebuck had been thinking the same thing and had already made up his mind to find out exactly how they were changed. "We have a consulate in Montevideo," he said. "I must go immediately."

Aaberg said, "And provisions, sir?"

"Yes," Roebuck said, glad Aaberg was thinking clearly. "Send for the purser. We will inquire after supply ships. If there are none afloat, we will manage the vittling ourselves."

Roebuck spotted what he guessed would be a safe anchorage. "Mr. Aaberg, let us sound out the possibility of lying to along the eastern bank of the island off our starboard bow."

"Aye aye, sir."

"And, ask Major Pemberton to prepare a detail of Marines. We'll row in at our first chance."

***

Once landed and walking again after so long with the movement of the sea underneath him, Roebuck felt like iron pins were bolted to his knees. It was always the same on land after so long at sea. Seven rowers had pulled him, Scoggins the purser, Pemberton, and five Marines in a launch to the wharf in Montevideo's harbor. Remains of the storm were all around. Carcasses of goats, sheep, and dogs rotted into a miasma of mud and scum on shore. Pemberton halted the Marines so Scoggins could retch for a few minutes.

Pemberton said, "Do you suppose it's the shit-stink, Captain, or the sight that offends our unfortunate purser's stomach?"

Based on the weakness of his own stomach Roebuck said, "The stink." And said, "Let us go," leading them toward an arched gate with a columned façade. He had read that this gate was the entrance to Montevideo's old city. It stood alone, no longer connected to walls. Roebuck walked around it. Pemberton and the others walked through.

Along the streets of the old city, people huddled for warmth, sitting or standing in front of lean-tos rigged from branches, wood rounds, and planks. Bonfires burned high on street corners as displaced Montevideans shouldered in and competed for warmth. A cart stacked with wood scraps stopped and people surged to grab hold of something they could burn or shelter under.

The *Savannah*'s crew crossed a wide plaza and Roebuck stopped to open a map of Montevideo's streets included with his orders. He hadn't expected to use it. The U.S. Consulate was just a quarter mile or so to their west. He started in that direction but quickly stopped, arrested by a whiff of roasting beef. It came from the open window of a red-painted home right next to them. Every Marine in the detail craned his neck toward it. They carried loaded carbines. Roebuck and Pemberton had cutlasses. There would be nothing to stop them from going in and helping themselves. Roebuck weighed it.

Pemberton said, "Son of a bitch and a donkey, that's a powerful good in your nose."

Something in how Pemberton said it brought Roebuck back from his hungry dreaming and they continued on their way. Their next stop was caused by two men in white jackets tossing a loud and obviously intoxicated old soldier from a public house. He yelled at them, "*Puta que te parió!*" startling a clutch of wrens from the arches of a nearby cathedral. The soldier rose without bothering to brush the dirt and leaves from the loose seat of his trousers.

Before leaving the *Savannah*, Roebuck had changed into his dress uniform and strapped on a cutlass. The old drunk stared at the Americans.

"*No vine a traer la paz, sino la espada,*" said the man, rubbing his eyes violently before resuming his stare.

"Had a little too much to drink, old-timer?" said Pemberton. "I wonder what the Dago's saying."

"*I came not to send peace, but a sword,*" Roebuck said.

Scoggins, over his retching enough to join in, said, "Sounds like a verse from the Good Book."

"Matthew 10," Roebuck said. "Can't remember the verse."

Pemberton, turning to Roebuck, said, "You understand that muck?"

"One reason I'm here."

"How did you come to talk like a Dago?"

"A pair of maids from Andalusia," Roebuck said, leaving out the part about his Dago mother.

Pemberton said, "Full of surprises, aren't you, Mr. Roebuck?"

The old soldier walked past them to the cathedral steps and lay down on his side, an unwashed child ready for bed. Roebuck and the detail turned west out of the plaza and down an alley.

Roebuck tried to remember the protocol as they walked. What had Perry said? Did a consul general take precedence over a naval commander? By the time they reached the consulate, Roebuck realized he could remember nothing about protocol because he'd never known anything about it in the first place. Perry had not mentioned it because he expected Roebuck's guns to do his talking.

Pemberton and the Marines waited outside as Roebuck entered a quiet foyer. Down the hall, light bled through the crack of a door left ajar. Roebuck knocked on the door and pushed it open.

A pinkish man was curled over a side table, fiddling with an open box. He jumped with surprise. "Well, sir," he said, recovering. "Welcome to Montevideo!" thrusting out his hand, "Hilary

Houghton, consul general of our glorious republic." The gesture was as unmilitary as it could be.

"Mr. Consul," Roebuck said, nodding, wanting to step backward, "Commander Robert Chase Roebuck of the U.S.S. *Savannah*."

"Come, young man, take hold, it's perfectly clean," Houghton said, pushing his hand nearly to the gold buttons on the front of Roebuck's frock.

They shook. Clean maybe, but clammy.

"Your arrival is unexpected, Commander. Commodore Nicolson assumed the *Savannah* had been lost in the storm. Won't he be pleased to hear otherwise?" Houghton looked down at his desk, picked up a ledger, and dropped it into the box, which he closed. "That notwithstanding, there was no mistaking his frustration at your tardiness, young sir. No mistaking it. With each passing day last week, the commodore grew angrier at your failure to join the *Savannah's* fifty guns to his."

"Fifty-two," Roebuck said.

"Fifty, a hundred, the point is you were not here. The day before the storm, Commodore Nicolson was angry indeed, more Vesuvius than man."

Roebuck said, "Where is the commodore now, and the squadron?"

"They put out to sea before the worst of it hit. Said he might pursue the French ships harassing merchants around the Falkland Islands."

This was dismaying. Would Nicolson still need the *Savannah's* guns? "Did he leave orders for me?"

"The commodore asked me to instruct you to remain in Montevideo in the event of your arrival."

"Does he not need assistance?"

Houghton shook his head. "No, indeed my handsome young sir. On that point he was quite emphatic. Your behind-handedness seems to be grounds for an inquiry. I recall that he even mentioned the possibility of a court martial. I do not exaggerate when I describe his anger as volcanic."

"Court martial? That can't be." Roebuck's heart dropped to his stomach. He assumed there would be consequences for not making rendezvous, but that?

"His words, sir, not mine. Court martial—it has a sinister ring, yes it does, and rather harsh, yes, but the involutions of military justice confound a mind, such as my own, ruled by logic. Reason, sir, that is the trick. I am a man born to it."

Houghton struck Roebuck as a muddy stream twisting into the dark.

"Officers," Houghton continued, "even those as young as yourself, are expected to see to the fulfillment of their orders. And you did not. Failure, Commander Roebuck, is most certainly not the trick."

Roebuck blanched and he felt his fingers curl. He said, "I need victuals. Are there any supply ships afloat?"

"None, but I have an excellent trading house under contract to supply our ships. Two blocks east there are stables and a carriage house, also under contract. They have the means to convey you. Ask for Mr. Guillory. He will recognize your uniform, sir, no calling card needed!"

"I'll need powder, too."

"That will be more difficult, as the conflict here has made a treasure out of that noxious black dust. But I will see what can be done. It may cost a little extra." Houghton rubbed his index finger against his thumb.

"Well, then," said Roebuck. "I will be off."

"No, no, stay put, Commander Roebuck. Please sit, my dark young sir." Houghton motioned to a chair before sitting on his own, castors squeaking under his weight.

Roebuck stayed on his feet.

"You must have seen the damage," Houghton said. "Montevideo has had a terrible time, simply terrible. What an unimaginable terminus for you, Commander, sailing for so long on a mission that has vanished into the sea at the very place of its genesis."

There seemed to be something gathered up inside of Houghton waiting to come out. Roebuck said, "What is it you wish to say, Mr. Houghton?"

Houghton tried a smile. "Well, then, my dear Commander, the commodore related to me that if you surprised us by arriving, you and your crew were to help the people of Montevideo through their tragedy until the Brazil Squadron returns. The commodore said this with such passion that I believe your future rests upon your ability to do it."

"He said that?"

"I think it would serve you well in any inquiry, by my word, I do. It was all over the commodore's face, to say nothing of his attitude. Sumatran, young sir, that is the word to describe the volcanic quality of his temper."

Roebuck wondered how Sumatran compared to Vesuvian. Roebuck looked at Houghton's eyes. They told him nothing. "The French continue to blockade?"

"They most certainly will when they return. They also left to protect their ships from the storm," Houghton said.

"What of the two captured American brigs," Roebuck said, "the *Eliza Davidson* and the *America*?"

"Lost upon the rocks."

"And the crew?"

"Gone, Commander. The cost of your tardiness, I fear." Pincers out again. "Drowned in the storm. Both ships broke open on the rocks. All of the men dead, not a single survivor."

"Good Lord." Roebuck dropped into the chair Houghton had offered earlier and slumped like something soggy. He could not believe the totality of this disaster.

Houghton said, "There is a point south of Montevideo called Yeguas. It is an ideal harbor to move food and fresh water from the interior to settlements along the coast where the storm has done the most damage. A road passes close by and the government has long wanted to build a spur that connects it to the harbor. I can think of no better way to help yourself in the commodore's eyes than by building that spur and bringing relief."

"We do not have the materials." Roebuck felt all the energy drain from his body. Until twenty minutes ago, he had been commissioned to free captured American ships and here Houghton was talking to him about digging around in the mud to construct roads.

"I'll see that the material you need is delivered. I am happy to assist with what may be your only opportunity to gain the commodore's favor."

CHAPTER 24

Pemberton stood next to a man gripping the reins of two pintos harnessed to a four-seat carriage. There was a second carriage behind it with worn leather seats and black paint chipped away from its side doors. Scoggins and two Marines sat in the box seat up front, looking bored, or maybe tired.

"What do we have here?" asked Roebuck, stepping into the cobbled street.

"This fellow has come to take us to suppliers for our vittling," said Pemberton. He nodded toward the man in a carriage. "He's an Englishman, Mr. Roland Guillory."

The man bowed slightly and said in a vaguely musical voice, "Welcome to Uruguay, Commander Roebuck."

"Your timing is faultless, Mr. Guillory," Roebuck said, not sure whether to be pleased or troubled. "News must travel quickly here."

"It doesn't have far to go."

"Major Pemberton," said Roebuck, "You and your Marines will please accompany Mr. Scoggins back to the *Savannah*." He needed time alone to consider all that Houghton had told him. Scoggins had drawn up a list so he knew what provisions the ship needed. "I'll go with Mr. Guillory."

Pemberton said, "Are you sure?"

"Kindly do as I ask, Mr. Pemberton."

Pemberton shrugged.

Roebuck climbed into the coachbox next to Guillory, who spoke gently to his horses. They started forward and the carriage rocked over the paving stones.

Guillory said, "Commander, please be warned that the storm hasn't left much behind in the way of provisions. There is little potable water on the coast, grain and corn is not widely available, and most livestock is either dead or inland."

"We must do our best," Roebuck said.

Once outside the city, the streets gave way to a smooth dirt track and Guillory's team fell into a trot. Low hills rose to the west, the sun high above them. The path narrowed first through a village and then through a small collection of cottages. A mile beyond, a ravine opened up and Guillory moved the horses onto a trail beside it.

"Why are we leaving the road?" said Roebuck.

"Commander Roebuck, how much do you know about conditions here?"

"Sounds like I am about to be educated."

"It may be important for you to know."

Roebuck nodded.

"The entire region from Brazil to the southern tip of Argentina, including Uruguay, is split into factions, nearly all at war with one another. Montevideo is controlled by the Colorados, who claim the right to govern. Outside of the city, Uruguay belongs to their rivals, the Blancos, under a man called Oribe, who claims with some justice to be the only honestly elected leader of this country. Brazil supports the Colorados while Rosas in Buenos Aires backs the Blancos, who have put Montevideo under a soft siege."

The carriage jumped up over a thick root and bounced Roebuck's bottom off his seat. He winced and almost groaned before composing himself and saying, "You feel we might be in some danger on the main road."

"French soldiers and Italian mercenaries allied with the Colorados patrol here. We'll see more of them if they know of your presence."

"The United States has no interest in the quarrel," Roebuck said.

"Your interest is that the French captured two American brigs, which now rest, it is said, at the bottom of the harbor."

The surprise in Roebuck's face must have been obvious. Guillory said, "It is no secret Commander. Far from that."

"And where does her Britannic Majesty stand in all of this?"

Guillory said, "The British are choosing against further involvement."

"So, the way is clear for the French."

Guillory nodded. "As they like it."

"The spirit of Bonaparte."

"Or the specter."

Roebuck remembered Perry's description of French actions. He had said the reason the French had been so bold in taking the two American ships was because they didn't fear the U.S. Navy, adding that if they thought the United States was too weak-willed to retaliate, they had good reason.

"Louis Philippe may be the Bourgeois King," said Guillory, "but his military is dominated by Bonapartists. They have reawakened France's colonial ambitions."

"Takes them far afield," Roebuck said.

"To the ends of the earth."

Roebuck said, "Who commands the French?"

"Admiral Leblanc is his name."

"Did LeBlanc serve under Bonaparte?"

"LeBlanc was one of Nelson's victims at the Nile," Guillory said. "He was captured and then paroled, as he tells the story."

"You know him?"

Guillory shrugged. "Montevideo is not large."

Roebuck had heard that Louis Philippe felt affection for the United States. The French King had even lived in Boston for several years as an exiled young man. Whatever his feelings toward Americans, Guillory was implying that the king could not control his military.

"Since the Spanish were ejected," said Guillory, "the tail of South America has proven a great temptation for the other empires of Europe. British ambitions to control the Paraná were thwarted by the Argentine navy several years ago. And the French have taken up against Argentina repeatedly, intervening on behalf of Peru and the Bolivian Republic in one war and now they do so again here."

"What do they expect to gain?"

"Weaken Rosas in Buenos Aires. And then either take control of Argentina or install a leader more sympathetic to their commercial interests."

"As they have done in Montevideo?"

"Yes."

"Your knowledge is encyclopedic, Mr. Guillory."

Guillory grinned. "There is no bliss in ignorance down here, Commander. Rather, it is fatal."

***

It was mid-afternoon before the carriage passed through a gate with a painted sign overhead that read "Nahomi." They moved down a way lined with leafless trees that soon gave way to neatly shaped hedges as high as the carriage wheels. The hedges on one side opened into a corral where horses with brushed tails and trimmed manes lolled and played. They were all pintos, shod so new the sunlight glinted off the iron.

They stopped at what looked like the main house of a great ranch. Roebuck climbed down stiffly. Guillory led him inside, where a Negro greeted them. He wore a crease pressed into wool trousers and a white cloth jacket fastened tightly with mother-of-pearl studs. Guillory returned to the horses while the Negro led Roebuck into a large room containing three mahogany desks, each one tidy as a captain's quarters and occupied by an equally tidy man reading papers or scratching out figures with a sharp quill. Roebuck saw through the glass panes of large undraped French doors into a walled garden where a fountain bubbled. He felt calm just to look at it.

Two portraits hung on the wall to his right. One portrayed a striking man with an uncovered head resting his left hand on a globe. His right hand seemed about to drop a scroll with a broken seal of red wax. In the other, a woman reposed on an elaborately upholstered chaise lounge. Her shoulders were bare in a blue gown and she looked directly into Roebuck's eyes. The artist had resorted to props to suggest something about the man. Roebuck supposed it was because he had little feeling for his subject. But she was different, beautiful, with a presence that the artist must have labored hard to capture—searching eyes, easy smile, the hint of something more. Roebuck felt a moment of pleasure, an odd feeling as if he, the artist, and this woman were slipping notes to one another in a schoolroom.

The clerks suddenly straightened, puffed out their chests, and glanced across the room, where a woman entered.

"Madame," said the Negro in Spanish, handing over Roebuck's calling card, "may I present Commander Robert Chase Roebuck of the frigate U.S.S. *Savannah*." To Roebuck he said, "I present Madame Doña Belén Saavedra y Mancera of la Compañía de Comercio de Overo."

She was older, but this was the woman in the portrait. If beauty was fleeting, its flight from Doña Belén had been glacially slow.

"Honored, Madame," Roebuck said in Spanish and bowed.

She said, "Commander, welcome to Nahomi," in English, obviously comfortable speaking it. "You have come from the consulate?"

"Yes, ma'am, we have a great need of supplies and the consul general suggested that you might be able to help." Roebuck also spoke English now.

"Mr. Houghton." A knowing smile to match her knowing eyes. "Well, we shall certainly try to meet your needs. What do you require?"

"Cattle and hogs, ma'am," Roebuck said, feeling awkward. "Flour and cheese. Salt, molasses, and whiskey."

"We can procure rum, but no whiskey."

"Rum suits."

"The cheese, salt, molasses, and spirits are close by. However, the meat and the flour will not be as quick. Will you slaughter and pack the meat yourself? It is something we can easily do for you if you wish."

"Using your barrels?"

"Of course."

"We already have a ship full of our own." Roebuck was uncomfortable negotiating with a woman, which, as he considered the feeling, was probably an advantage she was used to trading on. Probably why she had a corral full of groomed paints and what looked like at least two hundred acres of forage. He said, "May I inquire about the Don?"

"Don Justo? My husband?"

"Yes, ma'am, is he here?"

"He is in prison in Buenos Aires and will be, with God's grace, until the day he dies."

This answer didn't exactly increase Roebuck's comfort. "Permit me, Doña Belén, to ask how much per head of cattle?"

"Thirteen pieces of eight."

"Sink the offal?"

"Yes."

"Hogs?"

"Ten of the same."

He said, "Must be right fat hogs to command ten per head. What do you feed them, milk and molasses?"

She said, "Pork is an American passion, Commander, and not one that we share. We can give you a better price on mutton."

Roebuck knew that a return voyage with no chops or bacon would not sit well with the crew. And he had no love of mutton, especially the way the *Savannah*'s cook turned it into shoe leather. "I'll leave that for Mr. Scoggins, our purser, to decide," Roebuck said. "Maybe I missed the livestock coming in, ma'am, because all I saw were paints. You have some fine horses."

"Every pinto you saw is North American stock."

"I liked the black and browns. Don't see too many of those."

"How perceptive you are, Commander Roebuck. I bred those myself. Pintos are a passion of mine."

"It's a western breed, mostly," Roebuck said, pleased at the personal turn in the conversation. "Ranch horses. In the east we see bays, duns, and the like."

"You call them paints in your country, a good name for them."

"What is it about them, ma'am? If it's all right to ask."

"Ask whatever you like," she said with a laugh. "Pintos are not entirely one thing or another. Not a racehorse, but fast. Not a draft horse but good in the harness. There is something fine in that, no?"

Roebuck smiled.

She said, "What sort of horse do you prefer, Commander Roebuck?"

"I've never thought about it."

"Of course not. I must ask you about ships. Or perhaps it's too complicated for me?"

"It's simple enough."

"Well then, sir, tell me what kind of ship you prefer?"

"Whatever I'm sailing." Now her eyes surprised him, their curiosity. He said, "The paints suit you, I guess."

"You don't sound very certain." She was having fun now, and said, "The United States surprises me. A man so young to command a frigate in her navy."

He felt the heat rise to his cheeks. He said, "In the United States, it is an uncommon supplier of rum and hogs that requires commanding officers to account for their age," sounding to himself like a little prince.

"I'm afraid I have offended you, Sir."

"No." Was she toying with him? He felt six years old in her presence. She was older, twenty-eight or maybe thirty. He said, "I'm twenty-three years old."

"How nice," she said. "And thank you," she said in an amused way that snapped him right back to adulthood, "for saying that I am not common."

"Yes," he said and then stopped to consider that word, deciding it was somehow wrong. "I mean no. You are welcome. I mean not welcome but common." He exhaled sharply. *God. How many men had she made to feel so far off balance?* If it were a thousand, he was the thousand and first. He suddenly remembered something a commanding officer, Captain Parker, had told him in Tampico when a pretty Mexican girl had smiled at him and he'd responded with blushes and stuttering. Parker said how no harm ever came to a pure-hearted man who praised a handsome woman. Roebuck may not be pure hearted exactly, but the doña was nothing if not handsome. He said, "Uncommon does not begin to describe your beauty, Doña Belén."

"Well now, Commander," she said slowly, "that wasn't so difficult was it?"

"All due respect ma'am. The both of us know that it was."

He was suddenly conscious of the clerks. Their ears had probably grown with each word.

"May I ask when we might begin to slaughter the hogs and cattle?" he said. "And are you able to drive them to the beach north of the old city?"

"We can deliver them to Bahia Chico in a week."

He recognized the spot from the map, but the timing was a disappointment. "May I send you our answer tomorrow?"

"I would not expect otherwise."

He tried to think of a way to keep the conversation from ending. She was quicker.

"Mr. Guillory is waiting outside?" she asked.

"Yes. Is he a friend of yours?"

"An advisor and a friend."

"A fair coachman too."

She laughed. "A man of many talents."

Roebuck looked down for a moment, thinking she was just one step away, a step he wanted to take. "May I invite you and Mr. Guillory to be my guests on the *Savannah* tomorrow evening? Your presence would honor us," he said, wondering where he would get victuals for a decent meal.

"It would be an enchantment were it not for my work. I must find a way to move four hundred bushels of grain from the interior into the city before tomorrow night," she said.

"Of course. You must be very busy." Roebuck bowed. "I should leave before I lose any more of the day's light."

"Commander, in seven days I am hosting a dinner," she said. "Seven o'clock in the city at the Club Londres. Say you will join us."

Roebuck felt the blood pumping in his heart and experienced an idiotic fear she would hear it. "I look forward to it," he said. It was not much more than a croak, but he'd gotten it out. "Until then, madame," he added, returning to Spanish for some reason and bow-ing a little too deeply before turning and striding off with his back as straight as a bowstring, puffing up even farther than the clerks had when she'd walked into the room.

CHAPTER 25

The *Savannah*'s anchorage was in sight of a village called Buceo. Roebuck noticed that the village quay was gone, swept away in the storm. So too was the sand that had kept the waves from coming too close to the village. The surf's pounding had opened up hollows under some cottages, collapsing them and then washing their fronts away.

Two days ago, he had put Flynn the carpenter and a large detail of the *Savannah*'s seamen to work building groins that reached far into the surf to break its eroding effect. As they were completed, the seamen rolled barrels filled with sand and rock to the shore, emptying them into the spaces between the groins to help break the water. It was, he had realized, the only chance the remaining houses of Buceo had. Trees from a nearby grove provided the timber, as well as whatever had been salvaged from wreckage of ships lost on a wide crop of rock that jutted from the harbor's southern limit.

Roebuck had been told that the American brigs *Eliza Davidson* and *America* were among those wrecks, the ships captured by the French that had triggered the *Savannah*'s present mission. As the crew worked, Roebuck, accompanied by three Marines, cutlasses strapped to their sides, knocked on doors and visited shops to ask if the remains of any of the drowned Americans had washed up. None had. They left salt pork and cornmeal from *Savannah*'s stores behind after each of these visits.

At the same time, another group from the *Savannah* labored several leagues to the south at Point Yeguas, building Consul General Houghton's road spur. But Houghton was not satisfied with the progress and had sent a note reminding Roebuck that he could bring honor to America and to himself by building the spur as a sure-fire way to relieve the "terrible suffering" of the people of Uruguay, and that doing so would count heavily in his favor with Nicolson.

This very minute, Houghton was en route to see Roebuck here in Buceo. Roebuck was pretty certain that Houghton was coming to insist that the *Savannah*'s commander abandon work here and focus exclusively on the spur, for without it, Houghton was going to tell him, the villages along the coast would continue to suffer from a lack of food and fresh water.

After the first day of work in Buceo, patrols of French and Italian men in uniform as well as red-shirted locals, called Colorados, had appeared. Their appearance coincided with villagers no longer opening their homes and the shopkeepers shrugging when asked about drowned American sailors. Despite this, Roebuck and his men kept knocking and continued leaving behind food, whether the villagers opened their doors or not. Today, Malvey was in the village in place of Roebuck, accompanied by the Texan Cockrell, who spoke what he called border Spanish.

"Here it comes, Captain," called Ten'til, watching the southern approach.

The sound was faint, but Roebuck heard the squeak of carriage struts and the clop-clopping of iron-shod hooves. Eventually, the carriage arrived and stopped with a groan. The coachman jumped down to open a side door, where Houghton hunched looking around as if surprised to be out of the city.

Roebuck said, "I am busy, sir. I hope this will not take long."

"No greeting, Commander? I am obliged to visit this fish trap and not even a 'good day to you, Mr. Consular?'" Houghton turned both hands up in a gesture Roebuck guessed was meant to be amiable. The hands put Roebuck in mind of raccoon snares.

Houghton lowered himself awkwardly from the carriage and onto a stool opposite Roebuck. The wind blew long thin strands of hair around his head. Catching one expertly, he patted it down into place, before saying, "How goes our work on the rail spur at Yeguas, my dear sir?" His eyes expressed something that had as much to do with the words 'my dear' as a blue shark does a goldfinch.

"Slowly," Roebuck said, feeling pretty sure Houghton knew exactly how their work went.

"That is a shame, young sir. There are hungry people, women and children, who will surely hope for more of that grand old American can-do spirit. I daresay you should not trifle here in Buceo when faced with so much suffering. Commodore Nicolson will not approve, no indeed. Think, young sir, on the prospect of your court martial."

Roebuck dug into the dirt with a stick. He had been thinking of little else.

Houghton said, "Commander, please allow me an observation. A painful one, it is true, but one I must . . ."

"Go ahead."

"Well, I daresay there is something unfortunate about you."

"Unfortunate."

"Yes. I can't put my finger on it exactly. But you possess a deficiency of some kind. A fault of character, or perhaps the defect is spiritual. What I know for certain is that you would do well to reflect deeply upon it and seek a path toward improvement."

Houghton was an odd creature, but there was something a little deadly about him too. He confused Roebuck, who said, "Maybe I should join the Foreign Service."

"I suppose irony is the fashion among America's young people these days," said Houghton, illustrating that irony was the fashion for at least one of its middle-aged people, too. "One consequence of this defect, whatever its cause, is that you antagonize the French here and their allies in the Colorado government."

"I have not spoken to a single man among the French since the *Savannah*'s arrival. Perhaps my neglect offends them."

Houghton hovered, a big buzzing fly eyeing a place to land. "Would it not be better, Commander, for you to quickly complete your work and join Nicolson's squadron? The truth is that you are making yourself unwelcome and your progress on the spur does not impress."

Roebuck wondered what exactly this man wanted.

"You and your crew have been knocking on doors, Commander."

"Yes."

Houghton repositioned his weight on the stool, shifting his weight like a big bag filled with mismatched scraps of iron and tin and saying, "In search of crew from the wrecks, are you?"

Roebuck nodded.

"I have told you, those men are gone. The storm floated every one of them out to sea, so many fallen leaves on the stream. Departed, sir, departed."

Roebuck squinted toward the massive estuary of Rio de la Plata. The clear warm blue of the Caribbean was a fading memory, replaced by the South Atlantic's chilly gray. Breakers curled long and white. He imagined the contours of the floor beneath them.

"The Colorados do not approve of you harassing their citizens in their homes. And the French are unhappy."

Roebuck said, "We bring hungry villagers food from our stores. And we build. Nothing more," he said, looking back at Houghton now. "I have orders. They have to do with freeing American sailors. If I am to do that, I must find them. If they are dead, as you insist, I must bury them. Added to this are the orders from Commodore Nicolson, which you have reported to me as: help the people of Montevideo."

"Well, yes but—"

"I am bound by duty to follow these orders. The storm scoured away every grain of sand and most of the soil separating the cottages here in Buceo from the waves. The cottages need protection. Their occupants are hungry. So I ask myself, how can I do as the good commodore has instructed?"

"And your answer is to keep the surf from destroying homes and to feed the people."

Roebuck nodded.

"An act of charity, to be sure, but a small one, not commensurate with your rank and authority. You can best help the citizens of this marvelous country by putting all of your effort toward the road spur in Point Yeguas."

"We are working there," Roebuck said.

"But not fast enough. I tell you again, tarry no longer in this place."

Roebuck saw beads of sweat dotting Houghton's scalp, a nervous sweat. He stood and said, "No one has seen a single body wash up that they would describe as a seaman's. They've recovered the remains of many who drowned in the storm, but those were locals, women and children as well as men."

"This evidences the fact that those sailors are gone," Houghton said.

"Is it not strange to you that the sea only gives up the remains of locals, and not our sailors? If one surfaces, so should the other."

"The currents are unpredictable. I'm surprised you cannot see it. Those sailors now feed the crabs and other bottom-dwellers." Houghton quickly added, "May God deliver their souls."

Roebuck said, "We shall continue to look." He turned to watch three skiffs skipping over the waves, long white triangles of canvas leaning forward. Further out, more skiffs bobbed gently, their movement slower and more deliberate, trawling, probably first to the morning's riches. Roebuck said, "It's that simple."

***

It wasn't long after Houghton left that Roland Guillory, Doña Belén's assistant, surprised Roebuck with a visit, arriving in the saddle.

"Good afternoon, Commander!"

"Mr. Guillory, welcome, sir."

The Englishman dismounted.

Roebuck said, "Is that one of Doña Belén's paints?"

"It was until last week, but I bought him. I needed a fresh horse."

"Going somewhere?"

"Full of questions, aren't you, Commander?" Guillory said, extending a hand, which Roebuck took with a smile.

Roebuck said, "I do have questions, it is true. Because I have never been to a place where information is locked away so securely, and you just missed one of its most dedicated jailers."

"Mr. Houghton."

"You saw him leave."

"I did."

"Or rather you waited until he was gone?"

"I'm found out." Now it was Guillory who was smiling.

There was a loud crash. Crewmen were downing trees for timber in a grove of algarrobas. The algarroba was a dense tree with angry spines that had tormented the *Savannah*'s men until a villager demonstrated how to strip them with a machete.

"Follow me, Mr. Guillory."

They walked toward the grove. Guillory said, "Doña Belén has asked me to confirm your presence at dinner in two days."

Roebuck said, "You'll have no regrets from me."

"Splendid," Guillory said.

"Another officer will join me, if that is acceptable."

"Yes, of course. The doña will be pleased."

Roebuck smelled sap from the sawed trees, a clean smell. He looked over and saw a man pushing and pulling a very long saw, cutting a tree set athwart two squared logs.

"Extraordinary power," said Guillory. "How can he wield such a large tool?"

"Come closer," said Roebuck.

It was a long, two-man saw. One man was out of sight in a muddy pit, working the other end of it.

"He must be over eight feet down in that hole," Guillory said.

"Flynn the carpenter says ten feet."

The men pushed and pulled, one up and one down, a steel guide at the saw's cutting edge.

Teams of seamen with adzes squared freshly cut timber. Others rolled the finished timber lengthwise over round logs, with crewmen picking up the back rollers and running them to the front, a fine synchronization that kept even the biggest pieces moving all the way to the half-built breakwater sticking out into the bay's soft bottom. Flynn and his men had finished four of the groins and these were already having an effect, breaking the surf's eroding power. Roebuck intended to add four more.

"You govern the project efficiently," said Guillory.

"I have a team of carpenters and bo'sun's mates who take to this kind of work like beavers to a pond. And we've had no interruptions to slow us."

"I am afraid I have news of one."

The two men walked back toward Guillory's horse.

"Admiral Leblanc and his allies are unhappy with you, Commander. And they will stop you from further work here. The *Badine* has returned to port with news of your maneuver at sea."

Roebuck had been expecting this. If the French didn't have reason to be angry with him before, they did now.

Guillory said, "And you knock on the doors of those whom these men consider to be their allies and theirs alone."

"Our purpose is to do nothing but recover the remains of drowned brothers-at-sea. Anyone wearing a uniform, French or otherwise, will understand that."

"I wouldn't give Admiral LeBlanc any reason to cause you trouble. He'll take it if you do."

"Our work troubles no one."

"They see it as defiance, Commander, first as a result of your confrontation with the *Badine* at sea and now on land. Your search for the crews of the *Eliza Davidson* and the *America* challenges the French explanation of their fate."

Guillory's horse puffed and stamped beside them at the loud crack and splinter of another falling tree.

Roebuck said, "You are here to tell me what I should do," tired of the advice everyone here seemed so pleased to give. "So go ahead."

"Learn to live next to your bitterest enemy as though he were your sweetest friend."

"Love your enemies as you do your neighbors," mumbled Roebuck.

Guillory tilted his head.

"They're usually the same people," Roebuck said.

"Here they are," said Guillory. "The capital is under siege; the control of states is contested. This is no place to make enemies."

"My orders are to help secure the release of American sailors. But those sailors have vanished. What objection can be raised to my searching for them?"

"What does Mr. Houghton say?" said Guillory.

"He throws up his hands, repeats the word *yes* several times, then calls me young sir. He prefers we do nothing but work on the road at Point Yeguas."

"I'm sure he does."

Roebuck sensed that Guillory's real subject was at hand. "Tell me what you mean by that."

"Mr. Houghton and his partner, Don Justo, won a land concession between the harbor at Punta Yeguas and a mine where coal was recently discovered. Yeguas will become Uruguay's only coaling station for steamships."

"Doña Belén's husband?"

"Yes."

"The concession includes the road spur we are helping to build?"

"Yes," said Guillory smiling, "and you build it for free. It is a very generous thing to do."

"Does our Consular General have an interest in Don Justo's business?" said Roebuck, biting back his anger.

"I would describe what they have together as more of an arrangement." Guillory paused, about to say more, when they heard gunshots from the village. It was quiet for a moment. Then came the sound again.

"Muskets," said Guillory.

"Come to me, men!" called Roebuck, pulling the cutlass from its scabbard and raising it above his head. Twenty seamen left their work, grabbed pikes and cutlasses from a stand of weapons, and joined their commander, forming two lines with some effort.

"Mr. Guillory, you should stay here."

Guillory said, "Maybe I can help."

"On the double!" Roebuck said and they began to jog forward. As they rounded a bend, yells became audible and the smell of burnt powder was in the air. They passed into a small plaza where a scene of conflict opened up. One of the *Savannah*'s sailors was down on the street. Opposing Roebuck and his men was a platoon in a mix of blue and green jackets. Three mounted officers rode back and forth behind their line. The *Savannah's* detail was outnumbered two to one.

"Looks like Tom Eldridge, sir, on the ground. The gunner's mate," said Flynn. Blood pooled in the dirt where Eldridge was down. He writhed in shallow rolls.

Malvey, in a rage and struggling to break the grip of four of the opposing soldiers restraining him, yelled, "You water-shitting whoresons, let go or I'll cut out your puny hearts. Let go and draw your swords!"

Roebuck's men were moving toward Malvey when a green-jacketed officer on the other side shouted a command and half the platoon wheeled around, kneeling in line, raising their muskets. The other half filled in a standing rank behind them.

"Stop there, Capitán," called the officer in sneering accented English. "Or we will shoot." Drooping red plumes adorned his shako.

"What is this?" Roebuck called to the man.

"These men were breaking into homes and despoiling property," the officer replied.

"It's not true, Captain Roebuck," called Cockrell, who stood with the remainder of Malvey's detail between the two lines of men. "We were doing just as you said, offering salt pork and cornmeal and asking after the lost sailors."

"Captain!" Pemberton came up alongside Roebuck.

Roebuck raised his hand to Pemberton and called to Cockrell, "And Eldridge?"

"He was at the front. They shot him down, and Lieutenant Malvey ran at them."

"Tommy!" It was Ten'til, calling from the line that had spread out behind Roebuck.

"Stay where you are, Ten'til" said Roebuck.

The soldiers across from them were fidgeting with their muskets and looking at the small line of Americans across from them.

Pemberton said, "One volley from them would put an end to anything the *Savannah* might do here, sir. Outnumbered is bad enough, but they have muskets to our pikes and cutlasses."

Roebuck called, "Stay calm, boys."

"The mounted officer in the green jacket is Fabio Lechi," said Guillory. "He was a major in the Sardinian hussars and he's bloody murder with that sword."

Guillory called out in French, addressing another mounted officer as "Dufour", this one in the blue jacket of the French Navy. The officer shook his head. Guillory called out again and the man gently flexed his left calf, directing his mount to the right and showing his back to Guillory, who said, "They won't release your lieutenant."

Ten'til said, "Captain, we do nothin', Tommy he'll bleed out. Please, sir."

Roebuck remembered that Tom Eldridge was Ten'til's closest friend on the *Savannah*. Four of Lechi's soldiers ran out and grabbed Eldridge's wrists and ankles.

"Captain!" shouted Ten'til. "They're a-takin' him, sir. He'll die."

"Major, release the injured man and the lieutenant," called Roebuck to Lechi. "This is a misunderstanding."

"It's too late for that, Capitán," said Lechi. "Justice. We must have justice." The Italian nodded at his men and they began to carry Eldridge toward the two ranks of muskets.

"Stop!" Roebuck forced whatever authority he could into his voice. The soldiers paused, looking at Lechi. Roebuck continued,

"Major, if these men have done what you say, they will be punished. You have my word as an officer. Please release them, sir."

Lechi pursed his lips and shook his head. The men started again. Ten'til ran out, brushing past Roebuck toward the four soldiers and Eldridge.

Roebuck reached out to restrain him, but the foretopman was too quick.

Lechi raised his sword, shouting, "*Non sparare!*" and spurred his horse toward Ten'til. "Stop him, Capitán," Lechi called, "or you'll have more blood!"

Roebuck tried again. "Ten'til! Return or face the lash."

Lechi used his horse to block Ten'til from Eldridge. But Ten'til was quick and ducked past the horse's haunches. Lechi answered by leaning over and slicing into Ten'til's neck. It was a cavalry sword, big and heavy, and it dug deep. Lechi was more powerful than he appeared. He raised the blade again, blood dripping from its edge, steel catching the sun.

"Enough, man, for God's sake," called Roebuck.

Ten'til's knees buckled.

Lechi's eyes were unfocused and his head tilted backward as he swept the blade down, separating Ten'til's head from his shoulders. He said, "Now enough."

Roebuck felt a wild rage inside. He drew his cutlass and started toward Lechi, but Pemberton and Guillory held him back.

"Keep your head, Captain," said Pemberton. "Keep your head or we'll all be shot in seconds."

"Let me go, goddamn you," Roebuck said.

"This is not the time," Pemberton said. "The time will come, I promise you, but this is not it." Pemberton called to the Americans, "Hold your positions!"

Roebuck called to Lechi, "Cold-blooded murder."

Lechi said, "No, Capitán, I have saved you and your men from the muskets. Here is the consequence of an officer who has not the respect of those he commands. Control them or more will die."

Holman said to Roebuck, "Let me go instead of Eldridge, sir."

Roebuck nodded. He suspected Eldridge would receive no treatment and would die of his wounds if he were carried off. Holman walked out. Roebuck said to Lechi, "Take the midshipman instead of the seaman."

Lechi said, "*Bene*," and his men dropped Eldridge. Holman walked through a line of men that opened up to him.

The Americans surged. Roebuck jumped out ahead, turning and raising his cutlass. "Another step and I'll be the one doing the killing."

"But what that greasy bastard done, sir…" It was Flynn.

Roebuck nodded. "His time will come."

CHAPTER 26

The stone floor of the prison was rough. The mortar of its walls was moist and stained. Roebuck and Benoit, the surgeon, ducked into the artificial night of a dark room at its entrance lit by a few candles on the floor. A guard with the smell of an old man sat in the back. Roebuck showed him a silver real. The man didn't move. Roebuck showed another. The man looked at it. With the third real, the man rose and said wait here in Spanish.

It was ten minutes before a shackled Lieutenant Malvey emerged from a hall even darker than the room.

"Hello, Captain."

"How is it for you inside, Mr. Malvey?" Roebuck asked.

"I'd rather be in chains on the *Savannah*." Malvey tried a grin.

"Take these," said Roebuck, handing over a burlap sack full of salt pork, a quinine tonic, and lemons.

Benoit said, "How much water do you receive a day?"

"Two mugs, one in the morning and again about half the day later. Have you seen Mr. Holman?"

Roebuck said, "Not yet, but I have for him what I've just given you."

"How is your stomach?" Benoit said.

"I've got the shits." Malvey's lids closed. His face was cut and bruised. "Are they going release me?"

Benoit looked at the lieutenant's tongue and used a magnifier to examine his eyes. "Take your shirt off, Lieutenant Malvey."

"Rather not."

"Do it," said the surgeon.

Malvey pulled off his shirt.

Even in the room's darkness Roebuck could see the long-elevated scars criss crossing his back. He said without thinking, "You've been flogged."

"Aye, sir."

"When?'

"Years ago."

"For what?"

"Insubordination."

"It's a gift of yours."

"One I'd be pleased to give up."

Roebuck nodded. He wanted to ask how many lashes but didn't.

The surgeon spent thirty minutes treating Malvey's face and torso for cuts and feeling for broken bones. They looked in on Holman, who was faring better. Afterward, Benoit said Malvey had five broken ribs and if he was beaten again, one would poke a half-inch hole in his lung.

"They are beating him," Roebuck said. It wasn't hard to imagine Malvey asking for it.

"They are."

CHAPTER 27

Guillory cut a thick oval of mutton, laying it neatly atop a stack on a blue china serving plate. He then stuck the carving knife into the meat's flank, handle up. Doña Belén placed a triangle of rice pudding on Roebuck's plate, the smell of its clove and mace steaming up. Across the table sat the tidy, bewhiskered Senator Moises Montcalvo, who leaned over to fill Roebuck's glass, moving with a languor so complete it seemed otherworldly.

"Thank you, Senator," Roebuck said.

"It's Mendoza, Commander, from God's own vineyard."

"Mendoza?"

"Argentine wine," Montcalvo said. "Grown in the shadow of the Andes."

"They could grow it on the moon for all I care," Cockrell said. "Seems like a very fine bottle. But I'll need at least one more glass before I can properly adjudicate it. If you'd be so kind, Excellency."

"He's a Senator, Mr. Cockrell, not a king," Roebuck said.

An enormous fireplace with a pile of thick, burning logs took up the middle third of the club's wainscoted wall. Bright oil lamps ringed the room. Tables of diners filled it.

Montcalvo tipped the wine from God's own vineyard into Cockrell's glass.

Doña Belén said, "It has been a rare pleasure for us to work with the *Savannah*, Commander Roebuck."

"Mr. Scoggins has been very satisfied with the vittling, Doña Belén. So I thank you."

"Senator Montcalvo," Cockrell said, "we passed three groups of French sailors on the street. I couldn't help wondering what makes them so thick down here."

"They are as hungry as ever for territory."

Cockrell filled Montcalvo's glass.

Doña Belén said, "Have you ever known the unmarried son of a great family in reduced circumstances, Lieutenant Cockrell?"

Cockrell said, "Nary a son, ma'am. But I have acquainted myself with a daughter or two."

Her smile acknowledged the point. "I ask because sons like those prey on the unattached daughters of men who have made their fortune."

Montcalvo said, "There is a kind of exchange."

She said, "The merchants want the great name attached to theirs and the great name wants the merchant's money. France looks upon colonies that have recently gained their independence such as ours in the same way.

"They seduce us, or try," she continued. "If we are unwilling, they simply take us. The French are looking for a rich woman down here, Lieutenant Cockrell. They think it is how they will restore themselves to something like Bonaparte's glory."

Something was happening here, how Guillory had earlier let Roebuck know about Houghton, and now these two sharing something about themselves, their situation.

The doña froze as a disturbance rolled through the room like a wave. Cockrell began to stand.

Roebuck said, "Keep your seat."

Cockrell said, "Lechi's here, sir, in the flesh."

Roebuck fought the tide of his blood. "Alone?"

"Three others," Cockrell said.

Guillory said, "The French Captain Dufour is one of them."

Montcalvo looked immune to whatever effect the Italian had on the rest of the room. He said, "Major Lechi has made things difficult for you, Commander."

This would be a reference to the imprisonment of Malvey and Holman. The *Savannah's* enemies might push those two up against a wall and shoot them at any time. The threat of it put Roebuck at a severe disadvantage.

Roebuck said, "Lechi killed a good man. One of my best."

Montcalvo said, "They have been making raids into the heart of my country for the past six months, killing there too."

Lechi wore a green jacket. He hadn't removed the red kepi from his head. His trousers, *à la chasseur*, were a bright billowy red. What stood out to Roebuck was his sash, thick and also red, wrapped tightly around his middle like a very broad belt.

"Tell me about Lechi," Roebuck said.

"He served the King of Sardinia against the Mazzinian revolution," Guillory said. "But he killed a fellow officer in Sardinia, was arrested and escaped to join his king's enemies, including Garibaldi. When the revolution failed, both Lechi and Garibaldi were sentenced to die. So they came here."

"For what?"

Montcalvo said, "Power and glory."

"Unfortunately for them," the doña smiled, "both are in rather short supply."

Roebuck had heard the name of Garibaldi but couldn't place it.

Montcalvo said, "Mr. Guillory leaves out something important about Major Lechi."

The doña said, "Senator Montcalvo, it is enough, no?"

Roebuck said, "What is enough?"

"Major Lechi was Doña Belén's suitor," Montcalvo said.

"Was?" Roebuck said.

"The suit," Montcalvo said, "was unrequited."

She said, "He is a pig."

Guillory added with emphasis, "And Doña Belén is still married."

"This is something Mr. Guillory will not let me forget," she said.

Her humor came easily. She had charisma Roebuck felt down to his toes. He said, "And what became of this suit?"

"Nothing. He is nothing," she said.

Montcalvo shrugged. "When our Major Lechi sleeps, he dreams of the doña."

She said, "When he sleeps, he dreams of slitting throats."

Lechi sauntered over to the fire and tossed something into it, which flared and gave a loud pop. The diners gasped. A woman managed to cut off the beginnings of a scream.

"A charge of powder," Roebuck said, thinking what an odd thing to do.

"Major Lechi has a temper, Commander," said Guillory. "It has led him to kill three Colorado officers in duels, each with the sword."

Montcalvo said, "The doña has not been spared his temper."

Roebuck raised his eyebrows.

"He tells, shall we say, unflattering stories," Montcalvo said.

"About the doña?" Roebuck said.

"Of course," she said. "It is the sort of man he is."

Lechi sat down with a goblet of wine in his hand and stared at Roebuck. Diners were whispering as if that might spare them Lechi's notice.

"He is like a boy who has just discovered vile words," the doña said. "I cannot pass an Italian officer in the street without him grinning at me like a wolf."

"No one here believes Lechi's stories," said Guillory. "They know Doña Belén too well."

"Who cares what they believe?" she said, leaning back, raising her head, candlelight putting the shape of her shoulders and chest in relief. Something in her movement Roebuck hadn't seen before but recognized—defiance.

"The people of Montevideo take a violent interest in such stories," she said. "Nothing pleases them more than a man like Lechi bringing scandal and gossip to our village."

The ends of Montcalvo's mouth curled up, and there was a light in his eyes. "They say Doña Belén drinks."

The doña said, "She dashes around in the president's coach."

"And those rides on the French officer's mount," Montcalvo said, "she has no shame."

"Let them talk," she said.

"Doña Belén is a subject of interest to the people of Montevideo because she has helped so many in need," Guillory blurted. "She is a figure of respect and admiration."

"She seems a good deal more than that," Roebuck said.

"Thank you, Commander," she said with a slight bow, "for redeeming me from such a dreadful description."

"Apologies, madame," Guillory said, "I meant no harm."

"Worse than that," the doña said, and glanced at Roebuck. "He meant well."

Cockrell said, "Lechi keeps looking this way, Captain."

A bottle of French brandy arrived. "Compliments of Captain Dufour," said the steward in Spanish, showing it to Roebuck. Roebuck recalled Dufour as the mounted French naval officer Guillory had called out to before Ten'til was cut down. Tonight he looked somehow larger off the horse than mounted on it.

"I would expect him to bring it over himself and empty the contents onto your head," the doña said.

"Still time for that," Roebuck said.

Her eyes were wide open, fixed on him.

She said, "Perhaps he's decided he likes you."

"Let's find out," Roebuck said. "Steward," he called in Spanish. "Ask Major Lechi and his companions to join us for a toast."

Guillory leaned forward, hunching and looking worried.

Roebuck said, "Enemies and neighbors, Mr. Guillory."

Guillory leaned back and exhaled before saying, "One and the same."

Roebuck watched as the steward spoke to them, Lechi nodding his answer. Soon the waiters arrived with empty glasses and a small table. Lechi and the others followed. Dried mud and grease streaked their uniforms. A sour smell of violence clung to them.

Lechi said in rough English, "Bring us stools," nodding to Cockrell.

Cockrell ignored him.

"You," Lechi nodded again.

Cockrell tapped the two stripes and star insignia fastened to his left shoulder strap and said, "You know what this means?"

Lechi didn't look.

"Means I ain't your *chico*."

Suddenly two waiters were behind the four standing men, breathing hard, a stool in each hand.

Roebuck got to his feet, palms open. "Sit down."

Lechi grunted and sat. Dufour followed, and the two others.

Roebuck toasted King Louis Philippe.

Lechi said, "Your country has no king."

"We have a president," Roebuck said.

"Does he raise more pigs than the others?" Dufour said.

Guillory stood up suddenly and began a hasty salute to President Polk. Dufour toasted Joaquín Suárez, the head of the Uruguayan state in Montevideo, the glorious future, apparently, of this country.

The size of Dufour's hands made the brandy glass seem like it belonged to a child's tea set. He said, "Mr. Roebuck, I am captain of the *Badine*." This was the ship the *Savannah* had fired upon and left behind during the chase in the Atlantic. "You are a coward. You prefer to run rather than fight."

"Hold on now," Cockrell said.

Dufour said, "Maybe fifty guns is not enough for you."

"Fifty-two," Roebuck said.

Dufour carried a saber. Thick curved hussar swords hung at the sides of Lechi and the two others. Roebuck's cutlass dangled in its scabbard in his cabin on the *Savannah*. But he had his knuckled knife, and fingered its grip under the table. Cockrell had a pistol, but Roebuck knew it was not loaded.

Montcalvo said, "So you have returned from the interior, Captain Dufour. How did you find it?"

Dufour said, "Full of ignorant reactionaries and criminals. But there are fewer of them today than there were two days ago. And there will be fewer still by the end of the week."

Roebuck tilted the stem of his glass, rotating it, thumb and finger. The brandy left a clear, viscous ring near the rim, tacky droplets trailing down. "This is fine brandy," he said, "smells as good as it tastes," emptying his glass.

Dufour filled it.

Roebuck caught Cockrell's eye and touched his belt where Cockrell holstered his pistol. He said, "Lieutenant, kindly find the steward and ask him for cigars."

"Aye aye, sir."

Lechi drained his goblet and put it down, hitting the table hard. If he wasn't drunk, he wasn't far from it. But not Dufour; his eyes were chilly and clear. Doña Belén was motionless. Roebuck felt her eyes on him.

Dufour spoke again, his English was accented but not hard to understand. "Senator Montcalvo, is it not?"

"It is," Montcalvo said.

Dufour said, "A man who supports the reactionaries."

The smile hardened on Montcalvo's face. These two men were on opposite sides of something, maybe everything.

"The cause of man is progress, Senator." Dufour said it like he'd found a favorite subject.

"Is that what you call it?" Montcalvo said.

"I know your kind, Senator, gray beards and old faces bumping along with your backs to the future."

"Ah," Montcalvo said, "perhaps we walk that way to spare ourselves the sight of men like you laying waste to farms and churches and blowing out the brains of those who inhabit them."

"Owners of land misuse those who work it," Dufour said, starting what sounded like a lecture. "Priests and landowners fatten themselves on the superstition and labor of the people."

Montcalvo said, "Unarmed priests? Are they who you fight?"

Dufour's mouth turned up in an arctic grin. "Is it not an evil institution that does not suppose the people good? I speak, old man, of your church."

Roebuck stared at Montcalvo. The pointy-mustached son of a bitch didn't scare at all. He seemed to have grown by a foot before Roebuck's eyes. And Dufour, a man of politics.

Cockrell returned, caught Roebuck's eye, and touched his pistol grip. He then set an open box of cigars out on the table. "Your cigars, sir."

Roebuck said to the table, "Help yourselves."

No one moved.

Lechi said, "What do we have here?" pointing his nose at the doña. "I think maybe the lady spider is going to eat the hombre spider, the man," he said, turning to Roebuck. "She rides a horse like a man. Have you seen her?"

"I have seen her," Dufour said. "She has two strong legs."

"Yes," Lechi said, "but she makes her living with what's between them." He pointed at Guillory. "But not with that one. That one maybe can't do what she wants. No, she tempts the boy for that," nosing toward Roebuck. "The young spider. She's old and he's young, no?"

Roebuck said, "Captain Dufour. I think it's time for you to take this person," nodding at Lechi, "back to your table."

Lechi said, "Is this all you say? 'Return to your table'?"

"*Per favore*," Roebuck said.

Lechi said, "Maybe you're a coward after all, Commander, if this is all you do."

Cockrell said, "You needn't insult and fight with everybody you meet, Major."

"No one addresses you, *chico*," said Lechi, the last syllable of *addresses* a long, slippery *s*.

Cockrell said, "Making bad blood, quarreling. It will be a miserable life if you keep it up."

"And short," Roebuck said.

Lechi stood up, hand on hilt. "You threaten me?"

Roebuck giggled, not sure why.

Lechi said, "This is a joke to you?"

Cockrell said, "Sir, the major's red trousers are sorta funny."

"And the sash?" Roebuck said, feeling the grip of his knife.

Cockrell said, "Fortunately, the major has just the figure for it."

That was all it took. Lechi rose and came on, kicking away anything in his path, heavy hussar's sword up and swinging down at Cockrell. But Roebuck intercepted it, blocking with the blade and hilt of his knife. The force of Lechi's swing took Roebuck by surprise and a stinging vibration numbed him fingertip to elbow. He lost his grip and the knife flew from his hand, clink-clinking across the floorboards. Yet Cockrell lived.

Now Lechi squared his shoulders to Roebuck and raised his sword, the hall's diners kicking free, knocking over chairs and bottles. Goddammit, Roebuck's knife-hand was numb and worthless, but all his other sense screamed. The smell of pudding was so strong and the mutton—yes, oh God, the meat with that carving knife stuck into its flank. Roebuck grabbed it with his good hand and jumped into Lechi, stabbing straight for the heart, knife-tip breaking skin and penetrating. Lechi's sword fell. His hands tore at the knife. Roebuck stabbed again.

Now Dufour was coming, the other men right behind. Lechi falling back, blood shining and dark on the chest of his green jacket. Dufour almost on Roebuck.

"Not a step more, Captain." It was Cockrell at Roebuck's shoulder, his arm at full extension, pointing a pistol into the Frenchman's face.

Dufour and the others stopped.

Roebuck said, "Lieutenant."

"Sir?"

"You're half-cocked."

Cockrell quickly raised his left hand, drew back the hammer until it clicked and said, "Give me the word, sir, and I'll brain him."

***

Doña Belén said, "No."

Was that an expression of anger on her face? All Roebuck knew was he hadn't seen anything like it there before. She was talking to Guillory, speaking Spanish of course, raising her voice, commanding. Roebuck and Cockrell stood there in front of the Club Londres like two boys waiting to be let out of school.

Guillory gripped the reins of both carriage horses and was holding his ground. Doña Belén suddenly grabbed them. Guillory took a step away and turned his shoulder quickly, wrenching the reins away from her. She grabbed at them again and yanked hard, but he didn't let go.

Roebuck said, "Doña Belén, we can find our way back to the ship. We came here on our own and we can return the same way."

"No," she said, still looking at Guillory, but speaking to Roebuck. "They will kill you for what you have done. You were followed here. Did you know that? And now they will be waiting for you along every route between here and the harbor. You have given them what they most wanted from you, Commander, an excuse."

"This is a Christian country, isn't it? Why would they harm innocent men?" said Roebuck. "I acted to defend Mr. Cockrell from Lechi's blade, as witnessed by a room full of people. In any case, they would not," he added, wondering exactly whom she meant by *they*, "murder the commander of an American warship. That's more trouble than it's worth by a long shot."

Guillory said, "The doña speaks the truth. They will kill you when they find you. And they will find you soon. Your body will disappear with no trace, and without it there will be no evidence of your death and so it will be very difficult for your navy to do anything about it. Seamen desert all the time. It will be said, why not officers too?"

Guillory had told Roebuck about Lechi's allies among the Colorados, the faction that governed Montevideo. He wondered if LeBlanc was among them.

Roebuck said, "You can forget it, both of you. I am no pirate and won't run away as if I were."

Doña Belén said, "You just stabbed a very powerful officer to death with a carving knife. No one is asking you to run away, only to be prudent and not be such a fool."

"Doña Belén," Roebuck began, surprised by her use of that word.

"Listen to me," she said. "You and the lieutenant will ride to the south away from the harbor in my carriage. We have a place where we stage tallow and hides before loading them for shipment. You will conceal yourselves there until your men can come for you."

Roebuck was shaking his head. Hiding in the doña's greasy warehouse, waiting to be saved by his men would go a long way to justify the nickname Robby Run, even in his own mind.

"No, ma'am," he said. "We will be on our way. It's no more than 20 minutes from here to the harbor. A boat will soon be there to meet us, and the lieutenant has a pistol."

"And you do not even have a sword," she said. "You have caused enough trouble for one night. Just do as I say and make things simpler for all of us."

"And if I don't?"

"You will no longer be a nuisance," she said, "because you'll be dead. An unfortunate end to an evening that began with so much promise."

"At least we agree on that," Roebuck said.

"Captain Roebuck won't be persuaded, ma'am," said Cockrell. "I have learned that much."

"Let me have them," she said to Guillory, pointing to the reins.

"They will be looking for this carriage all over town, expecting these two to be inside it. It would seal their fate," Guillory said. "If they are to have any chance at all, I must deliver them to the tug pilot Fabini. He can take them away."

Roebuck said, "You two have your ears plugged. I say again, we are not going anywhere but to our ship and I already know the way. So," Roebuck bowed, "good night to you both."

It wasn't a look that she gave him so much as an inspection. Irritation had bumped the charm and poise from her face. Was this because she was afraid, concerned about his safety, or was it her nature? He didn't care for it, whatever it was.

Guillory said, "You must tell him, Doña Belén."

She attempted to ground Guillory into dust with her eyes.

He hesitated. It was clear how much Guillory wanted to avoid crossing her. Also clear that there was something she did not want Guillory to say. But he did it anyway, turning his eyes toward Roebuck with a surprising look of tenderness. "It is your sailors, Commander," he said.

Roebuck said, "My seamen on the *Savannah*?"

"No, I mean the men you have come here for, the ones who are missing. Those of the *Eliza Davidson* and the *America*."

Doña Belén growled at Guillory, no other word for it.

Guillory managed to put a little courage in his voice and said to her, "Admiral Brown. It must be Admiral Brown."

Roebuck said, "Admiral Brown?" dumbfounded that these two might be acquainted with Argentina's most famous man besides its ruler, Rosas.

Guillory said, "Yes, the admiral might be able to help you find those sailors. But you will need to go tonight—right now, in fact."

"They are alive after all?" Roebuck said, a feeling of vindication warming his insides.

Guillory said, "I am told they are. They have been enslaved to provide labor in coal mines in Argentine territory between the Uruguay and Paraná rivers."

Maybe Roebuck's apparent failure down here was not complete after all. He said, "Lead me to them, man, now." And then to Belén, "Thank you, madame, for a gratifying evening," hoping to retrieve a smile.

It didn't work. She said, "You have a friend it seems in Mr. Guillory."

Until now, Roebuck had believed she was a friend too. How long had Belén known about these sailors without telling him? She pulled a dip pen and tiny ink pot from her bag and quickly wrote a note, which she handed to him. Then Roebuck and Cockrell followed Guillory into the dark city.

CHAPTER 28

The pilot Fabini's tug was called *Perdita.* Her coal-fired engine sounded a low rhythm as it punched them through a headwind. There was no doubting her power, the way she made way against the current and through gusts that penetrated Roebuck's coat like needles of ice. Her sidewheels churned yellow foam. A thick stack chuffed smoke and her bow rolled dark water into white-pebbled windrows.

Lieutenant Cockrell, standing beside Roebuck, said, "What do you think, sir, five knots?"

"Seven, maybe." Seven knots or one hundred, Roebuck didn't care. Shipping on the *Perdita* was like riding in a sooty commode. According to Fabini, it would be another five hours on this trap before they reached Admiral Brown.

He and Cockrell stood at the rail, their breath steaming into the cold of Montevideo's antipodal winter. Roebuck's tired mind began a journey backward, first to the gunner's mates, calling him "Robby Run," then to the doña and how much less he understood her than he'd supposed, and then, as usual, back to Martin Roebuck, his father. After a while he found a spot on deck protected from the wind and lay down, shutting his eyes, waiting for sleep as smoke huffed up and out of the stack.

He must have dozed for some time because he awoke under a pile of cold air. Instead of rising, he pulled tight a moth-eaten wool blanket that someone had draped over him. There he shivered for a while before giving up and walking the deck to warm himself. The sun raised a sky over the big river's brown water, revealing leafless trees and waxen laurels on both shores. Beyond those were fields, some fallow and some littered with the chaff of harvest. There would be grain to feed an army here.

The Uruguay River formed the lower border of Entre Ríos, the most heavily disputed province in the civil war being fought between factions within Argentina and Uruguay. According to Guillory, the captive Americans were enslaved and forced to work at a mine somewhere in the Argentine territory of Entre Ríos.

Fabini was still behind the wheel; he must have stayed there through the night. Roebuck said to him, "How much longer?" Putting the question in Spanish.

"Soon."

Roebuck wondered what to expect. He said, "Are there ranches in the region?"

"Higher upriver. Here the land is very good for crops. It would be a waste to use it for beef. They can grow enough grass for feed in the highlands."

"The villages have beef?"

"Yes, of course, and lamb. Entre Ríos is full of meat."

"Game?"

"Game, too. The winter flocks will cover entire stretches of slack water, thousands upon thousands of fowl. Deer, too. But we don't eat venison so much. Why eat those pests with so many fat cows?" He laughed, pleased at such abundance.

No wonder the region was the object of competing attentions.

The clouds closed their gaps, blotting out the morning light, and rain soon followed. Roebuck beat his hands together for warmth. Further on, the mouth of another gaping river split the north shore.

"Rio Negro," Fabini said.

On a rise above the Rio Negro's mouth, men were mounted on big bays and roans. They had red blankets tied across their chests. Two wore bright red coats. Some slung muskets, others wooden clubs.

"Colorados?" Roebuck said, pointing to the men on horses. Colorados were the faction supported by Lechi, and as Guillory had hinted the night before, the French Admiral LeBlanc.

"Sí," Fabini said, without taking his eyes from the river. "Scouts."

The horsemen backed up and trotted off. The tug chugged past the river's mouth, staying on the Uruguay River.

Roebuck turned again to the pilot and said, "Are there always scouts here?"

"It is unusual."

"Any batteries?"

"Not before we meet Admiral Brown."

The tug sliced through shelves of fog and drizzle. A heron slowly lifted itself from a stand of reeds, flapping heavy dark wings.

Roebuck wondered about the mine Guillory had told him about last night where the crews of the *Eliza Davidson* and the *America* were enslaved and working. Was it defended? What chance did they have to find it? He needed to consider these questions in clean logical order, but the doña had left his mind agitated.

There were the questions Guillory had asked him about Houghton and the railway spur as well. Could he trust Fabini? He knew little about conditions here and had misjudged the doña. She had asked him so many questions. Now he was conscious of the fact that he should have been the one asking questions, trading for information rather than giving it away. He had been reticent with her and Guillory. Reticence was a weakness he had tried to rid himself of from time to time. Here was a good example of why. Because of it, he was ignorant of the war all around him, who held what territory, their strength, tactics. And unsure whom he could trust.

On the near bank a rooster strutted in front of a cottage, stopped to dig its beak into dirt, and gulped down what it found. Three dark-haired women had waded into the shallows and were scrubbing at something he couldn't see, skirts hitched above their knees, legs as brown as the water. They stopped and stared at the tug for at least a minute. A pair of mules brayed at their tethers.

The *Perdita* chugged upstream along the contour of a big dog-leg. Rounding the bend, she entered wide-open, slow-flowing water with boats in moorings along a shore village. Smoke rose from stubby stone chimneys.

"Sweet Lord," Roebuck said. Half a league ahead was a flotilla of ships arrayed across the river.

Fabini choked back the engine and said, "Here you find the great man and his ships. Admiral Guillermo Brown."

Roebuck knew of Brown. Every officer in this hemisphere did. Brown had founded the Argentine navy twenty or so years before and was famous for routing a Brazilian fleet of over thirty ships at Los Pozos. Roebuck was about to meet the New World's most successful living naval captain.

As they neared Brown's flagship, Roebuck pondered what the admiral would make of his predicament. Would he turn their tails and send them back? And as for the *Savannah*, by now everyone on board would be wondering about his disappearance. He could imagine their talk. "Robby's still running."

They reached Brown's flagship, Roebuck hoisting himself onto the deck through the entry port. He was greeted by silence, no ceremonial piping or side-boys to salute him. It was Roebuck's first time to board a ship as a visiting commander, and although he knew perfectly well that no one on board could possibly know his rank, he still couldn't stop feeling an odd resentment at the absence of ceremony. An officer led him and Fabini below to the ship's gallery, where Admiral Brown was at a desk scribbling with a pencil.

Fabini nodded and said, "Greetings, Admiral Brown," in Spanish, "may I present to you Commander Robert Chase Roebuck of the United States Ship *Savannah*. He comes with greetings from Doña Belén."

Brown rose and said, "Welcome." His tone was flat and maybe a little bored. He spoke with an Irish brogue tinged slightly by the Spanish he would naturally have acquired after so many years in Rio de la Plata.

"Doña Belén asked me to give you this," Roebuck said, handing Brown the letter she had written in haste the night before. The admiral looked at it for a moment, observing, Roebuck supposed, that it was not enclosed in an envelope.

Brown thanked Fabini and Fabini left, Roebuck suddenly worried that Fabini might be leaving for good. Brown unfolded the letter and read it out loud.

Thank you for your kindness in receiving this letter.
I was surprised and delighted to hear of your presence so close to us and wished we might have met.

I introduce Robert Chase Roebuck to you, an American officer in command of the USS Savannah. Although an American, he is neither dreadful nor an inveterate card player. In fact you will find that he is most trustworthy, has a complement of 350 men, and appears eager to put them to use in the service of your great cause.

Give my regards to your beautiful wife. I hope that she is well. Mr. Guillory continues in his prudent ways and sends you his compliments.

Your affectionate,
Belén Saavedra y Mancera

Roebuck thought it might have been a more courteous thing to read the letter silently, uncomfortable to hear himself referred to as if he weren't there.

Brown said, "She claims to be surprised."

"Yes, sir." The words dribbled reflexively from Roebuck's mouth.

Brown looked at him, calibrating. He said, "This letter is unsealed."

"It's real," Roebuck said, wondering if Brown recognized her hand. He thought he might, given the intimacy of the letter.

"The letter is hurried, your presence here is sudden, and you are alone."

"Well, yes, except for Lieutenant Cockrell." Roebuck did not know what to say. Guillory had suggested he avoid mentioning Lechi and not open this conversation with a request for help from Brown in finding the captive Americans.

"Where is your sword?"

"On my ship."

"An odd place for it," Brown said, and looked at the letter again. "I do not know that this is from Doña Belén."

"Perhaps you recognize her signature?"

"If I had another of her letters for comparison, I might. Unfortunately I must use memory, which decays rapidly."

Roebuck said, "Jonas Coe."

Brown started. "Say again."

"The name of your mount from her stables during your visit to Nahomi in January." When he and Cockrell left the doña outside the Club Londres, Roebuck thought Brown might question the letter's authenticity and so had asked her to tell him something only she and Brown would know.

Brown nodded. "Jonas Coe is an American, for several years my second in command. Now he is the admiral of the navy in Montevideo."

"So I have heard."

Brown sat down and motioned toward a stool in the corner. Roebuck pulled it out and sat.

"There's something you're not telling me," Brown said.

"How do you—"

"I'd rather you tell me now," Brown cut him off, "instead of later."

Roebuck was out of his depth. He had a feeling Brown could see in all directions at once.

So Roebuck told him. Everything.

***

Brown and Roebuck were sharing supper. Brown's hair was full and white. His chest and shoulders were a match for the bullion epaulets and gold-braided chevrons sewn to the front of his tunic. Roebuck wondered how he himself would look gray-haired, wearing his own admiral's uniform and was surprised by how much he liked that idea.

Brown was saying, "You'd do well to understand something about Rio de la Plata, Commander. No one is equal to your trust. Not a single solitary soul."

Although Roebuck liked Brown, he didn't care for it when a person told him what everyone else was like. He said, "Excluding present company, of course."

Brown's head tilted very slowly to the right and stopped. He held it there as if he were positioning a measuring instrument. "What are you doing here, Commander Roebuck?"

"I have told you, sir, we are here to recover a group of enslaved American sailors."

"What do you think is happening here?" Brown didn't wait for an answer. "If you are defeated or turned back, your failure will be described as a triumph over the greed of North American ambitions. You and your country will be mocked. The territory here is hostile. You know nothing about your objective other than it is somewhere within the vastness of Entre Ríos." Brown had a look of sympathy that was at odds with his words. "You won't last a day on the plains, if you happen to be pondering the idea."

That was precisely what Roebuck had been pondering. He said, "What do you suggest, sir?"

Brown mopped a plate full of gravy with a thick slice of bread. "There is a man, Chacón, who can help you. He commands a group of volunteers, gauchos."

Roebuck said, "What is a gaucho?"

"Horsemen," Brown said, "fighters. But for me to help you find Chacón, you must help me. That is fair, you agree?"

Roebuck didn't know what agreeing meant in this case but saw no other way. "Yes," he said.

"Here is how you can help me: Take your men to the upper Paraná River and deny the mercenary Garibaldi any resupply of powder and shot from his Unitario allies upriver. If you promise to do this, I can arrange for Chacón to help you. He will know how to guide you to the mine where Mr. Guillory and Doña Belén say the American sailors are. Nothing happens between these rivers that Chacón does not know."

Roebuck shrugged. He didn't like the idea of involving the *Savannah* or its men in Brown's war. It was exactly the sort of entanglement the U.S. Navy—or, as far as that went, the United States government—would do its best to avoid. The consequences to his career and reputation could be catastrophic. But that wasn't all. Roebuck had the irritating sensation of being manipulated, whether by the doña, whose position was an utter mystery to him, or by Brown, he wasn't sure. He had recently been struck by the idea that he would not be here at all had Lechi never shown up when Roebuck was dining with Doña Belén and her friends at the Club Londres. Had it been a coincidence? Who was on what side and for what reason? Rio de la Plata was a wilderness to him. Roebuck hesitated, the weight of it all unnerving him.

Brown said, "What chance do you have alone and operating entirely on rumors?"

"I see no reason to trust you," Roebuck said, "any more than I might a rumor."

Brown's brows worked themselves into sharp lines, his eyes a pair of blue sparks beneath them. He said, "You take chances, Mr. Roebuck." Then he said something that surprised Roebuck. "I believe Mr. Guillory may be right about what has happened to the crews of those brigs. France is a world away. Officials in Paris have little influence over what their naval commanders undertake down here. And we hear tales about LeBlanc's troubles in France and his acquisitive nature."

Roebuck said, "You suggest that LeBlanc is acting for himself and not for France?"

Brown said, "There's no abiding for men like LeBlanc. No rules of war. What they leave is ruin, believing so distant a place as this could not matter to their reputation in Europe or their honor. I tell you, young man, If you find those sailors and discover the cause of their disappearance, those responsible will do everything they can to grind you into nothing and make it as if you were never here."

This prospect did not sound very inviting to Roebuck so he agreed to Brown's proposal. Although he would not supply one hundred men as Brown had asked. He would not put the *Savannah* at risk by robbing her of that much of her strength.

CHAPTER 29

Brown had wanted one hundred men. In the end Roebuck agreed to fifty. He thought of Houghton's glee in talking about court martial. The possibility seemed more real now than ever.

Roebuck and Cockrell waited as Fabini returned to tow the *Savannah*'s fifty men behind the *Perdita* up the Uruguay River. Now in less than four days, the officers, including Pemberton and midshipmen Watt and Rowan, were climbing onto the deck of Brown's *Nueve de Julio*. It was a sight for sore eyes. A handful of the *Savannah*'s seamen and thirty-five Marines were doing the same on two other ships in Brown's flotilla called *Chacabuco* and *American*.

Once introductions were made, Brown told Roebuck and his officers that their first stop would be Gualeguaychú. His flotilla was carrying food and building materials for the people of that town. At suppertime, Roebuck, Pemberton, and Cockrell joined the admiral in his cabin and watched him carve a slab of beefsteak on his plate into neat slices and spearing several of them one after another into his mouth. When Brown had washed the last of these down with half a glass of Mendoza, Roebuck asked why the Europeans seemed to stake so much in this region.

"It is because we resist," Brown said. "The French and British tell us, 'Open your rivers to trade.' Our rivers have been open for the better part of twenty-five years, but only to those who respect our laws. The French presume to travel the Paraná as if it flowed through the Loire Valley.

If our ships sailed up the Seine without stopping to declare themselves or anteing up for the privilege, would they see it in the same way?"

"What of the British?" Pemberton said.

"Because we cannot allow the French, we must refuse the British. If not, the Argentine Confederation will be pulled to pieces by the great powers and their proxies here." He drained his glass. "It isn't just nations that plague us. This land between the Paraná and Uruguay rivers is disputed because of men like LeBlanc, Suarez the Uruguayan President, a man who stole the office, and the mercenary Garibaldi. These are men who see borders as a cause of violence and war.

"And what do such men say?" Brown said. "They appeal to universal principles. Republican ideals, they proclaim, must unite men. And under the force of these proclamations, they grab our land. Such men without limits, without borders, see themselves as bearers of a vision for mankind's future. But anyone with the first bit of sense," Brown continued, "knows that borders are necessary for peace and that without peace the people will never prosper. That before we gain the kingdom of freedom we must leave behind thieving and violence. We must have respect that stops others from taking what basic human morality and principle recognizes as ours."

Pemberton said, "And this is what brings you up these rivers so far from the sea?"

"First," Brown said, "we are here to deliver food and materials to those who have been burnt out of their homes and are starving in the aftermath of the mercenary Garibaldi's last visit. And next we will chase him from our land. For he has come in force to Entre Rios."

That name again, Garibaldi. It bothered Roebuck that he could not remember how he recognized but could not place it. As far as what Brown said, he didn't know whether it was true or not. Might be or might be otherwise; Roebuck wasn't in South America to find out. He said, "Do you face a strong navy?"

"Our navies are similar in size," said Brown. "But Garibaldi's ships are manned by very few Uruguayans." Brown paused to unfasten the top button of his coat. "They are crewed and commanded by mercenaries from Italy, France, and Britain, here for plunder and power. We Argentines fight to defend our homes." Brown said, "T

he last time Garibaldi traveled up this river, he stripped three towns bare of grain, clothing, and livestock. Drunken mercenaries from his ships put homes and churches to the torch."

"Where is he now?" Roebuck said.

"We lost him in a thick fog just past Martín García Island. I was certain he'd returned to this river. That's why we are here. But the audacious man instead chose the Paraná, and now he sails through the heart of our republic." Brown sounded impressed. "He is not in Argentina to strip away food and clothing this time. He's there for territory."

Putting both hands down on the table, the great Admiral pushed himself to his feet and grabbed his glass for a toast. It was empty.

Cockrell filled it, and lifting his own glass said, "To Argentina, may liberty dwell forever in the hearts of her people, peace inhabit her lands, and freedom flow in the stream of her rivers."

They all stood, touching glasses, Roebuck wondering what had happened to Cockrell's gift for understatement.

***

Soft rain fell in Gualeguaychú, a sprout of a town along the southern bank of one of the Uruguay River's tributaries. Brown chose an anchorage just south of town where a line of small boats, one tethered to the next, floated in the stream. A nag waded in to drink, its ribs visible beneath a black coat, bony withers jutting. On shore a few ancient boats shed paint in long jagged peels.

Onshore, Roebuck followed Brown, who walked with a forward lean, as if he were trying to cross a line chest first.

Brown turned and waited for Roebuck to catch up. "Look lively, man," he said.

When Roebuck was beside Brown, he asked how he would meet Chacón. Brown said, "I have already sent messengers by horseback to him with instructions to rendezvous tomorrow at dawn north of Paysandú, further up the Uruguay." Brown had decided on a new plan that started by combining Roebuck and his fifty men with Chacón upriver, where they would begin their move to free the American sailors.

Roebuck said, "Very good, Admiral."

"Afterward, you and Captain Pemberton's Marines will prevent attempts by Garibaldi's upriver allies to resupply him. I will send details when I have them."

"Aye aye, sir," Pemberton, who had shown none of the difficulty Roebuck had in keeping up with Brown's fast walking,

added, "You can depend on us."

They came to a long, burned-out building. Brown grunted and motioned Roebuck to go ahead of him through the broad entry. They both stopped past the threshold. The stink of the place was enough to melt the horns off a goat.

Families were lying about in small groups. A black-robed priest with a white sash high around his waist entered through a door to the left, carrying two buckets of water. He was followed by two men Roebuck guessed were acolytes, also carrying water. The priest emptied his buckets into a tub and a host of children ran over, dipping in wooden cups and guzzling it down. When the priest saw Brown, he smiled and came toward them, moving like a tadpole, still one second and darting the next. The men shook hands and grinned at one another.

"Father Cosme Damián Olascoaga is the vicar in the Diocese of Gualeguaychú," said Brown in Spanish. "Father, meet Robert Chase Roebuck, commander of the American ship *Savannah*."

Roebuck said, "A great pleasure, father," in Spanish.

The little man turned a warm smile to Roebuck, taking his right hand, and saying, "Welcome, welcome, Commander."

"Commander Roebuck has generously agreed to help our cause," Brown said and then he nodded at the scene in front of them, surveying the dismal state of the people in the vicar's care. "What is this?" He said.

"Their homes were torched, Admiral Brown, what else? I am hungry for some good news. What have you brought us?"

"Salt beef, beans, dried fish, tools, and almost two hundred crates of nails."

"We will store the provisions in the church," said Olascoaga. "Follow me." He scampered out and they headed into town.

The church anchored a broad, somnolent plaza where children huddled around a low, smoky fire. A woman in a faded coat and a long-hooped skirt crossed the square with an old fowling gun over her shoulder. A soft rain beaded on the bare arms and shoulders of two natives, bright orange bands holding up their black hair in thick piles. Each hauled a stack of spotted furs.

In front of the church, Brown said, "You can wait here, Commander." He and the vicar climbed stone stairs and passed inside.

Next door, a group of men in striped ponchos and odd felt hats worked on a domed adobe building with tall arched windows. Roebuck watched them for thirty minutes as they leaned a makeshift ladder against the face of the building, climbed up with a wire brush, and scoured away black scorch marks.

"It's a school, Commander," said Olascoaga in Spanish, walking quickly down the steps, Brown on his heels. "Garibaldi and his men looted the town and burnt buildings, including this one. Everything inside was lost. Desks, books, pencils. We even had magnifiers the students used to observe insects and sketch the details of flower petals."

Roebuck tried to see it, but the town suggested little besides black char and huddling people. He noticed a headless statue.

"The Virgin," said Olascoaga, following Roebuck's gaze.

The harsh smell of an extinguished fire wafted out the open doors of the church's portico. Roebuck realized that it had been torched inside as well as out. He said, "I can see commandering food and livestock to provision ships, but this?"

Olascoaga answered, "The church represents two things Garibaldi and his Republicans object to. The first is anything old, tied to the past. The second is authority. So what do they do? They replace old tyrannies with modern ones and dress them in a gown called Progress."

"A weak form of liberation," said Brown, "With its own superstitions fresh as their mother's milk."

It finally came to Roebuck where he'd heard of this Garibaldi. The Baltimore *Sun* had published an essay from Alexandre Dumas about Garibaldi's life in South America. Roebuck had been transfixed by the Dumas story *The Man in the Iron Mask*, in which a king's twin, born to a great name and towering social standing, was ultimately cursed. He remembered how the book ended. The twin was left with nothing, not his name, not even his face.

After that, Roebuck made a point of reading anything Dumas wrote, including the essay extolling Garibaldi's defense of republican ideals in Uruguay. Roebuck had formed a sympathy for the Italian based on this account and recalled a detail from the essay. He said, "Wasn't Garibaldi tortured in this very place, Gualeguaychú?"

"No," said the vicar, "it was Paysandú."

That was the town they would go to to meet the gaucho.

Brown hesitated, and then said, "So perhaps his motive is revenge. Not the noblest of man's sentiments."

"Alexandre Dumas claims that Garibaldi is a defender of justice and the right of men to govern themselves," said Roebuck.

"Garibaldi and his mercenaries have stripped four towns on this river bare of food, clothing, and animals," said Brown. "His men have torched homes, schools, and churches. He supported the overthrow of President Oribe, a man duly elected by the people of Uruguay. Burn a man's house to the ground, steal his livestock, and pull the shoes off his feet, and…" Again Brown hesitated. He seemed wary of the emotion creeping into his voice.

"What Admiral Brown means," Olascoaga said, "is judge a man by what comes of his actions, not by the virtue he or anyone else claims for them."

***

It was night when the *Savannah*'s men crowded onto the deck of the schooner that would return them upriver to meet Chacón. Stretching out on the deck, Roebuck squeezed all six feet of his length under a blanket. On the near bank, gray branches of great leafless trees loomed above him like winter spiders. He dozed thinking of webs.

Dawn came cold and wet. The day was half over by the time sunlight replaced rain, streaming through a line of bare trees to the east. The schooner passed the Uruguayan town of Paysandú for an anchorage a mile upriver. The sky lifted itself to reveal a single horseman high above the southern bank, the Americans were being shuttled ashore toward this man and his horse. In every direction but east, the ground was open, broad hills rolling up from the river.

The horseman motioned for Roebuck to come up to him.

"Let me take twenty Marines up there first, sir, to make sure there's no mischief," Pemberton said.

"Mr. Watt will come with me. That is enough."

Pemberton's onion-eyes bulged.

Roebuck continued, "We must signify our trust, Mr. Pemberton." He and Watt scrambled up, their breath steaming.

When they reached the man, Roebuck said in Spanish, "I am Robert Chase Roebuck, commander of the U.S.S. *Savannah*."

"Sí."

"And you, sir, who are you?"

"You know who I am."

"Commander Chacón?"

The man nodded, half of his face in shadow. "Tell me, Roebuck, can you ride a horse or do you only travel in water like a fish?"

Chacón wore a red Phrygian cap. A gold bauble hanging down from the tip made Roebuck think of a sleeping cap.

"I ride, but we have many men." Roebuck pointed to them down on the bank.

"And we have many horses," said Chacón, and called out "Oi!" without turning.

A company of gauchos rode up from a swale, churning a muddy path, most wearing fringed white pants, their feet wrapped in a thick white material. They carried lances with carved tips, charred to a hard point. Some had rifles holstered on their mounts. Half held the reins of unmounted horses; a fog of steam rose from the snorting animals.

"We have horses for those that ride. The rest will be in that," Chacón said, pointing at a wagon pulled by a team of mules. "Our camp is fifteen miles from here. Three hours if we leave now." His poncho was a rich blue embroidered with gold. He wore knee-length riding boots. Besides the pistols on either side of his waist, he strapped a saber to his horse. While not exactly bright, his brown eyes shone with a hard clarity.

Leaving turned out to be more difficult than Chacón anticipated. Only a score of the *Savannah*'s men could ride and the wagon was too small for all those who didn't, so many had to share a mount, their arms wrapped around a gaucho's waist. It was a picture that did not flatter the Americans.

Roebuck had learned to ride as a boy, his mother insisting that a gentleman must know horses. He had said he was no gentleman, and she was the daughter of money not blood. "Yes," she had said, "but in America, I am a noblewoman if I so choose, and my sons, princes. So you will ride a horse." His father, overhearing them, stepped into the room to say, "You'll ride, boy, and like it."

Roebuck rode but hadn't liked it. He was and remained bewildered by the sentiment so many held for their animals. Riding had always produced a feeling in him of desperation for which the only cure was the water and some wind.

The top of the bluff gave them a long view of an unbroken plain. Watt had his watercolors out and was sketching a group of the horsemen, the plain to their backs.

Chacón said, "Admiral Brown wants me to take you where the foreigners dig holes and like to play in the dirt."

"You know it?"

"Yes, I know it. It is where all forms of men go in, but only Frenchmen come out."

They rode through the afternoon on an endless flat pan of low scrub and dirt, Chacón turning from time to time to scowl at the *Savannah*'s riders and complain about their incompetence in the saddle. Roebuck's legs told him it had been too long since he'd been on a horse. After a time, trees appeared, tracing the line of a creek, then small groves, and soon after, woods. The gauchos rode easily, their silver bracelets jangling. Loose pants hid the shape of their legs and spurs peeked out from the bottoms. They didn't pin ribbons above the narrow brims of their felt hats, as cowboys did in the States, but feathered them with plumes of red, orange, and yellow.

Suddenly, three of the gauchos shot ahead of the column, two quickly branching off at ninety degrees from the trail, the third doing the same farther on. Roebuck saw a large creature in the space between the riders raise its small beaked head and start to run upright, carried quickly by two long bony legs, its neck a thick rope, the lilt of its head somehow out of rhythm with the rest of it. The third rider chased, but the creature was too fast, although maybe not too smart, because it ran straight into the other two who had positioned themselves to intercept it. They each whirled three balls connected by leather cord over their head before zinging them at the running beast. The first man was off target, but not the second. The cord entangled the beast's legs, tripping it. In seconds, the riders were dismounting and putting their long daggers to its neck.

"I tell them, 'Beef, eat beef, we have so much,'" said Chacón, "but they like to eat what they catch. It's their way. And they love the flesh of the rhea."

"What kind of beast is a rhea?" Roebuck said.

"A bird."

"Why does it not fly off?"

Chacón laughed out loud. "Fly?" and he turned back to his men, telling them what Roebuck had just asked. They cackled.

Chacón said, "There are fish that fly, are there not, Commander?"

"Yes."

"And the parrot speaks."

Roebuck nodded.

"This bird stands and runs like a man. No flying."

When those who'd killed the rhea caught up, Roebuck saw that they'd wrapped the chests and shoulders of their mounts. "Their horses are bandaged?"

"They cut the bird's meat into strips and wrap them flat on their horse as they ride," Chacón said. "Sweat cures the meat. Horse-cured rhea is something to savor, Commander." He reached into a small leather pouch and extended a hand that held something wrinkled and brown. "Try it."

"I ate biscuits and bacon on the ship," Roebuck lied.

"Eat it."

Roebuck shook his head.

"Now, amigo," Chacón said. He did not say it in a threatening way, but Roebuck understood that to answer 'no' would be useless, so he took the meat and bit into it. "It's sweet."

"Sprinkled with Brazilian cane, the world's finest," said Chacón.

Roebuck popped the rest into his mouth, chewed, and said, "Disgusting." The idea of horse sweat was lodged in his imagination. He was suddenly aware of the mounts all around him, how they stank, each one a fetid pool. Nausea pricked the back of his neck, his forehead bubbled with it.

Vomiting from the saddle would not impress his hosts. Wouldn't be a commanding image for his men either. Roebuck diverted his mind by tying knots in his imagination, starting with a double car-rick, then a sheepshank, going through ten of them before uncap-ping his canteen and taking a swig. He spat and tried to keep his stomach from total rebellion.

The road narrowed. Horses spread out, treading shrubs on either side. Their hooves became wet with green matter, the smell of camphor and sage replacing the stink of the animals. This was a relief and Roebuck didn't puke. Chacón splashed across a shallow ford and cut behind a buffer of low spiky trees. And out of nowhere, they were in a busy camp screened from the road.

Three hours on horseback had made tired little princesses out of the *Savannah's* men, full of complaints about chafing from the rub of their mounts, stiff joints, sore behinds.

A fire rose in a wide pit in the camp's center, where men piled on charcoal and propped an enormous iron grill over top. The grill featured large cuts of meat, black blood sausage, trussed birds, onions, and roots. The smell of cooking flesh and the sizzle of fat put an end to the complaints. Roebuck's appetite emerged from its rhea-induced retreat.

A man invited him and Pemberton into a round mud hut where Chacón was already seated on the huge skull of an ox, a fire kindled on the dirt in front of him. Fire-smoke escaped from a round opening above, but not all of it. A thin pall hung in the air. Chacón's captains were pulling beef from the spit and stuffing it into their greasy mouths.

"Come in, come in, amigos," said Chacón in Spanish. "Wine for these men," he shouted. "Or would you prefer rum?" He raised a hollow bull's horn in his left hand and drank from its mouth.

Roebuck said, "Wine for us both."

After swallowing a cut of beef, Chacón began dictating a message about the movements of the French and the Colorados to a man scribbling to his right. He paused for two swigs from the horn.

Pemberton said, "Why does he talk like that?"

"Probably can't write," said Roebuck.

All the horses were corralled in a pen just a few yards from the door. Their reek mixed with smoke and the smell of burnt drippings.

Roebuck needed something besides the taste of sweat-cured rhea in his mouth. The wine arrived and he guzzled the entire cup. Then came rough clay plates full of sizzling beef and some kind of green leaf. He dug in.

Chacón kept to his ox skull across the fire, eventually rolling a cigar the size of a small club. It wasn't long before his officers were doing the same, adding tobacco smoke to the haze. He cast a huge smoking, drinking, dictating shadow on the wall behind him, dispatching every matter brought to him with a nonchalance that seemed godlike. As one officer departed from beside the fire, another took his place. Here was a military base where operations did not seem to cease. When Chacón finished his dictation, he motioned Roebuck and Pemberton closer and gave them a smile that was light a few teeth.

"North Americans. Yes. Tell me why we in the south can't have what you have. Peace and men who depart the power of their office when it is time. Why must we down here be always at each other's throats?"

Roebuck began to translate quickly in a low voice for Pemberton, a good way to avoid answering.

"It is because you in the North are shopkeepers," continued Chacón. "The man with the biggest bank becomes president. And when you retire from president you go back to selling things, only now for much more."

Roebuck took a bite of blood sausage. Juices ran down the blade of his knife.

"My men were raised on the meat of spiders and fortified with scales scraped from living snakes," said Chacón. "For the first five years of my life, I ate nothing but dirt and drank only what fills the Iberá swamp, each gulp swimming with larvae."

After Roebuck translated, Pemberton said, "You mean to tell us that you're mean, meaner than us."

"What does he say?" said Chacón.

Roebuck translated.

"Mean? Hah! No, we are more than that. We are cruel, spiteful. Virtue has no appetite for the flesh of spiders or the scum of the swamp. But we know something you don't, you who come to us in the tall ships, the British, French, and now you North Americans. The Spanish during the revolution were the same. You come and you fight but soon go home, but the fight doesn't go with you. No, the fight is left for us to finish. But what finishes? Nothing. It never finishes because more come on the tall ships. Losing the fight means nothing to you. Just leave, go to someplace better. Napoleon loses and he keeps his head. He even comes back to rule France once more. What happens to France in defeat? They lose an island here, a colony there. So what?

"If I lose, we lose everything. Suffer everything. I have seen men forced to watch their daughters violated, watch their sons disemboweled as dogs feed on their intestines."

Chacón had dexterity. Roebuck had never seen a man who could drink and talk at the same time, pausing between sentences to take a pull of rum from the horn, enunciating every word with a mouth half full of liquid, his sentences short and clear. The amount of rum the man drank that night would have put down all five of the *Savannah*'s lieutenants.

"But with you it is a shopkeeper's war." Chacón drained another horn. "With us you must win and there is only one way to win, do you hear me?"

Roebuck said, "We are listening."

"It is easy to be hurt. To be shot, even. Easy. Risking that is nothing here. Victory is where the pain is. You have to make your enemy watch as you stick your cock into anybody he treasures, his women, children. You must be the one who feeds the dogs. This is not for shopkeepers or Napoleon or any other man who is not of this place."

"You fight like savages," said Pemberton as Roebuck translated.

"We feed on the hearts of savages," Chacón said. "Savages learned long ago to fear us. No, we must fight as only the devil himself can. We do this and give ourselves to him, no? We lose everything inside. A man here gains power, why give it back? It is his. He has it at the cost of his soul and that is something he can never get back."

Roebuck said, "There is a way back, Comandante, always."

Chacón shook his empty horn and it was quickly filled. "Way back, where? You must show me this way back because I know no one who has ever found it."

"The man's drunk." Pemberton shook his head.

Roebuck said, "What can you tell us about the mines?"

Chacón said, "You think the captives you seek are working in one of the coal mines in territory controlled by the Unitarios?" referring to the rebel Argentines supporting the French and Colorados.

"That is the information we have," Roebuck said.

"That is horse shit."

Roebuck used his knife to cut off a bite of beef. It steamed on the tip a moment before he eased it into his mouth. "Go on," he said.

"The coal mines are small, new. And in Uruguay, not here in Entre Ríos."

Roebuck swished the red wine in his clay mug. "Mendoza?" he said.

"What else?"

He gulped it down and a steward quickly refilled the cup. Pemberton raised his to be topped off.

Roebuck said, "This morning you said there was a place where men go in but don't come out."

"What I said was only Frenchmen come out. And perhaps a few of their Colorado dogs. It is a mine where they take something very valuable from the earth. Mining coal, they say, but that is no coal. The French work very hard to hide it. They move what they mine only at night in guarded carts to the Uruguay River. There they smuggle it to Montevideo or straight to French ships."

"When do we leave for this place?" said Roebuck.

Chacón said they would leave in six hours and ride through the night, unless Roebuck's fragile men broke into pieces in which case they would have to stop and sweep them up. Chacón said the mine was garrisoned with at least seventy men, and Roebuck could expect fortifications, wicker cages and gabions filled with dirt and stone.

"If it is silver or gold," said Chacón, "for every measure they find, they must move one million of the same measure in rock. It is why they must always find fresh men, like the sailors from your country. The life is worked out of them."

They slept there on the dirt floor by the fire, heads resting on pillows stuffed with grass. When they rose and began their ride, Roebuck felt the pain in his bottom. It was no ache, but a spike that shot up his spine into his head. Martin Roebuck had often compared his son's ass to his brain. Roebuck had until this moment assumed that was mere metaphor, but now he understood the connection. Most of the *Savannah*'s men had picked up thick wool in camp and wrapped it around their calves to protect against the chafing. The men riding in the wagon were jolted around enough to have complaints of their own.

After several hours, Chacón called for a halt by a shaded stream to rest and water the horses. Roebuck dismounted and walked to the stream to drink, moving like all his joints were fused together.

"Howdy Captain, how does your mount ride?" It was Cockrell, smiling for Christ's sake.

"All right, I suppose."

"Mine's fine for a mare, sir. These gauchos are iron-assed and do well enough in the saddle, if you think highly of riding like a Comanche. But they wouldn't do in Texas. That's where you find men who can handle a horse."

Roebuck had heard enough big talk. He turned away, wondering how much sand his men would show once the talk was over and the fighting started.

CHAPTER 30

The plains here were called Las Pampas for the wool-topped grass growing in tall, feathery clumps. When the sun went down, it was cold, and Roebuck shivered as he followed Chacón into the darkness, scrambling up a steep hill, occasionally slipping in loose rock and soil. Despite his stiffness, Roebuck was glad to be off the back of a horse, putting one foot in front of the other. Pemberton was with them, and two of the chieftain's captains. The others stayed hidden in the glen below.

The moon lit a shallow gully with a smooth dirt path cut into its side.

"Your mine, Capitan, is down that path," said Chacón.

"Let's go for a look," said Roebuck.

"I go no farther," said Chacón.

"Wha-what?" Roebuck stuttered.

"My men believe the place is cursed," Chacón said. "They are afraid to enter. Those who do are never seen again. This mine belongs to ogres or devils made to look like men, who consume the flesh of their enemies."

"You don't believe that," Roebuck said. "You said it was Colorados and the French."

"If I tell them, 'There is no reason to be afraid,' do you think that would cure their fear?"

"But you are here to help us."

Chacón said, "Help to get you this place and here you are." He turned to walk away but stopped to add, "We will wait here for you until it is one hour past the dawn and not a minute more."

"Impossible," Roebuck said. "That will not give us time to scout the mine, prepare, and attack. We need more time, Comandante."

"You have until then, pass the time as you like."

When Roebuck gave Pemberton the news, the Marine captain said, "What happened to sticking your cock into everything?"

***

Roebuck ignored his wet uniform. He ignored the winter air that felt like a suit of ice. A half moon was all but gone behind the western hills, casting just enough light to reveal a prodigious flow of river which separated him and his detail of men from the mining camp. His uniform was soaked because he and his men had just failed in their first attempt to cross. This failure occurred shortly after Pemberton had gone back to a position outside of the fortified entrance to the camp. That was where most of the *Savannah*'s men waited.

Roebuck and seven others concealed themselves behind the bushy heads of pampas grass across the river from the camp's rear. They were trying to get their courage up for another try at crossing. He and Pemberton had agreed that Roebuck would launch a diversion to pull the mine's defenders toward where he was now and away from the entrance. Crossing the river into the camp was the way they had decided to do this. Pemberton and his Marines would try to penetrate a front entrance weakened by the diversion.

Roebuck said, "We'll cross now." *Or try*, he thought, conscious that so much could go wrong between this bank and the other, a lot of ways to drown if you considered it.

Across the river were two squat adobe buildings, each barely lit by lamps strung from a porch beam. Roebuck had seen three men in nothing but blouses and drawers exit from these buildings to use the latrine. These were barracks filled with sleeping members of the camp's garrison, making it a very good place to start a noisy fight. The guard standing in lamplight swung his arms in an effort to keep warm.

"That's our landing," he said, pointing to a flat spot twenty yards downstream from the guard.

The Marines with him cradled .52-caliber Jenks carbines. Roebuck thought its levered side breach was odd looking, but Pemberton had assured him there was no weapon easier to open and close. Pemberton meant *loading* but hadn't used that word. A Marine could fire it twice as fast as a musket. Deadly from short range but not from a distance, no sir, a death wish is what Pemberton called it from a distance. So Roebuck had to fetch them close.

Five Marines were with Roebuck—the insurrectionist Vermont, Callahan, Rowe, and two men Pemberton had recruited from his Chickahominy tribe, called Sh'kook and Megedagik. Those two had been working to weave a float from tree branches and hollow stalks of pampas grass. It was flimsy, but flimsy would have to do.

"As you already know, the water is going to be very cold," Roebuck said to them. "You'll feel it in your chests. This time, don't let that frighten you. Just keep breathing, and slowly." He had seen frantic men lose the ability to inhale in the shock of cold water. It was a good way to die.

They waded in, each gripping the float with one hand and paddling with the other, heads above the surface. Roebuck's lungs constricted in the frigid water and he fought the impulse to gulp air. They had topped the float with six grenades, matches, carbines, and cartridge boxes in order to keep them dry. Roebuck kept his knuckled knife sheathed to his belt. He said, "Breathe deep boys but breathe easy and kick hard. Keep your feet underwater. Make no splashes," his voice carrying just enough for them to hear.

The current took hold, dragging them beyond their patch on the opposite bank.

"Harder, boys!" Roebuck said. "Kick, goddamn you!"

They kicked all right, more so as the current pulled them down. A stabbing pain went through the back of Roebuck's right thigh. It was rebelling against all the effort. He instinctively kicked it straight and grabbed the spot with both hands. Loosened from the raft, the undercurrent soon pulled him down. Despite his useless leg, he clawed with all his strength against the pull, going down and down, hitting the riverbed.

Arms exhausted, chest screaming, he pushed off the bottom with his good leg. But the current took him, saying, *stop fighting, preserve your breath*, his lungs expanding, exploding even. Was he up or down, bottom or top? And so what?

And then in an instant, cool air on his face, Roebuck staggered to his feet in a shallow by the bank. It felt like every one of his organs was pounding to get out. He turned toward the bank and tripped face first, the smell of mud and decay soon in his nostrils. He massaged his right leg and waited for the strength to return.

"Captain Roebuck!" Vermont was calling for him from upriver, barely audible.

"Here I am, Vermont." Roebuck rose and began to work his way slowly up the bank toward the Marine's voice. In a few minutes he was with the others, surprised to see how comfortable and easy they were, each with a carbine slung over his shoulder and a cutlass sheathed at his side. They had not experienced the river as he had.

Vermont said, "We thought we'd lost you, Captain."

"No such luck," Roebuck said. "We're here to attract the garrison toward us. Shoot and move, let them think we are more than we are." He would throw a grenade to signal to Pemberton. The Marine was not to make his move until he heard the signal.

He grabbed one of the grenades. The others did the same. Roebuck struck a match and touched it to the fuse. Bright sparks hissed. He jumped to his feet, heart racing, about to let it fly at the guard.

"Whoa, sir," said Vermont. "The fuses are cut for seven seconds."

Roebuck said, "Yes," and held on, controlling his breathing, measuring the distance against the weight he felt in his hand as someone said, "Make her count, Captain."

"Five, four, three—" He was aware now of his down-count, aware that he needed to let it go, *throw, goddamn it.* He pitched it hard and tried to make it straight. The grenade bounced once, turning over in the air, the nitrate smell of burnt match emanating from its fuse, trailing a boiled-egg quality in the smoke.

The guard had no time to dodge. *Boom!* The grenade exploded and Roebuck saw his contorted body frozen in its flash.

Uniformed men began to pour out of the barracks into the dark, their voices confused and afraid. Those of the *Savannah*'s men who were safe on the other bank began to shoot their carbines to make a diversion.

This was the first grenade Roebuck had ever thrown. It was a hell of a thing to see and it seemed to put the fear of God into their enemy. He wanted to throw another.

Megedagik rose up to throw his, aiming at a group running from the nearest of the two barracks. Roebuck couldn't see their uniforms clearly and he hoped to God they were French rather than Colorados, having no idea what trouble killing Uruguayans would cause. *Boom!* Another beautiful explosion.

Rowe threw the third grenade at the other barracks. Howls of pain resulted.

A firm French voice called out, an officer.

"He's having them fall in on the right, sir," said Vermont, translating.

They were French, all right, thank God.

"Sh'kook," Roebuck said, "Hold your grenade until they form and then put it right in the middle of them."

"Aye aye, sir," said Sh'kook, set to deliver the fourth missile.

The French came together in two tight ranks between the barracks, one kneeling in front of the other, close enough for Roebuck to hear the tear of paper cartridges and the scrape of ramrods in musket barrels. Sh'kook threw. The grenade bounced and rolled all the way to their line. The next moment was impossibly long as the French threw themselves to the ground, everyone waiting for the thing to go off. It didn't, a dud.

Roebuck said, "Down!" as the ranks rose up again and fired, the balls clicking loudly as they flew overhead. "Next grenade!"

It was Vermont's turn and his fuse was already lit. He reared back, not bothering to get up from his knees, and threw. The explosion opened a big gap in the line. The French broke, so many dark outlines turning to run. Vermont's grenade, its mayhem, was the tipping point.

Rowe and Sh'kook began to return fire with their carbines. More of the fighters arrived, some with torches, and spread out over the area. Had they come from the entrance? Callahan lit the last grenade and counted to four before quickly standing to throw it. Before the Marine could kneel again, musket balls punched him down the bank. Roebuck turned to see his lifeless body bobbing face-down in the current.

Roebuck guessed that maybe half of the garrison was now in the camp's rear, in front of him. It wouldn't get much better for Pemberton. He listened for the Marine captain's attack but could hear nothing above the din.

The French formed again and found the range. Balls snapped over them, getting closer. A coordinated volley forced Roebuck and his men down the bank, their boots in the river, musket balls plunking in behind them. They had to keep returning fire or watch the French walk over and load each of them up with musket balls.

Roebuck said, "Spread out. Shoot and move." He looked again toward Callahan, but the Marine had floated away.

They worked down the bank now. Vermont popped up and fired. Rowe stood to do the same, but immediately fell back, clutching his elbow. "Damn ball broke my arm," he called. "I can feel it. Oh God, oh Lord."

"Stay down," said Roebuck as he picked up Rowe's carbine. Roebuck rose to a knee, saw a soldier coming fast, sighted, and pulled the trigger. *Click*—nothing. The powder blister and charge had been dislodged. Sh'kook took aim and brought the running man down, close enough for Roebuck to hear the thud of the man's body as he hit the ground and then heard his groaning.

"I need your cartridge box, Rowe." The Marine had his eyes closed in a grimace.

"My belt is behind you, sir. I unhitched it."

Roebuck grabbed the belt and felt for the two leather loops attaching it to the cartridge box. He found them and yanked the box away.

He had only ever loaded one of these Jenks carbines at Fort Pickens. How did he do it? Goddamnit, he couldn't remember.

Rowe must have seen it. He said, "Raise the breech lever, sir."

Roebuck did this and the chamber slid open, withdrawing the block. Roebuck stuffed a linen cartridge in, smelling the nitrate as he did. He made it snug and pushed the lever closed. Next he fed the powder blister through to the nipple and lifted the weapon, much lighter and easier than any musket. He took aim by bringing a charging man into the V-shaped rear sight, aligning it with the nub. Then he pulled the trigger. The hammer sprung down, its mule-eared shape slamming the iron nipple. The powder sparked, and the chamber erupted in flame and smoke. The kick stunned him, and he missed high, the soldier diving for cover. Roebuck scrambled upstream and reloaded, firing when the legionnaire moved out into the open again. This time the man doubled over in a way that made Roebuck think he'd hit him in the gut. If he had, the man was a goner.

Roebuck reloaded once more, moved back toward Rowe, and rose up to fire. Three balls whizzed past. A fourth tore at his jacket. He dropped back down without pulling the trigger.

"Getting hot around here, sir," said Rowe.

Roebuck repositioned, popped up, and fired quickly, but a ball took the skin off a knuckle on his left hand. It felt like someone had laid hot iron on him. They would be shot to pieces if they stayed here. "To the bank!" he called and then went to help Rowe to his feet. They all ducked and waded down the river, trying to use the low bank for cover.

Vermont said, "Does it hurt, Rowe?"

"Hell yes it hurts."

"You a left-hander?"

"No, I ain't."

"Then you're a lucky man. You still have your good arm."

"That's a peculiar idea of luck, Vermont," Rowe said.

Vermont suddenly stood up. Then crouched again, buzzed by musket fire. "A sand bar here sir," he said.

"Follow it," said Roebuck.

The men splashed down the bar toward a high bank, the top of it above their heads. It was protection. Roebuck looked back at the barracks. Jets of flame showed at least fifty firing men, but their shots were spread all over the river. The soldiers had lost sight of them.

"Sir, I can see no place to get purchase," said Vermont.

"Keep moving," said Roebuck, one hand out against the bank's wall. The flow of the river had made the bank dense and smooth, no place to grab hold or dig in a toe. They waded farther down, Roebuck testing the firmness of the bed with each step. They came to a place where the river had exposed the roots of a big tree on the bank. Roebuck grasped the biggest root, ignoring the pain in his left hand, and pulled hand over hand until he was up and over the top, standing on dry land.

Soon all five men, including Rowe with his broken arm, were up and moving toward the sound of gunfire. Brambles and saplings began to thicket their way, too dense for them to make any progress.

"We're in irons, sir," said Vermont.

"Cutlasses," said Roebuck, shivering, his feet wet and numb. Using their swords, they cut through to a broad path where soldiers, eyes fixed ahead and carrying no weapons, ran pell-mell to the rear through the early dawn light, escaping what must have been Pemberton's attack.

Vermont took aim.

"No!" said Roebuck. "Leave them, they're running."

The path led to a small block of an outbuilding, its roof plaited with branches and reeds. Inside, soldiers were shooting from every opening they could push a musket barrel through. Next to the building, others had taken positions behind piles of gravel and a cart. Pemberton's men, coming up a wide path, were their target. The building and cart provided perfect cover for the soldiers concentrating their fire on the Americans, who hugged the ground and fired from their bellies, muzzle flames giving away their positions.

A large group of soldiers had gathered behind the building, the steel of their bayonets catching the last of the moon's bright light. An officer was calling them into a line, preparing a charge. They would cut Pemberton and his men to pieces.

"Don't like the looks of that, Captain Roebuck," said Vermont. "And where are the rest of our boys?"

It was true, only about half of Pemberton's force were visible. Had the others been wounded or killed?

A single high-pitched scream sounded from the other side of the house. Then more. The screams were short and loud and mixed together in a terrifying chorus. The French paused their firing for a moment. Roebuck saw a group of Marines and sailors crest a small rise to the right and come down on the French as a full-throated swarm. Pemberton had flanked the French and was at the head of the charging men, waving a saber.

"Let them have it, boys," said Roebuck, and the four of them began to fire into the French.

Dismayed at taking fire from their front and their left while being charged from the right, the soldiers flung down their muskets and ran. The rout was completed as Pemberton's maneuver collapsed the last line of defense at the hut.

"Mr. Pemberton," shouted Roebuck.

"Halloo, Captain!" said Pemberton.

"Where are the American prisoners?"

"Don't know, sir, we've been too busy with those rat bastards," he said, pointing at the last of the soldiers limping away.

"We must find them," Roebuck said, "and move out as quickly as we can." He guessed it would not be long before the mine's garrison regrouped.

"Captain!" It was Vermont, standing over a French officer who lay on the ground propping himself up on an elbow. He'd been shot and the left side of his uniform was soaked in blood. Roebuck sat him up and asked where the enslaved Americans were. But the man returned the question with an uncomprehending look. Vermont put it to him in French. And the Frenchman responded with a few angry words.

"He says that we can go to the devil," said Vermont.

"Ask him again."

Vermont did. "Same answer, sir, only he added that I speak French like an imbecile."

"Then I will gut him like a fish," said Roebuck, stepping forward, Vermont translating quickly. The man flinched backwards as Roebuck knifed at his bloody side, turning the blade away just before impact and striking the wound with the brass-knuckled handle. The officer bellowed. Roebuck pulled him up by the collar to his feet. The man bellowed again.

"Tell this son of a bitch I'm counting shots and if I hear ten before we find the prisoners, I'll kill him."

Vermont translated, listened to the response, and said, "Says he knows of no prisoners."

Roebuck turned to Megedagik, "Is that carbine loaded?"

Megedagik nodded.

"Fire it."

He did.

Roebuck said, "Nine shots left," holding up nine fingers. A musket sounded somewhere far off. Roebuck closed his index finger. "How do you say eight in French?"

Vermont said "*Huit*, like wheat."

Pemberton stepped forward, eyes looking ready to pop out of his face, thick veins lining his neck, and saying, "Wheat, you little cunt. Wheat."

This persuaded the French officer, who led them to a longish stone building with high narrow slits for windows.

"He says there they are, sir," Vermont said.

The man then showed Vermont and Megedagik where to retrieve the keys to a padlock and chains that barred a heavy wood door.

"Open it," said Roebuck.

The door opened into a single long cell full of men packed together, piles of straw under their feet, probably bedding. They were filthy and hollow-faced, eyes registering more confusion than life. Roebuck's orders had led him to expect over sixty men, but the number here was well short of that.

"I am Commander Robert Chase Roebuck of the U.S.S. *Savannah*," he said. As he finished these words, half the men dropped to their knees. Some wept.

"I thought we were lost," said a tall, gaunt man, coming forward. "Dear God, I was sure we were lost." He took Roebuck's wounded hand, shaking it violently. Roebuck grimaced and yanked it away.

"Which of you captains the *Eliza Davidson* or the *America*?"

"Richard Warren was captain of the *America*, but he died in the mines 2 weeks ago. I am David Russell. The *Eliza Davidson* is mine."

"Time is short," said Roebuck. "Rally your men, if you please, Captain Russell."

"We are ready to go now. All we have is what you see on our backs."

They moved outside and Roebuck said, "Can they run?"

Russell said, "We have six men too sick to walk. As for the rest, we shall have to see."

Cockrell arrived. "Sir, Pemberton has deployed at the entrance to cover your retreat, but we have to be fast. The French appear to be regrouping."

Vermont and Megedagik loaded three of the sick men into handcarts they'd found beside the outbuilding. Roebuck took one of the sick men on his back. Cockrell and several Marines helped the last of them.

"Off we go! On the double!" Roebuck said.

They lumbered away.

The sun was just beginning to show, shining low light into the camp. Whatever fear they had put into the French in darkness would evaporate in the light of day.

When they reached the line of Marines, Pemberton said, "Christ Almighty, Captain, you took your sweet time. Did you stop for breakfast?"

Roebuck said, "It was hard to move quickly," as two Marines grabbed the man he carried on his back.

Captain Russell of the *Eliza Davidson* looked at the scattering of Marines taking cover behind a gabion and a loose stone wall and said, "Where are the rest?"

"We have another line that way, formed beyond the first bend in the road," said Pemberton.

"How many?"

"Maybe a few less than you see here."

Russell said, "Are you mad? They have three times your number. This is how the United States frees her citizens? Sending a boy and an old man with a handful of soldiers?"

"Marines," Pemberton said, "not soldiers. You'd feel better if you understood the difference. And I'm younger than I look."

Roebuck said, "Keep moving, Captain Russell. You need to get behind the second line as soon as possible. Get your men to keep moving."

As Pemberton called for his pickets to pull back, Roebuck heard a Jenks discharge up ahead, and then another. Pemberton had pickets out to alert them to an attack and Roebuck saw them backpedaling into view, one stopping long enough to raise up and fire again. Then the French came.

"We have good cover here," said Pemberton. "But once they come at us with bayonets they'll make goddamned short work of us."

"You'll delay them here?" Roebuck said.

"Nothing more."

Roebuck nodded.

Pemberton shouted, "Hold your fire!"

The French stopped at the sight of gabions. One fired a speculative shot. A Marine returned it.

Pemberton stood up and pointed his pistol at the man. "Next one who shoots before I say, dies."

The French came in two ranks, stopping when one of their officers gave an order. The first rank knelt, the second stood. The officer raised his hand, and the muskets came up.

"Cover!" yelled Pemberton. His men ducked for safety.

Both French ranks fired and then launched themselves forward in two disciplined lines, leveling their bayonets and chanting, the sound as menacing as the sight. Roebuck didn't know what would come next, and he wanted to ask Pemberton, but knew the question was pointless, a matter of fear.

"Steady, Marines. Fire on my command and fire low," Pemberton said. "Aim at their nuts."

Roebuck turned to see the released prisoners shuffling toward the bend, not even halfway there.

"Present!" yelled Pemberton, and any carbine not already raised came up. "Fire!"

Flames jetted from the muzzles. Powder smoke engulfed them. The line of their enemy wavered under pressure from a wave of .52-caliber balls. The officer remained standing and shouted. The enemy closed ranks and came again.

"Fall back!" yelled Pemberton. "We'll meet them with cutlasses at the next line."

The Marines turned and made for the road at a dead run, blades out.

"Marines, present!" It was the voice of Mace, Pemberton's sergeant. Mace had brought the second line of Marines to a position this side of the escaping prisoners. He yelled, "Fire!"

The French attack shuddered again but recovered and came faster, their blood up, their turn to do the killing.

Pemberton said, "Go on, Roebuck. You must join the others," and drew his saber. Bastard had a nice long sword.

Roebuck drew his knife in one hand and cutlass in the other. He turned to the Marines. "We have to hold them here, boys. Be strong!" Saying to himself, *Robby's not running this time.* Thinking, *what a stupid place to die, not even a war.* Pemberton was shouting but Roebuck couldn't hear what he said, a wall of sound coming toward them. The ground started to vibrate. Hooves. A roar now and he turned just as Chacón's gauchos rode through them and spread out to begin the slaughter. There was no match for these superb riders and their lances. In minutes all the enemy were dead or dying.

Chacón circled around and looked back at Roebuck. Red stockings of blood covered his mount from hoof to hock.

"Fortune spreads her legs," Pemberton said and sheathed his unsoiled blade.

CHAPTER 31

Captain Russell led Roebuck and several of his men to where the camp's mules, wagons, and carts were housed. These would enable the *Savannah*'s detachment to move the freed prisoners as well as their own wounded, which included Rowe and another eleven men, across the plain, *Las Pampas*.

Roebuck had freed the American sailors and accomplished his mission in a way that gave him pleasure to contemplate. But when he considered that he had just fought a battle with French and probably Uruguayan soldiers at a time when the United States was at war with no one, he knew he would soon be answering for it.

There were three wagons side by side. Cockrell climbed into one of them and began to throw mining tools out the back. "Captain," he said.

"What is it?" Roebuck was almost too exhausted to answer.

"I think you need to take a look at this."

"You don't," Roebuck said, "have the wit to describe it?"

"Be easier to show you, sir."

Roebuck climbed very slowly into the wagon, where Cockrell hunched over an opening in the floorboards.

"It was open just a hair. If you put it back…" Cockrell said, fitting a tapered block into the opening. It was a false floor.

Roebuck got down on all fours to peer inside. The real floor was maybe a foot and a half below, where long white sacks bulged from the front of the wagon to the back. A few pieces of metal were loose on top.

Roebuck picked one up, an ingot. "Silver," he said. "Stamped 85% pure."

***

Camp was hours away and Chacón's men looked nearly as miserable as Roebuck's did. This gave Roebuck a pleasure he was not proud to feel. His uniform was damp from the night's river crossing, his socks too, and a cold wind blew over the plain. Rocks and gullies jolted the men on carts, the sick and wounded sounding off in ejaculations of pain. These expressions embarrassed Roebuck one minute and made him heartsick the next.

Estancias dotted the territory. Livestock grazed. They passed through a village and turned northward on a road that was little more than a pair of wheel ruts in the high spots and gummy mud in the low ones. Soon the largest of the wagons was caught deep in the latter. The muleteer cracked his whip and his mules jumped forward. The mud made sucking sounds but didn't yield. They tried again. The mud farted loudly and the men laughed.

"Dismount!" called Pemberton. "And start digging."

The Marines dug with whatever they could find. Those who found nothing used their hands, but the morass had a life of its own, oozing back into whatever they cleared.

Chacón pulled his mount alongside Roebuck. "The area will soon be alive with Unitario patrols. Are you and your men waiting here to save them the trouble of finding us?"

Roebuck said, "I can't control the mud. A passable road might have made for a better route."

Chacón said, "Your damn wagon has sunk into the mud like they're full of rocks, not men." Then as if surprised by that idea, his expression changed and he tugged violently at the reins and to come around to face Roebuck.

"Amigo, be so kind," Chacón said, "as to unload the wounded." His eyes were on the wagon's bed rather than its wheels.

"Why don't we harness a few of these horses," said Roebuck. "We can probably pull it free with just two of them."

"If you want, I'll have my gauchos unload the wounded and sick," said Chacón, "But they may not be gentle."

Roebuck nodded and soon the Marines had removed seven men from the wagon. It still sat heavily in the mud. Chacón put his right hand on the grip of his pistol and said, "Tell me, amigo, what weighs down your wagon?"

"Maybe you know already," Roebuck said.

"That is possible. But I have asked you a question."

"Silver."

"From the mine," said Chacón.

"Didn't fall from the sky."

"It is Argentine silver."

Roebuck said nothing but moved his right hand to the hilt of his cutlass.

"Come, Commander, what need is there for the sword?"

"How you grip that pistol's what."

Neither moved.

"Were you going to tell me about this treasure?" Chacón said.

"Hadn't made up my mind."

"You're a thief, Commander, no different than the French."

Roebuck examined Chacón's face. He looked tired, the man's perpetual energy low and fading.

Chacón said, "It belongs to the people of Argentina."

Roebuck said, "You mean you want it for yourself."

Chacón's brown eyes turned black. "Bring it to me when we make camp."

"I will do with it as I see fit."

"Then we will take it," Chacón said.

Roebuck said, "We killed the devil in the mine, ate his heart, and it gave us strength to slaughter the ogres."

"You would have died if not for us."

Roebuck said, "What you fought were men, and we were about to do to them what we'd done to the devil." He leaned toward the chieftain. "What will your men do when I say the strength of the devil still dwells inside us and that we will use that strength to cut out their puny hearts and feed them to dogs and vultures?"

Chacón considered this and said, "Harness four horses. Two would only make it worse," and rode back to the head of the column.

Roebuck released the hilt of his cutlass and watched the flow of blood bring color back to his hand.

***

Roebuck awoke. He rubbed his eyes. A blurry black form moved inches from his face. He blinked and thought about pulling the blanket tighter. The form had six legs attached to a torso as thick as his thumb. Its antenna twitched, pincers opening and closing on a squirming ant. "Good God," Roebuck said, sitting up and kicking away.

"Top o' the morning to you," Pemberton said, sitting on a log. Steam rose from a cup in his hand. "Bad dreams?"

"A beetle," Roebuck said, standing up quickly and shaking his head. "Where the hell's my belt?"

Pemberton nodded toward a spot a few feet away.

Roebuck fastened it around his waist and felt for the handle of his knife. There it was. Looking around he remembered where he was, Chacón's camp. Only now it glowed under a velvet of morning mist.

Roebuck smelled coffee and looked at Pemberton's kettle balanced on three stones over a glow of embers. He poured a cup and took a sip so bitter it could have been biting him. Roebuck spat it out and said, "For Christ's sake, man, why don't you just suck on the beans?"

Pemberton said, "You like it a little weaker, maybe."

"I like it so it doesn't taste like you've been chewing lemon rinds and just pissed in my cup."

Two dogs wandered over. The first dropped to its haunches and scratched the side of its head with a hind leg. The other squatted to pee, a bitch. Mangy fucking animals. Marine Sergeant Mace, sitting on the far end of Pemberton's log, spat on a gingham square and polished his boot, goddamn him. Watt sketched with a piece of charcoal. Roebuck looked over his shoulder, failing to see a picture in Watt's black marks.

Last night Roebuck had walked into Chacón's tent and tendered two bags of silver, calling them payment for provisions, even though he knew Brown and not Chacón had supplied them. Chacón had paused from his dictation and his rum-filled horn long enough to nod. He might even have smiled, but it was hard to say in the firelight.

He thought of Rowan, the other midshipman on this mission. After reaching camp yesterday, Rowan took the freed prisoners and the *Savannah*'s wounded to a nearby village on the banks of a deep creek. With the help of a guide, Rowan and several Marines would take two boats to Gualeguaychú and seek out Vicar Olascoaga. Rowan also carried most of the silver with him and a letter from Roebuck entreating the vicar to tend to *Savannah*'s wounded and to use some of the fortune in silver Rowan carried to help those in the towns who had lost their homes and livestock to Garibaldi's raids. Roebuck wanted to ensure that the silver would do some good before lining the pockets of men like Chacón.

"Mr. Watt," Roebuck said.

Watt stood up, still in his shirtsleeves. "Morning, sir," he said.

"You and Sergeant Mace prepare the men to march in fifteen minutes. Not turned out, mind you, but ready. Commander Chacón has provided a hundred pounds each of jerked beef and venison, as well corn cakes and ten skins for water. Make sure the latter are filled from the stream. Load everything onto the carts."

"Aye aye, sir."

Now it was morning and Chacón emerged from his shelter, not looking any the worse for his methods. He whistled in three shrill bursts. The gauchos came to life, ready to move in minutes. Roebuck steeled himself to the miserable prospect of another ride.

"Commander Roebuck," Chacón said in his rough Spanish. "I have word that Admiral Brown moves up the Paraná to a place called Costa Brava, where Garibaldi is anchored."

"We go to Costa Brava?" Roebuck said.

"First we must capture a ship, *Diana*, anchored to the north."

Roebuck nodded.

As they rode north to capture Brown's ship, Roebuck had time to consider the last six days. The *Savannah* had been dispatched to help the Brazil Squadron free two American merchantmen and especially free their crew. He believed his action in the mine camp had mostly accomplished this, but at a cost of six dead men and twice that many wounded. Would the Navy say the price was too high? He reckoned they would. Roebuck hadn't just failed to avoid the Gordian knot of alliances in Rio de la Plata, he was in the heart of it, deciding his country's role in a civil war. And what would happen if Brown lost his confrontation with Garibaldi? Roebuck and his men would be captured and probably executed.

Here was a thought that brought him back to the business at hand. He had to do whatever he could to keep Brown from losing. The *Diana* was anchored by the town of Esquina in a branch of the Paraná River. According to the agreement with Brown, Roebuck and his men had to turn her seven guns against any effort to resupply Garibaldi from the Unitario stronghold of Corrientes, upriver. This was the American part of the bargain struck during their meeting on the Uruguay river.

Now, according to Chacón, a small flotilla with a load of powder and shot had embarked from Corrientes the previous night to resupply Garibaldi. No details about the flotilla's size, but Roebuck didn't care. He was elated at the prospect of getting his rear end out of the saddle and his feet back on deck.

***

They reached Esquina before dawn. The gauchos dismounted to cool their horses as they strolled through town. With much more difficulty, Roebuck's men followed suit. Up the street, a man staggered toward them and slurred the words of a song. Another man goaded a team of burros. Both became silent as the gauchos passed.

At the town's harbor on a narrow branch of the Paraná River, Roebuck left his mount and stepped onto the wharf with Chacón. A ketch with two masts of fore and aft sails was anchored with a cutter tied to her stern. It was the *Diana*, the ship they had come for. Her rigging and low draft would be ideal for river sailing. Her port battery faced the town: two twenty-four-pounders, a carronade, and a swivel gun. The latter would be a menace if loaded with grape and could cover both sides of the ship. The carronade was fixed and only covered the port side. Roebuck counted four watchmen on deck.

"*Los colores*," Chacón said, nodding at her banners. "*Unitarios, rebeldes.*"

"We need to take the ship, but we have no boats," Roebuck said.

"We'll find boats."

"No time," Roebuck said. It was almost dawn. "The time to take it is before the deck comes to life with first light. We surprise them now, they won't be able to bring their guns to bear."

"Then that is what we shall do," Chacón said, hustling back to his mount. From horseback, he called out, "Men, come to Papa!"

The gauchos came quickly, walking their mounts.

Chacón pointed to the *Diana*. "I will have that *flechera* or die! Let those who dare follow Papa!"

He rode a little way to a low bank and spurred his horse into the river. The beast stepped through the shallows and then began to swim. His men mounted their horses and followed the tips of their lances in the air. They began to scream like animals, about forty of them on mounts that paddled like four-footed ducks. Bells began to ring the alarm on the *Diana*. The watchmen jumped over the rail when they saw Chacón and his men coming toward them. Even the caiman alligators scrambled out of the river and away.

"A fright for man and beast alike," Cockrell said, walking up.

Roebuck was fascinated.

When the horses reached the ship, their riders stood on their saddles to boost themselves on board. The ship's Unitario crew rushed to the deck, as many jumping ship as staying to fight. Chacón and his men stabbed and jabbed in a fury while taking fire from pistols and muskets. Their mounts turned around and paddled back.

It was over in minutes, no prisoners taken, the wails of those brought to Chacón's justice filling the ears of the Americans as they came aboard. Unitarios were propped against bulwarks with slit bellies, their entrails yanked out. Some moaned, some gasped, but most were dead.

A featureless corpse wearing a coat with a captain's stripes had his stomach cut open, nose and ears cut away, and the skin peeled from his face. Blood drained from the deck through scuppers. Roebuck shivered at the memory of what he said to Chacón over the silver. Roebuck had asked for trouble like a fool without any idea what he was asking for.

CHAPTER 32

Chacón and Roebuck watched from the *Diana*'s deck as the Gauchos on shore employed long narrow-bladed facón knives, still dripping with Unitario blood, to pry pebbles loose from the hooves of their mounts. Others wiped their animals down, drying withers and backs. Some even brushed and curried the beasts as if smoothing knots from a child's hair.

"*Bueno hombre*," Chacón said, "let us go."

"But there is still another fight," said Roebuck.

"*Sí,* always another fight."

"The admiral is relying on you to screen his sailors as they tow his ships upriver."

"There is no end to what the admiral needs. We are tired. Our horses must rest," Chacón said. "Commander, when you first arrived, we thought you and your men were the same as those that had come before. The British or French, or those rodents, the Spanish. Now my men say yes, they have two arms, their pricks swing between two legs, but they can't be mortal, how they walk right into a devil's den and kill him."

They both laughed. Chacón said, "I think maybe you have the gaucho's heart."

"But not the gaucho's ass."

"No, you have asses of porcelain," Chacón said, slowing his words, "but you are not afraid to fight."

Roebuck said, "If our orders lead to that. But your men, following you into the river."

Chacón said, "They have the courage of free men. They fight because they fight, not because of orders."

"Yes," Roebuck said, turning back to the gauchos, "the freedom."

"You see it, don't you? Maybe these plains are like the sea with fathoms of their own."

Roebuck thought of the *Diana*'s captain, eviscerated and faceless.

They shook hands and Chacón climbed down to the cutter. Four of the *Savannah*'s men rowed him to shore through morning mist.

On the *Diana*'s deck, the *Savannah*'s men started their work to get her under way. There was no boatswain, no master gunner, but one of Chacón's lieutenants had found them a *baqueano*—a river guide. When the man came aboard, Roebuck squeezed a dollar's worth of silver into his hand, saying do well and there's more. The *baqueano* stared at it and said he'd go over the Iguazu falls for two more just like it.

"She's ready, sir," said Murchison, the *Savannah*'s foremast captain, one of the few seamen who had made this journey.

The *baqueano* took the tiller to steer. Roebuck grasped it just below the man's hands and smiled. The *baqueano* nodded deeply and stepped away. The resin burnish of the wood had a pleasing opulence. Roebuck measured the current through vibrations traveling up the rudder ropes and through the wood in his grip. He knew he could feel his way to the main channel before turning her over to this man. "Release the gaskets, Murchison," he said. "Get us under way."

"Heave short," Murchison called out. "Loose and hoist the mains'l."

A tremor shook them, a breath across the deck and into the sail.

The booms gave a little and Roebuck pushed the rudder alee to gather more of the breeze into her canvas triangles. The *Diana* nosed around to the channel and quickened on its current. Roebuck wet his lips, sensing a cool breeze. The sun peeked over a line of trees to the east, warming his face and lighting his steaming breath.

When they emerged into the main body of the Paraná, the *baqueano* took back the tiller. Threads of mist hid the far bank. Roebuck imagined the river's shoals and felt a strong sense of relief to have this guide who brought them around so the *Diana* took full hold of the breeze, shooting across the current and tilting downstream.

Before long, they came to a long narrow island that divided the Paraná into a pair of broad branches. Roebuck told the pilot to take them close to a point on the island he spied toward its end. Finding a dead spot in the current, they backed and filled into a position that Roebuck liked and dropped anchor.

Their anchorage would conceal the *Diana* from any ships traveling downriver and it gave her batteries command of either branch. It was as good a position as any to intercept the vessels Brown had told Roebuck to expect, the ones he was here to prevent from reaching Garibaldi with shot and powder for his guns.

The next day after the sun had already passed its peak, two barges appeared. They were full of powder kegs and crates that Roebuck assumed were filled with shot. Escorting the barges were a pair of yawls each armed with a swivel gun. The barges were long, flat and narrower than the sort he had often seen on the Chesapeake. The low rise relative to their freeboard meant that there wasn't much of a target for the *Diana*'s guns to hit. The barges were crewed by three men, one on a tiller and two pushing off the river's bed with long poles, reminding Roebuck that they wouldn't need the same depth to travel the river as the *Diana*. They'd move easily over shallows in a way that the Americans could not.

The *Diana*'s battery launched three warning shots toward them. Roebuck hoped to put the fear of God into their crews, loaded up as they were with explosive powder.

On the first barge, two men ducked as the shot whistled over them. But the shot had a different effect on the crew of the second barge. All three of them jumped ship and began to swim for the far shore away from the *Diana*'s island. The men on the yawls quickly followed them. The Diana fired again at the first barge and it's men steered into shallow water, jumped over the rail, and waded ashore.

Roebuck took the barges and their cargo of shot and powder in tow, leaving the yawls. It was the simplest thing he and his men had done since weighing anchor in Pensacola and he hoped this was a sign of easier things to come.

CHAPTER 33

The *Diana* made way down the Paraná river to link up with Brown. Roebuck wondered whether Brown and Garibaldi had already clashed. For Garibaldi, there would be no way to avoid Brown and his ships. Roebuck prayed that Brown would prevail if he hadn't already, because if Garibaldi defeated Brown, the future for Roebuck and his men was grim.

It was a day and a half before heavy plumes of smoke appeared in the distance and another four hours before they heard the sound of cannon.

The *baqueano* eased the wheel, causing the *Diana* to fall away to starboard and clear a long and low shrub-topped island. More of the battle sounds were audible now. Roebuck's sinuses were beginning to burn with smoke from green wood and spent powder.

The crew turned quiet as the river dilated into the shape of an enormous pear, the battle presenting itself as a spectacle of fire and sound. The *Diana* was at the pear's stem. Downriver at its widest point were twenty vessels at least. Roebuck brought up the glass to scan their masts for colors. Most flags were hazed over, but the red flag of the Uruguayan Colorados, yellow sun in its canton, flew over one of the ship's closest to the *Diana*, and below it was a commander's banner. It had to be Garibaldi. His fleet formed a "T" less than a thousand yards away. A line of smaller ships, local *zumacas* and *faluchos*, made the T's trunk, which pointed toward the *Diana*. The crown was a line made up of a three masted ship, a corvette, and two armed sloops, their starboard batteries facing downriver at what Roebuck recognized as Brown's flotilla.

"Admiral Brown has him outgunned," Roebuck said.

"I expect so, given that we possess the mercenary's shot and powder," Pemberton said, referring to Garibaldi as Admiral Brown did.

Brown's flagship, *Nueve de Julio*, had formed a line with the ships he recognized from his meeting with Brown on the Uruguay river: *American*, *Chacabuco*, and the *Echagüe*. The last of these anchored the line at the north bank, making it impossible for any of Garibaldi's vessels to outflank them.

The men of the *Savannah* watched for two days as Brown and the Argentines defended their positions on the river with the ferocity of wolves. For Garibaldi's part, how could he escape? Roebuck saw no way.

***

Watt had broken out his watercolors and was observing the battle with an artist's repose. Roebuck studied his work before saying, "It is so much like what we see, Mr. Watt, but with a difference."

The artist, surprised by the attention and probably conscious all at once of his position as a midshipman, dropped his little brush and began to rise.

"As you were, as you were," Roebuck said. "Maybe the difference is what gives your paintings their grip."

Roebuck might have used the word *disquiet* instead of *difference*. "You have a way of making it as if we were present in your picture."

"It's the shape of the trees maybe, sir, how they frame it."

Roebuck nodded. There was always something—trees, masts, even people—framing Watt's paintings and always something odd in the shape of those frames. Watt gave them movement, as though they could slither away at any moment and leave the view stripped and rampant.

"Your renderings are oddly satisfying, Mr. Watt."

"This is an oddly satisfying place, sir." Watt smiled and returned to his watercolors.

Roebuck's mind had lately been twisting itself into knots over each additional hour they passed away from the *Savannah*. As if each hour was a unit of failure by which the U.S. Navy would measure his command. The battle was a spectacle, an escape from these thoughts, but it was also a barrier to their movement. Roebuck and his men could not return to Montevideo and the *Savannah* until the battle was over because they could continue downriver to the sea.

Brown's men were on shore, towing the *Nueve de Julio* upriver, closing on Garibaldi's battered ships. Roebuck used his spyglass to watch an officer aboard that ship handing out boarding pikes to marines on deck. By contrast, the men on Garibaldi's ships crawled over decimated timbers and splintered planks to spread gunpowder and splash liquid.

"May I?" It was Pemberton.

Roebuck handed the glass over.

Pemberton looked for a few moments and said, "A sad carnival."

Roebuck said, "What do you suppose is in those bottles they are emptying on deck?"

"They have the shape of brandy bottles. What a goddamned waste," Brown said, handing the glass back to Roebuck. Roebuck saw two men standing side by side on Garibaldi's ship. One passed a bottle to the other who tipped it to his mouth. They were drinking whatever it was straight from the bottle.

"You could buy all the smarts on that ship right now for a nickel and get four pennies back," Pemberton said. "More drinking going on than fighting."

Roebuck said, "They're about to get paid in shot and steel."

Without warning, the men on Garibaldi's decks began to leap over the sides, ten at a time, swimming for shore. Some were too noodle-legged with brandy to move. Others were dead drunk, their supine forms as much a part of the wreckage on deck as broken yards and battered gunwales.

Roebuck searched the north bank. Some of Garibaldi's swimmers were already pulling themselves out of the river. Others waded chest-high, holding their trousers and blouses above their heads. A man with a very full beard emerged from the river. Others began to entreat him, pointing to their ships and gesticulating at Brown's approach.

This man calmly pulled on a pair of gray trousers and a brilliant red shirt. It was Garibaldi. Roebuck had seen him over the past two days commanding the quarterdeck and had guessed his identity. Brown must have been witnessing the same thing. Sure enough, the admiral ran out his guns into position to fire on these waders as they heaved themselves up on shore. Two broadsides of canister would grind the lot into a mottle. But Brown did not fire.

Next, Garibaldi pulled on a striped gaucho's cloak, tugged what looked like a nightcap onto his head, and walked into the woods.

Every other man still on his feet followed him. Then came the explosion, an immensity of fire that caused Roebuck to wonder for a wild instant if river water was its fuel. The men around Roebuck covered their heads as splinters of timber and pieces of metal fell from the sky.

PART THREE

CHAPTER 34

Thousands of cheering voices echoed across the Plaza de Mayo in Buenos Aires. Streamers flew from thousands of hands. It was a big plaza—huge, in fact, but not big enough to contain all of those who had come to celebrate Admiral Brown's great victory. They overflowed into the streets.

An elevated stage had been assembled in front of the broad entryway to the Teatro Colón, where what was near a fifty-piece orchestra played a march Roebuck didn't recognize. There was even a piano striking chords, with the harmonies bright and clear. Admiral Brown stood smiling in front of the band. The march ended but not the cheers. That took some time. Buenos Aires had been alive with celebrations ever since Brown arrived that morning. His sailors and marines were the men who had saved the confederation. They were heroes.

The magnitude of Brown's victory seemed to expand as the celebrations wore on. In the morning Brown was the Almirante Grande, the Great Admiral; by noon he was Argentina's Nelson. A few hours after that, Nelson wasn't fit to shine Brown's boots. If this continued, by midnight he might have to turn water to wine.

Here was a chance to fill the plazas and streets with eating, drinking, singing, and dancing. These were not the kind of people to beggar the chance. The British, the French, and now the Colorados had all tried their luck with invasion. None had succeeded. *We are a chosen people,* they said to one another, and maybe they were.

Brown gestured to quiet the crowd and began to speak, his big voice echoing across the plaza. He described acts of courage from several young officers lined up on the stage behind him, a Lieutenant José Maria Mayorga and two midshipmen who were brothers, Mariano and Bartholomew Cordero. These two looked young enough to be chasing fireflies. The crowd cheered them on.

Brown leaned forward. His face heavy as granite. The plaza hushed. "The conduct of those mercenaries," he said, referring to Garibaldi and his men, "has been like pirates rather than warriors belonging to a civilized people, looting and destroying every creature or thing that had the misfortune to fall under their power."

An angry roar from the crowd.

"They forget the Supreme Power that sees everything, and that sooner or later, rewards or punishes us according to our actions."

The crowd cheered more. Brown was a part of these people, knew their hearts. And they listened to him.

The admiral gave way to President Rosas, or the Dictator, as he was known to his opponents. The man's eyes were as rich as the royal blue of his jacket. His epaulets were thick-fringed slabs of gold bullion. And the broadest red sash Roebuck had ever seen covered his big trunk. Most men would have disappeared in that uniform, but Rosas seemed comfortable wearing it.

He decorated the men Brown had mentioned and several others as well, pinning medals to their chests. Young dark-eyed girls came forward to give flower bouquets to these heroes and a neat peck on each of their cheeks, the crowd shouting *"¡Olé!"* as they did.

Brown had come to stand beside Roebuck and whispered in Spanish, "Ready yourself for a long night's fiesta, my friend."

***

Roebuck danced with a lovely young citizen of Buenos Aires and it was bliss. She had pinned rose blooms to the trim of her gown. Her hair was pulled back and shining, her face flushed. The powdered tops of her breasts moved up and down at each step. He had forgotten what to call her but hadn't forgotten Cockrell's advice, which was to call any girl whose name he did not know "Maria" because they all seemed to have it listed at least once in the paragraphs they called names.

"Maria," he said.

"*¿Sí?*" she answered, looking into his eyes in a way that made him think if they were pools, she'd jump in.

"I must give some of the others a chance." Roebuck said, his feet beginning to cramp.

"We must dance one more," she said. "Please, this music has been so dull. I have not even begun to dance." She squeezed his arm, quite a grip.

Looking around, he saw Watt unaccompanied, tried to catch the young man's eye, but failed. The music stopped and he felt a tap on his shoulder. Cockrell. Good man.

"I'd be pleased to have the next dance, if the lady allows."

Maria looked him over and was satisfied. Cockrell's fine blond hair had attracted more than his fair share of attention among these beautiful brown-eyed women. Roebuck bowed, she curtsied, and the deal was done.

Roebuck watched the couple, Cockrell looking happy, his gift for bluff putting him through when the steps escaped him. Most of the women dancing held their hair in place with elaborate combs and some wore lace mantillas. Men stood with glasses of wine or smoked long clay pipes, the women taunting them loudly. This was half ball, half barn dance and therefore to Roebuck's taste.

"Commander Roebuck." The British in this voice was familiar.

Roebuck rose, "Mr. Guillory! How surprised I am to meet you here!"

"And pleased, I hope."

"Of course."

Guillory turned toward Admiral Brown and smiled.

"You are friends?" Roebuck said.

Guillory nodded and said, "Admiral Brown has arranged a quiet place for us to talk. Will you follow me?"

Seeing Guillory somehow reminded Roebuck of being away from the *Savannah*. It had been eight days.

As they walked, Guillory said, "You've been busy."

"You're well informed," Roebuck said.

"Old habits, as they say."

Roebuck followed him through an archway into a hall. They stopped at a broad door trimmed with a pattern of the fleur-de-lis. The crown was a lily painted in gold against a deep red, lovely. Roebuck remembered that the fleur-de-lis was a symbol of France and wondered if the French capacity for beauty was twinned in some mysterious way to their mania for violence.

Guillory opened the door and passed into a room bright with oil lamps. Through a window, Roebuck caught sight of the plaza, where thousands still danced and whooped, ate and drank.

A man rose to his feet and smiled, "sir", he said. It was Rowan, the midshipman who had delivered the silver to Vicar Olascoaga in Gualeguaychú. He must have read the surprise on Roebuck's face because he offered a genial, "I am pleased to see you, Captain."

Roebuck suppressed his surprise enough to say, "And I you Mr. Rowan."

A woman beside Rowan remained seated, her face hidden by his broad shoulder, but Roebuck knew immediately it was Doña Belén. Her presence filled the room.

Admiral Brown, who had been trailing Roebuck and Guillory, said, "Your friends from Montevideo."

"Yes," Roebuck said, and he bowed to the doña as she moved out of Rowan's shadow.

"How pleased I am to see you so well," she said.

"Very well indeed, madame. Thank you." Roebuck had wondered almost every day since coming upriver who she was, how she could seem to be both a friend and something else at the same time. He turned to Rowan. "Mr. Midshipman, sit down please."

Brown gently laid his hand on Roebuck's shoulder and guided him into an open chair, saying, "Commander, Mr. Guillory and Doña Belén have transported Mr. Rowan here to see you."

As Rowan made his report, Roebuck felt enormous relief. After Gualeguaychú, Rowan had returned to Montevideo and the *Savannah* and described how Commodore Nicolson's Brazil Squadron was anchored there at the edge of the harbor. After the storm, the French had not managed to concentrate enough ships to try even the weakest version of a blockade. Rowan described the safe conduct of the American sailors freed from La Gaucin mine to Nicolson's flagship, the *Independence*.

Guillory and Brown nodded as the midshipman spoke. The doña stayed still as a cat. Rowan reported on the condition of the *Savannah*'s wounded men and how Malvey and Midshipman Holman were still imprisoned.

Roebuck wondered about the silver, but kept his mouth shut, not sure what the others knew. They knew enough, though, because Guillory himself raised the subject by asking Rowan if his commander would like to hear about it. Rowan paused before saying, "Yes sir," and told Roebuck how they had found Vicar Olascoaga and delivered all the silver to him, and how Mr. Guillory had aided their return to the *Savannah* from that town. Rowan ended his report with an assurance from Lieutenant Aaberg that all was well and that they hoped to see the captain safely aboard the *Savannah* soon.

An odd quiet followed this report and Roebuck wondered what had come over such a collection of talkers. The silence dragged into something wooden. Brown focused his attention on Guillory and Roebuck waited for the Englishman to slip something clever into the void, but Guillory did not provide. The room wound itself in Roebuck's direction, their eyes on his. It came to him that they had business for him alone, so he invited Rowan to find Watt in the ballroom and enjoy the festivities. Rowan stood up, bowed with ceremony, and hustled off, every part of him looking like a young naval officer on his way to a large room full of women.

Doña Belén rose, waist tapered sharply above full skirts, hair pulled back. There was something about her that seemed to comprehend the world. Taking the seat next to his, she leaned in.

"Commander," she said, "Admiral Brown has been flattering in his description of your quality as an officer."

"You came through very well for us on the Paraná," Brown said, "and we know how you dealt with the French at the mine."

"Major Pemberton had a great deal to do with that," said Roebuck. "And the gauchos."

"Yes, the gauchos," Brown said. "Chacón believes you could pull teeth from a dragon."

"If I had stayed with Chacón any longer, I'd probably have to," Roebuck said. Whatever was happening here, they weren't coming right out with it.

Guillory looked at Brown and then the doña. "Are you not young for a commander?" he said.

An irritating question. "I am."

"How did it happen?" said Guillory.

"The *Savannah*'s captain was called to personal matters and the Navy needed someone to command."

"Midshipman Watt told me of your eluding the French razee and two corvettes," Brown said.

Roebuck wondered if Watt had also mentioned the six dead topmen or his dive into the bucket of tobacco spit.

The doña said, "Uruguay needs an admiral for its navy."

"I thought that was Garibaldi," Roebuck said. He looked at the door.

"Not the Colorados," she said. "We need an admiral for Los Blancos for the government of Oribe."

Her sympathies in the civil war were with Los Blancos and Oribe, then. He hadn't known for certain until now.

Brown said, "We have the ships for such a navy in Buenos Aires. Additionally, with your help I believe we will relieve Admiral LeBlanc of his corvettes and the razee."

Roebuck shook his head.

"What I mean," said Brown, "is that Uruguay needs a man like you. A man who leads, a man who knows rivers and the sea. The navy will be yours."

Brown, Guillory, and Doña Belén were solemn. Not just solemn, they were fraught.

Guillory said, "Admiral Jonas Coe is an American, as you are. He commanded the navy of Uruguay before he was relieved by the usurper Suarez. Suarez gave the navy to Garibaldi. You arrived *in medias res*, only here for the second part."

Brown said, "South American navies abound with English and American officers, myself included, although I am grateful to call myself Argentine now."

"Robert," Doña Belén said, "You are twice the captain Jonas Coe is."

At least twice, he almost said.

She put her right hand on his. Something rose in his chest and throat. And his mind felt as if it was chasing its tail.

She said, "We need your help."

"I did not know you sympathized with Oribe," Roebuck said.

"That is because I do not," she said. "I sympathize with the choice that Uruguayans must make about their future. They chose Oribe. We are a nation, Robert, with something wonderful ahead of us, a future befitting an enlightened and free people. But only if we have selfless men to lead who respect the law, as I believe you would.

Brown said, "There is honor and glory to be won, Commander."

***

Back in the ballroom, Doña Belén sat beside Roebuck close enough to touch. It caused his stomach to feel like it was walking a tightrope. Brown and Mrs. Brown, Pemberton, Guillory, and a Major Seguii, also with his wife, shared the table. President Rosas had decorated Seguii earlier in the day for bravery. The man's nose was crooked and his eyes looked pulled together as if by an uneven magnetic force, but the decorations pinned to his chest glittered. The doña's proposal kept coming back to Roebuck, the idea of his own navy. Such a thing could only happen in a place where August is cold and birds run upright like men.

It was late. The band had thinned to just an accordion, two guitars, and a pair of skins. They were playing loose and fast. Roebuck thanked God for music and its power to distract. He wanted to stop his thoughts from chasing after the idea of commanding his own fleet. He needed to enjoy this moment.

A line of men danced, tapping their feet and turning a full circle. They followed a rhythm clapped out by an opposing line of women. The men stepped toward the women, pulling bandanas from their belts and holding them out. Their backs were straight, chests out, each body a bass clef on a sheet of music.

There was so much to feel here, the joy, the passion, to feel as these people did. The men spun their bandanas, flashing them toward the women. Each man faced a woman and they stared at one another in a way that agitated Roebuck. The men pushed out their chests even farther and spread their arms wide. The women also held bandanas, forming triangles that covered their faces up to the eyes, stepping to their own rhythm. The men and women coupled at long last, intertwining, then pulled apart, eyes fixed on each other as they waved the bandanas above their heads. Roebuck avoided looking at any of his companions, embarrassed by all this.

The doña said, "Zamba is what it's called."

He turned to meet her eyes.

Madame Seguii pulled her husband onto the floor, the room cheering them. She added bravado to the dance by tearing a medal from her husband's chest and holding it instead of a bandana above her head. The ballroom erupted. Madame Seguii's head went back and she laughed.

Each movement in the Zamba, each gesture, pulsed with a meaning that Roebuck couldn't miss. It made him think of dances in America. Had they ever meant anything like this? Their refinement and formality barely teasing at what this Zamba made impossible to ignore.

"Commander, your expression makes me wonder," the doña said. "Do you disapprove so much of what you see?"

His face felt hot. "What sort of thing do you think I disapprove of?"

"What a pleasing subject," she said.

"I was thinking of our dances back home, madame. Their beauty and elegance."

"You are struck very gravely by thoughts that give most men pleasure."

"I was also thinking that our dances have come to mean very little other than themselves," he said.

"And thinking ours means something more," she said. "Is that not so?"

Roebuck turned toward Major and Mrs. Seguii on the floor and said, "The major's wife adds something interesting of her own."

"Yes, she does."

The dance ended and the Seguiis moved off the floor, retreating to a dim corner with long tables topped by pitchers and glasses. Roebuck watched them drink.

"What did he do exactly in Bajada?" said the doña, also watching them.

Roebuck said, "Admiral Brown tells me Major Seguii commanded a small battery on shore that fought off Garibaldi's ships as they tried to land."

The Seguiis moved to an alcove with a lamp sputtering low light. He sat while Madame Seguii remained standing. She leaned over her husband, pulled the comb from the back of her black hair, and shook her hair loose, letting it fall over his face. Then she sat down. Roebuck and Belén watched as her husband, unwary, rose and put his mouth to the nape of her neck.

Roebuck looked away.

Not Belén. She watched them for a while. Then she gestured, palm up, toward the dancers. "Indulge me, Robert," she said, rising.

"I don't know a step."

"Then you must do whatever comes to you."

"Wait."

Roebuck went over to some of the *Savannah*'s officers seated with their Argentine counterparts, their table a mess of carafes, mostly spent, and two bottles of brandy.

"Brandy," he said.

One of the Argentines laughed and poured a glass full.

Roebuck emptied it and asked for another. Then, returning to the Doña, he said, "God help me," as they went out on the floor.

The guitars vibrated in his chest, the drumming in his toes. He faced her in a state of confusion. She began to move. He looked into her eyes—that part was easy—and tried to follow her.

"In America this dance would cause a scandal, no?" she said.

He nodded. "Everyone within a mile would be church-bound for a week and then they'd find a field for a revival just to be sure." He felt himself unclenching.

"But this is Argentina, so no scandal," she said. "How does it feel?"

"Like I'm a damned fool."

She brought her lips together and pushed them out so he couldn't miss the full red glory, and said, "It feels good, Commander, no?"

Yes, it did.

He knew he couldn't do this dance, but maybe all he needed was its spirit, the unity of man and woman. He kept his eyes on hers, matching her movements. His body resisted, wanting the steps. But he was feeling what they all felt when a man and a woman came close like this, with their bodies pressed together. He closed his eyes and opened them. Belén stared at him, robbed for the moment of any cleverness.

He moved without the dance's postures, no outstretched arms or puffed chest, no bandana in his hand. He had to make it down to the two of them.

The hall became quiet, an uneasiness on the floor as he stripped the Zamba to its bones. Belén stumbled, her poise fractured. He wondered what it was she wanted people to believe about her, wondering why he had never thought of this before. They danced just once and left, moving in a poet's dream. She grasped his hand, squeezing until it hurt, and grabbed his jacket, pulling him in as they walked.

He said, "I have been thinking about your navy."

"After," she said and led him to her rooms.

She removed his uniform jacket and pulled off his blouse, unbuttoned his trousers and pulled them down to his feet. He stepped out of them. Servants had heated water for her bath, in a large drum kettle over the fire. She scooped it out in pails, pouring them slowly over him as he sat naked in her porcelain tub. She washed under his arms, between his toes, making him clean, the muscles on his back and shoulders. She didn't skip a single spot.

Toweling off, he watched her reflection in the mirror as she gathered his uniform, holding the pieces close, breathing them in. He was getting hard that feeling of being split in two as she pulled him into her chamber.

CHAPTER 35

He woke before she did and watched her as she slept. Could he tell her about his father? About Martin Roebuck? About his father's shipyard partner, Roland Mann? A man who drank corn whiskey in a way you could set your watch to. Slurring by one, stumbling by two, wandering away by three, and on one unfortunate day dead by four, drowned in the shallows of the Chesapeake Bay.

After Mann's death, Martin hired an artist to paint an advertisement on the side of a large barn visible from the main road connecting them to Annapolis. Instead of Mann's Shipyard were the words Roebuck & Son and a three-quarter view of one of the clipper ships their yard was known for. It was the only step his father had ever taken toward redeeming the name of his family, which he had ruined twenty-seven years before during the War of 1812 while commanding a hodgepodge of vessels with a few guns known as the Chesapeake Naval Militia. When the British arrived, led by Admiral Cockburn, Martin announced that his militia was too weak to resist. Cockburn sailed in, dropped anchor, and rowed to the eastern shore, plundering whatever towns he didn't burn. Roebuck concealed his little flotilla farther north in one of the Chesapeake's narrow fingers, discharging nary a shot in anger.

If that wasn't enough, Martin had delivered the same performance when Cockburn returned for another round a year later.

So great was Martin's disgrace afterward that the name of Roebuck became a byword for the kind of cowardice that leads to the burning of towns, the death of civilians, and national humiliation.

When the painter completed the Roebuck & Son barnside advertisement, Martin showed it off to his wife and his sons, Matthew and Robert. Martin Roebuck had stood there gazing at it for two solid hours, shedding all at once two and a half decades of shame.

Unfortunately, vandals whitewashed it later that same night. Undeterred, Martin ordered it repainted, but again before first light it was washed white. Martin tried once more, even staying up to guard it with Matthew and Bobby, each of them with a shotgun in hand, Martin carrying a fowling piece. However, this time over fifty men came, not bothering to disguise themselves. The Roebucks could do nothing but let them white the painting out again. One of the men, a cooper they had often worked with from Easton, said, "You have no name here." And the wall stayed white. Everyone continued to call the enterprise Mann's Shipyard. It was known as Roebuck & Son nowhere but the Talbot County registry.

Belén awoke, kissed his forehead, and left the room, returning after a while to sit beside him in bed, moving the dark hair away from her face with a fingertip and saying, "It seems that Mr. Guillory awaits us in the drawing room."

Roebuck sat up. "Does anything escape that man?"

They dressed and went out, Roebuck first and the doña a minute after, as though showing up separately would make a difference.

Guillory's smiling aplomb had given way to a drawn look and haste to speak. "Commander Roebuck, Admiral Brown asks that you take the *Diana* down to Colonia de Sacramento as soon as you can assemble your crew."

"What of his own crews?"

"Most were granted leave and have gone off."

"What could be so urgent?"

"LeBlanc is almost in Colonia. He has gone to find Vicar Olascoaga and retake the silver."

"I don't see what this has to do with us," Roebuck said.

"If LeBlanc reaches the vicar before you do, he will certainly kill him and anyone with him."

The silver might mean the vicar's death, and the silver had come from Roebuck. He had to go, that was obvious, and moved quickly toward Guillory and the door, but stopped, turning to Doña Belén, who backed toward her chamber. He went to her, pushed inside, and shut the door.

"I'm sorry," he said.

The black of her eyes flashed.

"Doña."

"My name is Belén. You said it once," she said, backing away as he reached toward her.

"I have to go. There's a man going to die."

She shooed him with both hands. "Go then," she said, "go."

He wanted to stay. Never wanted anything more. But that was a dream and it was ending as all dreams do.

***

Something made the morning feel heavy, the gray sky maybe or the churn of the estuary's pale brown water. The *Diana* had managed to carry the last of the morning's land breeze slowly across to Colonia and had dropped anchor. LeBlanc's *Badine* was there, hove-to three cable lengths from shore. If Roebuck and his men had arrived earlier, had reached LeBlanc and his crew in town, they might have stopped them, but afloat, the *Diana*'s six guns were no match for the *Badine*'s twenty-eight.

Roebuck watched the *Badine*'s crew rig a derrick and boom to hoist and lower crates into the hold. He recognized the crates as those taken from the mine in Entre Ríos, crates of silver. A man looking every inch like an Admiral—had to be LeBlanc—Dufour, and several of the *Badine*'s seamen emerged from below, leading five prisoners in irons to the bow. Despite the irons, Roebuck recognized Vicar Olascoaga's small, decisive movements.

When Olascoaga and the other four reached the entryway, LeBlanc pulled a pistol from his holster and handed it to Dufour, who turned to one of the chained men and raised the barrel to his temple.

"Lord, no," Roebuck said.

Cockrell standing beside him said, "Why, Captain Roebuck? Why would he do it?"

A puff of smoke was followed immediately by the pistol's report and the man fell to the deck.

"Cold-blooded murder," Roebuck said.

A very young man, an acolyte by the look of his robe, was lashed face-to-face to the lifeless body of the murdered man. Several of the *Badine*'s crew lifted and threw the two of them, one dead, one living, over the rail. The crew jeered the acolyte as he struggled for a time before sinking into the brown water.

Dufour shot the next man while Vicar Olascoaga was making his peace. The vicar was lashed to the fresh kill. Then he too was over the rails, struggling and gone. Dufour prepared to shoot the fifth and last of the prisoners, but LeBlanc stopped him and instead had the man launched on a small jolly boat with a pair of oars. The man was frantic as he pulled toward shore, moving in ragged arcs until calming himself enough to row a straight line. Freed, no doubt, to spread the word of what happened, a messenger for LeBlanc to spread the word: *Do not defy me.*

"They need to pay for that," said Cockrell.

"It's up to us to make them," Roebuck said.

Chapter 36

Belén was returning home from Buenos Aires by carriage rather than horseback. She needed to keep her mind on business instead of on her mount. Here it was day two of her life without Justo, the man having been executed by firing squad yesterday morning.

Her servant Rocio sat beside her chattering away with her other servant, Anna. Belén never knew what to make of these two girls. She wondered how their lives would be different without Justo on the prowl and hoped they would be better. Guillory, seated across from her, buried his head in a pamphlet from Valencia describing new techniques for budding orange trees. The pamphlet was hardly new to him. He had submitted a proposal to her weeks ago based on a thorough reading of its contents. What he was doing now was using the pamphlet for cover, hiding from the attentions of Rocio and Anna. It never failed how brazenly they vied for his interest, which never failed to confuse him. Well, she thought, Mr. Guillory was an adult and must fend for himself.

The subject for her consideration right now was the connection between her trading company and the American consul general, Hilary Houghton, which had come through Justo. Justo had been nothing more than Admiral LeBlanc's rather dull tool. That meant LeBlanc was the one who had made the connection. Houghton had brought their trading company much needed revenue from American naval ships. She smiled at the thought that Houghton had also brought them Robert Chase Roebuck, the agent of the apparent collapse of their conspiracy. She had heard LeBlanc refer to Robert as the schoolboy and wondered what he would call him now. No, what she really wondered was what Robert was going to do. Would he stay with her?

The American Commodore, Nicholson, had returned to Montevideo with his squadron, coming to her with a massive order for the victualling of his ships. Houghton would be due a commission for this, that was their agreement, and she needed to work out what she should do, given Houghton's connection to LeBlanc and his crimes. Rather than a commission maybe Houghton deserved a bullet—or ten, like Justo.

The scope of LeBlanc's conspiracy had become clear to them all. The man was nothing if not ambitious, and ambition was not something she normally faulted. This brazen French Admiral had hoped to command Uruguay's navy, strengthened by captured ships and fortified with silver from the Gaucin mine. And then there was the fortune he would acquire by marrying the freshly widowed Belén. A woman was not capable of running such an enterprise, he had said, claiming to feel an obligation to help her given the death of Justo, even though she had been managing the estancia Nohemi for nine years without assistance from Justo.

Justo's part in the conspiracy had been his promise to bring the support of the Spanish crown to LeBlanc's scheme. This delusion had helped LeBlanc diagnose Justo's juvenile nature, making it simple to arrange his death in order to clear a path for his obtaining the wealth of Nohemi. Lechi was to lead Uruguay's army. Once all of these plans were in place and LeBlanc had consolidated his position, he would effect a coup d'état, installing himself as Uruguay's leader. Uruguay was a weak state, divided and in need of direction and LeBlanc had recognized a chance at the kind of power few men in the world ever wield.

But now Lechi was dead, killed by Robert's hand at the Club Londres. LeBlanc was disgraced and hiding, although in possession of a fortune in silver. But what of the American, Houghton? How did he fit in? She now realized how deeply he was involved. Why hadn't she worked it out before? Was it the income he brought them that had caused her not to think more deeply about his part? Of course it was. Justo had been ruining their business, her father's life's work. Now she realized how few limits there were to her own desire to keep it from dying.

In time, her carriage passed through the Estancia Nahomi's gate and she felt a sensation of home like she hadn't in years. Justo's absence, the man finally answering to God's judgment, made the place welcome again. But when they rounded the bend before the pasture where she wintered her pintos she saw no horses grazing. The grass had grown high. Had the farrier told her that some of the beasts were due to be reshod? Maybe that is where they were.

In front of the main house, many unfamiliar mounts stood hitched to the post. Uniformed men, French sailors with a few Colorados among them, were at the door. She looked toward Guillory, who was already staring at her. Rocio and Anna had stopped talking. One of the uniformed men went into the house as another offered to help her down from the coach.

She said, "Who are you?"

"He is with me, Doña Belén. And he joins all of us in welcoming you home."

She did not need to see the man to recognize his creamy voice. She turned to see LeBlanc come out from the big house. "My Admiral," she said, ignoring the uniformed man's outstretched hand as she stepped down from the carriage.

LeBlanc bowed and smiled. "At your service, madame."

He had taken her completely by surprise. She had to be careful because LeBlanc was more dangerous than anyone she had ever known.

"I did not see my horses in the pasture," she said.

"The painted ones?" LeBlanc said, referring to the markings of her pintos, prepared for this.

"You have done something with them?" she said.

"They now have the honor of serving your country," he said, "as mounts in a company of dragoons."

"Colorado dragoons?"

"Of course. The Blancos being traitors to Uruguay and to the principle of justice." He looked amused.

She said, "You have sold my horses."

"You will no longer need them, my dear. So I have found them a worthy home."

"I hope you negotiated a good price."

"Well," he said looking at his fingernails, "I am no merchant."

She wanted to say, *No, you are a thief and a murderer.* Instead she said, "I will thank you to pay me what those horses earned."

"Doña Belén, I will give you much more than that," he said.

"Very well," she said, "I'll take it now."

"In time, my dear, I will give you something much greater." She had to admire the way LeBlanc presented himself as though there were nothing new in the world to trouble him. He was not a man given to anxieties.

She began to direct the uniformed men to unload her luggage.

LeBlanc said, "Do you not wish to know what it is?"

She said, "You have stolen and sold my horses. They were very dear to me. So my curiosity is curtailed by the feeling that you are about to tell me something else that will displease me."

"You know in your heart," he said as calmly as ever, "we want the same thing. And I know that you have the wit to give thanks that I am here to see we get it."

She winced inside. He was referring obliquely to their flirtation, which she had never discouraged. In fact, she had very nearly become his lover, and he was the kind of man to know this. A man who paid attention to women, who had paid attention to her, a man who took time to see their desires. Now he was saying that yes, he knew something about her she had not admitted even to herself, that she also desired power and that this was the same desire they had for each other.

There was no denying how good it felt to have such a man want her and even try to see her for who she was, for better or worse. LeBlanc was even attracted by the worse. After nine years as Justo's wife she could not imagine what LeBlanc saw, but she wanted to know, so far she was these days from understanding herself.

"Yes, my dear," he said. "You know it is true. I see it in your face. It is there in your silence. We must have the same thing, you and I."

What a dangerous soul. She had to get away from him. He was no different than Justo, nothing more than another corrupt man, and she had had her fill. Belén smiled and nodded, afraid to say even one word in reply. She suddenly felt Roebuck there beside her—a useless but happy fantasy.

"You must be hungry," LeBlanc said. "Your cook has prepared dinner, so let us eat to our hearts' content. Then we shall work out our future."

Two of the uniformed men gripped the bridles of the carriage team. Another climbed up to take the reins from the coachman.

CHAPTER 37

"Do I understand that you were on the *Independence* with Commodore Nicolson yesterday?" Guillory said, carefully picking his way over cobblestones wet with rain in Montevideo's old town.

Roebuck had benefited from the Englishman's knowledge about the French and their intentions. Now he had the sensation that Guillory knew no less about the Americans and had probably been learning most of it from him.

"Those of my interactions with the commodore that concern you, Mr. Guillory, I will relate with no delay. As for the rest..."

Guillory began to respond to this, but Roebuck waved him off. It was true that after Roebuck had returned to the *Savannah*, Nicolson invited him aboard the *Independence*, a razee serving as the Brazil Squadron's flagship. The commodore wanted to hear what had happened in the interior. He also wanted to hear what Roebuck had learned about U.S. Consul General Houghton, a man whose corruption had come to light, Nicolson said, and must be dealt with.

Surgeon Benoit was walking beside Guillory, the three of them on their way to Montevideo's prison. Two weeks had passed since Malvey and Holman's imprisonment and Roebuck was anxious about their condition.

A guard showed them into an office with a wainscoting of handsome grained wood. The warden sat behind a desk cut from big hunks of cherry, burnished to a high shine. The room looked like it belonged in a Philadelphia bank.

The warden rose and said, "You have returned." He wore a coat that had a lot more shoulder than the warden himself did. Its wide lapels were fringed with shiny black fur. His red vest was trimmed with an oriental pattern and a thick gold watch chain hung from its pockets. The warden shifted and the gold waved.

"Yes, sir, we have returned," Roebuck said, answering the man's Spanish.

"I don't know why. Very little has changed," the warden said.

"We are here to ask you about the trial," Roebuck said. "When will Lieutenant Malvey and Mr. Holman be tried?"

"Nothing is scheduled. They are prisoners of war."

"America does not fight in any war."

"They attacked a company of soldiers."

"You know that is not true," Roebuck said.

"Do I?"

This man infuriated Roebuck, but what good was that? He said, "You have no reason to hold my men and if you persist there will be trouble."

"Yes, well, trouble being what it is," the warden said, "I can't say that such a thing is desirable." He rang a small bell, and a guard came to lead Roebuck and the surgeon down to the cells. The guard wore rags for trousers. He wore a blouse smudged with dirt and oil, probably from his pores. He carried a sooty torch as he led them into a tunnel underground. The smoke soon had Benoit coughing.

Roebuck's nostrils were filled with the smell of decay. A soft flapping sound came and went.

"Bats," said the guard in Spanish. "They eat flies and mosquitoes, so they stay. Our guests." A shortage of teeth did not discourage the man from grinning.

They stopped at a narrow opening barely wider than the surgeon's shoulders and barred with iron. The guard keyed the lock and pushed the bars open. Holman, crouching in a corner, stood up quickly and squinted into the torchlight. He looked worn out.

"Hello, Mr. Holman."

"Hello, Captain Roebuck, sir." Holman called him captain, Roebuck's title, as all in the navy did. He had been called Commander, his rank, by everyone here in Rio de la Plata. It pleased him to hear the title.

Benoit put one end of a rubbery tube about eighteen inches long over Holman's heart.

Holman looked at it and said, "What in tarnation?"

"Snake ear trumpet," said the surgeon. "Breathe in."

Holman looked at Roebuck. "You're getting us out, sir?"

"I'm not here in the asshole of Montevideo for any other reason," said Roebuck, wondering if it would help Holman's spirits to wink.

"Lieutenant Malvey is sick, sir," Holman said, "The shits have him, can't keep anything inside. He used to come out and walk around the yard with me, but not now. Not for five days."

The surgeon finished with Holman. They went to Malvey. His cell was foul, with two wooden buckets in the corner. Soupy brown liquid topped one and had dried to a crust on the stays.

Benoit examined Malvey, asking, "How often do they empty those buckets?"

"Don't know," croaked Malvey. "Last time was some days ago. How long have I been here?"

"Couple of weeks," Roebuck said. He could taste the vomit pushing up his gullet.

Skin draped the bones of Malvey's face like a damp sheet. "How's Holman?" he said.

"Not bad," Roebuck said. He could think of nothing else to say. "Not too bad."

"Am I leaving this morgue, sir?" Malvey said.

"We are all leaving." This statement caused Roebuck to understand that he had to make it true.

"And Mr. Holman? I hope his stomach's not as angry as mine," said Malvey.

"Boy has innards constructed of brass. Healthy as a crow," said Roebuck. "He's been waiting for you out on the grounds."

"Captain, you have to find a way to get me out. This is no place for a man to die."

Malvey was pale and thin. The ironic and angry light in his eyes, a source of such danger for so long, was gone. Roebuck had hated that light but now decided he didn't want it extinguished unless he was the one to do it.

They left Malvey and followed the stinking guard toward the warden's office. Benoit said, "The lieutenant's dysentery is advanced and he has a fever. He'll be dead in three days if he stays."

"Don't need a goddamned snake trumpet to know that," said Roebuck. They returned to the office, where Guillory waited for them outside.

They entered the office and the warden said, "Sit down," motioning to blue velvet cushions on his chairs.

Roebuck gripped the chair handles hard enough to bend their brass as he lowered himself to sit.

"You've wasted your time, Commander," said the spider to the fly.

"One of your prisoners is dying, sir," Roebuck said.

"He arrived in poor health, Commander. Nothing here has caused his illness."

Guillory pulled out two bottles of French brandy from a sack he'd brought with him. Roebuck put down five silver reales.

"A gift?" said the warden.

"A token of friendship," Roebuck said, thinking of the buckets in the corner of Malvey's cell.

The warden opened one bottle with a pop and poured some out. He sniffed, then swallowed. "Too sweet. A poor choice," he said while placing the bottles in a trunk next to his desk.

Roebuck felt Benoit's eyes on him.

"The reales are enough to buy the prisoners fresh bread and water for a week," said the warden.

"We want them both released today," Roebuck said, the rise in his voice nearly getting away from him.

"Quite impossible," said the warden. "If freedom were so important, best avoid losing it in the first place, no? Better to follow the laws of the country where you anchor."

"We are past that are we not?" said Roebuck, wondering how this bootlicking viper's neck would feel in his grip.

The warden nodded.

Roebuck said, "So tell me, what is the price for one so far gone?"

The warden's chair let out soft, rocking squeaks. "Wheels of justice must turn, señor."

Roebuck placed a bag on the table, saying, "We would like to donate this for medicine and food or whatever good it might serve." He had two more bags like it in his coat pockets.

The warden leaned forward, untied it and tapped our two silver reales, before covering the bag with his left hand. "Do you have another?" pinching his lips into a grin. Such mirth. "It can make things better for your men."

It wasn't clear what this man intended. At a loss, Roebuck placed another bag on the table.

"Commander, your generosity proves your intentions, but I have to tell you that if I release these men, the Colorados and the French will certainly bring all manner of unpleasantness down upon me." His words were as elegant as the gold-ringed hand that shot out to cover the second bag.

A shark was a shark, ass in soft velvet and smelling of French brandy or not. This one had bite. Roebuck recalled Malvey's collapsed features and let his rage flow. He drew his knife and stabbed down with all his power into the desk's cherry top. The handle stood straight up and quivered right between the warden's two hands.

Roebuck said, "It's their unpleasantness later or mine now."

The warden tried to stand, but Roebuck pushed him back down, whispering, "Which is it going to be?"

***

Soon after this conversation, the warden had experienced a change of heart, sending for a teamster, two horses, and an ambulance. The surgeon and Guillory would look after the *Savannah*'s two freed officers while Roebuck hastened toward the consulate, where he and Commodore Nicolson were planning to visit Houghton. Roebuck expected Nicolson to share the Navy's consternation with him for his upriver gambit. His hope for some acknowledgement from the commodore for his success had during previous conversations been disappointed. If Roebuck didn't get the Navy's praise, what would he get? He expected the worst and prepared himself for Nicolson to fill his ears with trouble.

As he walked, thoughts of the Doña took over. Their night together was a youth's fantasy. Something that could not possibly happen within the sorry limits of an adult's life, except that it had happened and, by some miracle, happened to him. Could he see her again? He was desperate to believe he could.

Two Marines saluted him as he passed through the consulate's entrance.

Two more guarded the door to Houghton's office, one of them a sergeant, who asked, "Commander Roebuck?"

Roebuck nodded.

The sergeant knocked once before opening the door.

Nicolson was seated at Houghton's desk.

Roebuck said, "Commodore Nicolson, good afternoon, sir."

The commodore grunted, "Umph," and then, sounding like he'd swallowed a plate of gravel, said, "Why does it seem that I am always waiting for you, Mr. Roebuck?"

Nicolson had left the top buttons of his white vest unfastened, revealing a red silk scarf wrapped neatly around his neck. Roebuck had heard about the scars. A surgeon had removed splinters from Nicolson's throat during the fight when Lawrence lost the U.S.S.

Chesapeake to the British after a fight off of Boston some thirty years ago. Nicolson's vocal cords had never fully recovered and were still famously likely to fail him. As a consequence, he had developed an unusual talent for communicating his thoughts in grunts and vibrations.

"Something's amiss here, Commander Roebuck."

"Sir?"

"Ummm hmmm."

Such a reflective *ummm hmmm.*

Nicolson raised his chin like an agitated horse does its muzzle and nodded toward a closed door.

Roebuck walked over, opened it, and staggered backward. Houghton was hanging perfectly still in the center of the small room, suspended by a leather belt. One end looped through an exposed ceiling beam and the other around his neck. It was shocking, but worse was how the man had been left there to hang.

There was a chair under Houghton that had been knocked onto its side. Roebuck set it up and called, "Commodore, kindly send in the guards." The two Marines were soon beside him. Roebuck stepped up on the chair, pulled his knife, and cut through the belt's leather. The Marines grabbed the body as it dropped.

Houghton's face was unrecognizable, a contortion of purple and blue. This man of prestige and authority was unmade, without so much as the features of his own face remaining to tell you who he had been.

Nicolson hunched over Houghton's desk. Roebuck didn't want to look at him, afraid of what he might say.

"A waste," Nicolson said.

"Yes."

"Errphhh." Nicolson pointed at an unfolded paper at the desk's end. Roebuck picked it up and read.

Sir,

As you have requested of me to give a full account of the silver mined from La Gaucin, I hope that you will do me the kindness of acknowledging your inability to control the commander of the Savannah and the disaster this has visited upon our operation.

I myself have been forced to abscond from Rio de la Plata in a manner befitting a common criminal. Given this accumulation of failures it is in the instance impossible for me to affirm your request for assistance.

Furthermore, I feel it is a matter of just and righteous principle to withhold from you the thirty thousand reales our agreement specified as your due. These I hold as indemnification for the depredations of your navy and for the insult to our flag and, moreover, for the painful lack of competence you have manifested in every discharge of your duty to our enterprise. Please be satisfied with the ten thousand reales that you have in hand.

I am, Sir, very respectfully, &c, &c,

Rear Admiral J. D. LeBlanc
Ship Perle

"Houghton and LeBlanc were partners?" said Roebuck.

Nicolson nodded.

"So you left him hanging by his neck."

"I'd have left him hanging by his testicles," Nicolson paused for a moment to clear his throat, "if I suspected he had a pair. He was a disgrace and when the people of Uruguay and Argentina discover what has ha—" Nicolson paused again, lifting his chin to straighten his throat.

Roebuck was not in a mood to wait. "Happened," he said.

"Yes. And they will discover it, I can—" More shaking. Nicolson stomped the floorboards twice. A Marine soon entered with a large mug of beer. The commodore drank half of it, moving his head forward and backwards several times.

There was a knock at the door. Nicolson called, "What is it?"

"Senator Montcalvo to see you, sir."

"Ummm." Nicolson made this noise to himself, but the displeasure in it was clear. "Show him in."

Senator Montcalvo entered looking as crisp as ever, although more serious. He nodded to Nicolson.

Nicolson said, "Welcome, Senator."

"Commodore," Montcalvo said, clipping the greeting, and then to Roebuck, "Commander."

Roebuck nodded.

Montcalvo stared at Roebuck for a few moments before facing Nicolson and said, "You have not told him."

"The matter does not concern him," Nicolson said.

"Does not concern him? It concerns him more than it does anyone else." Montcalvo looked back to Roebuck and said, "Admiral

LeBlanc has recaptured all the silver you found at La Gaucin and murdered Vicar Olascoaga."

"I was there to see it," Roebuck said.

"And failed to prevent it," Montcalvo said.

The statement jolted Roebuck. He saw for the first time how much this urbane man was fighting to control his anger.

Nicolson interrupted, "Senator, please try to consider it from our position."

Montcalvo ignored Nicholson, keeping his eyes on Roebuck's. He said, "LeBlanc has also kidnapped Doña Belén Saavedra y Mancera, proprietor of La Compañía de Comercio de Overo. Mr. Guillory witnessed the abduction."

Roebuck stood up reflexively. There was not a moment to waste. He said, "They sail north?"

Montcalvo said, "Yes. LeBlanc has friends and property in Brazil."

Roebuck said, "How many ships?"

"Dufour commands the *Badine* and LeBlanc himself leads the *Perle*. There are no others."

"When?"

"He provisioned his ships from the doña's stores and left this morning."

Roebuck turned to Nicolson and said, "There may still be time, Commodore. I can have the *Savannah* ready in two hours. I will leave then."

Nicolson said, "You'll do no such thing,"

Roebuck was still standing, looking down at Nicolson, suffering an anxious need to hurry. "Sir," he said, "we will need every second to overtake them."

Nicolson said, "Our work is finished in Rio de la Plata, Mr. Roebuck. What LeBlanc does is France's problem."

Montcalvo said, "Intelligence informs me that Leblanc has sugar plantations in Bahia. Should he reach it, he, Doña Belén, and the silver will vanish into Brazil's hinterlands. Not you or anyone, including the French, will be able to do a thing about it."

Nicolson said, "Mr. Roebuck, I will have enough trouble explaining the loss of life from your ship, eleven men so far. I will have to explain this to the Naval Commission. They will greet this news with unfriendliness. I have no intention of allowing you to make this any more difficult for me than you already have."

Montcalvo said, "Commodore, you answer to a naval commission?"

"As most commodores do."

"And who does the commission answer to?"

"What do you mean?" Nicolson said.

"The President of the United States, perhaps, has installed a Lord of the Admiralty as is done in England?"

Nicolson said, "The Secretary of the Navy." There he paused to swallow some more beer to clear his throat. He added, "We are fortunately spared from lords in the United States."

"A political appointment?"

"Naturally," Nicolson said, "appointed by the president."

"And who does your president answer to?"

"I see what you're after," Nicolson said. "You mean the people of the United States."

Montcalvo shook his head, impatience lining his face.

"I believe he means the newspapers," Roebuck said.

Montcalvo said, "Yes, I do. Commodore Nicolson, if you take no action to recover what you have lost to LeBlanc, the goodwill that Commander Roebuck has won among many of the people here in Rio de la Plata will be squandered. Your country will be disgraced in the eyes of our people. You will be seen as complicit in LeBlanc's theft of our nation's wealth. And worst of all, complicit in the abduction of one of our most beloved citizens, Doña Belén Saavedra y Mancera."

Nicolson said, "What does this have to do with the newspapers?"

"It will be news from one end of your country to the other. I will see to that. I have an American nephew who edits the *National Intelligencer* and he is a great friend of Duff Green of the *Republic* in New York. This will be a story that Americans want to read."

"Sir," Roebuck said, "The clock is ticking."

Nicolson said, "No," but didn't sound very certain now.

Montcalvo said, "Your name will be connected to Houghton's forever in our history and in your politics. The infamy will stick to your naval commission unless they can attach the blame to you."

"Fine, goddamn you, fine," Nicolson said, "but I will have nothing to do with it. It's your ship and your neck, Mr. Roebuck." Turning an angry eye on Montcalvo, he said, "And to hell with you, sir."

Montcalvo smiled, put his hand on Roebuck's shoulder, and said, "Be quick."

Chapter 38

Back on the *Savannah*, Roebuck had let his officers know about Doña Belén and about the urgency of their new mission. They had responded by making the ship ready to weigh anchor in less than two hours. A stiff land breeze blew and Roebuck had taken advantage of it, making way out of the harbor with the help of a red-cheeked pilot whose clipped, indecipherable Spanish sounded as if spoke while biting into an apple.

Roebuck cast one final look back at the old city. His eyes lingered on the gleaming steeples of the cathedral before moving to the quay, where stevedores moved cargo. The dark-haired figure of a woman crossed the dock, reminding him of the doña, and whatever pleasure he felt at shipping back out to sea turned gray and bloodless.

"Captain, where do you reckon we'll pick up the sea breeze?"

It was Cockrell, calling down from the forecastle, asking this simple-minded question, typical of the way all the officers, even his lieutenants, had come to trust in what they believed was Roebuck's magical gift to predict the presence and direction of wind. He'd seen two ships that morning picking up speed on the edge of the bay. It was easy to suppose they'd grabbed a sea breeze there, whipping up from the south. His savant-like powers nothing more than two eyes and the sense to use them.

"Once we draw down the southern limit of the harbor," said Roebuck, "it will pick up, and when it does," he turned to Aaberg, "whistle all hands, if you please."

"Aye aye, sir."

Out in the bay, the ship met her breeze and the crew surged to clewing up and sheeting sails, bracing yards. In an hour, the *Savannah* was easy as she leaned into swells, her bow turning the surface over in white folds of foam. Montevideo was gone from view, replaced by a journey that opened up before them again, this time taking them back toward native soil.

"Captain, what chance d'you give to see *Perle* and her vipers again?" said Cockrell, eyes shining with pleasure.

Roebuck said, "I'd say they were good," with no idea at all how good.

Nicolson had said he didn't care whether Roebuck caught LeBlanc or killed him. What he did care about was returning the silver to Rio de la Plata. He conceded that this was an opportunity to reverse the loss of American pride and reputation to the corruption of her consul general Hilary Houghton.

Using silver from La Gaucin as well as proceeds from the sale of cargo stolen from captured merchant ships, LeBlanc had apparently purchased sugar cane plantations in Bahia, Brazil. This is the area where Roebuck hoped to find him. The *Savannah* would have to be fast. LeBlanc and his ships had a two-day advantage, but the French ships weren't manned by sailors so much as a collection of mercenaries and thieves. His own crew was Roebuck's only hope, because he knew if he didn't catch LeBlanc at sea, there wouldn't be any catching him at all.

How had Houghton and LeBlanc, such different men, come together? Guillory had said that LeBlanc had a legion of creditors in France who made it impossible for him to return without the prospect of living out his twilight years in debtor's prison. As for Houghton, Guillory had said he suffered from the same delusions as the typical American adventurer, only a little grander. Greed made for strange bedfellows.

Two decks below the main deck's bow was a compartment barely large enough to hold a litter of dogs. They called it the sick bay and it was where Roebuck was visiting First Lieutenant Bernard Malvey, who rested in a hammock. Benoit had been treating Malvey with sweet water drawn from springs in the hills above Montevideo, and soups made from the broth of herbs, roots, and a misshapen species of fish that Roebuck didn't recognize. Benoit had also prescribed slow walks on deck for fresh air and pastes concocted from the organs of that same odd fish. When Malvey's fever had broken in a prodigious sweat, the surgeon deemed his system "purged."

"You look like a new man, Mr. Malvey. You'll be on the mast tops soon," Roebuck said.

"True, sir, very true."

Malvey had become friendly, even solicitous, since his release from Montevideo's prison. Roebuck hoped this new spirit would last but had his doubts. The pleasure Malvey took in subversion had seemed as much a part of him as the spots freckling his cheeks.

"I am glad to see you so well, Lieutenant," said Roebuck.

"Surgeon says I can walk the quarterdeck alone tomorrow. Be at my post again in days sir, I can feel it. Take more than the shits to keep Bernard Malvey off duty, excusing my language, sir."

"We'll be able to count on the best of Bernard Malvey?"

"That you can, sir, surely. Yes, indeed. I owe you that." Malvey looked quickly away. "Feeling a little worn out sir, sorry." He closed his eyes.

Roebuck had the impression that Malvey had just thanked him in those few words, which had been awkward but earnest. How many reasons had Malvey been given to thank someone during his lifetime? Probably very few.

"Well then, I must check with the officer of the watch, Mr. Cockrell, I believe."

"Best be on your way then, sir, before he runs our prow right into Brazil."

"Until later, Lieutenant."

"*Vaya con Dios*, sir." Malvey smiled in a way that was as close to reticence as Roebuck ever expected to see.

***

A week later, Roebuck was on the quarterdeck as dewy morning gusts blew from the southwest, cooling him through the cloth of his trouser legs. Every day since leaving Montevideo had been a nearly perfect replica of its predecessor, driving them closer to the Bay of Bahia and the center of Brazil's sugar trade. The *Savannah* had made good time.

The horizon was a damp impenetrable muddle. Roebuck, answering a sensation that prickled the back of his neck and forehead, had given word for tubs of cutlasses and pikes to be placed around the main deck, and for magazines and filling rooms to be readied. Malvey was healthy enough to be at the guns again and had just put his crews through an exhausting drill. Malvey was very pleased to have so grand a supply of fresh powder, haranguing the men in a way that demonstrated the extent of his recovery. Roebuck could see that crews didn't need much encouragement. There wasn't a man on board didn't know what had happened to the Americans at La Gaucin or to the vicar, a man of compassion, and his acolytes in Colonia. They badly wanted this fight.

Drawing closer to the city of Salvador in the state of Bahia, the *Savannah* began to encounter trading ships and slavers. The sugar trade's insatiable need for slave labor was well established.

The next morning had been warmer, the equator getting closer and closer. The day following that was warmer still. According to Roebuck's calculation, Bahia lay directly west.

"Halloo deck!" It was the foresail topman. "Ship off the port bow. She's a full-rigger sir, on a starboard tack and bent our way."

Several minutes passed before another of the topmen sighted a second contact eastward.

The first topman called again. "Halloo deck! The bigger of the two has hauled and loosed her mizzen royal three times." This Roebuck suspected was a signal when distance or conditions obscured hand held flags.

Roebuck brought up his spyglass. "Looks like the *Perle* and she's standing toward us," he said. "I suppose the signal was to combine." He snapped the glass shut.

"Canvas, sir?" Aaberg said.

"They press full-sailed."

"In a hurry, I guess."

Roebuck said, "Let them come." He wanted to seem calm and took a moment to simmer down before saying, "Time to crowd on sail. We'll make for the starboard ship. Get us there quick, Mr. Aaberg, before they combine."

"Aye aye, sir."

"Helm down, young man, hard," said Roebuck to the wheel's quartermaster.

Aaberg called to the mizzen and main mast captains, telling them to set studding sails. The widened spread of canvas shot them ahead so quickly that the first of LeBlanc's ships altered her course away.

"Clear the decks, Mr. Aaberg." Roebuck turned to one of the boys. "Beat to quarters, Billings."

The boy rapped a loud emphatic drumbeat as men cleared the deck of anything that might interfere with the operation of the guns.

"Run the guns in!" Malvey was up on deck now, answering the call of the drum. Gun muzzles were pulled back for loading.

"Lieutenant Malvey. Our first chance will be with the *Perle*," said Roebuck, pointing, "with our bow chasers."

"I reckon so, sir," said Malvey. "She won't want to face us alone. She'll try hard to link up with the other."

They continued along a direct line toward the *Perle*, LeBlanc's forty-eight-gun razee.

It was another hour before Malvey called, "We've closed to the range of our long eighteens, Captain."

The *Savannah* was to the *Perle*'s wind, an advantage Roebuck hoped to use to disable her, or at least deal a blow, before her consort arrived. But he'd underestimated the speed of the second ship. It was Captain Dufour's twenty-eight-gun *Badine* and had closed the gap with surprising quickness to join LeBlanc. Roebuck knew there would be a price to pay for underestimating the corvette's speed. He said, "Haul the stuns'ls and royals."

Aaberg gave the command and the crew jumped to it, reducing the ship's sail for battle.

"Ready when you are, sir!" shouted Malvey from his position over the two eighteen-pounders.

"Fire at will, Mr. Malvey."

The *Savannah* had her nose toward the *Perle,* and her two bow chasers fired one after the other. The first was short by two hundred yards, the second by fifty.

"Mr. Malvey, you are wide right, sir, by some margin," Roebuck said, nerves causing him to state the obvious. "Do you have the centerline of those guns?"

"Yes, sir," Malvey said. "Those two shots were to compensate. These next will tell."

They reloaded and Malvey again called for discharge. Chain shot spun out of the gun in a burst of smoke and fire. It missed, twenty yards to the right, but the range was good. Roebuck said nothing, feeling like his head might explode. Nerves warped him, had him seeing each miss as the difference between victory and defeat. Malvey adjusted the gun himself, taking a few extra seconds. He yelled, "Here's one for Ten'til!" The crew roared as he pulled the lanyard. Two balls separated by a foot of chain whipped through the air and split the *Perle*'s spanker vangs, freeing the yard and sending the huge canvass trapezoid of her spanker into a flapping luff.

The gun crew cheered. Malvey told them to shut their mouths and keep working. The next shot crashed through the *Perle*'s mizzen topsail and then parted a buntline on the main.

"Whadduya know, Mr. Malvey!" said Roebuck, in a shrill with relief. "What do you know!"

"Damn, Mr. Malvey, if you couldn't take the rag off a bush." It was Cockrell.

"I'll give you enough rags to pattern your old mother a rug when I'm through," said Malvey. He turned to sighting and firing two more rounds as they closed, doing the targeting himself. After the first three misses, the eighteen-pounders didn't put a shot into the sea.

The *Perle* had started to come around, trying to bring her broadside to bear on the *Savannah*. Malvey's eighteens fired down the *Perle*'s length, shredding her rigging.

"Mr. Cockrell, check that Major Pemberton has readied the Marines in the tops. He must have enough cartridges to fill the *Perle*'s deck with lead."

The *Perle* finished her swing to the wind and gathered way. As Malvey's angle of fire flattened, the difficulty of finding the target grew.

The *Badine* had gained enough to come in line with the *Perle*.

"Mr. Aaberg," Roebuck said, "we will wear around."

"Aye, aye, Captain," Aaberg said, adding, "We hurt her, sir. She'll be slower."

Roebuck nodded, thinking that they were about to receive the same sort of treatment from the *Badine*, a consequence of his miscalculation, only from closer in and from fifteen guns instead of two. He knew there was no maneuver left but to bring his starboard battery into position. This meant the *Savannah* would suffer raking fire from the *Badine*'s port battery and fire from the *Perle*'s stern chasers.

If handled well, LeBlanc's and Dufour's guns could ruin them before Malvey could do any of the damage Roebuck so wanted to do.

The *Savannah* began her turn with the *Badine* close enough for Roebuck to see her gun captains looking down the iron barrels of their carronades, sighting targets on the *Savannah*. As commander, he would be among those targets. He contemplated his violent death for a second before silently praying that the enemy would try to shoot up the rigging instead of clearing the deck. He prayed again, before shouting, "Steady, boys!" as much for himself as the crew. "Stay at your guns and we'll have at this little brig. But you must stay at your guns. Mr. Watt!"

"Aye, sir?" Watt had placed himself at the ship's waist with a cocked pistol in his hand, which Roebuck had lent him, and another in his waistband.

"Answer any man who abandons his post with your pistol."

"Aye aye, sir."

The first of the *Badine*'s cannons boomed, flame licking the lip of its muzzle and a thick tail of smoke following. It fired at an angle over their portside bow, smashing the *Savannah*'s lower mast yards. Another gun fired. Chain shot ripped through rigging. Blast followed blast. Men dropped from the *Savannah*'s tops like branches cut from the crown of a tree. The tenth and last gun hurled bar shot down the length of the ship, shearing braces from the lower fore and main yards. The *Perle*'s guns had targeted the rigging and the damage done had proven that choice. Edwards the boatswain and his mates leapt to the work of repair.

The *Savannah* was less than halfway through her turn, helpless to do anything except present herself as a slow, meaty target. Soon the *Badine* began her procession of fire. Double-shotted canister and grape cleared bloody swaths across the *Savannah*'s deck. Two men from the number four gun were ground to a pulp. Withering volleys of metal fanned out. Roebuck felt the wind on his cheek from a clutch of lead balls that lodged themselves in the white pine of the mizzenmast behind him. He watched as the *Badine* prepared another blast, this one clearly aimed at him.

Pemberton shouted, "Roebuck, get yourself behind that mast, you welp. They'll cut you to ribbons."

Roebuck ignored him and shouted, "Hold fast," as much to himself as anyone, fighting the fear and the urge to hide.

"Goddamn you," Pemberton said, sprinting toward the quarterdeck. He put himself between the *Badine*'s gun muzzles and Roebuck just as another burst ripped across the deck. This one lifted Pemberton up and threw him backward, absorbing cannister headed for Roebuck. Pemberton's hands reflexively clutched at his mauled face. His right ear was gone and his eye hung out of its socket by a knotty thread.

Roebuck knelt beside him. "Stretcher!" he screamed. Then gently to Pemberton, "There's not a mark on your uniform, Mr. Pemberton, and you have all your limbs."

"My ear," Pemberton said, touching the void. "Do you see it? Will you take it to Benoit to sew back on?"

Roebuck watched his friend the great Marine major die with half of his face smeared across the quarterdeck.

The *Savannah* completed her turn and Roebuck brought her to heel in a position parallel to the line of LeBlanc's two ships, but in between.

The *Badine* was captained with iron poise. Roebuck saw Dufour on her quarterdeck with sword in hand.

The *Savannah* fired her foremost guns into the stern of the *Perle* and her aftmost guns into the bow of the *Badine*. For the moment the *Savannah* had an advantage, carrying more guns into the fight. But she was taking terrible fire both fore and aft. It would not be long, Roebuck knew, before LeBlanc would find a way to bring more, probably many more, of his guns to bear.

Malvey called from the bow, "The *Perle*'s just lost her mizzen-mast cap, sir."

Roebuck said, "Now see if you can't cut her mast down, Lieutenant."

"I'll try, sir."

If Malvey could dismast the *Perle*, the balance would shift in the *Savannah*'s favor. He needed this because LeBlanc had backed the *Perle* to bring more of her guns to bear on the *Savannah*, firing them with effect; she would soon be in position to savage the *Savannah* with a broadside.

"Keep an eye on the *Perle*'s main and mizzen masts, Mr. Aaberg. Any sign of her backing any further, holler."

"Aye aye, sir."

"Sir, the corvette is crowding on sail, readying to stand toward the *Perle*," said Edwards.

The *Badine*? No! Roebuck hadn't expected her captain to take such a risk, but here she came, shooting forward. The Perle herself moving forward and out of the way. The move was well synchronized and once the *Badine* was where Dufour wanted her, she punched the *Savannah* with a broadside, smashing the gun deck. Roebuck had been outmaneuvered.

"Give me a report, Mr. Cockrell," Roebuck said, almost choking on the words.

Cockrell aye-ayed and backed quickly down the hatch to see what damage had been done.

The *Savannah* blasted back, but her crews had prepared for the *Perle* to back, not the *Badine* to jump ahead, and all but a few of her twenty-four guns were leveled too steeply for the bigger *Perle*. Their shot sailed through *Badine*'s rigging and splashed wastefully into the Atlantic far to the lee.

"We've been hulled, sir." Cockrell was back and out of breath.

"How many?"

"Two holes, sir, Mr. Flynn is trying to fill them. Also, the sixteen and eighteen guns are disabled."

"Their crews?"

"Dead or wounded."

Hulled. This would be the first time an American frigate had suffered that indignity in decades. Defeat at the hands of the *Badine*, a ship carrying fewer than half the *Savannah*'s guns and probably crewed by as many landsmen as sailors, was staring him in the face, utter failure.

Gun smoke grayed them in, and Roebuck could see very little of his enemy. But he could hear them, the commands of their gunnery officers and the grind of iron-rimmed wheels as cannon rolled into position for another round.

Malvey called, "The *Perle,* sir, her mizzenmast is sagging," pausing for a moment before he said, "Why, she's taking off, sir, cracking on sail."

"All guns, fire them now," called Roebuck. "Both batteries! Mr. Aaberg, cut us under those people." He pointed at the *Badine*.

The simultaneous eruption of all the *Savannah*'s guns hid them in thick layers of smoke. Visibility was reduced to a few yards in any direction.

Aaberg called to the mast captains, "Ready to brace about," and soon after, "Starboard the helm for stern-board, hoist the jib, port sheet aft."

Aaberg waited as the seamen heaved up canvas, timing his next order. "Square the after yards."

"Mr. Malvey," Roebuck called, "Mr. Aaberg will soon have us luffing across their stern. When we are, I want every shot on her rudder and chains."

"We'll set her adrift, sir?" Malvey said.

"Set her adrift and board her," Roebuck said. "Mr. Cockrell, tell Sergeant Mace to prepare a boarding party."

If they slowed across the *Badine*'s stern and Malvey had time to make the shots count, they might damage her tiller or the chains that controlled it. Then they'd turn straight into her, grapple, and pull her close.

"How will we find our way, sir, when we can't see a thing?" It was Aaberg.

Roebuck had the *Badine*'s last speed and heading burned into his mind. He would feel his way around her. But what kind of answer was that? He ignored the question.

The *Savannah* lurched back. "On my word, Mr. Aaberg, we'll swing away from the wind as close to square as we can." Roebuck waited, feeling her. "Now!"

Aaberg gave the orders, and the crew hauled the sails close again.

"Starboard the helm, hard now," said Roebuck. "Another man for that wheel, goddammit!" He felt frantic to put the *Savannah* at the angle needed to bring them within a grappling throw.

"Hard a-lee," called the helmsman.

Smoke cleared as the *Savannah* nosed around, paying off as well as Roebuck could hope. The nub of the *Badine*'s spanker boom suddenly pushed toward them through the smoke.

"Mr. Malvey, aim twenty-five feet below the end of that boom!" yelled Roebuck. "Luff, Mr. Aaberg! We must crawl past her."

But they were too fast, nearly to the number-five starboard gun before they were ready to fire. Eight shots wasted.

"Slower!"

The remainder of the *Savannah*'s guns began their assault on the *Badine*. Smoke again thickened.

Malvey said, "I'd wager she's opened up below, sir, and I doubt there's much left of her rudder and chains."

If it was true, the *Savannah* had destroyed the ability of the *Badine* to steer. But that was only the first step. Now they needed to bring her athwart.

Sergeant Mace, Pemberton's second, appeared to say, "Here to report we've handed out the pikes, cutlasses, and pistols and we're ready to board, Captain." The Mace's eyes were shining, the prospect of the fight making him look half drunk.

"How many?"

"We'll take forty and leave ten sharpshooters aloft."

Roebuck looked over the side to the *Badine*. Her normal complement would be about 140 men, but he suspected that LeBlanc's mercenary crews were undermanned and piecemeal. "Mr. Cockrell, gather ten of our best seamen to join us in the boarding party."

"Aye aye, sir."

Aaberg said, "Captain Roebuck. You do not intend to board with the party?" There was something both inevitable and irritating about the Aaberg's good sense.

"I do, Mr. Aaberg, and I ask that you remain to manage the ship in my absence." Roebuck turned to Edwards and Midshipman Rowan, saying, "As you are my witness, I am appointing Second Lieutenant Aaberg to take command in my absence. I fear Lieutenant Malvey's illness may still weigh too heavily upon him."

Aaberg was well and ready. And if command distracted Malvey from his management of the guns, they would have no chance. Besides, the crew trusted Aaberg, even if they admired Malvey's brass. Smoke cleared, revealing the *Badine*'s crew swarming to repair her tiller and chains.

Roebuck said, "Fill our sails, helmsman, and fetch us alongside." The *Savannah* caught the fore tack and jumped forward. "Mr. Aaberg, brace the main and mizzen tops'ls flat aback, and then shake all forward, let the jib fly." The ship eased into position to unleash a broadside. Canister and shot swept the *Badine*'s deck.

The crew took to the braces again, swinging the yards around, the helmsman meeting them with the wheel, steering the *Savannah* into the *Badine*'s port side.

"Hah! We have her, sir!" said Aaberg, excitement betraying him for once.

The Marines heaved grapples at the *Badine*'s rigging and rails, hooking and heaving her toward them. The *Badine*'s crew tried to keep the *Savannah* away with handspikes, but the *Savannah* was too heavy and they were too few. Roebuck drew his cutlass, climbed onto the rail, and leapt at the French ship with a group of Marines, all of them hacking at the *Badine*'s boarding nets, trying to clear the way. The French poured a volley of musket fire into them and several Marines fell back. Roebuck felt lines begin to give, the nets springing upward and open. Another volley came, a dull wap-wap sound of bullets hitting flesh. The Marine to his right grunted and fell between the hulls of the two ships into the Atlantic.

Roebuck pulled himself onto the deck amidships and faced a mass of the *Badine*'s marines and sailors readying a charge. He drew his knife with his left hand, cutlass ready in his right. The *Savannah*'s men were still clambering on board as the French came at them. Roebuck parried a pike thrust and smashed down on a seaman with the knuckles of the knife. He saw Mace take another by the hair and the waist of his pants and toss him over the side. Cockrell fired his pistol, howling like a moonstruck dog as they pushed the *Badine*'s crew back. Now the men of the *Savannah* charged. Roebuck drove his cutlass into a French marine's shoulder. It was a mad scramble in a smoke and haze that made it almost impossible to see whether you cut an enemy or friend.

A scream caught Roebuck's attention and he turned aft to see Dufour slashing his saber at one of the *Savannah*'s Marines, who tried to block. Like an acrobat, Dufour stepped left, raised his sword, and drove the tip into the Marine's chest. The saber was curved and caught a little as Dufour tried to yank it from the man's flesh. Putting boot heel next to blade, Dufour kicked the Marine back and the blade came free.

Roebuck sprinted at him. Dufour sensed it and thrust his saber with such speed that Roebuck barely parried it away. Dufour slashed with a high backhand. Roebuck blocked with his cutlass but slipped like a man on ice over the deck's bloody surface and fell.

Dufour came in quickly, too quickly, hurrying the killing thrust and missing as Roebuck rolled away, sat up, and kicked his feet to propel himself backward toward the *Badine*'s mizzenmast. Dufour slashed down to the left. Roebuck ducked right, wrapping his left arm around the mast and levering himself up. Dufour leapt in, but instead of stabbing he brought the brass pommel of the saber's hilt down on Roebuck's temple with shocking power. The pain staggered Roebuck and before he could recover, Dufour did it again.

Fear and fear alone kept Roebuck on his feet. Dufour drew his saber back. Roebuck saw an opening and stabbed his knife into it, but Dufour sprang away, escaping with nothing more than a few threads cut from his coat. Both of them up now and panting, Roebuck feeling pain, Dufour with his flattened blade out, flicking the tip. The saber was a full six inches longer than Roebuck's cutlass.

Dufour watched Roebuck's eyes. Roebuck made a move for cover behind the mast and the Frenchman followed easily, but this time it was Dufour who slipped on the blood. Roebuck thrust at the fallen man with his cutlass. Dufour flicked it away but didn't see Roebuck's knife as its brass-knuckled handle smashed into his brow. Roebuck slashed again with the cutlass, but again Dufour was too quick, parrying and raising his free hand to clear his vision of the blood beginning to flow from the cut above his eye. It was a chance, the best one Roebuck would have, and he leapt at Dufour, driving his knife into the man's belly, turning, pulling, and stabbing again and then again as they tumbled over. Dufour still had the strength to push Roebuck away, slashing madly as he did. Roebuck scrambled to a sitting position and stared. He felt weak, like he was floating in a warm pool. His temple throbbed. The weight of his head seemed to be supported by silken cords. He felt a churning nausea.

His vision tunneled as he watched Dufour trying to stand, putting his knees under himself, unsteady but somehow rising. Dufour came toward him now as if from a great distance, his right foot out in front, but unable to raise his left. He looked down and grabbed the knife Roebuck had left in his belly by its handle, pulling it out.

This Frenchman wasn't finished fighting. He had willed himself up and now he willed himself forward. Roebuck was finished, without enough energy to roll out of the way as Dufour raised his saber for one final blow. Then suddenly a sword tip showed through his chest and Dufour pitched forward. Malvey, out of nowhere, stepped on the man's back and yanked his killing blade free.

"Just easing the poor froggy bastard past his suffering," said Malvey. Then he rifled through Dufour's pockets.

CHAPTER 39

Bright sunlight reflected off the dome of Benoit's bald head as he moved in to examine the bloody pulp of Roebuck's head wound.

"You must come below where I can treat you," the surgeon said.

Roebuck was seated on a stool on the quarterdeck. "Treat me here."

"You have to lie down so I can clean the wound and apply sutures."

"Do it here, now," said Roebuck. If he went down to the sick bay or his cabin or anywhere but here, he was afraid he would be dead the next time he came back up. "Young man," Roebuck called to the boy on watch. "Send for Lieutenant Malvey."

The boy sprinted off.

"Captain, you must lie down."

"God damn your eyes, would you have me lie on deck planks?" He was not going to let Benoit cut so much as a half inch of skin from him, that much he was sure of.

Benoit moved off with a look that made Roebuck think the surgeon was as likely to let him die as save him. Except Roebuck understood that the man's enormous professional pride wouldn't allow that.

"Hallo, Captain Roebuck." It was Malvey. "What a big French bastard he was."

"Captain Dufour was his name."

"Can't fault him for how he handled that saber," Malvey said. "Gave as good as he got, didn't he?" The lieutenant stared at the blood-soaked wrapping around Roebuck's head.

"Until you arrived," said Roebuck. "And then he just got."

"What he deserved, the bloody bastard. I'd give it to him every day of my life the same way if the Lord willed it. Toady-fucking bastard."

"It felt good didn't it, putting steel into a motherfucker such as he," Roebuck said, lightheaded and carried away by Malvey's enthusiasm.

"Aye sir, as good a feeling as I've ever had cutting someone."

"Tell me, Lieutenant, how does the *Badine* float?"

"She was kind enough not to sink, sir. And sweet enough to give up her treasure." Malvey showed Roebuck a large nugget of silver between his forefinger and thumb.

"Good, Mr. Malvey, very damn good."

"That's not the best of it, sir." Malvey grinned at Benoit. "It's the lady sir. She was below on the *Badine*. And she ships with us now."

Roebuck felt nausea and panic. He had been certain she would be on the *Perle*.

Malvey must have noticed, because he said, "She is fine and tending to some of the wounded on the *Badine*."

Roebuck wanted to rise up and hug his first lieutenant. "God bless you, man, and God bless this crew."

Malvey said, "She has asked to come aboard and see you. In fact, she has asked many times. You have done it, sir," Malvey said.

"Recovered four chests of silver and freed the Lady plus her two girls. All that remains is to welcome her aboard."

Roebuck's head throbbed and his mind was weak. He wanted to lift his hand to his hair. He knew it was plastered to his head by blood and sweat. He would under no circumstances receive her looking like this. He said, "If the *Perle* arrives, the *Savannah* will be her target, not the *Badine,* so the lady is safer where she is."

"Doña Belén will insist, Captain. She has insisted already."

"Then you have done well, Mr. Malvey, to resist her." Roebuck meant it. Most men fell all over themselves to please her. Malvey wasn't that kind. "And how does the *Badine* fair?"

"We put four holes in her stern, sir. If she were Portsmouth-built, she'd be sunk, but the French are masters of the bulkhead, so she remains above water."

"She's seaworthy?"

"Aye, sir. With twenty men at the pumps, rotating in fives, spending themselves with the effort. We're overloading the bow, sir, moving the guns and ballast forward. See if we can't raise her aft so we get her holes out of the sea."

"How much water does she carry?"

"Five feet, sir, and gaining."

"She'll keep above water if we tow her to Salvador?"

"How far is that sir?"

"Six leagues, maybe less."

"Wouldn't want to speculate on that, Captain."

"Consider the speculation an order, then, Mr. Malvey."

"Well, yes, sir." Malvey said. "With care I believe she can."

In Salvador they could secure Doña Belén's safety and repair the *Badine* to make her a prize. This would be an enormous boon to every man on the *Savannah*. The thought reminded him. "And the *Savannah*?"

"Her rigging has been badly fouled. We must patch all the courses and replace one in three of her yards."

"Masts?"

"They have held up well, Captain, yes indeed they have. The foretopmast was hit but if we don't load her up too much, she'll stay aright. And the darling Mr. Flynn has reduced the flow of water through the holes shot into her bilge."

"Prisoners?"

"Secured below."

"Who captains the prize crew?"

"Lieutenant Brimblecorn, sir. Midshipman Enderby is his second. They have sixty of the crew."

"Excellent, Mr. Malvey," said Roebuck. "The *Savannah* is fortunate to have such experience as yours aboard. We'll take the *Badine* in tow, see to it immediately."

"Before we've finished repairing her and the *Savannah*?"

Fogged with pain and loss of blood, Roebuck's mind was still clear enough to know that they had to reach the safety of the harbor at Salvador as soon as possible. They must avoid LeBlanc or face annihilation. He said, "Yes, we'll refit as we move." The *Perle* had lost the top of her mizzenmast and had much of her rigging knocked down, but she would have replacement spars and could refit and be ready to fight in a matter of hours. Repairing the *Savannah*'s would not be so tidy. Their best chance was a safe harbor.

Sailors arrived with a cot. When they attempted to lift Roebuck off his stool and into it, he said, "Hands off me, and get to work. With all that has to be done, it takes four of you to carry one cot?"

Roebuck rose, staggered a step and then dropped into it. Looking at Benoit, he said, "You have everything you need to clean and sew?"

The surgeon nodded. "Take this," he said.

"What is it?"

"Laudanum for the pain."

"None of that. You'll not put me any further out of my right mind, sir, and if you cut one ounce of my flesh away, I'll return the favor ten times over."

"You're as stubborn as a toddling child," Benoit said, "Take this, then," and handed him a leather strap.

"For what?"

"To bite when you feel my knife. I intend to remove some flesh around your wound." Benoit doused the cut with liquid.

The pain was sharp and immediate. "God damn you, you'll kill me before you even get to the knife."

"It's a mixture of absinthe and vinegar. The ancient Greeks used something like it to cleanse a wound."

"It's devilry and tortu—"

The surgeon stuffed the strap in Roebuck's mouth about as violently as anyone had done anything that day. "Hold him down," said Benoit, and then he began with his scalpel.

Roebuck immediately regretted turning down the laudanum. He tried to communicate this with a series of grunts, but his mouth was too full of leather and his arms were under the control of two burly seamen. He'd remember the big bastards, make them pay later. The scalpel carved a ring around the tender flesh of his wound and his head throbbed mercilessly. Roebuck tried to yell as loud as he could for the laudanum. It did no good. If the surgeon and the others thought these were cries of pain, they were not entirely wrong.

"The skull is fractured, Captain. I must align the pieces."

Roebuck felt the cold metal of Benoit's instrument like a dagger of ice. He bit harder on the leather as the pain rose, even his sweat tormenting him as if they were tiny extrusions of molten lead.

Benoit shook his head doubtfully. Roebuck thinking that a bedside manner might be something the man could improve upon.

Benoit said, "That should do it. I rather like the work I've done, Captain. I'll wrap it tight now to hold it in place and to keep it clean. Good thing I picked up the extra gauze in Montevideo." Benoit said this with cheer in his voice so flimsy that everyone within earshot ground their eyes in embarrassment. The surgeon removed the leather strap.

Roebuck hissed, "Get yourself below, Surgeon. Your work is just beginning." If he were a snake he'd bite Benoit. If he were a gator he'd take off an arm, the one with that godforsaken scalpel still in hand.

As soon as Benoit was gone, Roebuck stood, went noodle-legged with pain, and stumbled. Edwards and a mate caught him and helped him to the stool, where he passed an hour waiting for his mind to clear. The rising sea was becoming a threat to the ponderous and waterlogged *Savannah*. Roebuck listened as the carpenter's mates plugged more of the hull's shot holes by pounding in wooden cones smothered in tallow, thinking that the bilge would be too full of water to permit them to do the job properly. The hull would continue leaking, weighing the *Savannah* down through the waves.

"Mr. Aaberg."

"Sir?"

"Shift the men from repairing the jib and spanker to securing the gun ports instead." The fore and aft sails could wait.

"Aye aye, sir."

Sealed gun ports meant that they would lose the firepower of twenty-eight cannon on the gun deck. But Roebuck could see no other way. The sea would soon be high and splashing through those ports and, not long after that, flowing through them.

All hands were engaged in refitting the courses with new canvass, repairing blocks, setting new spars for the yard arms, but the *Savannah* wouldn't be anything close to ready for action if that action came soon. It was a fatiguing thought to Roebuck. His cot beckoned.

As he watched from the stool, he felt like a visitor, a spectator. Watt came with a grim list of eight dead and twenty-three wounded. Roebuck noticed Pemberton's name among the former and his own among the latter. He knew that many of those twenty-three wouldn't live out the day. They'd be buried at sea quickly to clear space for others. How strange to think that Roebuck himself might soon be wrapped in canvas, weighted by iron shot, and sinking to his grave. There was none but God to decide now. Was never otherwise. His mind was as inundated as the ship as he began imagining bloody stumps of arms and legs sawn off by the *Savannah*'s very careful surgeon. If any of the procedures had been novel or required some unusual technique, would Benoit diagram them? Roebuck had once seen the surgeon's journal, its pages full of drawings detailing nearly every malady, every surgical complication the man had encountered during his years at sea. Benoit was so much better than every one of the bone-sawing shysters Roebuck had shipped with in the past.

He dozed a little, drifting from wakefulness to something like sleep. He knew this was dangerous. The *Perle* was out there and he must force himself to consider how they could survive if she found them. Even so he could not help it and it went on for some time.

Malvey appeared in front of him again. "Captain, sir, the gun decks are good and tight."

"What is our speed?"

"We've taken the *Badine* in tow and her drag is prodigious."

"Our speed, please."

"A knot, maybe two on a gust."

Roebuck suppressed a groan and said, "Our heading?"

"Northwest by west, sir. The wind bears northeast now and steady. We've been making way for close to six hours."

He calculated that this meant that they would still be hours from Salvador and safety. Roebuck said a quick prayer that LeBlanc give up the fight and asked for his glass. A boy handed it to him. He had hoped to see the shadow of Brazil's coast to their west, but there was only sea. He set the glass on deck and let the lids of his eyes shut.

He sat like that, unsure how long, until the call came from one of the tops, "Hello deck! Sail ho. Dead ahead."

Roebuck watched Aaberg lift his glass up and hold it there for some time, before saying, "It's the *Perle*, sir. Three masts, two decks, and flying French colors. Same ship as yesterday, I'm sure of it."

"How far off?"

"I'd say six maybe seven miles."

"What of her mizzenmast?"

"Refit, I guess, Captain. She's carrying sails on all masts up to her t'gallants."

"What is her attitude, Mr. Aaberg?"

"Close hauled and standing for us."

Roebuck took a look himself. What he saw was confident, aggressive sailing. LeBlanc had doubtless detected the limp in the

Savannah's way and noticed that she was awash, sitting low, half her guns sealed in.

The *Perle* would be in range long before they could reach a safe harbor. Roebuck used the restorative power of fear to concentrate his addling mind on what to do next.

"Sir, the *Perle* is tacking to point her nose sou'-sou'east."

Roebuck said, "She's headed to the wind."

"Yes, sir," Aaberg said. "The admiral probably wishes to move out from under our lee."

LeBlanc was choosing to bring his sails even closer to the wind, sacrificing the *Perle*'s speed in order to gain the advantage of a windward position.

Roebuck said, "Helmsman, take us a-weather, bring the breeze over our port beam."

Malvey had been listening to the exchange and said, "Shall I set the *Badine* afloat, sir? We'll treble our speed at least without her."

"No. But ready a couple of hands with hatchets. When we have to cut her loose, we will."

"Aye aye, sir."

"And Mr. Malvey."

"Sir?"

"Clear the decks for action. The guns are yours again."

Malvey smiled, "We'll make the *Perle* rue the day, Captain"

When Malvey had gone, Roebuck asked for his chair to be brought up to the quarterdeck so he could lean on its back in order to remain standing. He did not like the idea of sitting on a stool during what was bound to be a frightful battle. The pain in his head had subsided by degrees, although there was still more than enough of it.

Roebuck wondered if they should lighten the *Savannah* by tossing out the water caskets. No, her lower profile was worth preserving, less of her hull above water for the *Perle* to target. She would never be quick in this condition, caskets or not.

LeBlanc commanded a much fitter ship. He had her on course to take advantage of the wind. If Roebuck let him, the *Perle* could have her way with them, and could sink them easily. But LeBlanc did not know whether the doña shipped on the *Badine* or the *Savannah* and the same was true for the silver. The admiral was here to recover both and could not risk sinking either ship. Greed was something you could count on, and Roebuck had seen enough of it in LeBlanc to figure the admiral would try to board and capture each of the two wounded ships to get what he wanted. Putting them downwind now would make it easier, where LeBlanc could neutralize the *Savannah* by killing her crew with canister and grape and dismasting her. If he succeeded, there would be aught for the Americans but to heave to and surrender. Given the *Savannah*'s condition, LeBlanc could be forgiven for thinking that the fight was already won.

"Mr. Edwards," Roebuck said.

"Aye, sir?"

"I want you and your mates to reeve double-blocked lines to as many of the grapple hooks as you can."

"Block the hook line, sir? Is that what you mean?"

"It's what I said."

Roebuck watched the gap between the two ships slowly close over two cycles of the hourglass. Each grain of sand that fell seemed to pile tension up on deck. He tried to think of a way out, of something to change the balance weighted against them. But nothing came. The *Badine* was dragging them to a crawl. And even counting the *Badine*'s cannons and carronades, the *Savannah*'s closed gun ports meant that LeBlanc outgunned them. Roebuck sat down and gazed across the rising ocean at the enemy. LeBlanc would be doing the same, taking the *Savannah*'s measure, maybe congratulating himself.

When the fight was nearly on them, Roebuck saw the line of Brazil's coast in his spyglass no more than three pitiless leagues away. He watched as the *Perle*'s crew loaded her guns and loosened her braces in preparation for the move a-weather. Then his mind warmed with the germ of an idea. Gradually he saw what he must do.

"Sergeant Mace!" he shouted, forgetting for a moment the gash on his head. He twisted a grimace of pain from his face. "Join us here on the quarterdeck." Malvey and Aaberg were there already.

"Coming, sir." Mace answered from the ship's waist where he and his Marines were preparing themselves for the fight. Mace slowed as he drew near, hesitating, slit-eyed. Roebuck guessed this was because it was strange to find the ship's commanding officer seated and unable to form his syballs, or rather syllables, correctly.

Roebuck plunged forward and addressed the three officers gathered beside him. "When we begin this fight, the ship, the crew, Marines, all of us, must act in perfect unity. If we do, victory can be ours." That was a reasonable start, although Roebuck noticed that the word *together* had come out as "arleger." Still, the sequence was good and he hadn't detected any bewilderment in their eyes. "The *Perle* will have to come about in order to complete her run to the wind. When she does, cut away the *Badine*, port the helm, and we'll run under the breeze right up into the *Perle*, stem to stern. Is this clear?"

Aaberg thought for a moment before a grin wrinkled his weathered face and he began to nod. "When she starts to bear away, sir?"

"That's right, Mr. Aaberg."

"Cutting away the *Badine* might just give us the lift we need," Aaberg said.

Roebuck nodded.

Malvey aye-ayed and Mace nodded.

"Mr. Malvey, as soon as you can train your aftermost gun on the *Perle*'s port, let fire all, double-shot grape and canister. I want her deck clear."

"Too many men on her deck for that, sir," said Malvey. "Let's not wait, but jump her rails, board her like we did her consort."

Roebuck glared. Even now they questioned him, maybe they always would.

"As long as there is a thimble of blood flowing through my veins, I command, Mr. Malvey, do you hear me?"

Malvey quickly looked at Mace. But Mace kept his eyes on Roebuck. "I guess you'd command on a half a thimble," Malvey said. "And I'd gladly follow you if you did, sir."

"Sergeant Mace, you will prepare every grappling hook onboard and throw them into the *Perle*'s shrouds, stays, backstays, anywhere we can gain purchase. Use the grapples that Edwards has reeved. Hook the *Perle* and then pull her to us as fast you might raise a sail."

Mace nodded.

Good. Nothing there but mute acquiescence. "Fit as many men as we can in the fighting tops to suppress their fire. Arm them with carbines and especially grenades and darts. A match tub on every top, please. Use incendiaries, Mace, abundantly. We'll burn them out like rats from a hole. If we kill them enough, they'll lose the means to board."

"Won't they sink us then?" Malvey said.

"And lose all that silver?" said Aaberg. Mace gave a half snort of pleasure.

The *Perle* probably expected to fight a weak and inert opponent. The *Savannah* might— had to—confound that expectation.

"Mr. Aaberg, soak every exposed piece of canvas, wet the decks, and fill the water buckets. We'll want to avoid a fire," Roebuck said. "Five pieces of eight for any man drops a grenade into a hatch and twenty for a man that explodes her."

Mace said, "Hell, maybe I'll do her myself."

Roebuck said, "Iss you, Sergeant, I'll make it thirry," his light-headedness robbing him of control over his tongue. He nodded the officers away and observed as incendiaries were carried up from the magazine as well as boxes full of carbine charges. Roebuck saw Vermont move to the foremast.

When Aaberg took his place again on the quarterdeck, Roebuck asked, "Are we ready?"

"We are, sir."

"Mr. Edwards?"

"Yes, sir. Just waiting for your word."

All eyes were on the *Perle*. What if she stayed her course? Was he seeing what he wanted to see rather than the reality behind the *Perle's* movements? If she didn't tack, what then? Roebuck mouthed another prayer. They were coming thick and fast now.

"Mr. Aaberg," he said, "don't let me sleep. If I start to fade, find a way to keep my eyes open. That is an order."

Aaberg didn't move.

"An order, Mr. Aaberg."

"I understand, sir."

"Hallo deck," came a voice from the maintop, "She's started around!"

When the *Perle* was nearly in irons, Roebuck said, "Starboard the helm!"

And Aaberg nodded to Edwards who called to the stern, "Cut her away, boys!"

Two boatswain's mates quickly hatcheted through the heavy towline, and the *Badine* floated free. As soon as she did, *Savannah* lurched forward, turning away from the wind, her sails starting to gather the breeze.

Aaberg called, "Let go the braces, square the yards and then sheet her home." The *Savannah*'s sails were wide open now and filling quickly. The ship veered toward the *Perle*, gathering speed.

"Sir." It was Malvey. "There'll be no broadside like this. Our bow needs to line up to their stern."

Aaberg said, "They've run out the guns, sir."

Had LeBlanc anticipated them? The crash of thirty-two-pound shot from three of his carronades flew the length of the main deck, plowing down two of the number-eight gunners. A succession of explosions followed as the rest of the *Perle*'s guns rocked them.

Roebuck looked down and saw teeth and skull fragments on the deck. His trousers dripped with mottled gray flesh.

Whose brains were these? Not Aaberg's. The second lieutenant was still standing, unperturbed, at least outwardly. Holman, the midshipman?

"Mr. Aaberg, brace the fore sails about," called Roebuck. The *Savannah*'s forward momentum broke with a shiver.

"Mr. Malvey, hold fire until your last gun bears."

When they were in line with the *Perle*, less than half a cable between them, Roebuck heard Malvey yell "Fire!" The *Savannah*, heavy and nearly awash, barely shook as her broadside blanketed the *Perle*'s deck with the iron of grapeshot and the slash of canister. The *Perle* answered, smashing them and splitting more planks than Roebuck imagined a ship could lose. The *Savannah* staggered but held. Her wounded began their wailing. Roebuck had no stomach for another sight of teeth and brains over the deck so he kept his eyes on the enemy.

Marines swarmed the tops, adding carbine fire to the din. Mace was on the rail, calling them to fight. At least twenty grappling hooks with their burr-tipped arms flew from the *Savannah*'s deck, catching the *Perle* here and there. But the *Perle* was throwing hooks into the Savannah's rigging. LeBlanc was ready and wanting to board the *Savannah*. The crews heaved the massive bodies together, needing every pound of leverage the lines provided.

The hulls collided, and Roebuck thought of a huge sledge smashing the staves of a barrel. The crackling sound of long oak fibers separating fascinated him. Blood trickled down his cheek. Would this pain ever go away?

"A deft move, sir," Aaberg said. "Our mizzen yardarms and their foremast rigging have come together and we are tangled."

"Entangled?"

"Yes, sir."

LeBlanc may have guessed that the silver had been transferred from the *Badine* to the more seaworthy *Savannah*.

The *Savannah*'s Marines fired into the *Perle*'s deck from the tops. But LeBlanc had his men piled up along their starboard bow, squatting to avoid being hit. Both sides had raised the boarding nets to protect their ships from boarders but Leblanc had cut away a wide passage through the *Perle*'s nets and his men poured through it, the first wave leaping across the now narrow chasm, armed with boarding axes, and cutting the *Savannah*'s boarding nets from their fastenings. In seconds they were on the *Savannah*'s deck at the stern, fighting off attacks from a small band of Marines armed with pikes trying to drive them back over the rails. Roebuck was stunned by how well LeBlanc had responded to the *Savannah*'s maneuver.

Moreover, LeBlanc himself was among the boarders. While not in the front, there he was shouting directions, unmistakable in a plumed admiral's hat. Mace responded by rallying those of his men not shooting from the tops. Roebuck drew the cutlass in his right hand and the knife in his left and took off after Mace, shouting for every seaman within earshot to follow him. But they did not follow Roebuck. They were ahead of him. Moving fast and with decision toward the enemy. When the two bodies of men collided, Roebuck saw Leblanc leading a group of his own marines toward the aft hatch. LeBlanc probably already had an idea of where the silver might be below, wanting, Roebuck supposed, to grab it and go, rather than fight it out here. LeBlanc had served a lifetime on ships just like the *Savannah* and wouldn't take long to unpuzzle where the riches had been stowed.

Roebuck felt a hand grasp his shoulder. "Captain Roebuck, stop. You must stay on the quarterdeck, sir, to command." It was Aaberg, who knew very well that Roebuck commanded practically nothing with his addled mind. But Roebuck could swing a blade. That didn't take such a clear mind.

"Let go of me, Aaberg," Roebuck said, attempting a growl.

Aaberg said, "The surgeon insists—"

"Damn that man's eyes," Roebuck said. "He would have swaddled me and put me in a crib. And damn your eyes, Aaberg. Let me go."

Aaberg released him and called a group of Marines to Roebuck's side. "See that our young commander is not overly rash."

That was bold for such a neutral man as Aaberg. *His blood is up. Fine*, thought Roebuck, *fine*.

Roebuck and his keepers chased LeBlanc and his thieves down two levels to the orlop deck. Roebuck called out when they were finally close enough. LeBlanc turned and laughed when he saw Roebuck, bloody-headed and looking dazed, possibly unstable. The two groups of men came together except for LeBlanc, who scooted away toward a set of locked enclosures where he tried to pry one open. He smashed at a lock with the hilt of his sword, and when this had no effect, he pulled an iron hammer from his waistband.

"LeBlanc!" Roebuck said.

LeBlanc, not taking his eyes off the lock, said, "The day is ours, Mr. Roebuck. It would be wise for you to concede and save the lives of your men. You will be given safe passage."

Roebuck, staggering toward him, wondered what would happen when he got there.

LeBlanc squared his shoulders, sword drawn and straight like Roebuck's own cutlass but longer. He looked confident, the blade like an extension of his arm. *Oh boy*, Roebuck thought, *another damn Frenchman who can whip me with a blade*. What was he doing? Why hadn't he listened to Aaberg? But there was this other feeling, how he wanted to defeat this man, kill him, jealous somehow of whatever attraction the doña had felt for him, and remembering how the vicar had suffered and died.

LeBlanc took several steps quickly forward and raised his sword. Roebuck flinched and backed up. The Frenchman would have more skill and experience with a blade, no doubt. But Roebuck was young and even with a throb in his head and fog in his mind he was quicker and stronger, and that mattered. He had to use this advantage—the faster and wilder, the better. He sprinted and leapt at the admiral, trying to take him by surprise, swinging his cutlass at LeBlanc's side.

LeBlanc parried easily, shaking his head *no*, and saying, "You must stab me, Roebuck, for I will block every one of your attempts to cut." He grinned. "Try again."

LeBlanc seemed to be on stage, performing the part of savoir faire. His act made Roebuck feel like an oaf and Roebuck hated that feeling. He lunged this time, taking the man's advice. LeBlanc easily knocked the cutlass aside and as Roebuck's momentum carried him past, LeBlanc swung the iron hammer down, aiming at Roebuck's head for a killing blow. But Roebuck sensed it coming and ducked. His head throbbed and although this fight had just begun, Roebuck knew he could not last, the haze rising again inside his mind. He stood, thinking, *I might lose this battle. The* Savannah *might be sunk. But if I can kill this son of a bitch, that will be enough.*

He stared at LeBlanc, his mind befogged but working differently now, seeing something he had had not seen before. The hammer was heavy and had unbalanced the Frenchman. Roebuck swung his cutlass wildly at LeBlanc's left side, missing, and staggered past. Again LeBlanc tried to top him with the hammer. But Roebuck's move had been a feint, and this time when LeBlanc swung and missed, Roebuck was ready. As the Frenchman regained his balance by extending both arms outward and shuffling his feet. Roebuck punched viciously with the knuckled knife in his left hand, aiming at the man's chin. LeBlanc partially blocked the blow with his sword hilt, but the brass of the knife handle still connected, dazing him. Roebuck swung the cutlass, LeBlanc instinctively protecting his side with his sword and thwarting the attack.

But Roebuck was already smashing the bottom of the knife hilt with a backhand swing into LeBlanc's right temple. Then he turned the knuckles and delivered a pair of quick jabs into LeBlanc's brow. It knocked LeBlanc silly, but not off his feet. So Roebuck put his boot heel into LeBlanc's chest and kicked him over backward, leaping atop him as he fell, smashing those knuckles again and again into the man's face, remembering LeBlanc's grin, his sangfroid, recalling Chacón and the *Diana*'s mutilated Unitario captain. Roebuck continued to pulverize LeBlanc's face until one of the Marine's pulled him off and said, "He's dead, sir."

When the boarders realized LeBlanc had been killed, they tried to fight their way back to the *Perle*. Most were killed or captured on the way.

Roebuck turned to the boatswain. "Lash me to the mizzenmast."

"Sir?"

"Waste no time, Mr. Edwards."

"Captain, the surgeon, he said—"

"Now! Or shall I put you in irons?"

Edwards did it, rigging Roebuck into a standing position, lashed to the mast by cord thickly wrapped in rags to keep it from rubbing away Roebuck's skin.

Incendiary darts and grenades poured from the *Savannah*'s tops, raining fire down on the *Perle*. Roebuck saw men from the *Savannah*'s foretop shooting at the *Perle*'s men aloft. The quick-loading Jenks was murder at this range.

Sparks trailed one of the flaming darts, followed by an explosion of burning hooks and barbs that burred into the *Perle*'s tarred standing rigging, catching fire. Roebuck saw Vermont heave an explosive, the throw reaching longer than imaginable. A massive jerk and a tremor shook both ships, as the *Perle*'s twenty-four-pounders lay into the *Savannah* from a range close enough to span with a broomstick.

The *Savannah* returned fire. There was no aiming, just repetition, sounding more and more frantic. Load, fire, load, fire from both ships. Roebuck's mast bowed and straightened again and again with the impact, each round hurting something awful. It must have been the same for the *Savannah*. He was sorry for her, knew that she was being opened up and ploughed through.

He felt as though he hadn't slept in a year. His eyelids kept closing. Each time he opened them again it felt like he wouldn't bother next time. Aaberg was moving up and down the quarterdeck, commanding. He admired that, but at the same time believed Aaberg would not mind if he closed his eyes. So he closed them again, but the ship was rocked by another blast and the vibrating energy of the battle concentrated in his head wound. If he could sleep it would be fine. He would wake up and be refit, whole again. He drifted away, even as another blast rocked them, thinking, *Good, I can sleep through it now.* But no, he swallowed a lungful of powder smoke and heat and was racked by coughing.

Next thing he knew, Lilywhite was tipping brandy into his mouth. A hand splashed a bucket of water on his face. Roebuck said, "Easier ways to kill a man than drowning him."

The hand said, "No sleeping, Captain, you don't want to do that."

Roebuck straightened his spine and spoke through his teeth. "How does it go on the mizzen top?" That was where they would win or lose.

Edwards said, "Our yards are out over their deck, sir. Vermont and two others have crawled out on them to drop the grenades straight down. Every time the *Perle* gathers men to board us we send them running with grenades and the Jenks."

"Vermont," Roebuck said, for a reason he couldn't think of.

"Aye, he throws bolts of lightning."

"Zeus."

"No, sir, Vermont."

"Yes, I know."

Roebuck felt for his own sword. It wasn't there. "Fetch me my cutlass," he said to the seaman standing beside him. His head throbbed and he shut his eyes.

A seaman said, "Sir, we're a-taking you away from here."

Roebuck opened his eyes, "Wait, let us see Admiral LeBlanc once more," and he looked toward the *Perle*'s quarterdeck but there was no admiral, just another officer Roebuck did not recognize, who picked up a grenade that had been tossed from one of the *Savannah*'s tops, a stinking piece of rotting fruit, and tossed it, fuse still sparking, over the side. "A man of unusual poise," Roebuck said.

"LeBlanc is dead, sir," said Aaberg. "You dispatched him."

Roebuck wasn't sure about that, although he did remember fighting Dufour. A very large man who had whipped Roebuck with a sword. Not a very glorious memory. Had he fought LeBlanc also? He liked the report of this victory. His head throbbed. He wanted to sleep.

The same seaman as before said, "We're a-taking you below."

As they lifted him, a massive explosion rocked the *Savannah*. The deck was beautiful with fire and Roebuck watched his men move in threads, entangling, some snapping. He heard his ship's roar, a miserable coda concluding a miserable passage. Aaberg was screaming, absolutely screaming. Roebuck smiled. Man's come out of himself for once. Aaberg bellowing *Cut them away, cut them away, away, away.*

Another voice, his father's, saying *Climb up, boy. The sweetest are higher yet, boy, higher*, then the snapping sound of a bad branch. And a burning away like chaff in a field, fire rising and rising.

CHAPTER 40

Each day Belén walked to the hospital in Salvador where the Americans were being treated, repeating to herself that the commander was going to leave her, no matter under two rods of dirt or at sea on the *Savannah*, so why bother?

Four days ago, upon her first visit, Belén had asked to see him. The ship's surgeon Benoit led her to where he lay in a hot, ripe room. His face looked both fevered and lifeless at the same time. A rat had run by, escaping out the open door. By the scratching sound coming from under the bed, she guessed that there were others. Benoit said without much interest how there were too many of them to worry about. At that moment, she understood that the *Savannah*'s wounded had little chance here and had asked Benoit what they needed, expecting him to say something along the lines of "God's mercy." Instead, he listed the requirements as easily as a boy reciting his letters. First and foremost was a place with clean rooms and a circulation of air.

Belén spent the next three days searching for rooms that met the description. Yesterday, late in the afternoon, she found them in a partially rented three-story boarding house. At first the landlord balked at her offer of three months' payment in advance for every room on the top two floors at seventy-five percent the normal rate.

So she turned her back to him and walked down the steps, not reaching the street before he called her back, an apologetic woe-is-me note in his voice. She and her servants would lodge there to help Benoit. Belén had been tempted to ask for a padlock for her servant's door with all these sailors afoot, but didn't. She would have to trust Anna and Rocío. The boarding house sat on a hill across from the customs house and offered an upstairs view of the harbor. She selected a room with a broad balcony for Robert, sensing that his revival might depend on the smell of the sea and the sense of its salt.

That was how Doña Belén Saavedra y Mancera, sole proprietor of the La Compañía de Comercio de Overo, came to spend two of the most precious months she ever lived caring for wounded and dying American sailors beside a man who adored her.

CHAPTER 41

Rocío and Anna bathed each of the wounded men, except Robert. He was Belén's. She would not allow another woman's hands on him, even found herself restless and resentful when the surgeon touched him. It was she who cleaned his head wound, forcing herself to scrub it even as he recoiled in unconscious pain, and changed its dressing. When she could no longer stand the loom of death in his face, she stayed away, but never for more than a day. Some evenings, Benoit helped her wheel him onto the balcony, where they sat, the Atlantic breathing cool gusts over them.

Two weeks passed and one day Robert's eyes twitched open just long enough for her to see their sparkling blue. Since then, even while helping the surgeon on his rounds, she thought of nothing but the possibility of seeing those eyes again. If they opened once more, she knew he would not die.

A tall midshipman named Mr. Watt came to see Belén. He looked assembled from mismatched parts, most of them too long. This included an endless chin that he shaved clean and often rubbed between his thumb and forefinger, a gesture that gave him the appearance of the world's leanest philosopher. She imagined him in robes like Socrates, only too short to cover bony white ankles and wrists. Yet the young Mr. Watt had a charming freedom from the self-consciousness often part of a tall, thin young man's disposition. He looked directly into her eyes and asked if she would stand for a painting. Belén was flattered.

Watt started by drawing her on Roebuck's balcony. After two days and several sketches, he began to paint using oils and a large rectangle of canvas beside the bow of the captured *Badine*. A week later, he said she no longer had to stand, that he could complete the painting on his own, thanking her with such formality that it seemed impossible for him to be a North American. Belén teased him by saying so, and he said that was because he wasn't, he was a Virginian.

Another time, Mr. Watt took her aboard the *Savannah*. The sight of so many half-naked crewmen sweating as they worked to refit her made Belén ashamed at first and she wanted to debark, but Mr. Watt insisted that she see the ship, telling her the story of what had happened, first with the *Badine* and then the *Perle*. His eyes were wet and gleaming as he described how the captain had been lashed to the mast. She felt her own eyes fill with tears, but not for Roebuck's suffering. These were tears of happiness that Robert had the devotion of this loving young man, to have earned such a friend. The story itself was impossible and she was desperate to think that soon the whole world would know of what the commander had done. It is just such tales that are told and retold and spread across oceans. She hated the thought of the world soon discovering his strange magic. The world was bound to fight her for him.

The *Savannah's* refit had been steady in its progress and she was almost seaworthy again. A Captain Perry had arrived on the ship *Macedonian* to inspect her. His presence was apparently a great surprise and an agitation. The *Savannah's* crew had become consumed with talk of what might happen to them, to the ships, and their officers.

Lieutenant Cockrell came to see Belén. He was very tidy. All the buttons of his jacket were fastened and the leaves of his collar flat and spotless. Even his boots blazed under a new coat of polish. He had come with an invitation for Belén and Mr. Benoit to join him for dinner with Captain Perry. A few hours later, Cockrell and Aaberg met Belén and the surgeon on the dock. Six seamen rowed them through Salvador's harbor to Perry's ship the *Macedonian*.

Belén was pulled up in a lift and greeted by several adorable, uniformed boys who made a line, drumming and bugling what Mr. Cockrell called ruffles and flourishes. She knew a little of the traditions naval men so adored but could not imagine that it was customary to salute the arrival of a woman married to a man with no military or diplomatic status and who happened to have been recently shot as a traitor to his country.

As they were led to the captain's cabin, Cockrell leaned over and said that those honors were very rare indeed and normally reserved for a consul or chargé d'affaires but were done especially for Belén because Captain Perry believed she was the most deserving friend the United States had in all of South America. Her first reaction was to dismiss this as another of Cockrell's blandishments, but he seemed earnest. It reminded her that she knew these men on land, not on ships where they lived their true lives and were their true selves.

She expected to be revolted by the smell of the ship below, but all the ports were open, and a sweet breeze drifted through. It was not as dark as she remembered her visits to Admiral Brown's ships, although the space felt terribly low and she had the sensation of moving through a shallow box.

A steward announced them, and Perry offered a "Welcome!" in a throaty voice, smiling and rising from his seat. "Doña Belén, how pleasant to meet you."

"Captain Perry," she said, "Mr. Cockrell tells me that your greeting on deck has done me a great honor. Thank you."

Perry grunted, waving his hand in a way to suggest she should think nothing of it. The five of them sat and chatted for a time in a surprisingly aimless fashion. Belén tried to imagine how Robert would host a lady and three juniors for supper. The conversation would not be aimless, she was certain of that.

After a time, Perry rose with a glass of Mendoza in his hand—Americans seemed quite content to drink Argentine wine—and said, "To Doña Belén, a woman whose beauty is exceeded only by her kindness and generosity." He impressed her somehow as an old stallion lying down in clover.

Belén was about to say how she would prefer that he reverse this formulation when the other three rose and offered a surprisingly aggressive set of hurrahs. It was at this moment Belén knew she had something to fear.

The food was hot and plentiful. The wine with its rough edge and depth matched the beefsteak and buttered potatoes. The lieutenants did most of the talking and drinking, Perry amiably replying with smiles and encouraging expostulations between sips of tea.

During a pause, he turned to Benoit to ask what the surgeon thought about the condition of the men. Mr. Benoit hesitated a moment. Something Belén had never seen him do in their month together.

Benoit quickly recovered his usual direct and ready self, saying, "The men are healing well. We have only lost two since moving to Doña Belén's boarding house. Before the move, we lost seven men. It can be reasonably asserted that the *Savannah*'s wounded owe their lives to the ministrations of Doña Belén as well as to Anna and Rocío."

He always addressed Belén's servants with a certain regard. At first, she was embarrassed for him, speaking to those two in that way, but Anna and Rocío had started to behave more like nurses than menials. The more he spoke to them, shared details about healing, asked them for explanations of what they saw, the more this was true. Back at Nahomi, Belén wanted them to be servants, but for now the surgeon's way was probably for the best.

Benoit said, "The doña has certainly saved the life of Captain Roebuck. I expected him to be dead a week after developing sepsis."

Belén said, "I can hardly take credit for your work, sir."

"Please do not take it amiss, madame, if I say that you are quite wrong. I may have kept Commander Roebuck from dying, but you brought him back to life." The statement electrified the cabin, everyone leaning toward Benoit.

Captain Perry said, "And what sort of life is that, Mr. Benoit?"

"A life, sir, which he might live like any other man who has not suffered as he has."

"So he will come to?" It was Cockrell.

"He is closer every day."

Perry nodded toward the cabin door, and Cockrell invited Benoit and Aaberg to inspect the ship's rigging. It was obvious that the time had come for the captain to speak to Belén in private. She suspected everyone knew what for and she was suddenly conscious of the menace in the red cast of Perry's complexion.

"Doña Belén," Perry said, "our navy owes you a debt of gratitude for the care you have given our men. We would have to save the lives of people who are very important to you if we wanted to perform any commensurable service."

"Your navy has rid Uruguay of Admiral LeBlanc," she said, "a scoundrel and a man who abused us whenever he wished. And you have helped to bring corruption into the light of day."

"Corruption that was partly ours."

He referred to Houghton. She said, "That is all the more reason you might have ignored it. And at great cost in blood and suffering, you have returned treasure that belonged to my people."

Perry beamed, obviously pleased by these words, and said, "Very soon, a Captain Fitzhugh will be in Salvador. Fitzhugh will return to the United States with the *Savannah*. And we hope that Commander Roebuck will return on the *Badine*."

Belén nodded but said nothing.

"At home, the United States Navy will be very keen to celebrate the commander's victory. His healthy presence in our capital is paramount."

"Naturally."

"Madame, may I ask you if you have heard rumors that some among the people of Rio de la Plata hope to enroll Commander Roebuck into their navy? Put him in charge of their fleet?"

"They could do worse," she said.

"And mostly do." These words issued without irony from Perry's sun-cracked lips. "But, my dear, young Roebuck is not ready for command of a frigate, much less a fleet. I am not certain he is ready for any command at all."

"A joke?"

"He has something unique, a kind of genius. But command requires much more than that."

She said, "I am a proprietor of a trading house. Why do you feel this is of any interest to me?"

"Madame, you have a reputation that puts you a little past that." He took a long sip of tea, and produced a sound she believed was meant to reassure her. Instead, her spine tingled. "I want you to know that Commander Roebuck must return with the *Badine*. He is a commander in the U.S. Navy."

"You say that as if it were written in the stars."

"Maybe not in the stars, but it is written as clearly as a man's destiny can be."

"He is not like you, Captain, not just another officer." Belén wanted to tell him what was different about Roebuck, how he might help her country realize the greatness that was its right. She wanted Perry to know how shocked people were by Robert's unwillingness to keep any of the treasure he had captured in La Gaucin. His reputation as an incorruptible man was sealed among the people of Uruguay. They understood him better than did block headed North Americans like this one.

"My dear," Perry looked into her eyes. "You cannot conceive the admiration I hold for Commander Roebuck for winning the loyalty and affection of a woman such as yourself. But I tell you truthfully, Commander Roebuck *is* like me."

She said, "He is no instrument to be used according to the whim of your navy."

"Well then, what is he?"

"He is himself." What were the words to end this man's certainty?

"In the Navy, we are all instruments, Doña Belén. This is what makes the commander like every other of our officers. It is so because that is what we chose to be."

"But inside of him—"

"—Is where he is most like me, and like the others," Perry said.

There was something terrible about the gray of Perry's eyes.

"He is not as you know him, my dear," he said, "because he can only be himself at sea. Maybe you think I do not understand Commander Roebuck. That a middle-aged man such as I cannot see what separates him from the others. But I do.

"Imagine how it feels," he continued, "to be master of these magnificent ships, to feel the sea as he does. It is his future to be master of all other masters of these ships. Commander Roebuck can feel what is in front of him. And the U.S. Navy will make this true for him in a way that Uruguay never can, but not yet."

Belén said, "If you would be so kind as to call for the *Savannah*'s lieutenants, Captain, I must return. And the surgeon, too. There is still work to be done." She was beside herself and needed to escape.

"Will you take some coffee first?"

"No, Captain. I thank you for dinner and the honor of your company, but I must go."

As they were rowed back, the *Macedonian* fired three guns in a salute. This so surprised Mr. Cockrell that he said he'd never experienced such an honor in his life, even though he knew it wasn't for him, and he asked if Belén would come again tomorrow to see if the two of them couldn't talk Captain Perry up to seven guns. But she did not experience the guns as a salute. They were pure damnation, offered in exchange for her future.

CHAPTER 42

Although he was not conscious to hear her, Belén told Roebuck how Mr. Watt had described the *Savannah*'s victory over the *Perle* and how a host of local boats had taken the incapacitated *Savannah* and *Badine* in tow to their harbor after the *Perle* had sunk. She repeated this each day as she bathed and fed him.

One afternoon a storm brought on an ugly sea, wind and rain blowing hard from the east. She wanted the commander to feel it, hear the fullness of its thunder, and called for Rocío and Anna. They moved him to the balcony, where she again told him all that Mr. Watt had described, how the crew admired Roebuck's courage when he was strapped to that mast, fighting through the pain. She finished the story and walked to the balcony rail to look out over the harbor, when a clear and strong voice, his voice, said, "And you believed him?"

CHAPTER 43

The sun had set, and the hallway was quiet. An hour had passed since Benoit's final rounds for the day. Roebuck watched the Doña in lamplight. "When I saw the squall yesterday, I thought I might be in hell," he said, "but then I saw you and thought, 'It's heaven,' only I had always pictured heaven as a sunny place peopled by winged angels carrying big glasses of port. It took me a moment to sort out what you might be doing there. But without you I would never have thought of heaven in the first place."

"And what would you have thought of?"

"A Brazilian boarding house inhabited by a collection of stump-legged tars."

"Not exactly heaven."

"Not hell either, especially with this view." Roebuck was on his back in bed but gestured to the French doors. "I cannot imagine how I could have stayed asleep for a month."

"Not asleep, Commander," said the doña. "Unconscious and fevered."

"And snoring like a hog after an hour at the trough, I'm sure."

"Two hours and two hogs is more like it."

Roebuck was fighting to get past the sheer humiliation of his condition, of her caretaking, and all she must have put up with. It mortified him. "Benoit says that I owe you my life," he said.

She said, "He denies any responsibility for it himself?" She was smiling, although he knew the conversation did not please her.

"As you seem about to do now."

She looked at him with no change to her expression.

He said, "Well, I thank you for it." But he resented her seeing him in a condition akin to a helpless bawling baby, shitting, pissing, sweating, stinking, dependent on her for life itself. But he had to thank her for it—what else could he do?

"Well, I am sorry. I think you perhaps deserve my apology for how I've come to you. Throwing myself into this must seem very…" The doña was caught on the next word.

He knew she wouldn't rush, waiting until the one that perfectly focused the world and her place in it came to her. That was how she spoke, how she did everything. So he waited. Then it came to him. She might have the word, but hated to use it, and then, because he was beginning to understand her, he said, "Desperate?"

She blanched, and he experienced a moment of clarity. She felt as exposed and abject as he and was now struggling not to spit in his eye.

She said, "You were more charming on your deathbed."

"Too late now."

"You might learn otherwise." She got up to go.

"You have just arrived. Can you not spare more time for a recently dying but fully recovered man?"

"I'd say you were hardly recovered at all with such a confused mind." She paused. "But the dying phase seems to have passed."

"Thanks to you."

"Don't say that," she said. "Do you think me ignorant of your resentment? Every time you look at me, I see it."

"My darling girl, I love you despite your saving my life," he said, smiling. And he did love her, seeing her like this, them both like this.

"I'm a girl now? I feel I've aged ten years in the last month. And I am many years your senior already."

"Barely a few, I'd say."

"Arithmetic is not one of your strengths."

"You're my beautiful girl."

"Your fever has returned to confuse your mind and this time I feel tempted to feed it."

Roebuck sat up, quickly grasping both her hands, pulling her toward him. "Feed it then, *querida*, don't fight it."

***

The next morning, Aaberg arrived, hat in hand, to deliver what had become his daily report. "The *Savannah*'s refitting is done, Captain. She's better off than she was the day we left Rio de la Plata."

"I'm feeling fit myself," Roebuck said. "When will you begin work on the *Badine*?"

"Tomorrow, sir. The carpenter has been making plans and we have what we need to get started." Then Aaberg's face wrinkled.

"Go on, Lieutenant."

"Has Captain Perry been to see you, sir?"

Roebuck shook his head.

The Norwegian-born lieutenant fussed with the lining of his hat for a moment and eyed the floorboards. "Or Captain Fitzhugh?"

"Fitzhugh?" Roebuck was acting as the *Savannah*'s commander, but Fitzhugh was her commissioned captain.

"Aye, sir, he arrived two days ago."

"On what ship?"

"A dispatch ship, the *Seneca*."

"So he came with no command."

Aaberg shook his head and removed himself from the room as soon as he could, leaving Roebuck to contemplate the meaning of Fitzhugh's arrival. The Navy was taking the *Savannah* away from him.

***

It was midnight. Roebuck's head rested on the doña's naked stomach as they lay in bed together. Her breasts quivered as she breathed, and he reached up to trace the outline of her nipples. He kissed them. First the left then the right. The contrast of their dark wadding against the soft cream of her breasts fascinated him, same as the downy black triangle below the white of her stomach.

He moved his lips to her stomach, and she breathed in quickly. He shifted his body up so they were stem to stem, his body so much lighter now than when they were together in Buenos Aires. The doña drew him into her, and he felt that strange pull, a thread unspooling from the back of his head to the arch in his feet. She pulled it from him, wrapping them together until he fell back, afraid of the exhaustion, fighting it, fighting to take more of this impossible pleasure, this happiness.

As they rested and his strength returned, he felt something leaden between them, had felt it now for several days, the sharp edge of a question. He wanted to ask her if he could stay with her, command her country's navy, be with her. She had not mentioned it again and he was so afraid she would say no. He could not bear the idea of that, of losing her again. Her breasts, her nakedness on his, her love and the life it had returned to him. He couldn't bring himself to risk it, risk the way she absorbed his torments, softened them until they were loose and ragged and flowed away in pieces.

With her, he might command a navy of his own. What twenty-three-year-old officer had ever done that? He knew deep inside that there was no one in this world like her, none even close.

CHAPTER 44

Belén loved the wounded crewmen in that boarding house and had grown to consider them as her boys. She loved them in their vitality and will to live. There were exceptions, of course, such as Margraf, who in addition to being a seaman was a lecher and an imbecile.

The clock struck nine at night. It was Anna's turn to visit each wounded man to fill his pitcher with water, extinguish his candles, and urge him to sleep. Belén knew that Anna would also visit her Robert. Belén sometimes wondered if Anna saw what she saw when she looked at him. It was obvious that Anna felt something for him, obvious in the way Anna flushed whenever he said anything to her. This knowledge gave Belén a strange pleasure because he would never be Anna's. He was hers.

When the sound of Anna's movement between the rooms stopped and her door latched with a click, Belén lit her smallest candle and flipped the hourglass on the stand beside her bed, watching the granules flow from top to bottom. She lay back and thought of him, and then of her and him together, imagining the backs of his fingers and then their tips over her breasts. He knew how that made her feel.

Granules dropped through the neck of the glass in a beautiful rush, piling up, some tumbling like tiny puffs of cloud down a perfectly shaped mountain, others catching at the peak, balancing, right there. His hands touching her differently now, firmly and faster, not stopping until her cheeks were flushed and her breath came in sharp draws and pushes, the last grain through the glass.

She dried the perspiration with a towel and fanned cool air over her skin. Justo had told her many years ago, "The world emanates from the bedroom," something she had never understood until now. She felt a sweet certainty that Roebuck also understood.

Pulling on a shift, she smiled at the voice inside her saying how very bad Belén was to think of her Robert in this way. That a woman who truly loved him would remember he was unconscious and nearly dead from septic fever seven short days ago and that he must preserve his energy for himself. She had learned to ignore this voice and reject it for the sad and lonely soul it represented. Roebuck's energy was her energy. It gave her life as much as it did him.

She climbed the stairs in the darkness, feeling the cool between her legs. Going to him, going to do it again, only there would be no grains of the hourglass, no need for her wicked imagination. His touch was real, the way he found places in her, making her feel in a way she had never imagined. And she would try to do the same for him, wanting to know him like he in his magic knew her.

She lay down beside him and they embraced, another voice in her whispering, *We are so alone, so perfect, so gone from this world and all its everything, and we and we and we.*

CHAPTER 45

The doña had come to his bed each of the last four nights, but tonight would be different. Roebuck needed to know if she would have him or not, if this time of theirs together was no more than a pause to the grind of life or something greater. In Salvador she had not breathed a word about the possibility of his returning with her to Montevideo. Nor had she spoken of the offer she and Admiral Brown had made to command Uruguay's navy. And yet here she was every night.

She opened the door and slipped under the covers beside him.

"Are my fingers cold?" she asked, caressing his chest.

Nerves constricted his throat. He couldn't speak.

She kissed his lips and grasped his prick, saying, "Let me warm them here."

His body produced no response, and he sensed her stare in the darkness.

"You're shaking, Robert."

Unmanned, he stood up and faced her.

"What's happened?" she said. "Why are you like this?"

"I want to be your admiral," he shut down his thoughts and said. "To be with you. I see our future."

He heard her laugh, a sound of such warmth.

She said, "Well then, Admiral Roebuck, think of this as your commission," pulling him back to her.

It was new again, the intensity of it and his desire for her.

CHAPTER 46

Robert said, "I must be mad to leave my commission and country for a married woman." He said the same thing every afternoon. Belén could hardly tell if he was teasing or serious.

She said, "Why do you make me repeat myself so?"

"Madness," he said. "Am I mad?"

"Yes," she said, "but your madness is not in coming to Uruguay with me, it is that you doubt me. My husband has been shot, executed in Buenos Aires. And there is not a soul who regrets it, except maybe the overworked prostitutes he called servants, and they'll just miss his money."

"He has no friends in Montevideo?"

"The destitution of his condition is perfect, as I told you. No friends, no family that will claim him, his allies loathed him, his countrymen wished him dead."

"But he had a wife."

"Yes," she said, "although I look upon the firing squad as a form of annulment."

Why was he so fascinated by her husband? At first Belén had believed it was jealousy, and the idea was delicious, but she had come to understand it as something else. Robert was fascinated by the notion of a powerful man with money and position so utterly destroying his own life. He never tired of hearing how Don Justo had betrayed the people of Uruguay as well those of Argentina by acting as an agent of the Spanish, trying to persuade them to retake the colonies they had lost in Rio de la Plata. Not a shred of honor to be found anywhere in the man.

As for herself, she knew Justo was little more than the sum of his appetites. There had been some pleasure in those appetites when he counted her among them, but such things do not last.

He said, "How do you know I am not like him?"

"I know."

"But am I not betraying my country?"

She said, "The country you have given such glory?"

"That is not how they will see it."

"But you are doing nothing wrong," she said, "nothing illegal."

"Nothing illegal, that is true," he said, rising slowly, not quite steady yet on his feet. "As for the other—"

"Well then, stay with your navy and your Cockrell and your foul water and your boys and your salted pork and—"

He said, "Lieutenant Cockrell would suffer to know you rate him with salt pork and foul water."

"Lieutenant Cockrell hasn't suffered a day in his life."

Robert smiled, and something in her flared.

"Why don't we leave tomorrow? Why wait?" he said. "If I am strong enough to prevail upon your virtue every night—"

"You pig."

"As I have—"

"Silence that wicked tongue," she said, "or you won't see me again in this room after dark."

"Not another word."

She said, "Captain Perry has asked me aboard the *Badine* tomorrow."

"The old lecher."

"Your vow of silence?"

"Overwhelmed by my sense of outrage," he said, and laughed until the pain in his side stopped him and he grimaced.

"That is your punishment," she said. She knew how much it vexed Roebuck that Perry was seeing her a second time before once visiting him.

"Well, remind the man that I am still among the living and am lonely for some good company."

"What am I?"

"I don't have to tell you."

***

The *Badine* was no longer a battered, sinking hulk. She had been transformed into a beauty, with a freshly painted yellow streak reaching from bow to stern against a shining coat of black. Robert had told Belén how he liked his hulls yellow because it made them look fast in the water, faster than they actually were. He loved the *Savannah* but hadn't liked how she was painted, saying she's fast but hardly looks it.

Captain Perry was waiting for her in the *Badine*'s captain's cabin. It was smaller than the *Macedonian*'s cabin, a little bigger than a closet. He said, "Doña Belén, we meet again," each syllable sounding to her as if hacked out of the air with a jagged blade.

"Captain Perry." She curtsied.

As soon as he had lowered himself into the chair, the steward appeared with a bottle of wine.

"Will you have a spot?" Perry said.

"Thank you, no,"

"A credit to you, madame." He shook his wattles and the steward backed out with the unopened bottle.

"So, captain, what have we to discuss today?"

His narrow gray eyes rounded into an almost thoughtful expression. "Well, we have a surprise that I hope will please you."

He then asked about the condition of the wounded men. She told him the surgeon had just that morning said all were ready to sail, although many would not be of much service as seamen anymore.

"The Presbyters in Pensacola," Perry said, "have set up a Lord's Benevolence for the *Savannah* Relief Fund for widows of the dead and to supplement the pensions of those too injured to continue service."

"Presbyters?"

"Church people. A very popular denomination in the United States."

So confusing, all the churches in North America, as though every man and woman had a ministry catering to their particular idea of the Lord and his creation. Belén said, "I shall ask my servant Rocío to bring one hundred reales for the fund tomorrow."

"I thought you might be inclined toward such a gesture. The men will love you all the more for it."

"An affection I fully reciprocate."

The man bowed his head. "I want to show you something I received from the Naval secretary by dispatch yesterday." Perry spread five newspapers on the table between them, the *Washington Evening*

Star, the *New-York Daily Tribune*, the *New York Herald*, the *Baltimore Sun*, the *Boston Post*, each dated from over a month ago. "These are powerful newspapers in our country. They represent the views of both major political parties."

She tried to look interested.

"Read them please, madame."

She said, "Which one would Commander Roebuck read first?"

Perry didn't hesitate. "The paper from Baltimore."

A big, black-lettered headline across the top of the front page read, *Savannah Captures Badine, Sinks Perle*, and in smaller print: *Our Bobby Chase: America's Nelson?* The *Washington Evening Star* read, *Savannah Whips the French* and beneath it, *Sinks One, Takes Another*. The New York newspapers were likewise emphatic.

Perry said, "Commander Roebuck is being celebrated in every town in the United States of America. He is universally acclaimed."

She stared at the headlines and then at the captain. This was horrible. If Robert did not return home, if he stole away from his country at this moment when its people honored him… leaving with an older wealthy widow to serve her country's navy… Her eyes pooled, and her lungs tightened.

"The Navy has not enjoyed such affection among our people for thirty years," Perry said.

Belén stood up. "I must go. I must. I'm sorry, Captain."

"I can see you understand what this means, madam. Commander Roebuck has no choice but to return home. His country looks to him in a way they haven't looked to anyone in years."

She was at the door, her hand on the knob.

"Please let me show you something else, my dear, before you go. I beg you."

Her tears would not be denied.

"My dear, do not cry," Perry said. "You have so much."

"Every tear I shed is out of nothing," she blurted from a blind need to be understood. "Every one a call to God." Perry had his hook in and was yanking hard, ripping Robert out of the perfect warm pool of their love, taking him from her.

Perry waited until she was out of tears. Then he said, "See this," and pulled away a cloak covering a framed picture behind him, a portrait. Belén had to rub her eyes to see that it was her standing before the *Badine*.

"Mr. Watt's work. It will always hang in this cabin, Commander Roebuck's cabin. He has a commission to command this corvette, *Badine*."

All Belén heard was *we are taking him from you, we are taking him*. She saw that Roebuck must go home or face a lifetime of shame for himself and especially for his family. She rose and took the first steps toward spurning the heaven that had moved her to this hell, nearly falling as she debarked. Without the quick hands of the boatswain and his mates she would have dropped like a bundle of rags into the water. With their help she made it to her boat. As they rowed her to shore, she thought of that cruel loveless decade with Justo.

She had been written out of the stars for Commander Roebuck. What was written in them for her? Was she not meant for loving him and for being loved by him? If not, for what then? For what? For the ashes and dust of one more failed love.

CHAPTER 47

The doña had not said goodbye, not left anything of herself to him, not a word. Now he understood why. After two days of heartbreak and confusion, Roebuck understood why she had left on a Navy dispatch ship.

Captain Perry was on the way here and Roebuck was forcing himself through the pain of donning his uniform. Pemberton's blood had been cleaned from the white duck trousers and his own blood from the blouse and coat. But the stains could not be scrubbed away completely and they combined with jagged repair seams to give the impression of something defeated.

Perry arrived and Roebuck welcomed him in, noting the curiosity on Perry's thick, fleshy face. They sat and Roebuck poured tea from a white porcelain service. Molecules of steam rose from the cups, catching morning sun in the swirls.

"Ghastly," Perry said after a sip. "No wonder South Americans have such affection for coffee." He spread five newspapers out over the table. Their stories reached a level of hyperbole that embarrassed Roebuck, proclaiming each in its separate way that Bobby Chase was America's best man.

"Bobby Chase," said Roebuck.

Perry nodded.

"I hate that name."

"It suits you."

"Gunners mates on the *Savannah* called me Robby Run. Mocked me, their way of saying, 'He's a coward.'"

"They had it wrong. But won't again, I wager."

Roebuck said, "You showed these to the doña?"

Perry nodded.

Roebuck's mouth was dry and he swallowed. "You chased her away."

"Didn't have to, son. She understood what it meant."

"And if she had never seen them?"

"She did it for you, Mr. Roebuck. Prevented you from being foolish and bringing ruin to your reputation among your country-men and multiplying the disgrace of your father."

Perry sipped again, pushing air through his teeth to register dis-taste. "I wrote a dispatch to the Navy Secretary recommending that your brevet rank of commander be reversed," said Perry.

"I am to be a lieutenant again?"

"That was my recommendation." Good news is that I also rec-ommended you and the *Savannah* be commemorated with a silver medal for your success in freeing our merchant sailors, an extraordi-nary honor not conferred since 1813. I also requested that you be given command of a brigantine. Your eventual rise to captain is most probable if you develop the judgment and wisdom needed for com-mand. Your skill in seamanship and your courage, while very great, are not enough."

Roebuck sat mutely, thinking, *In the last thirty years, what American captain has sunk or captured ships as I have?*

"More good news is that your fame has made my recommendation against your promotion to the permanent rank of commander impossible. The Navy Secretary sees an opportunity to bring attention and glory to the service through your accomplishments." Perry waited, probably expecting some acknowledgement from Roebuck. None came.

"You are now a full commander, Mr. Roebuck, despite your questionable risk-taking and hasty judgement." Perry handed three documents across the table. "Here is the letter signed by Secretary Bancroft, and here is your commission, and here are your orders. Congratulations, this makes you the youngest commander to serve in the Navy in twenty years."

What Roebuck wanted was to be beside Doña Belén, not in this son of a bitch's navy.

Perry apparently still felt the need to explain, because he went on, "Few men have ever been commended with the permanence of a medal minted by our nation's treasury. These medals will be sold throughout our nation. Your deeds and those of your men will be thus represented in thousands of households across our great democracy. It is fitting to honor your success."

Roebuck shook his head before saying, "Yes, sir." While wondering what tub of rot Perry would give him to command.

***

When Perry told him that he was commissioned to command the *Badine*, Roebuck knew he should be glad but still it left him ice cold. He had been using newfound strength by pushing lieutenants

Malvey and Cockrell, who had asked Perry to serve under Roebuck, each day to ready their ship.

His orders were to join the *Savannah*, which had set sail a week ago, at the Washington Naval Yard as soon as possible. The wind obliged him the next day and with the *Badine* shipshape more or less, they would weigh anchor within the hour and be sailing back to the United States.

Roebuck was writing at his desk when Watt knocked and called through the door, "We're ready, Captain Roebuck."

After gathering the last of his papers, he and Watt hastened down the hill, joining up with Cockrell along the way. Roebuck congratulated Cockrell on his new status on the *Badine* as second lieutenant and Watt for his promotion from midshipman to lieutenant. Cockrell was giddy, which was no surprise, but the smiles flowing out of such a hard head as Watt's was.

"Did you know, sir," Cockrell began, and then perhaps not satisfied, started over with "As you know, sir, the Navy purchased the *Badine* from you and from us as a prize. Well, the money arrived just yesterday."

"Well, that is very fine indeed," Roebuck said. Malvey had already delivered this news, but Roebuck saw no reason to ruin it for Cockrell.

"What will you do with your money, sir? It's a right pretty sum."

"I'm not sure, Mr. Cockrell." Roebuck had asked Perry to see that half of his prize money would be donated to the Presbyters Benevolent Fund. Perry had objected to this, saying that a commander needed to maintain a certain standard in his cabin. "You are their commander, not their preserver. Don't mistake one for the other." Perry the Pontiff, purveyor of truth and wisdom.

On the quay, the crew gathered in front of the *Badine*. Roebuck felt dread at the prospect of what seemed about to happen.

"As a matter o' fact, sir, 'tain't just the prize money," said Cockrell. "What's more is the *Badine*. She's got a new name."

Roebuck tensed.

"Yes, sir, the ship has been rechristened in a way that goes a little off the straight and narrow. Was us, the *Savannah's* officers, that put the Navy up to it. We wanted to see her christened afresh. Commodore said the secretary back in Washington agreed, given the unique circumstances of your success and such."

Roebuck knew Cockrell wanted him to ask what the new name was, so he didn't. He looked at the ship and had to admit she looked good.

Vermont led the hands in a hip-hip hurrah for Roebuck and then two more. They gathered around him—a little too familiar, their hands out, patting his back, congratulating him. An old sail was draped from the ship's bowsprit, covering her front. He was about to demand what the hell it was doing there when Malvey stepped forward to speak. *Good*, Roebuck thought, because Cockrell was irritating him. Roebuck was pleased to consider how Malvey had surprised everyone and asked to ship with him rather than Fitzhugh.

"Let us celebrate our captain's return," said Malvey.

"Huzzah!"

"And let us do honor to South America's most beautiful woman and a true friend to the American seaman. No queenlier woman ever trod the Lord's creation."

"Huzzah!" The enthusiasm was universal.

Two sailors on the bow pulled back the canvas, uncloaking a freshly painted figurehead. Roebuck saw immediately that it was

Doña Belén, barefooted and standing on the wings of three carved angels. She was bare-shouldered as well. "Commander Roebuck, may I present to you the U.S.S. *Belen*."

Roebuck stared for a second and said, ". . . What?"

Cockrell must have read this distress because he leaned in and said, "Mr. Watt and Mr. Flynn did it for you, sir, with the help of all the *Belen*'s crew. And especially they did it to honor her. Would you find a word to say?"

Roebuck realized the men expected something from him, a new kind of duty. "Very fine, boys, very fine," he said. "The ship looks gorgeous, but nothing compares to the original article. Three cheers for Doña Belén!"

They cheered more loudly than ever.

***

Onboard, Roebuck said, "Mr. Cockrell, did the doña know about the rechristening?"

"I don't know for certain, sir, but I suspect Captain Perry told her. She was to rechristen the ship herself but was taken ill and left suddenly."

Roebuck pictured the scene and knew what had happened, how she would feel and react to the grim irony. It was a picture that did him no good, so he pushed it away and bore into his work. In his cabin Watt, Malvey, and Cockrell had presented him with a portrait of the Doña Belén which hung on the wall. He managed a feeble smile and thanks, but it fooled no one and his officers left with concern on their faces.

Navy Secretary Bancroft had personally requested that Roebuck detail in writing all that had happened. But before he could put ink to paper he took down Watt's portrait of the doña and leaned its face against the back wall opposite his cot. The last thing he needed was to see her eyes.

He worked steadily at the report for two weeks, alive to the Navy's intention for its use. Heroic tales repeated by a grasping press would do the navy nothing but good. Roebuck tried to neuter the more exciting parts and make the report as plain as possible. It was the Navy, after all, that had engineered his separation from her.

Or had it? Maybe Belén had sensed something about him she didn't like or want, something hidden. Maybe that was the cause of her leaving.

On a morning when the ship carried a slow wind over an easy sea, Lilywhite's voice came through his cabin door. "Captain, sir," followed by his ever-insistent knock.

"Yes, what is it?"

"Lieutenant Malvey here to see you."

"Let him in."

Malvey entered. "This afternoon is inspection, sir."

"Well?"

"Will you come topside for it, sir?"

Roebuck said, "When I am ready."

Malvey walked across the small cabin and put his hand on the edge of the framed portrait on the floor facing the wall. "Sir, if it's all the same to you, we'd like to hang this in the wardroom."

"Take it."

"Mr. Watt did such a fine job of capturing her."

"Are you going to take it, or talk about it?"

When the *Belen* reached the Leeward Islands, Roebuck set a course for the port of San Juan to reprovision. A dispatch ship arrived while they were at anchor in San Juan's harbor, bringing mail as well as copies of a new resolution from Congress nicknamed the "Bobby Chase Naval Construction Bill."

> *Be it enacted by the Senate and the House of Representatives of the United States of America in Congress assembled, that for the gradual increase of the navy of the United States that the sum of 1 million dollars per annum the President is hereby authorized to cause to be procured steam engines and all the imperishable materials necessary for the conversion and refitting of seven United States sailing ships, 2 with not more than 10 guns, 3 with not more than 30 guns and 2 with not more than 50 guns. Also to procure materials necessary to increase the size of the New York shipyard to twice its current dimension by addition 2 dry docks, and 6 buildings for storage.*

The bill did not include a single new keel to be laid down for sailing ships. Worse, seven existing sailing ships were to be fit for steamers, all in his name. How soon before every captain in the service commanded ships that chuffed coal smoke and clanged engines? Steamers would smoke up the harbors as train engines as did rail yards, mariners no better than greasy, soot-faced engineers.

Back at sea with Florida nearly under their lee, warm gusts whipped around Roebuck, Cockrell, and Watt on the quarterdeck.

When they had weighed anchor in Salvador one month ago, the crew had been proud of their victory and happy at the prospect of returning to native soil. Each had received his portion of the prize money and each would be recognized as a hero at home, able to make the rare claim in the U.S. Navy of winning glory in battle. Forever after, they could say they had been with Roebuck on the *Savannah*. Unfortunately, Roebuck on the *Belen* wasn't much to brag about. He had been morose, reclusive, and all but unwilling to acknowledge them.

Cockrell said, "Captain, Lieutenant Watt has some business with you and I would like to join in. Can we visit you in your cabin this evening to discuss it?"

"Business?"

"Mr. Watt must supply a picture for your medal of honor, sir, and we must decide on the subject matter so's he can draw it up for the mint in Washington."

"Is this true, Mr. Watt?"

"Yes, sir. One side must be your profile and the other a scene from your victory."

Roebuck said, "Lieutenant Malvey will manage the quarterdeck?"

"Yes, sir," Cockrell said. "And he has encouraged us to come to you."

"Very well, you may come down this evening at two bells."

"Gladly, sir, yes indeed."

The appointed hour came too soon for Roebuck. Cockrell and Watt arrived at his cabin together, Watt with his sketchpad and Cockrell with a sack from which he produced two bottles.

"Brought a little taste for you, Captain," Cockrell said. "We know you didn't get to enjoy Brazil quite as much as we did."

Roebuck moved his eyes from Cockrell to Watt, who didn't seem like the type to enjoy himself in the way Cockrell implied.

"Or rather, as much as I did," said Cockrell, catching the doubt in his commander's face. "Watt here couldn't enjoy himself on a Polynesian island full of large-titted girls in nothing but grass skirts."

"That right, Mr. Watt?"

"I've never been partial to grass skirts, sir," Watt said.

Cockrell nodded, a grin blossoming on his face.

Watt continued, "I believe a man like Mr. Cockrell here could find a way to enjoy himself on the night before his hanging."

Roebuck said, "Wouldn't be surprised if it comes to that."

Cockrell said, "Well, sir, life is what you make it."

"Mr. Cockrell, are you going to tell me what is in those bottles?"

"Cachaça, sir. Think of it as Brazilian rum."

Roebuck pulled three glasses from a drawer. Cockrell filled them.

Watt said, "Sir, I'd like to show you a sketch I have tried for the back of the medal."

Roebuck sipped as Watt untied the silk bonds on his leather pad, opening it to a pencil drawing.

"What on earth is that?" Roebuck said.

"It's you, sir," Watt said, "tied to the mast, as we engaged the *Perle*."

"My mouth is open as wide as a hogfish. And my eyes are slits."

"Just a sketch sir."

"It's ridiculous."

"I have another." Watt opened his pad to a picture of the *Perle* exploding, the *Savannah* strapped to its stern quarter. Mixed into the smoke and fire of the blast were pieces of planks, sail, chain, and men.

Roebuck stared. "Is this how it was?" He was being carried below when it had happened.

"Aye, sir," Cockrell said. "Vermont threw a dart down into their hatch and it sparked powder. They were bringing up a box of charges, is what Vermont said. The charges went up and then their magazine. It was just as Mr. Watt has it here."

Roebuck said, "I wonder what that was like for the *Perle*'s men."

Cockrell said, "Hot, I reckon."

"This picture will do," said Roebuck. "Thank you, Mr. Watt."

Cockrell said, "Mr. Watt, why don't you show Captain Roebuck the sketches you've shown us."

Watt flipped three long pages and stopped at a sketch of Doña Belén's profile. The three of them stared at it for a while. Cockrell was nodding. Watt began to flip to a different sketch, but Roebuck stopped him and continued to look at her. Eventually he said, "Any others?"

Watt flipped to one showing three quarters of her face and her half smile, its warmth. His heart began to beat more slowly and his room seemed to expand. He was pleased to have these two officers with him as friends and realized he must carry forward the good feeling he had for them and for his other men too, Vermont, Malvey, all of them. But especially he must remember Pemberton and what that ornery old Marine had done for him.

Next Watt showed a watercolor, a profile from the other side, a strand of black hair hanging loose over her cheek.

"Quite a woman, sir," Cockrell said. "The men could not be prouder to serve on *The Doña*," using the ship's nickname that had caught on with the crew. "For half of them it feels like they ship on a brig named after their mother, for the other half it's their sweetheart. Reminds a man of the beauty in the world."

"Beauty," Roebuck said, "is a fine thing."

"So is love, Captain, nothing finer. To Doña Belén."

They toasted her.

Roebuck said, "To Major Pemberton, a man who gave his life for mine."

"Hear, hear," Cockrell and Watt said.

Next day, on the quarterdeck, Malvey approached Roebuck. They stood together staring at the low rise of Florida's coast.

Malvey said, "Good to be home, isn't it, sir?"

Roebuck nodded. He wondered what home meant to the others, especially to Malvey. They seemed excited to be close to American soil again. And he wondered why it meant so little to him. For now it was enough to be among men he could consider friends.

"Mr. Malvey, kindly find Lilywhite and have him hang Doña Belén's portrait again in my cabin."

***

www.ingramcontent.com/pod-product-compliance
Lightning Source LLC
Chambersburg PA
CBHW030057310726
48970CB00004B/1046